Defiant Ecstasy

By

Tiana Washington

Copyright © 2019 Tiana Washington

No part of this book may be reproduced by any means without the written permission of the author.

All Rights Reserved.

"Defiant Ecstasy"
Written by
Tiana Washington

www.amazon.com

Amazon Author Page

https://www.amazon.com/Tiana-Washington/e/B00DXL05L2?ref=sr_ntt_srch_lnk_4&qid=1564246787&sr=8-4

Published by
Creating Design
P.O. Box 1785
Columbus, IN 47202

Dedication

To my amazing and handsome husband, Daniel, my handsome son, Tylon and my beautiful daughter, Thijs...thanks for loving me as much as you do!

In Special Memory of my beautiful and fabulous mother, Regina Washington and my courageous daddy, Jeffrey Farr, I will cherish you, adore you, and love you forever in my heart! We did it! Kisses and hugs from your little girl!

Chapter 1

Charleston, South Carolina 1878. Jackson Harding had traveled nine days on a passenger liner from his home in London, England back to his childhood home in South Carolina. After many years of living the life of a bachelor and at the urging of his mother to marry, Jackson thought it would be best to return to the states to meet and perhaps wed Sara Williams, the daughter of his father's childhood friend. Jackson hadn't seen Sara since he was a boy of seven years old. His parents disliked the fact that Jackson had rather play with the slave children that his family owned instead of the other wealthy white children. His defiant stubbornness angered his father and embarrassed his mother. Their course of action and punishment, aside from the beatings that he endured by his father's hand, was to send him to London to learn how it was to be a proper gentleman. Jackson was sent to an extremely strict school for boys where lashings were the way to control disobedience and wayward ways. Jackson had known many of those lashings in the many years that he attended school. With every lash that he received, his anger toward his parents grew. He swore that he would never forgive them for sending him to this hell. He sent letters pleading to his parents to allow him to return home. He would only be allowed to come home when he understood that whites were superior to any and all blacks. Refusing to believe in such nonsense, Jackson's father refused to send anymore allowance to support his son. Jackson, however, would not be deterred. He ceased all communication with his family for several years. As soon as he was able to leave the horrid school, Jackson thought it best to study law. He had saved a great deal of his allowance and put himself through law school. He became a very prominent attorney and had made a name for himself by becoming appointed a Justice of the High Court. With every success he garnered, Jackson made it his duty to send word to his mother of his many accomplishments, and of course, in great detail, he bragged on the size of his earnings along the way. From the responses to his letters that he would receive from his mother, it was quite evident that his mother was a woman of high social standing and lavished the fact that she was a pampered woman. There was no doubt in his mind that his mother would not be able to resist engaging the other women in her social circle into conversing with her to tell of her son's amassed wealth and prominent standing in the English courts of law. Jackson's assumptions were correct. With every new letter he had sent his mother, she replied with the names of women who came from impeccable families most eager to make his acquaintance. The highest ranking on her list was that of Sara Williams.

Jackson Harding was one of the most eligible, wealthiest and powerful men in all of London. Aside from his social status, he was definitely handsome. He was extremely well dressed and tall in his stature. His eyes were hazel and his blondish brown hair was styled very short to his head. He had a brooding scowl to his face that drove the young ladies of high society into a frenzy. The deepness of his voice was more than enough to have any woman lose her senses when he was near. Jackson often noticed the seductive glances and he received many offers to share the beds of the hot-blooded women. He accepted more offers than he denied. Often leaving those who sought marriage; in heartache. The ease of how he acquired some of the most beautiful and sought after women into his bed angered his competition and on many occasions resulted in attempts on his life and his accusers jailed for attempted assassination on a Justice of the High Court. His rebellious nature in school led to many altercations. His adversaries quickly learned that he was not one to take lightly. But in truth, Jackson was bored. He wanted a real fight. He wanted a woman who would not so easily allow her to be bedded. So far, he had found none.

When word reached Jackson that the United States were in the midst of a civil war to end slavery, he finally considered writing to his family. After receiving word from his father, who was adamantly against freeing of the slaves, and was siding with the southern Confederates, Jackson hoped that the north would prevail and would put an end to the barbaric act of enslavement. In a return letter to his father, he had told his father such. Receiving no response from his father, Jackson was sure that his father was upset at his words. His father's displeasure in him meant nothing to Jackson. In his opinion, his mother and father were only that in name. He had, however, somewhat forgiven them for abandoning him those many years ago, but he felt no emotional bond with them. In the meantime, Jackson continued on with his life in England, all the while keeping up with the goings on in America and their now heated civil war.

After years of reading article upon article about the war, Jackson and several of his Union supporting friends, were elated to hear that the Civil War had ended and that the North had won and that slavery had truly been done away with in the United States. Jackson was even more surprised to receive a letter from his mother in New York. In the letter she had written to inform him that she and his father were forced to free their slaves and had fled up north as to not lose everything that his father had worked so hard for but that they would be returning back home to South Carolina to rebuild. She asked that he would pray for their safe travels and hope that their home was not ruined by the savage and merciless Yankees. In closing, she wished him well and that she longed to see her son. She informed him that she would write again as soon as she and his father were settled. Jackson set the letter aside on his desk in his office and continued reading the details of his impending case.

Georgina Harding kept true to her words. Thirteen years after the Civil War ended, Jackson received yet another letter from his mother requesting that he come home. She apologized on the lengthy time to contact him. She wouldn't dare invite him home until their home was restored to its former immaculate glory; fully staffed and their home's gardens blooming with colorful flowers. Jackson had to scoff at his mother's descriptive words. However, the fact still remained that he was ever so bored with his routine life. A holiday to his childhood home could be just what he needed. He had to admit, that he was more than anxious to meet some of those robust and prominent young women that his mother spoke of. Jackson smiled to himself. He had broken a good many hearts here in England. Why not change things up a bit? What could possibly happen? He highly doubted that any of his mother's hopefuls were a challenge. Honestly, he had yet to meet any woman that could keep his interest. They were all the same; rich, spoiled and annoying.

Brilliant! Jackson thought to himself. His mind made up. He would pass on his upcoming cases to another justice, book passage on the next ship sailing to the United States, and venture across the Atlantic to dabble in a little southern charm.

Chapter 2

Hialeah Nokosi began her morning as she always did. She prepared herself a simple breakfast of buttered bread, a poached egg and tea. After her small meal, she tidied up her cozy two room home. It wasn't much, but she was grateful to have her own home and small bit of land left to her by her former employers. She was even more grateful that they had left her with a few hens, a rooster for mating, one cow, a horse and their worn down wagon. The wagon wasn't the best but it got her into town to sell her goods. She was running low on flour and sugar and a few other items that she was in need of. Hialeah hoped that the mercantile owner, Mr. Nesbit, was tending the store today and not his venom-spewing wife. Mr. Nesbit was kind enough to purchase her eggs that her hens produced. Hialeah made it a point to choose the best eggs as to not offend Mr. Nesbit. His was, after all, the only store she was allowed to frequent. The other shop keepers were quick to call in the sheriff. She was considered a trouble maker and her kind was not welcomed in their stores.

Hialeah quickened her pace. She grabbed her bag that contained her sewing utensils and made her way to the small chicken coup to gather Mr. Nesbit's eggs. She was allowed to purchase her items as long as there weren't any white customers in the store. If there were, she had to wait until every white customer and non tainted black customer had been served. His white customers were known to make a fuss if they saw her in the store.

Hialeah chose the very best eggs she could find and carefully placed them in the basket. She covered the eggs with a small cloth and set them aside to hitch up her wagon. With everything in place, Hialeah climbed onto her wagon and made her way into town. She stopped her wagon in front of Mr. Nesbit's store just as he was unlocking the door. Mr. Nesbit was a slightly thin middle-aged man about average height. His hair was still full and very blond. He took pride in his full head of hair; always running his hand through it. His eyes were the brightest of blue and he prided himself in his appearance. He was always nicely dressed. Hialeah quickly jumped from the wagon and grabbed her basket of eggs and hurried toward Mr. Nesbit with a satisfying smile on her face. She was relieved to see him and not his wife. "Mornin', Mr. Nesbit, sir." Hialeah said. "Miss Nokosi." Mr. Nesbit returned the greeting. "Now be quick you hear?" Mr. Nesbit warned as he opened the door. "Yes sir." Hialeah said as she scurried inside of the store. She set her basket of eggs on the counter to be assessed by Mr. Nesbit and hurried off toward the sewing threads. Hialeah grabbed the colored threads that she needed and requested her usual amount of sugar, flour and bacon. Mr. Nesbit always paid her sixty cents for her eggs so she knew what her total purchase would be. On her way back toward the counter, a pair of black boots caught Hialeah's attention. She stopped in her tracks and set her threads down next to the shoes. Hialeah picked up one of the boots admiring it. She then looked down at her feet, a frown appearing on her lips. Hialeah turned her foot side to side. Her boots had holes forming in the heel and the soles were beginning to detach themselves. Hialeah held the boot up for Mr. Nesbit to see. "Mr. Nesbit, how much these here boots?" Hialeah asked. "One dollar fifty." Mr. Nesbit replied. Hialeah set the boot back down and picked up her threads. The boots would have to wait until she earned some more money. She had made it thus fair with her worn out pair of boots, another week or so wouldn't matter much.

Hialeah walked to the counter where Mr. Nesbit had already placed her sugar, flour and bacon in a bag. She set the threads down on the counter and Mr. Nesbit picked them up and placed them into the bag as well. He then walked over to the candy jars and pulled out one piece of red licorice and handed it to Hialeah. She always completed her shopping with a piece of licorice. Hialeah took the candy and smiled. "Thank you." Hialeah said. "See you soon." Mr. Nesbit replied. Hialeah took her bag of purchased goods and headed toward the door. Almost as an after-thought, Mr. Nesbit called Hialeah's name. "Did I forget something?" Hialeah asked confused. "No, I did. Hold up a minute." Mr. Nesbit said and went into the back of the store. He quickly returned with a roll of fabric in his arms. "What do you think about this?" Mr. Nesbit asked. The fabric was dark yellow and brown plaid. It wasn't the most attractive fabric that Hialeah had seen and she was unsure as to why Mr. Nesbit was showing it to her. "It isn't exactly eye catching, but it's yours if you want it." Mr. Nesbit stated. Hialeah's eyes widened. "Mine sir?" Hialeah replied surprised. "I can't do anything with it. The truth of the matter is, the wife ordered this from a catalogue from a store that has since gone out of business. We've tried to sell it, but it's just so unsightly, we had to pull it from the shelves." Mr. Nesbit said. "You sure you want me to have it all?" Hialeah asked. "Absolutely. Please get it out of my store." Mr. Nesbit replied. Hialeah smiled, grateful for the free fabric. Eye catching or not, it was hers and she could definitely use a new dress. She was growing tired of wearing the tattered one she had on. "I'll take it." Hialeah said smiling. "Perfect." Mr. Nesbit replied. "I'll carry it out for you." Mr. Nesbit said.

Mr. Nesbit and Hialeah left the store. Mr. Nesbit placed the fabric in the back of Hialeah's wagon, happy to be rid of the eye sore while Hialeah placed her small bag next to her on the seat. Hialeah was pleased that she had finished her shopping just as the town was beginning to wake up. She had left Mr. Nesbit's store just as a group of chattering white women entered. Hialeah sat atop her wagon and watched the people coming and going. The hot rays of the early morning June sun were shining down on her as she continued to people watch. She wouldn't sit for long. She couldn't risk her bacon spoiling in the sun's heat. Hialeah decided to go home, drop off her items and return to town. Surely someone would be interested in hiring her for her mending talents. She was the best seamstress in town or at least that's what she told herself. Hialeah spotted the sheriff and his two no good deputies across the road. She didn't want any trouble with the foul man. Hialeah signaled for her horse to get going and she made her way out of town.

After arriving to her small home, Hialeah quickly took her items inside and set them on her table; tossing her bacon into the icebox before hurrying right back out of the door. Folks were coming into town in droves and if she wanted to find work, then she had better make it back into town right away. Surely someone would take her up on her offer to mend their garments. Most of the town folk wanted nothing to do with her, but she had to make some money. Mr. Nesbit only took her eggs whenever his wife was not in the store and she was already out of money after her venture. She was owed three weeks worth of pay from Mr. Grisby, the tavern owner, for mending the gowns of his working girls but whenever she tried to collect her wages, he gave her ridiculous reasons as to why he could not pay. His main reason was always that the tavern wasn't doing well, even though it was always a full house practically every night. And if she dared try to make a fuss, he threatened her with the sheriff. No matter, Hialeah thought to herself. She would make her money one way or the other. She climbed back onto the seat of her wagon and headed back toward town.

By the time Hialeah made it back into town, the upcoming county fair banner had been hung and the streets were buzzing with people. The smells of fresh baked bread, pies and fried ham from the town restaurant teased her nostrils. No sense in getting excited over the delicious smells though, the restaurant was another place she wasn't allowed. It didn't matter too much to her. There were plenty of places for her to dine on the colored side of town. That is, when she had money to dine; this wasn't too often. Hialeah put the thought of food out of her mind and jumped down from her wagon with her sewing bag in tow. She walked down the sidewalk greeting people as she normally did and began offering her services. She even showed her hopeful employees her new sewing threads. Only to be told that they would never do business with the likes of her. Some folks didn't even acknowledge her presence and the few that did threatened her with the sheriff for harassment. Sheriff Dale Willard didn't take too kindly to colored folks speaking to the good white folks. He especially didn't take to Hialeah. He considered her worse than a regular colored because she had as he called it, 'savage' blood in her veins. In his eyes, a colored mixed with savage blood was lower than a colored mixed with white blood. He made his feelings known every chance encounter he had with her. He promised he would lock her up or worse if he caught her bothering white folks in his town. His anger was fueled even more when she challenged his right to lock her up. Her uppity nigger attitude made his blood boil. Hialeah made it a point to avoid him at all costs.

Hialeah continued her quest to find work. She spotted Sheriff Willard and his two deputies making their rounds. Distracted by their presence, she was nearly hit by a carriage. Lucas, the Harding's colored male driver, yelled at her to move on. Hialeah's angry retort was drowned out by the sound of a stagecoach pulling up. Hialeah waited on the sidewalk. She was anxious to see who the passengers were. If they appeared to have money, then she would introduce herself and offer up her mending services. Lucas hopped down from his seat and opened the door for his passengers. Hialeah immediately recognized Georgina and Henry Harding. They were some of the wealthiest people in South Carolina. They had once owned the most prosperous cotton and tobacco plantation. She had heard stories about how they fled up north to keep from losing their money before the Civil War could ruin them. Since the war's end, the Hardings were once again top suppliers of cotton and tobacco, but since slavery was now over, they had to pay colored folks to work their land. Aside from the Hardings emerging from the carriage, Hialeah also recognized the young woman in their company. Sara Williams. Sara stood mere inches shorter than Hialeah's five foot nine inch height. Her auburn curls were always fashionably styled and her dresses always seemed to show much of her breasts. Her brown eyes were those of her father's, Judge Harland Williams. It was no secret that her father sided with the wealthy white folks any time there was a trial that involved coloreds or poor whites. Most colored folks considered him as 'crooked'. Hialeah had her own personal reasons for despising the Williams. After his passengers were safely on the sidewalk, Lucas climbed back onto his seat.

  Hialeah stood back and waited to see what brought the Hardings and Miss Williams into town. The stagecoach driver opened the door for his passengers while his assistant began to unload the passengers' bag. Hialeah watched as two women and three men stepped out of the coach. Hialeah was able to catch a glimpse of the tallest of the three men. Although white men had never much appealed to her, this newcomer was a most handsome man; dark in his demeanor and domineering in height. Hialeah found herself taking in a breath of nervousness. She thought he could give the sheriff and his low-down deputies what for. His brooding gaze was enough to keep Hialeah frozen in her spot. She watched as the stranger folded his coat over his arm. She averted her attention back to the Hardings and Miss Williams. They looked seemingly lost; confused. Mrs. Harding caught the driver as he was climbing back onto the stagecoach. "Excuse me, but just where is my son? My Jackson?" She asked authoritatively. Hialeah watched the exchange between the driver and Mrs. Harding. The handsome stranger caught her attention as he casually strode his way over to Mrs. Harding with a sly grin on his face. He stopped behind her and leaned into her ear. "Hello mother." Jackson said deeply. Georgina Harding spun around on her heels to put voice to face. Jackson's sly grin was replaced with a huge smile. "Mother." Jackson said. He watched as his mother's eyes grew the size of saucers. "Jackson!" Georgina exclaimed loudly. "My Jackson?" Georgina asked. "Indeed I am." Jackson replied. Henry Harding walked over to the pair just as Georgina threw herself into her son's arms squealing in utter surprise. Sara remained where she stood. She didn't want to interrupt the reunion. Jackson embraced his mother. It had been far too long since he had laid his eyes on her. Although she was his mother, Jackson felt as if he were embracing a distant relative.

When Georgina Harding finally released her son, Jackson gave his mother a good looking over. Her eyes were still as blue as he remembered them. Her once blond hair now had traces of gray and her figure had gone from the slender form of a young mother to an ample-sized woman in her middle ages. But she was still as beautiful as he remembered. Jackson then turned his attention to his father. It was as if Jackson were looking into a mirror at his older self. He was the spitting image of his father. He was slightly taller than his father, but his eyes and hair color was a perfect match. Jackson, however, felt nothing in his father's presence. He could do nothing but extend his hand.

"Father." Jackson said. "Jackson." Henry replied with the same emotionless tone to his voice. Hialeah watched the painful greeting. "You've done very well for yourself." Henry said. "Yes sir, I have." Jackson replied meeting his father's gaze. The same icy gaze that he was told many times that he displayed. Sensing the tension between her son and husband, Georgina hooked her arm around her son's and led him away from his father to where Sara stood waiting. "My darling Sara, this is my Jackson; Justice of the High Court appointed by the queen herself." Georgina said proudly. "Why I don't know what to call you." Sara said coyly. "Jackson will do just fine." Jackson replied smiling. "Jackson." Sara remarked sweetly, extending her hand out to Jackson. Jackson took Sara's hand and placed a kiss on the back of it. "It is a pleasure to make your acquaintance once again, Miss Williams." Jackson replied. "Oh I just love it!" Georgina squealed. "Sara doesn't he sound like a proper English gentleman?" Georgina beamed. "Why yes ma'am he does and just as charming I'm sure." Sara replied. Georgina clasped her hands together in joy. "I declare, you two make such an excellent pair." Georgina remarked happily. "Why Jackson, the wedding will be the grandest affair in all of South Carolina." Georgina said gleefully. Jackson forced a smile at his mother's words. While he did find Sara Williams most attractive, he wasn't about to just jump into marriage at his mother's whim. "Well before you have me at the altar my first day home, would you know of a place that could repair my coat?" Jackson asked lightly. "Your coat?" Georgina asked confused. Jackson removed his coat from his arm. "I was in a bit of a scuffle on the ship." Jackson replied. Jackson showed his mother the rip underneath one of the arms of his coat. "A scuffle? Are you hurt?" Georgina asked in utter shock. "I'm quite unharmed." Jackson replied. Georgina turned toward her husband. "Henry, do get over here. Jackson was assaulted." Georgina said. Jackson chuckled at his mother's words. "I assure you mother, I was not harmed." Jackson replied.

"Well you must entertain us with your account of this scuffle." Sara said. Jackson waited for his father to join them before telling his story. Hialeah waited impatiently for Mr. Harding to join his family. She too wanted to hear the story. Georgina grasped her husband's arm dreading the awful tale. Jackson fought hard not to burst into laughter at his mother's expense. She was clearly one for the dramatics. "Well do go on." Sara urged. "It was nothing really. I merely stopped some mad man from accosting a woman passenger on the ship. He meant to do great harm to the woman. He didn't like my interference and threatened me with a knife. He then lunged at me and as I stepped back, his blade ripped through my coat. I then grabbed his arm, wrestled the knife from his hand and gave him a swift blow to the head. He fell to the ground and was seized by members of the crew. No harm done." Jackson said. "You could have been killed." Georgina replied fearfully. "Well my coat took the worst of it and is sorely in need of repair." Jackson remarked lightly. "Charming and brave." Sara said. Jackson nodded his head in Sara's direction in appreciation.

After having heard Jackson's story, Hialeah was quite nervous about approaching him. She did, however, need the money. She had nothing to lose. Besides, she had been turned down for her services before. If he declined her services, it wouldn't be the first time. Hialeah took a deep breath. She waited for several passersby to clear the sidewalk before she slowly made her way toward Jackson, her sewing bag in tow. Hialeah stopped about a foot away before softly clearing her throat to find her voice. "Excuse me, sir." Hialeah said softly. Jackson turned around at the sound of the soft voice coming from behind him. He was taken aback by Hialeah's presence. Jackson immediately noticed her long straight black hair and her light brown eyes. He also noticed that her dress was sewn together by several patterns of fabric and her shoes were practically worn through. He also noticed that she was absolutely breath taking. "I can repair your coat for you. Mend it good as new." Hialeah said. Before he could speak, Georgina angrily stepped in front of him blocking Hialeah from getting any closer to her son. "How dare you address my son!" Georgina snapped. "I free to speak to anybody I please." Hialeah replied defiantly. "You will not speak to my fiancé." Sara remarked harshly. "Ain't no law 'gainst it." Hialeah replied matter-of-factly and proceeded to dig through her sewing bag. Hialeah produced the new sewing threads that she had just purchased to show Jackson. "I got new sewing threads too." Hialeah said proudly. Outraged by Hialeah's disobedience, Sara lashed out viciously. "Why you filthy little savage whore!" Sara replied angrily. Sara raised her hand to slap Hialeah. Jackson swiftly grabbed Sara's arm preventing her from striking the innocent woman. "Don't." Jackson said sternly staring Sara down. Surprised and shocked at Jackson's defense of a colored, Sara snatched her arm away. "Well I never. You're a nigger lover." Sara remarked in shocked anger. Jackson's actions not only surprised Sara and Georgina, but Hialeah as well. "Henry, go fetch the sheriff quickly." Georgina ordered. Henry trotted off to do as his wife demanded followed by an offended Sara. "Mother, I am sure that is not necessary." Jackson said. "Why it most certainly is. She knows better than to harass decent white folk." Georgina replied smugly. "Harassed?" Jackson asked incredulously. "It's alright, sir, I use to it." Hialeah replied softly. Before Georgina could utter another word, Sheriff Dale Willard, whom was close by having breakfast at the town's restaurant, and his two deputies came barreling down the sidewalk followed by Henry Harding and Sara. Georgina left Jackson's side in a huff and quickly grabbed Sheriff Willard's arm and led him toward Hialeah.

Dale Willard was a proud southern man. He stood about five feet eleven inches tall and was grossly fat for a man his height. His stomach hung over his trousers, which were held up by black suspenders. His thin lips were pursed together and his eyes were a dull blue. His once dark brown hair was balding around the middle and was always covered by his signature wide brimmed Gambler hat. He took pride in being the town's sheriff and no matter what he wore; his silver badge was attached to every shirt or coat front. "Sheriff, I want her arrested." Georgina demanded. Sheriff Willard nodded his head at his deputies signaling for them to grab Hialeah. She had been warned one too many times. This time, she would be spending the night in jail.

Jackson stepped in front of Hialeah before Sheriff Willard's deputies could put their hands on her. Both men stopped in their tracks. Confused, they both turned to their boss. "Sheriff." Jackson said. "That's right, and who are you?" Sheriff Willard asked. "Sheriff Willard, this is my son, Jackson Harding. He's been living in Europe; England to be exact. He's made quite the name for himself as Justice of the High Court." Georgina boastfully replied. "Well Young Mr. Harding, as your mother said, I'm Sheriff Willard. Dale Willard and these two fine gentlemen are my deputies. This here is Deputy Willie Calhoun and this is Deputy James Blake. We do our very best to protect our fair community." Sheriff Willard said proudly. Jackson wasn't interested in introductions. He didn't like the looks of either Willie or James. Although both men were quite dapper in their dress, and appeared to be around the same age as Jackson, they both rubbed Jackson the wrong way. He despised crooked shifty men and these two were just that. Willie was a tad bit shorter than James. Both men had dark stringy blond hair that they brushed back and covered with their hats. They were also both average in built. Willie's eyes were gray whereas James's eyes were green. They had the same smug look to their faces as did Sheriff Willard. Jackson decided at that moment, that he would not trust the lot of them. "Sheriff, I believe my mother called on you prematurely. There's no trouble here." Jackson remarked. "Oh, there's definitely trouble. That one right there is nothing but trouble." Sheriff Willard replied. "I ain't done nothin' wrong. I just come by to offer my services. Offer to mend his coat." Hialeah said. "I don't give a damn what you're offering. You get going, or I'll have my deputies throw you in jail where you and your kind belong. You hear? Now get out of here." Sheriff Willard replied. Hialeah looked around at the crowd of white faces that had gathered around to witness the Sheriff's and Georgina Harding's tirade. Humiliated, she ran across the road and didn't look back. Tears stung her eyes as she climbed onto her wagon and rode out of the town.

Jackson was disgusted by not only Sheriff Willard's treatment of the woman, but his mother as well. Sara's attempt to strike the woman and her attack on his person was the beginning of the end of their so-called engagement. Satisfied with ridding Hialeah of their company, Georgina thanked the sheriff and his deputies. Sheriff Willard turned to walk away after receiving his praise from Mrs. Harding, but Jackson had questions that he wanted answered. "Sheriff." Jackson said. "What can I do for you Mr. Harding?" Sheriff Willard asked. "You can start by telling me what the bloody hell is going on." Jackson replied harshly. "Jackson. Your manners." Georgina replied. "No worries Mrs. Harding. It'll be my pleasure to inform your son about that one there." Sheriff Willard replied. "Please do." Jackson remarked heatedly. "That there isn't no regular colored. She got savage blood in her. She's what I call a mutt. You see it's one thing to be a nigger, but when you mix nigger blood with Injun blood, well that's the lowest kind of nigger there is. She's tainted twice." Sheriff Willard remarked smiling. Jackson could feel his blood boiling hearing the disgusting words spewing from the sheriff's mouth. He found no amusement in the sheriff's description of the woman and he wanted nothing more than to pummel his smug face. Sheriff Willard opened his mouth to continue, but was cut off by Jackson's next word. "Enough." Jackson said gruffly as he angrily walked by the sheriff and his mother. Jackson unceremoniously grabbed his two pieces of luggage and made his way to the back of the carriage. Lucas hopped down once again from his post and opened the doors for the Hardings and Miss Williams before joining Jackson at the back of the carriage. Once out of earshot from the ladies, Sheriff Willard followed Jackson to the back of the carriage. Jackson and Lucas were attempting to secure Jackson's luggage in place. Jackson ignored the sheriff's presence. "I do believe I've offended you Mr. Harding." Sheriff Willard said. Jackson didn't bother to look at the sheriff. "Hardly." Jackson retorted the annoyance evident in his voice. "Good. Good. I only thought to warn you against the likes of that rebellious trouble maker. She's a wild one. A thief and a working girl." Sheriff Willard replied, his words now catching Jackson's attention. "A working girl?" Jackson replied curious as to the sheriff's meaning. "Oh I don't mean a working girl like she claims. I mean the kind that does her best work…shall I say, on her backside." Sheriff Willard remarked smugly. Lucas had finished securing the luggage and left the two men to finish their conversation. "She mentioned nothing of the sort." Jackson said. "Now why would she? Being in the presence of your dear mother and all." Sheriff Willard replied. "Why she works in a very seedy part of town for a man named Grisby, Terell Grisby." Sheriff Willard continued. "Who's he?" Jackson asked. "He runs a business where fine young gentlemen, such as you, go to seek pleasures of those other than their wives." Sheriff Willard replied. Jackson had heard enough. The sheriff's antagonizing tone of voice was too much for Jackson to bear. "Good day Sheriff Willard." Jackson said heatedly. Sheriff Willard merely nodded his head.

Jackson climbed into the carriage. He couldn't wait to get home to see Mama Lilly and have some of her fresh lemon pie. He had written to her over the years and was quite anxious to see the woman who had kept him sane through his trying times away from home. Most people referred to her as Miss Lilly but to Jackson, she was mama

Chapter 3

After several days in his mother's company, Jackson was near his wit's end. Georgina Harding had taken her son to every social outing she had been invited to, and every social event had consisted of her boasting of his accomplishments in London as a queen appointed Justice of the High Court, how rich he was, and how he was home to wed Sara Williams. She made it a point to reiterate that fact to the young southern belles who were glaring at her son with wanton looks on their faces. She did, however, manage to embellish the incident on the ship. Jackson's one on one fight went from one assailant to three, sometimes four or five. What was driving Jackson even more to the brink of insanity was that every gathering he attended, the same faces were in attendance. Jackson was positive that every person who had made his acquaintance through his mother had to have been absolutely bored to death from the same story that she had been so proud to tell over and over. He was desperate to get away from the boorish snobs that his mother held in such high regards. Sara Williams was included on that list. Yes, she was a fairly attractive woman, but Jackson couldn't stomach the conversations that they shared. He was repulsed by the way she treated the black servants that were serving the white guests. He couldn't for the life of him see himself married to a woman with such a vile and wicked tongue. Besides, he had been to enough of these sort or gatherings in London to last a lifetime. He wasn't about to spend his holiday in his hometown surrounded by the very people he had wanted to get away from in London. Jackson excused himself from the party and decided to walk through the gardens of the host. As he walked through the garden, he was immediately reminded of his conversation with Sheriff Willard. What he needed was more lively company.

After a somewhat peaceful dinner with his mother and father, Jackson took to his childhood bedroom. It had been a long time since he had seen his old room. His first night home, Jackson reacquainted himself with his old home. He walked the fields where the slaves toiled for hours in the hot sun. He found himself visiting the old slave quarters where he played with the many slave children when he was a boy. He relished the short-lived friendships he had with the children of the plantation. Now, those same children with whom he had played with were grown men such as he and were long gone. Nothing was the same any more. The slave quarters were eerily haunting now and Jackson could no longer bear the disturbing memories that they held.

Jackson waited until his mother and father were asleep and the house was still before he crept out of the house into the night. He didn't want to be questioned by his mother as to his late night escapade. She would no doubt disapprove of him going to a tavern with such unscrupulous people. Before going out to the barn to saddle up a horse, Jackson grabbed his pistol and holstered it in his gun belt. It was nearing 10:00. Jackson was sure that whatever was going on in the unsavory part of town was a lot better than what he had endured thus far in his mother's company. With that thought in mind, Jackson mounted his horse and feeling free, rode off into the night. He couldn't help but to wonder if he would run into 'her'. Jackson was curious as to why other than the fact that she was mixed with Indian and black blood, what exactly made her a troublemaker. A half sly grin played across his lips. He liked troublemakers. He, in fact, was hoping to get into a bit of trouble.

As Jackson rode more into the rougher side of the town, he could smell the odor of cigars wafting in the air. The loud sounds of piano music, laughter and what appeared to be several fights, no doubt over gambling echoed in his ears. The shear excitement of it all was thrilling. Clearly, Grisby's Tavern was the place to be. Jackson was curious as to how many of the so-called men of high social standing were out cozying up with the low-brow women of the tavern. The very thought made him laugh out loud. His mother would no doubt swoon if she ever knew. He wondered if his father ever frequented this place. Holy shit; would that be one hell of a fight between his parents that he would love to witness.

Jackson dismounted his horse and tied the reins to a post. He looked around before entering the tavern. Jackson was thoroughly pleased at what he was witnessing. Drunken men stumbling out of the tavern after one too many drinks and several more patrons were being tossed on their asses for whatever reasons. Jackson found himself amused at the sights. He needed a good stiff drink and a beautiful woman to serve it to him. Yes, indeed. This was going to be an interesting night.

Jackson entered Grisby's Tavern and found an empty table yet dirty table. He sat down but before he could catch the attention of the blond woman serving drinks at a nearby table, loud voices from the back of the tavern caught his attention. Clearly some bloke had angered one of the women in the tavern. When the dueling pair came into view, Jackson was surprised and yet pleased to discover that the angry woman was the same woman who had approached him on the sidewalk on his arrival. She was being led roughly by her arm by a well dressed man to the doors of the tavern. Jackson stood from his table to get a better view and to make sure that whatever happened, no harm came to the fiery woman. From what he could make out amidst the ruckus of the tavern, money was involved. Jackson was sure that the man in question was no doubt, Terell Grisby, the tavern owner. "You'll get paid when I say so!" Mr. Grisby yelled. "I want what's due me!" Hialeah yelled in return snatching away from Mr. Grisby. The once boisterous tavern had gone silent. "I work hard; three weeks and I wants what's mine!" Hialeah fired at Mr. Grisby. "You get outta here or I'll fetch the sheriff!" Mr. Grisby warned. Hialeah fired back at Mr. Grisby with a hot-tempered tirade in her father's tongue to which Mr. Grisby was none too pleased. "You get the hell outta here with that savage talk or I'll throw you out! You god damn filthy savage whore!" Mr. Grisby yelled. Hialeah was seething with rage. She knew Mr. Grisby would make due on his promise to have her arrested. Once again all eyes were on her as she looked around the tavern. Angry and defeated, she stormed out of the Mr. Grisby's establishment. Arrogantly satisfied with his victory, Terell Grisby pulled out the cash that he owed Hialeah from his coat pocket and waved it in the air to the amusement of his patrons before cheerfully insisting that everyone go back to their drinking and good time before disappearing to the back of the tavern.

Jackson noticed the tattered dress she wore and the devastated look on Hialeah's face as she left the tavern. He was none too pleased. He downed his drink and left his table. Jackson closely followed Mr. Grisby to his make-shift office in the back of the tavern. Mr. Grisby entered his office and just as he tried to close the door, Jackson entered startling him. As soon as Mr. Grisby turned around, he was met by Jackson's fist. Mr. Grisby fell to the floor from the swift blow and Jackson wasted no time in retrieving the money from his coat. Jackson casually exited Mr. Grisby's office and made his way back to the front of the tavern. He grabbed a drink from a tray as a serving girl walked by and downed it quickly. He set the empty glass on the bar and left the tavern.

Jackson stepped into the crowded road in search of Hialeah. He left his horse hitched and started down the road on foot. Hialeah walked absentmindedly down the road ignoring the angry yells of frustrated drivers as she slowly walked in the middle of the road. Jackson reached Hialeah and grabbed her by the arm pulling her from harm's way just as the driver of the wagon was preparing to run her down. Hialeah broke Jackson's hold of her arm and turned on her unwelcomed rescuer. She hastily dug into her sewing bag and pulled out a knife. Hialeah quickly removed it from its sheath and pointed it at Jackson keeping him at bay as she began yet another heated tirade in the same language that she had used on Terell Grisby. By the fierce look in her eyes, and her weapon drawn on him, it was anything but pleasantries. As Hialeah's verbal attack continued, Jackson slowly reached into his pocket and pulled out the money he had taken from Mr. Grisby and presented it to her. "I believe this belongs to you." Jackson said calmly undaunted by Hialeah's weapon. Hialeah could barely see her rescuer's face from the dim light of the moon, but she immediately recognized the foreign voice of the man who had come to her defense against Sheriff Willard. Jackson continued to hold the money out for her to take. "I'd gladly give it to you if you'll put your weapon away or would you prefer to kill me on the street?" Jackson asked. "Mvskoke opunakv opunayetske omv (Muh-z-go-gee obo-naguh obo-na-yetz-gee oh-muh)?" Hialeah replied. "I'm sorry. I don't understand your language." Jackson remarked. Hialeah ignored Jackson's statement. She returned her focus back to the money he held out. "What that for?" Hialeah asked suspiciously. "You're the working girl from the tavern are you not?" Jackson asked. "He give it to you? Mr. Terell give it to you?" Hialeah asked curiously. "Something like that." Jackson replied casually. Hialeah didn't know what that meant and she didn't care. She snatched the money from Jackson's hand and shoved it into her sewing bag. She was, however, curious as to what someone like him was doing at Mr. Grisby's tavern. "What you doin' in this part of town?" Hialeah asked suspiciously. "I needed some air." Jackson replied casually. Hialeah felt no need to pry any further. She had her money and that's all that mattered. She returned her knife to its sheath and slipped it back into her bag. "Well, I thank you." Hialeah said and turned to walk away. "What did you say to me? That language you were speaking, what is it?" Jackson asked. Hialeah turned back to face him. "It be Creek. My daddy's tongue." Hialeah replied proudly. "I give you a good tongue lashin' for touchin' me without my say so. Then I ask you do you speak Creek." Hialeah remarked. "A tongue lashing? Consisting of what exactly?" Jackson replied lightly. "I say to you what I tell any white man." Hialeah remarked. "And what would that be?" Jackson asked casually. "That you got no right to touch me. None of you. I ain't no slave. Ain't never been no slave. If'n you want my company, it gonna cost you." Hialeah replied sternly looking up to meet Jackson's gaze in the moonlight. "Then you are a working girl?" Jackson asked. "That what the good sheriff tell you?" Hialeah replied. "Is it true?" Jackson asked. "That my business." Hialeah replied harshly. "May I know your name?" Jackson asked. "That my business too." Hialeah replied defensively. She placed her hands on her hips. "Alright, then I'll simply address you as Miss." Jackson remarked looking Hialeah up and down. He was entranced by her long sleek black locks and amused by the moccasins she wore on her feet. Jackson's silent gaze over her body unnerved Hialeah. "What you lookin' at me that way for?" Hialeah demanded. "Just taking in a most enchanting view, Miss." Jackson replied smoothly. "What view?" Hialeah remarked suspiciously. "You." Jackson replied simply. "Well you keep your eyes lookin' elsewhere. I don't care for men like you lookin' at me with strange eyes." Hialeah remarked defensively. Jackson chuckled at her Hialeah's words. It was quite obvious what she meant but Jackson thought it'd be amusing to hear Hialeah object to his viewing of her because he was white. "Men like me?" Jackson asked mockingly. "White men." Hialeah said matter-of-factly. "Ah, so then you take offense to white men admiring you?" Jackson asked. Hialeah crossed her arms ignoring Jackson's question much to his amusement. "Do me a favor." Jackson replied. "What's that?" Hialeah asked curiously. "Stay clear of this part of town. You're far too good for the likes of that place." Jackson replied.

Hialeah spun on her heel and walked away from Jackson. Before she could get too far ahead of him, Jackson called out to Hialeah. Jackson couldn't help but to chuckle at her stubbornness as she continued walking; ignoring him. Jackson playfully rolled his eyes and hurried after Hialeah. Quickly catching up to his new found challenge, Jackson walked around Hialeah until he was standing directly in front of her barring her path. Hialeah let out an annoyed huff and crossed her arms yet again. She was briefly distracted by the aroma coming from the local restaurant. It wasn't the finest establishment in town nor was the patrons who frequented it, however, the tantalizing smells coming from the restaurant was enough to make Hialeah's stomach growl after having gone quite some time without a bite to eat. Hialeah glanced toward the restaurant's entrance and inhaled before returning her focus back to Jackson. "Why you come pesterin' me again?" Hialeah asked sternly. Jackson caught her quick glance toward the restaurant. "I'd like to buy you a drink." Jackson replied. "I don't care for that poison." Hialeah remarked. "Then perhaps I may escort you to the county fair in my honor tomorrow?" Jackson replied. "Monks. (Mo-ngs)" Hialeah replied simply. "Monks?" Jackson remarked curiously. "It mean no." Hialeah replied firmly. "Then you have an escort already?" Jackson asked. "I ain't got no escort cause I ain't fixin' to go." Hialeah replied sternly. "Besides, there's plenty of uppity white women willin' to fall all over themselves for your attention and I ain't one of 'em." Hialeah remarked stubbornly. "I have no interest in their attention." Jackson replied smoothly. "Say what you want. My mind's made up." Hialeah remarked adamantly.

"Alright, well then how about joining me for a late supper?" Jackson asked nodding his head toward the restaurant. Hialeah hadn't eaten in hours, yet she didn't trust anyone whose skin didn't match her own and even then she was cautious around her own kind. Hialeah raised a curious brow. "Why you wanna have supper with a colored woman?" Hialeah demanded crossing her arms. "I don't care to dine alone." Jackson replied simply. Hialeah walked away from Jackson. She headed toward the restaurant and peered through the window hoping to find colored diners. She was thoroughly surprised to see a few tables occupied with people that looked like her enjoying their meals. Jackson followed Hialeah unsure of what she was looking for. Hialeah quickly turned away from the window when Jackson approached her. "You think I gone owe you or somethin'..." Hialeah began defiantly. Her tirade was cut short. Jackson rolled his eyes mockingly and took a hold of Hialeah's arm and led her into the restaurant.

The restaurant was filled with drunkards, unruly patrons, and simple folk hungry for a good meal. Jackson found a small table near the rear of the restaurant. Hialeah could hardly hear herself think. She hurried to take her seat before Jackson could pull the chair out for her. Glancing around the room, it was obvious that Jackson was the finest dressed man in the whole place. Jackson took his seat and hailed over a waitress. They were greeted by a busty brunette carrying a tray with two glasses of water. Her less than appealing apron was covered in grime and her stringy hair had fallen loose from its bun. Hialeah thought it best to keep her opinion to herself but clearly the woman had seen better days. "What can I get you?" The waitress asked somewhat yelling over the crowd as she set the two glasses of water down on the table. "What's your special?" Jackson replied. "Fried chicken, pickled beets, green beans and corn bread." The waitress remarked. "We'll have the special please and a whiskey." Jackson replied. The waitress nodded her head and scurried away. Jackson leaned back comfortably in his chair and stretched his long muscular legs crossing them at the ankles much to Hialeah's surprise. She was taken aback by Jackson's relaxed demeanor. A man of his caliber sharing a table with a common nobody like herself; a colored nobody at that. He surrounded himself with ruffians and persons of ill refute like it was commonplace.

Hialeah found herself quite intrigued by Jackson Harding. She still didn't trust him but she was very much intrigued.

Hialeah never once stepped foot into the shabby restaurant or any restaurant. This was all brand new and rather exciting. She was, however, baffled as to the real reason why someone as wealthy as Jackson Harding would be doing in the worst part of town. Before Hialeah could ask her question, their waitress returned with their drinks. Jackson wasted no time in indulging himself with his whiskey. He placed his lips on his glass and took a leisurely sip. Hialeah frowned in Jackson's direction. She never understood the appeal for such drinks. Jackson placed his glass back on the table. Hialeah could hold her tongue no longer. She leaned in toward Jackson and narrowed her eyes. "What you really doin' here cause I don't believe for one minute a fancy man like you come for air." Hialeah said. Jackson took his time with his answer. He took another sip of his whiskey and nonchalantly began tapping the side of the glass with his fingers. He mimicked Hialeah's gesture and leaned toward her. "What's your name?" Jackson replied teasingly. "I ain't fixin' to say." Hialeah remarked. "Very well then." Jackson replied with a grin on his lips leaning back in his chair once again. "Very well then, what?" Hialeah asked. "Your name is your business. What I'm doing in such an unsavory part of town is mine." Jackson replied casually. "This part of town is full of trouble. Gamblers and loose women and the like. Rich men like you come here lookin' for those women when your wives don't please you none. That why you here?" Hialeah asked curiously. Jackson chuckled and leaned in once more. "I'm here for fried chicken and to know your name and seeing as how you refuse to tell me your name, I suppose I'll have to settle for the fried chicken." Jackson replied mockingly. Before Hialeah could respond, their dinner arrived. Jackson sat straight in his chair to allow for their food to be set on the table. Hialeah waited until their waitress had left them alone before bowing her head to say her grace. Jackson cocked a brow and followed suit. He bowed his head as Hialeah said grace. He didn't know the name of the exotic beauty before him but he was almost certain that she was a church going woman. A church going woman that spent time in a whore house? She was indeed a mysterious woman.

Hialeah finished her grace and inhaled the smell of her food. She waited until Jackson picked up his fork and took a bite of his dinner before doing the same; a gesture that didn't go unnoticed by Jackson. "What was that?" Jackson asked curiously. Hialeah quickly hurried to swallow the bite of green beans she had taken. "Your hesitation?" Jackson replied. "Just the way my mama learned me is all. My daddy always took the first bite." Hialeah remarked. "Before you or your mother?" Jackson said. Hialeah nodded her head before continuing her meal. Jackson wanted to know more. He asked Hialeah several questions about her life. Most of his questions went unanswered. By the time they had finished their meal, he still knew very little about her. Hialeah's aloofness piqued Jackson's curiosity even more.

After having paid for their meal, Jackson escorted Hialeah back to where they had met. He seized the moment to inquire about the fair once more and just as before, Hialeah rejected his offer to allow him to escort her to the big event. "Well that it is a shame." Jackson remarked in mock defeat. "How so?" Hialeah replied. "A fair in my honor and no charming escort to enjoy the festivities with me. Utterly disgraceful. Perhaps another time then?" Jackson said casually stunning Hialeah as he took hold of her hand and placed a soft kiss on the back of it. "I'll leave you to your affairs." Jackson remarked smoothly with a nod of his head. He stepped aside so that Hialeah could continue on her way.

Hialeah remained in her spot briefly as Jackson left her side. The calm yet deepness of his voice and his domineering presence made her tremble. She found herself absentmindedly caressing her hand. She didn't dare look back but she couldn't resist. She quickly looked over her shoulder just as Jackson peered over his. Hialeah looked away hastily and Jackson chuckled having caught her taking a last moment glance at him. Hialeah nervously continued on her way. She thought to herself that perhaps this Jackson Harding weren't so bad. He did come to her defense against the sheriff and kept that awful woman from striking her. Jackson noticed that Hialeah no longer walked down the middle of the road.

Jackson walked back to his horse with a devilish grin to his lips. He was looking for trouble and he was sure after this meeting he had found it. He had no doubt that his new challenge would show up to the fair with fire in her eyes after the little stunt he had just pulled on her. Jackson mounted his horse thoroughly pleased with his performance. He returned home and entered the dark house as quietly as he had left it. Jackson kicked off his boots and laid in his bed fully clothed with his arms folded behind his head staring into the darkness. He found himself still smiling at his encounter with the woman whose name he had still yet to find out. Jackson couldn't help but to let out a small chuckle as he lie in his bed. He had come back home to find a woman that would challenge him. Jackson was now more sure than ever that after his encounter with the stubborn minx she was indeed the challenge that he had been looking for. He was, however, still curious if she were truly a working girl as Sheriff Willard had mentioned. She hadn't exactly answered his question when he had asked her. Indeed, Jackson thought to himself, she would definitely be his challenge and he was always up for a good challenge.

The next morning, after soaking and bathing in a refreshing tub of warm water, Jackson readied himself for the county fair. He hoped that he would run into his new stubborn challenge but after speaking to her the previous night, he doubt that she would attend. Jackson denied his mother's request to join her and his father for breakfast. Instead, he chose to have his breakfast in the kitchen with Miss Lilly. He always felt more comfortable around the servants. When his mother requested that Jackson attend the fair as the family, he denied that request as well stating that he wanted to avoid the long lines. In truth, he had no desire to be in the company of his mother or Sara Williams after their disgusting display in town. Mounting what was his favorite horse, Jackson rode off toward the town. He was dressed in khaki colored trousers with a matching coat, a simple crisp white shirt and black boots. The combination of the sun's rays and the cool air made for a most refreshing ride into town.

After finishing what needed to be done around her small home, Hialeah bathed and dressed and sat in her rocking chair contemplating whether or not if she should attend the county fair. In the short time that she had lived in South Carolina she kept to herself and only went into town when necessary. She found herself thinking about what Jackson had said as she caressed her hand with a smile on her face. It truly would be utterly disgraceful for a man of his caliber to show up with no escort and he wanted her in spite of her being poor and colored. Besides, she had nothing else to do. Why waste such a beautiful day sitting at home? The fair came around only once a year. Perhaps doing something other than her usual routine could be refreshing. Convincing herself to come out of her shell, Hialeah dug into her sewing bag and gasped in horror. She quickly emptied its contents on the table. Her money was missing. She bit into her bottom lip in shear aggravation. She knew exactly who the swindler was and he would not get away from taking what was hers. Hialeah jumped to her feet and furiously raced out the door.

When Hialeah arrived at the fair she had one thing on her mind and that was to confront Jackson Harding and get her money back. Swarms of people had filled the fair ground. There were colored vendors selling their goods on one side and white vendors selling their wares on the other. Delicious aromas of assorted treats wafted through the air and the booming music from the county fair band rang in Hialeah's ears but she was determined to keep her mind on what mattered. She wanted what was hers and if that meant causing an uproar then so be it.

Hialeah jumped from her horse and angrily bee-lined her way through the fair's entrance. She turned in several directions scanning the crowd for any sign of Jackson Harding. Jackson, on the other hand, had been keeping a sharp eye anticipating Hialeah's arrival waiting patiently near the fair's entrance. He chuckled to himself as he blended in with the crowd as she made her way through the gate. Jackson was quite amused by the angered expression on her face. He was also entranced by Hialeah's sleek black locks flowing down her back. Jackson cocked a surprised brow at what he was sure was a smile on his hot tempered minx's face as children ran by her carrying balloons and stuffed animals that their parents had won for them from the various games on display. He found himself smiling watching Hialeah's face light up as if she too were a child. Jackson casually strolled up behind Hialeah and tapped her on the shoulder. Hialeah turned around to a grinning Jackson. Her own smile quickly faded. "Beautiful day is it not, Miss?" Jackson said simply. Hialeah was enraged at Jackson's audacity. "Don't you beautiful day me, you…you thief!" Hialeah spat. Jackson placed his hand over his heart in mock surprise by her attack. "Thief?" Jackson replied teasingly. "You stole my money and I want it back." Hialeah growled out. "I assure you, Miss, your money is safe." Jackson replied. "Then hand it over or I'll have you arrested." Hialeah remarked heatedly. "Arrested at my own fair in front of so many children? Now that would be rather cruel." Jackson replied sarcastically. "You a down-right thief, Jackson Harding." Hialeah spat. Jackson raised an amused brow. "Ah, so you know my name?" Jackson asked. "I know your name. Everybody in town know bout the Harding name." Hialeah replied matter-of-factly. "So you know my name, yet I've still the pleasure of knowing yours or would you have me continue to address you as Miss?" Jackson replied teasingly. "Don't make no never mind what my name be." Hialeah remarked stubbornly. Jackson crossed his arms. "Alright, then I suppose you'll have to have me arrested. The sheriff's standing over there." Jackson replied simply with a nod of his head in Sheriff Willard's direction. Hialeah followed Jackson's nod and let out an annoyed huff. She didn't dare attempt to have Jackson Harding arrested. "Why you care to know my name?" Hialeah demanded. No one of Jackson's status had ever bothered to inquire of her name. "It's proper manners to know ones' name when you make their acquaintance…in our case, for the third time." Jackson replied simply. "I weren't lookin' to make your acquaintance the first time. I was lookin' for work. Weren't lookin' to make your acquaintance last night neither. I only want what you stole from me." Hialeah remarked sternly. "And you shall have it provided you tell me your name and allow me the honor of your company as you so kindly did last night." Jackson replied casually. "You have my word. Besides, you're already here." Jackson said. "Folks don't want me here." Hialeah replied. "I want you here, Miss…" Jackson trailed off. "Nokosi. Hialeah Nokosi." Hialeah replied stubbornly. "Hialeah Nokosi. May I call you Hialeah?" Jackson asked. "If it get me my money back, Mr. Harding." Hialeah replied annoyed by Jackson's arrogant demeanor. "Jackson."

Jackson remarked peering into Hialeah's eyes. "Say my name, Hialeah." Jackson said low. His intense gaze made Hialeah tremble. She swallowed hard trying to find her voice. Jackson's stance and hazel eyes weakened her very being. "Say my name." Jackson said smoothly. "Jack…Jackson." Hialeah stammered softly. "Good. Now that we've gotten the hard part out of the way, and you'll not object to a white man such as myself escorting you, we'll take in this wondrous fair. Perhaps, Miss Nokosi, you may even enjoy yourself." Jackson said lightly.

Hialeah now crossed her arms in defiance. She stubbornly stood her ground. "No worries." Jackson said. He left Hialeah alone contemplating her decision. She desperately needed her money. Exhaling in defeat, Hialeah followed Jackson to the ring toss game and stood next to him. She immediately eyed a little rag doll with red hair made of yarn. She wore a blue dress with black shoes and pouty red lips that matched the color of her hair. "What will it be? The doll or the stuffed bear?" Jackson asked. "It be my money." Hialeah replied sternly. Jackson cocked yet another amused brow. Hialeah crossed her arms. If she wanted her money she had best play along. "The doll." Hialeah gritted out. "Alright, the doll it is." Jackson remarked confident that he could win the game. "Hoping to find you." Jackson said simply. Hialeah frowned, unsure of what Jackson was speaking of. "Last night you asked what business I had on the unsavory part of town. Now you know." Jackson replied casually. He removed his coat and offered it to Hialeah. "Would you please?" Jackson asked. Hialeah took Jackson's coat and draped it over her arm. She couldn't help but to notice the sinewy outline of his muscular frame through his white shirt. Was it the heat causing her cheeks to warm or the very true fact that Jackson Harding was indeed extremely handsome? Handsome and overbearingly arrogant yet searching for her. Shaking her head to clear the thoughts that were coursing through her mind, Hialeah found herself crossing her fingers as Jackson pulled two cents from his pocket. He handed the money to the man running the booth. In return for his two cents, Jackson was handed three rings. Hialeah said a silent prayer as Jackson rolled up his sleeves. She took a few steps back to allow Jackson room to toss the rings. One throw after another all three rings landed around the bottles. Hialeah's eyes widened. She could barely contain her joy. She squealed in utter delight as the crowd of people watching Jackson clapped behind him. Reveling in the moment, Jackson bowed to his admirers.

Jackson pointed to the little rag doll and received a roar of laughter from the men in the crowd. He handed the doll to Hialeah and the immediate sound of laughter ceased as several women inhaled their breaths in shocked disbelief as they realized Jackson Harding was in the company of a colored woman. "For you, Miss Hialeah Nokosi." Jackson said grinning slyly. He ignored the shocked whispers and mumbles as he escorted Hialeah to the man selling balloons. After purchasing four red balloons, they strolled over to the carousel. Hialeah walked onto the platform and chose her horse. Jackson sat across from her. Hialeah held on tight to her balloons and her prized doll as the carousel began to go around. Jackson glanced over at Hialeah. He was taken in by her smile. Her ice cold demeanor from the other night and the murderous look she had given him near the fair's entrance had melted and revealed a child-like innocence.

When the carousel came to a stop, Jackson climbed from his horse and reached out his hand to assist Hialeah from the ride. "Once more." Hialeah said. Jackson laughed. "If you don't mind, I'll watch you from outside the carousel." Jackson replied. "You fixin' to faint?" Hialeah said with a furrow of her brows. "Men don't faint, but yes." Jackson replied jokingly before stepping off the carousel. Hialeah remained on her horse as other riders joined her on the ride. Jackson handed the man in charge of the ride more money and took a few steps back as the carousel began to move for the entertainment of the passengers. The first go around, Hialeah decided to wave to Jackson as she went by. Her second go around, Jackson made a humorous face and Hialeah burst into laughter. She could barely contain herself anticipating what Jackson would do next. As the carousel made its way around once more, Hialeah's bright smile faded. Jackson was no longer standing alone but in the company of Sara Williams and a circle of her friends all gushing over him. Hialeah couldn't take her eyes from the lavish yellow sundress worn by Sara or the matching parasol that completed her ensemble. Hialeah glanced down in disgust at her hand sewn dress pieced together by discarded scraps of fabric. Oh how awful her appearance must be to Jackson in comparison to Sara's expensive dress.

When the carousel came to a complete stop, Hialeah climbed from her horse with her balloons and rag doll in her hand and walked by Jackson. She caught Jackson's eye but said nothing. She didn't wish to make a fool of herself in front of such a crowd. Jackson, however, caught the glimpse of disappointment in Hialeah's eyes as she hastily made her way toward the fair's exit. Jackson excused himself from Sara and the overbearing chattering of her friends and raced after Hialeah much to Sara's shock and dismay. Jackson ignored the calling of his name by Sara and kept his focus on Hialeah's red balloons. Not wanting to draw attention and attract any gossip mongers, Jackson refrained from calling Hialeah's name. He matched her stride and quickly caught up to Hialeah as she hurried through the crowd of fair goers. Jackson reached out and took hold of Hialeah's arm ceasing her hasty retreat. Fearing the hand on her arm belonged to Sheriff Willard, Hialeah froze and braced herself for a humiliating and public verbal assault. She took in a deep breath and closed her eyes.

Jackson furrowed his brows confused by Hialeah's rigid stance. He released her arm and casually walked around to face her. Surprised to see Hialeah's eyes closed, Jackson crossed his arms in front of him and grinned. "What are you doing?" Jackson asked calmly. Stunned to hear Jackson's thickly accented and low voice instead of Sheriff Willard's southern drawl that made her skin crawl, Hialeah inhaled a deep breath and immediately opened her eyes. She raised her head to take in Jackson's full height. Hialeah was relieved yet upset to see Jackson's grinning face before her. "Why you frighten me like you did?" Hialeah demanded. "My apologies." Jackson replied smoothly. "You keep it it mean so much to you." Hialeah remarked adamantly. Jackson was perplexed by Hialeah's outburst. "What you stole from me." Hialeah replied heatedly. "Besides, Miss Sara and her fancy dress waitin' on you right over there." Hialeah remarked nodding her head toward the carousel. Jackson glanced in the direction of where Sara still stood with her friends. "Ah, I see. You're either jealous of a dress or the person wearing the dress. Which is it?" Jackson said simply. "I must look an awful sight next to her." Hialeah replied pitifully. "Miss

Nokosi, I didn't commit robbery in hopes that you'd come here wearing some ridiculously frilly dress, or that you resemble Miss Williams. If I wanted to be in her company, then I would be. However, if you wish to leave then so be it." Jackson replied nonchalantly before slyly and quickly slipping the rag doll he had won for Hialeah from her unsuspecting arms and walking off with it. "But you'll leave without this." Jackson called out over his shoulder waving Hialeah's doll over his head. Taken aback by what had just happened, Hialeah rushed after Jackson. "That's my prize, sir." Hialeah said sternly. Jackson stopped short and Hialeah nearly collided into his backside. Jackson turned to face his disgruntled fiery minx. "You'll have it back and your money after you've joined me for some cold lemonade and peach cobbler and stop this ridiculous talk of dresses. Otherwise, I'll look pretty foolish walking around with a red haired doll. Agreed?" Jackson asked with a cock of his brow. "You think cause you rich and handsome you can do whatever suits you?" Hialeah replied accusingly. "Precisely." Jackson remarked matter-of-factly before continuing on his way with Hialeah close on his heels. He stopped short again taking a moment to ponder Hialeah's question but this time Hialeah was ready. She side stepped avoiding Jackson's backside. He turned around a naughty smirk on his face. "So you think I'm handsome?" Jackson asked teasingly. "That ain't what I said." Hialeah replied defensively. "I'm pretty sure you did." Jackson remarked. "Well I ain't mean it." Hialeah replied stubbornly. Jackson leaned in close. "I'm pretty sure you did." Jackson remarked playfully before marching off toward the lemonade stand. Hialeah found herself smiling as she followed after Jackson. She had never had anyone pay her any mind especially a man of Jackson Harding's caliber. She liked it...a lot.

    Jackson escorted Hialeah to one of the many tables set up for the colored folks while he went to purchase two cups of fresh lemonade and homemade peach cobbler. Hialeah tied her balloons to the chair and waited patiently for Jackson to return. She watched as he casually strolled into one of the colored lines without so much as a care that he was white and struck up a conversation with the thirsty patrons standing in front of him. Hialeah was in awe of Jackson Harding. He spoke to coloreds like they were his equal. Hialeah had no idea what was being said but it was enough to make Jackson throw back his head in laughter and pat the colored man on his back like they were the best of friends. The man in line tipped his hat to Jackson and went on his way after purchasing his goods. Jackson was handed two plates of peach cobbler and Hialeah hurried to assist him with their cold beverages. Once seated at their table, Jackson placed Hialeah's doll onto the table before digging into his sweet treat. Hialeah reached for her doll and placed it on her lap. She noticed the many eyes of several colored fair goers watching her and Jackson enjoy their desserts and refreshments, no doubt curious as to why he would be seated amongst them. Hialeah squirmed in her seat feeling uneasy. She leaned in toward Jackson. "Don't it bother you none that folks are watchin' you?" Hialeah asked in a whisper. Jackson glanced around him and returned his attention to Hialeah. He leaned in toward her. "I suppose they too think I'm handsome." Jackson replied in the same whispered tone as Hialeah. His response brought out laughter from the both of them. Jackson was happy to have brought several smiles to Hialeah's lips but the sound of her laughter was pleasing to his ears. "Beautiful sound your laugh." Jackson said smoothly. Hialeah could feel the blush of her cheeks as she looked down at her dish of peach cobbler. "I embarrassed you." Jackson said. "It's okay." Hialeah replied softly. Jackson dug into his trouser pocket and produced his wallet. He removed Hialeah's money and set it on the table between them. "As I promised." Jackson said. Jackson nodded his head as he stood to take his leave. "By the way, you look perfect, Miss Hialeah Nokosi." Jackson remarked with a wink of his eye before leaving Hialeah alone at their table.

Hialeah sat motionless as Jackson disappeared into the crowd. She slowly reached for her money and absentmindedly placed it into her sewing bag. Taking a moment to glance around, everywhere Hialeah looked people was enjoying the fair. Wives hung on the arms of their husbands laughing flirtatiously. Children were running wildly and there she sat alone and miserable. The sudden feeling of emptiness was too much to bear. Hialeah buried her head in her hands and softly sobbed unaware that Jackson had returned and stood over her. "Sobbing at a fair?" Jackson said casually. Startled, Hialeah quickly glanced up to a grinning Jackson. "I take it you'll be staying a tad longer?" Jackson teased. Hialeah nodded her head and hastily wiped her tears from her cheeks. "I'd like that very much." Hialeah replied. Jackson untied Hialeah's balloons from her chair and handed them to her. Hialeah picked up her prized doll and Jackson assisted her from the table. He held his arm out to Hialeah. Without hesitation and giving no thought to the watchful eyes of the onlookers seated around them, Hialeah graciously took Jackson's arm.

Jackson and Hialeah carried on with the entertainment that the county fair had to offer. They stopped to watch the apple pie eating contest. They took a moment to cheer on several children entered into a pig chasing contest and Hialeah was quite enthusiastic with her applause and whistling as Jackson handed her his coat to compete in an apple bobbing contest winning a free ride on the fair's much anticipated spectacle; a hot air balloon ride. Albeit she had never heard of a hot air balloon, Hialeah was thrilled for Jackson just the same.

Making their way to the hot air balloon site, Hialeah continued to be in absolute awe of Jackson. He was the only man of great wealth that took part in the apple bobbing contest and cared not of what the other snobs thought of him. He welcomed the praise, wise cracks and pats on his back for winning. Drenched in water, Jackson took it all in proudly. His calm and casual demeanor put Hialeah at ease as she walked by his side. She suddenly found herself ignoring the gawks of people as they walked to their destination.

Hialeah's eyes widened at the sight of the colorful balloon attached to a large basket. The balloon was tied down on all four sides. Hialeah was truly entranced by the balloon. She couldn't take another step. "Have you ever seen such a thing?" Hialeah asked in wonderment. "Once. In London." Jackson replied. "What it do?" Hialeah asked. "You climb into the basket and the balloon lifts you to the sky." Jackson replied. Hialeah lifted her head to the sky and inhaled. "Way up there?" Hialeah remarked as if in a daze. "Would you care to join me?" Jackson asked walking toward the balloon. "I think I best watch you from here." Hialeah replied. Jackson chuckled as he walked back toward Hialeah. "It's perfectly safe. Trust me. There's nothing like it." Jackson remarked. "I trust you. Still terrified though." Hialeah replied nervously her eyes fixated on the massive balloon. "I'll protect you." Jackson said. Hialeah looked up into Jackson's confident eyes. She wondered if he feared anything.

Jackson retrieved his coat from Hialeah and put it on. He handed her balloons and rag doll to a little colored girl watching and waiting for the balloon to take flight. He pleasantly asked the little girl if she would take care of Hialeah's things. The little girl smiled and nodded her head. Jackson nodded his head in appreciation before escorting Hialeah to the balloon amidst the crowd that had begun to form to witness the balloon's launch. Hialeah was hesitant to climb into the basket. She felt herself trembling. "I decided to stay right here." Hialeah said her voice quivering. "How about you join me and if we fall you land on me?" Jackson replied teasingly. Hialeah envisioned Jackson lying in the dirt and her on top of him. What a sight that would be! That would surely get folks' tongues wagging. "I fixin' to land good and hard on you too." Hialeah remarked. Jackson cocked a brow; a devilish thought roaming through his head. He would much rather have the hot tempered temptress lying beneath him but for now an exhilarating balloon ride would have to do.

Dismissing his thought of having Hialeah in his bed, Jackson surprised Hialeah as he lifted her over the basket's edge before joining her in the basket. Jackson seemingly ignored the gawks and stunned inhaled breaths from the crowd. Hialeah's stunned expression having been hoisted over the balloon's edge was lost on him as well. "Are you ready?" Jackson asked excited to lift off. Before Hialeah could utter a word, they were joined by the gentleman who would be flying the balloon. He informed Jackson and Hialeah how the balloon worked and that they would only go as high as the ropes allowed. Hialeah looked over the edge of the basket at the long thick ropes tied down by even thicker spikes. She felt her knees giving away beneath her but tried to regain her composure next to Jackson. The sound of the roaring fire released by the instructor startled Hialeah. She practically leapt into Jackson's arms as the balloon began to slowly rise. Jackson welcomed the opportunity to comfort Hialeah. He placed his arm around her waist and smiled down at her. "No worries." Jackson said soothingly. Hialeah closed her eyes briefly as she nodded her head.

Jackson's arm around her waist immediately put Hialeah at ease as they continued to float from the ground.

The cheers from the crowd below emboldened Hialeah to look over the edge as she held on tightly to Jackson. "Amazing isn't it?" Jackson asked. "Look around you." Jackson said. Hialeah was speechless at the overwhelming view from the balloon. She could see the tops of the buildings and the whole county fair. Although her heart was pounding in her chest, riding in the massive balloon with Jackson was the single most fascinating thing she had ever done. "It's so beautiful." Hialeah replied in awe. "Shall we jump?" Jackson asked teasingly. "Have you gone plum crazy?" Hialeah rushed out. Her outburst made Jackson and the instructor throw back their heads in laughter.

Word of Jackson Harding winning the first ride on the hot air balloon spread like wild fire across the county fair. Sara had taken this grand opportunity to boast to anyone in ear shot how her fiancé had won them the ride and how thrilled she was to be the first to go up in the balloon. With her equally spoiled and overbearing friends rallying behind her they all made their way to the balloon pushing anyone aside that stood in their way. The hearty applause and cheers from the crowd halted their steps as they simultaneously raised their heads to the sky. Sara inhaled a stunned breath in shear disbelief as she witnessed her fiancé in the balloon's basket with his arm around the waist of a colored woman smiling and waving to the onlookers below. "Oh Sara, how humiliating for you." One of Sara's friends said. "Shut up." Sara spat before storming her way through the crowd with her friends on her heels. She was seething with rage as the balloon carrying Jackson and Hialeah was being lowered back to the ground by the balloon's crew members.

Although still reeling from the rush of her first time in a balloon, Hialeah was thankful to be back on the ground. The little girl who had taken such good care of Hialeah's things raced toward Hialeah and Jackson to return them back to her. Jackson lifted Hialeah from the basket and smiled at the little girl as she handed Hialeah her gifts. Jackson thanked the little girl for her generosity and dug into his pocket to reward the little girl. He knelt down to her level and held out a shiny dime for her to spend at the fair. Beaming with excitement, the little girl hugged Jackson before racing off to spend her reward. When Jackson stood to his full height he was met by a visibly furious Sara Williams. "Miss Williams." Jackson said simply. "How dare you humiliate me by carrying on with this wretched half-breed filth for all the town to see? Have you no decency?" Sara spat angrily.

Embarrassed and shammed before what appeared to be the whole town, Hialeah ran through the crowd with tears stinging her eyes. "Miss Nokosi!" Jackson yelled as he ran after Hialeah following her red balloons as she pushed her way through the onlookers. Disgusted at herself by allowing Jackson to charm her, Hialeah dropped her rag doll and released her balloons into the air. Jackson stopped for a brief moment as Hialeah's floating balloons distracted him. He felt a tug on the back of his coat. Jackson turned around to find his little assistant holding up Hialeah's rag doll. Jackson took the doll and nodded his head in thanks. Noticing the little girl's eyes widen, Jackson turned around to find Sara staring daggers into him with her hands on her hips. "Well?" Sara demanded. "Well what, you despicable bitch." Jackson growled out before shoving his way through the stunned crowd to get as far away from Sara as possible. He was beyond livid at her treatment of Hialeah. His pleasant day now ruined and utterly clueless as to where he could possibly find Hialeah, Jackson left the fair ground, mounted his horse and rode for home cursing Sara Williams to hell.

Hialeah rode with break neck speed away from the fair and from the horrible scene of everyone gawking at her. She couldn't be bothered with the stream of tears that ran down her cheeks as her tiny house came into view. Her only thought was getting home and locking herself away. She jumped from her horse and raced into her home slamming the door behind her. Hialeah collapsed against the door and burst into tears. Oh how she despised Sara Williams. For the first time she felt welcomed and not ignored and in mere seconds her joyous day was bashed in front of her eyes. How could she ever be so foolish to believe that she could be seen with Jackson Harding and not ruffle the feathers of Charleston's socialites? Hialeah promised herself no matter how nice Jackson was to her, she would never be seen with him again. That ol' Sara Williams could just have him. She didn't need that kind of attention. Jackson Harding was a man of power and prestige and she was just a simple nobody. Surely after what had happened today, he would forget about her.

After his horrendous encounter with Sara, Jackson spent the rest of the day fuming. He took his supper in his bedroom and avoided conversing with his mother. He was sure she had heard about the day's events and would no doubt side with Sara. He wanted no part of it. What he did want, however, was to find Hialeah. If he had to go to town every morning with her doll and make a complete fool of himself then that's what he would do.

Jackson kept true to his plan. He went into town each morning for a week in hopes that he would find Hialeah. He kept her rag doll in his saddle bag but with each passing day, he returned home feeling empty. He didn't dare ask anyone in town her whereabouts. Hialeah had been humiliated enough. He wouldn't add to her cruel treatment by allowing gossip to circulate about her. He would wait patiently until she had a need to come into town.

Hialeah shied away from town as long as she could but she was in desperate need of a few items. She made it to town at her usual early time. She had already brought her eggs for Mr. Nesbit, but she was eager to spend some of her earnings that Jackson had obtained for her from Mr. Grisby in Mr. Nesbit's store. She had her eyes on the nice pair of shoes that she had wanted to purchase on her previous trip and now she had more than enough to buy them. She kept her four dollars safely tucked into her sewing bag and calmly hopped off the seat of her old wagon and walked up to Mr. Nesbit's store. Her calm demeanor faded at the very sight of Mrs. Nesbit minding the store instead of her husband. Hialeah exhaled a breath and prayed that just this one time Mrs. Nesbit wouldn't treat her so cold-heartedly. The store had already acquired a few customers both white and colored and Mrs. Nesbit was busy assisting one of the white ladies. Hialeah opened the door and slipped inside but the ringing of the small bell above the door caught Mrs. Nesbit's attention and her eyes grew the size of saucers at

Hialeah's presence. Mrs. Nesbit let out a huff and left her customer as she bee-lined her way toward Hialeah. "You get out of my store." Mrs. Nesbit said angrily. "I won't cause no trouble." Hialeah declared as she dug into her sewing bag. She produced her money to show Mrs. Nesbit. "I got money." Hialeah said. "Your money or you are not wanted here." Mrs. Nesbit replied heatedly. Every customer in the shop stopped their shopping to watch the spectacle. "Please ma'am, I'll wait my turn." Hialeah pleaded. "You'll do no such thing. Now leave my store. Your kind is not wanted here." Mrs. Nesbit replied heatedly. "What you mean my kind? I colored just like them." Hialeah replied nodding her head toward the other colored women in the store. "They're regular colored folk. You're tainted with savage blood." Mrs. Nesbit said smugly. "You got no right to treat me this way." Hialeah replied fighting back tears. "I same as you." Hialeah continued. "You're nothing like me. Now you leave my store or I'll have the sheriff on you." Mrs. Nesbit warned. Once again, shamed and humiliated, Hialeah shoved her money back into her bag and ran out of the store.

  Jackson let out a long sigh of relief. His week-long search had finally paid off. From across the road, he watched with a smile on his face, as Hialeah drove into town and parked her wagon a short distance from the Nesbit's General Store. He dug into his saddle bag and hurried across the road to place Hialeah's rag doll onto the floor board of her wagon before deciding to wait for her outside of Mr. Nesbit's store. Jackson had barely enough time to place Hialeah's doll in her wagon before she came barreling from the store. Blinded by her tears, she unknowingly collided into Jackson. Her eyes cast down, Hialeah was oblivious to Jackson's presence. "Excuse me sir." Hialeah said tearfully as she hurried to her wagon without looking back. "Miss Nokosi." Jackson said. Recognizing the familiar voice once again, Hialeah continued on; wiping her eyes as she hurried to her wagon with Jackson trailing behind her. Matching Hialeah's stride it took no time for Jackson to catch her. He reached for Hialeah's arm only to have her pull away from him. Hialeah spun on her heel to face Jackson. "What you follow me for? Ain't I humiliate you enough in front of your fancy white folk?" Hialeah spat. Jackson ignored her question. "Are you alright? What happened?" Jackson asked. "Why it matter to you?"

Hialeah asked stubbornly. "Don't make no never mind. Estonkes os (Is-don-ges oh-s). I'm fine." Hialeah replied her eyes welling up with tears of hurt. "What happened?" Jackson asked soothingly. Unable to bear Jackson's hazel gaze and calming voice, Hialeah fell victim to her tears. She began to explain to Jackson what had transpired in Mrs. Nesbit's store. Jackson gently placed both of his hands on Hialeah's shoulders. "I beg you Miss Nokosi, do speak English." Jackson said. Hialeah was so distraught; she was unaware that she was speaking in Creek. She forced herself to look up at Jackson. Her lips were trembling. Hialeah took a deep breath to calm herself. "She throw me out. She says my money not wanted in her store. She tell me I tainted." Hialeah said through her tears. Jackson absentmindedly wrapped his arms around her to comfort her. Across the road, Sheriff Willard watched their embrace.

Jackson released Hialeah from his supportive embrace. She was a fiery one but she didn't deserve such cruel treatment. Hialeah wiped at her eyes once more. "Come with me." Jackson said. "Where we goin'?" Hialeah asked confused. "Shopping." Jackson replied with a devilish smirk on his face. "I ain't goin' back in there with that woman. She fixin' to send for the sheriff if I return." Hialeah rushed out worriedly. "No need to worry about the sheriff." Jackson replied. He held his arm out and nodded his head for Hialeah to take his arm. Hialeah hesitated before reluctantly linking her arm around Jackson's.

Jackson entered Mrs. Nesbit's store with Hialeah on his arm. He could feel her shaking but said nothing. Jackson had yet to meet Mrs. Nesbit but was feeling quite enthused about his impending performance. The little bell above the door rang and alerted Mrs. Nesbit to a new customer entering her store. Mrs. Nesbit opened her mouth to protest but was cut off by Jackson. "Good morning ladies!" Jackson said boisterously. Once again the store went silent. "You get that woman out of my store." Mrs. Nesbit replied heatedly. Jackson approached Mrs. Nesbit with Hialeah still silently linked to his arm. "Ah you must be the enchanting Henrietta Nesbit." Jackson said smiling. Mrs. Nesbit was taken aback by the compliment. "Excuse me." Mrs. Nesbit replied slightly flustered by the compliment. "Jackson Harding." Jackson remarked. "Jackson Harding? You wouldn't happen to be…" Mrs. Nesbit began. "Indeed I am. Georgina Harding's boy." Jackson replied. Excited whispers and giggles from the other ladies in the store caught Jackson's ear. Jackson thought to take his show a little further. He took Mrs. Nesbit's hand and placed a kiss on the back of it. Feeling overwhelmed by the attention she was receiving by the handsome Jackson Harding, Mrs. Nesbit nearly lost her composure. "It is an honor to make your acquaintance I must say." Jackson said. Hialeah kept her eyes on Jackson. "My dear mother was just raving about you." Jackson said smoothly. "About…about me?" Mrs. Nesbit asked proudly. "Absolutely. She was boasting to me what an exceptional Christian woman you are. I believe her exact words were that all of Charleston would benefit greatly if we followed your path of righteousness." Jackson replied. "Which is why I simply had to come meet you in person, and in doing so, as you can see, I was nearly ran over by this poor woman who had been brought to tears. Why I was nearly dumbfounded when she explained to me moments ago that she was tossed out of your fine establishment and threatened with the sheriff. I simply refused to believe that the very woman my mother had only just referred to as an exceptional Christian would do such a horrid act to a woman in dire need." Jackson remarked. Mrs. Nesbit began to blush hearing such high praise of her person coming from the Hardings. "You must forgive me. I have been under the weather and quite frankly out of sorts all together." Mrs. Nesbit replied in her most southern genteel accent. "I thought as much. A fine woman who cherishes the Lord as you do simply would not turn her back on one of the Lord's less fortunate souls." Jackson remarked. "I assure you I would not." Mrs. Nesbit replied proudly. "Then you surely wouldn't object to my escorting this dear soul as she look over your fine merchandise? And I promise, as a gentleman, she will abide by the rules." Jackson asked charmingly. "Of course, Mr. Harding, of course." Mrs. Nesbit replied. Jackson nodded his head in appreciation and led Hialeah away from Mrs. Nesbit.

Hialeah was so eager to finally be able to shop amongst the other ladies she didn't know where to start. Jackson watched as she happily picked up some scented soaps and from there, she reached for the shoes that she had wanted when she brought in her eggs to Mr. Nesbit. Jackson was very much aware that he was being watched by the women in the store. He nodded his head and smiled and received flirtatious looks from some of the older women and blushing giggles from their daughters. Jackson even winked at some of the colored women in the store who walked by blushing. Hialeah, however, was oblivious to the reactions that Jackson was stirring up in the women. She stood in line with her arms full with her soon to be purchased items. She could hardly wait to try on her new shoes and bathe with her new soaps and put on her new nylons.

When it was finally her turn to pay for her items, Hialeah thought she would faint from excitement. Jackson stood by her side and smiled charmingly at Mrs. Nesbit, whom couldn't concentrate on her adding to give Hialeah an amount on her purchase. "Two dollars fifty." Mrs. Nesbit blurted out. Hialeah dug into her sewing back and handed Mrs. Nesbit her money and waited for her change. Hialeah grabbed her bag of purchased goods and thanked Mrs. Nesbit before leaving the store, but Jackson wasn't done having his fun at Mrs. Nesbit's expense. He leaned over the counter and whispered into her ear how much he craved older women before kissing Mrs. Nesbit on the cheek. As he exited the store, a loud thump was heard behind him but Jackson kept walking with a humorous smile on his face. He could hear several women announcing that Mrs. Nesbit had fainted.

Hialeah was several steps ahead of Jackson by the time he had left the store. He caught up with her and Hialeah stopped and turned to him a confused look on her face. "What?" Jackson asked. "You fancy that woman or somethin'?" Hialeah asked. "Fancy her?" Jackson replied lightly. "Mrs. Nesbit. You take a likin' to her?" Hialeah remarked. "Hardly." Jackson replied. "Then why you say all those nice things to her?" Hialeah asked genuinely confused. "Why not?" Jackson said. "Cause she a mean witch." Hialeah replied. Jackson laughed at her choice of words. "She isn't so bad. Besides, even mean witches need to hear that they're enchanting once in awhile." Jackson said. "She downright wicked." Hialeah replied as she started walking towards her wagon. Neither of them spoke until they reached Hialeah's wagon. Jackson took Hialeah's bag and set it on the seat. "There, you're all set." Jackson said. Hialeah gave Jackson a suspicious look. "Why you help me? How come you don't treat me like the rest of the folks in town?" Hialeah asked. "Would you prefer it if I treated you horribly?" Jackson replied. "Don't think you could." Hialeah said climbing onto her seat. "Why is that?" Jackson asked. "Cause you maybe take a likin' to me." Hialeah replied matter-of-factly. Jackson smiled at her bold assertion. "Perhaps." Jackson teased. "What you want from me?" Hialeah asked curiously. "The mere pleasure of your company." Jackson replied casually. "That's all?" Hialeah remarked. "Indeed. Now do try to have a pleasant day Miss Nokosi and be mindful that you don't step on your passenger." Jackson said. Hialeah frowned confused as to what Jackson was referring. She looked down at her feet and gasped in surprise at the sight of her rag doll. She bent over and picked up her doll. "I've come into town everyday hoping to reunite the two of you and to apologize for Miss Williams' ill manners." Jackson said. "I accept." Hialeah replied. "I'm honored to have made your acquaintance." Jackson remarked. "May I ask you a question?" Hialeah replied. "Depends on the question." Jackson remarked smiling. "You like fishin'?" Hialeah asked. "Fishing?" Jackson replied with a raise of his brows. "I haven't gone fishing in quite some time." Jackson said. "I was fixin' to go tomorrow mornin'. It'll be a good day for it if you'd like to come along. Only got one pole though." Hialeah said. Jackson pretended to ponder over her request for a moment. "Alright. Fishing it is." Jackson said. "Milliner's Pond bright and early." Hialeah said. "I'll be there on one condition." Jackson replied smiling. "What's that?" Hialeah asked. "That you'll not attempt to stab me if I don't catch any fish." Jackson replied teasingly. Hialeah smiled at Jackson's teasing as she remembered their first encounter after her ordeal with Mr. Grigsby. "Cehccvres (Zee-hee-zah-les). I'll see you again." Hialeah remarked before commanding her horse to move on.

Jackson watched as Hialeah rode away before heading back to his horse. He found himself still smiling as he climbed onto his horse. His smile instantly faded as he noticed Sara Williams and two of her friends watching him with smug looks on their faces. "What a waste of a perfectly good man. Handsome and charming and a disgusting nigger lover." Sara Williams said smugly. "Why I don't know what's worse, being born a complete nigger or half nigger half dirty savage. And to think, I would share your bed." Sara continued her friends giggling.

"Allow me to solve your riddle. I'd say being born white trash with a mixture of sickening fat sow. Oh, and I assure you Miss Williams; I had no intention of allowing you in my bed. You're not worth the fuck." Jackson replied heatedly before turning his horse. He could hear Sara screaming in outrage as he rode away. He was sure his mother would scold him for his behavior. The very thought of his mother reprimanding him like a child brought a smile to Jackson's face.

Jackson made it home just as his mother and father were being served lunch. His mother called to him to join. He didn't care to converse about his whereabouts to his mother, but he had missed breakfast and he was very hungry. He opted to have lunch with his parents and make the best of it. Jackson sat across from his mother and waited to be served. His mother looked as if she were ready to burst. She clearly wanted to know what he had spent his morning doing. Georgina Harding's frustration grew even more evident as she began to tap her finger tips on the table. Jackson picked up his glass of lemonade that had been served to him and took a long swig of it. Jackson set his glass back on the table and Georgina burst. "Jackson Harding would you care to tell me and your father just where you were this morning?" Georgina asked visibly upset. "Not particularly." Jackson replied casually. "Well, I had the unfortunate pleasure of being told by Sally Higgenbottom..." Georgina began. "Sally Higgenbottom? Oh yes, the sweet lady..." Jackson's words were abruptly cut off. "Sweet lady indeed! She's the biggest gossip in town." Georgina snapped. "And she was all too eager to stop by this morning and spread her vicious gossip about my son." Georgina stated. "That is unfortunate." Jackson replied mockingly. "Do you think this humorous? Do you think for one moment that I relish the fact that my son has been gallivanting around town with that heathen woman?" Georgina asked heatedly. "Heathen woman?" Jackson replied teasingly. "You know precisely whom I am referring to." Georgina spat. "I can assure you mother, I spent no time in town with Miss Williams. I did, however, enjoy the morning in the company of Miss Nokosi." Jackson replied calmly. Before Georgina Harding could lash out at her son, the thundering sound of horses approaching caught the Harding's attention. Confused, Georgina Harding stood up and peered out of one of the massive windows of their dining room. "It's Harland

Williams." Georgina said. She turned to her husband. "Are you expecting him?" Georgina asked. "He hadn't make mention of dropping by." Henry Harding replied. Before another word could be uttered by any of them, the Harding's front door was swiftly swung open. The crashing of the door against the wall startled Georgina and brought Jackson and his father to their feet. "Where is he!" Harland Williams yelled angrily his voice booming throughout the hall. "Why they's havin' lunch, Mr. Williams." Miss Lilly, the family's cook, responded from the foyer. "I'll see if Mr. Henry is finished with his meal." Lilly said anxiously. "I'm not here for Henry. You bring me that scoundrel. That Jackson!" Harland Williams spat. Henry and Georgina Harding both turned toward their son. Unbothered, Jackson took another sip of his lemonade and once again simply set the glass on the table. "Excuse me. I do believe I have company." Jackson said calmly before leaving his parents in the dining room. Henry and Georgina Harding exchanged looks of confusion and hurried after their son.

Jackson casually strolled out into the foyer, his hands clasped behind his back. "Judge Williams, I wasn't expecting you." Jackson said teasingly. "You smug bastard!" Harland Williams spat. "Bastard?" Jackson replied mockingly. "Bastard!" Harland yelled. Jackson turned to face his mother. "Mother, am I a bastard?" Jackson asked sarcastically. "Jackson, don't use such vulgar language." Georgina replied. "Harland, just what exactly is this about?" Henry Harding demanded. "He knows damn well what this is about." Harland replied heatedly keeping his eyes on Jackson. "Your nigger lover son insulted my Sara." Harland continued angrily. "My Jackson would never do such a thing." Georgina replied offended at the very notion. "My daughter came home in tears. She said Jackson referred to her as a hideous cow." Harland remarked. Jackson burst into laughter. Georgina Harding stamped her foot in outrage at her son's utter disrespect. "Jackson, for God's sake, your manners." Georgina said annoyed at her son's childlike behavior. "Forgive me mother, but I assure you, I did not refer to the good judge's daughter as a hideous cow." Jackson replied smiling. "You see there. A simple misunderstanding, of course." Georgina replied relieved. "Then you're calling my daughter a liar?" Harland demanded. "I wouldn't dare think it. I am, however, calling her hard of hearing." Jackson replied casually. "Jackson." Georgina remarked shocked. Jackson ignored his mother. He kept his eyes focused on Mr. Williams. "It wasn't a cow, sir. I referred to your daughter as a sow, a hideous sow." Jackson replied matter-of-factly.

Harland Williams' anger had reached its peak. He would not stand idly by and allow his daughter to be insulted. Harland grabbed Jackson by his shirt front; an act that sent Jackson's temper over the edge. He broke Harland's hold on him and swiftly grabbed the older man by the neck. Jackson ferociously slammed Harland's back against a wall; his hand tightly around his neck. Georgina Harding screamed in shear fear. Henry Harding raced toward the two men. He pulled at Jackson's arm to no avail. Jackson's hold on Harland's neck was relentless. "Take your bloody hands off me!" Jackson yelled at his father; his menacing eyes still locked on Harland's now terror filled ones. Henry released his hold on his son's arm. Jackson was now fully focused on Harland Williams. "Don't you ever think to put your filthy hands on me again. Judge or not, I'll break your goddamn bloody neck." Jackson vehemently spat his warning. He roughly released his hold on Harland Williams' neck causing him to stumble. Harland regained his footing and gasped for air. Neither Henry nor Georgina Harding moved from their spots. After filling his lungs with enough air to speak, Harland turned to face Jackson. "I'll have you arrested for this." Harland wheezed out. "Do it sir, I dare you." Jackson threatened. With nothing left to say, Harland Williams stumbled out the front door.

Jackson stopped what was sure to be a scolding from his mother before she could even open her mouth. "Don't." Jackson said angrily as he headed for the back door. "Where are you going?" Georgina persisted in asking. Jackson kept his back to his mother and father. "To the slave quarters, mother. I've always felt more home there than here." Jackson replied his voice still full of anger. "This is your home Jackson." Georgina replied. Jackson turned around to face his mother. "No mother. This ceased being my home when you agreed with that man…" Jackson began as he pointed to his father. "To send me away as a mere boy." Jackson continued his voice hate filled and bitter. "Jackson you must understand. Your father and I had good reason to send you away." Georgina replied pleading for her son's understanding. Jackson scoffed. "Pray tell mother. What reason could there have possibly been for a mother to send her only child away from the only home he had ever known?" Jackson replied sarcastically. "Jackson, you were spoiled, disobedient. You were an unruly child." Georgina remarked. "Why?" Jackson asked, his voice booming in the massive hall. "Because I refused to believe that whites were better than coloreds?" Jackson replied heatedly. "People were beginning to talk." Georgina remarked defensively. "Oh of course." Jackson replied again full of sarcasm. "And people's idle gossip warranted beatings from my own father, sent off alone to a country I knew nothing about, to a school where I endured even more beatings?" Jackson spat. "Abandoned by my own parents!" Jackson yelled. "Jackson we never abandoned you." Georgina replied sympathetically. "Then where were you when I cried out for you!" Jackson asked angrily. "When I cried for my mother!" Jackson remarked viciously his chest heaving with rage. Unable to bear her son's cruel outburst any longer, Georgina turned away from Jackson. With nothing left to be said, Jackson left his mother and father standing in the hall.

  Jackson spent the rest of the afternoon and well into the evening in an abandoned slave quarter. Lying on his back in the dark on an old bed with his head rested on his arms, Jackson thought of absolutely nothing. He had fallen asleep dreaming of the times he had spent driving the slave mothers insane; wildly playing with their children. He was awakened by the sound of footsteps approaching and the dim light of a lantern. A soft knock on the slave quarter door brought him to his feet. "Mr. Jackson, you in there?" Lucas called from the other side of the door. "I wish to be alone." Jackson replied. "I's got yo' dinner. Miss Lilly says to bring it to you. Says not to bring this here plate back unless it's empty." Lucas replied. Jackson went to the door and opened it. He remembered quite vividly that Miss Lilly was a no nonsense type of woman. She was nurturing and stern and very much the disciplinarian. She was a dark skinned woman with black hair that she kept in a bun. She was roundly in her figure and taller than the average woman. Her glares were enough to keep any spoiled child in line. Jackson knew better than to leave a plate of Miss Lilly's food untouched. She had been cooking for his family since before he was born. Jackson adored her tremendously. She was an excellent cook and he was pretty hungry. Lucas entered the slave quarter holding Jackson's tray in one hand and the lantern in another. Jackson retrieved his tray from Lucas and set it on the small table in the room. Lucas set the lantern down next to Jackson's tray. He then went to his bag and pulled out a bottle of whiskey and set it on the table. Lucas looked at Jackson. "Not sure if you're a drinkin' man, but after what I heard, I think you need this more than I do." Lucas said. Jackson offered Lucas an appreciative smile. "Thanks." Jackson replied. Lucas simply nodded his head and turned to leave. "Care to join me?" Jackson asked sliding the bottle in Lucas's direction. Lucas sat down at the table and Jackson followed suit. Jackson removed the lid from his dinner. Roast beef and potatoes. One of his favorites. Lucas took a swig of the whiskey and slid the bottle back over to Jackson. Jackson took his turn at the bottle and wiped his mouth on the back of his hand. He then turned to Lucas. "May I ask you a question?" Jackson asked. "Yes sir." Lucas replied. "Why are you here?" Jackson remarked. "Not sure what you mean sir." Lucas replied. "Here. You're a free man. Why are you here working for my family?" Jackson asked. "After the war, I needed work. I got me a wife and two boys to provide for. I came here and offered my services to your daddy. He pays real good. Saved enough money to buy my own land." Lucas replied. "Why didn't you go north?" Jackson asked. "No need. This here my home." Lucas said. "Was mine too once." Jackson replied. "Never should have returned here." Jackson said somberly. "Then you never would have met her." Lucas said. "Do you know her?" Jackson asked. "Seen her in town lookin' for work. White folk don't pay her no mind though. Hear she real good at mendin'." Lucas said. "Mending?" Jackson replied. "You know, sewin' and the like." Lucas remarked. "My wife lost out on the job for Mr. Grisby cause she sew better than my Ruthie." Lucas said. "Then she's not a working girl?" Jackson asked curious. "Mr. Grisby hire her to mend dresses and such. She don't keep gentlemen company." Lucas replied. Jackson was relieved to hear the news. Lucas stood up from the table. "I best be goin' now. My Ruthie don't take too kindly to me missin' dinner." Lucas said. "Your Ruthie's a lucky woman." Jackson replied. "No sir. I be the lucky one." Lucas said. "Thank you." Jackson replied. "I knows it ain't my place, but if you takin' a likin' to that girl, you best get her outta here before they's trouble." Lucas warned. Jackson simply nodded his head and Lucas left him alone.

Chapter 4

    Jackson had finished Lucas's bottle of whiskey and woke up feeling out of sorts. He was covered in sweat from the summer's heat and his head was pounding. Jackson swung his legs over the tiny bed and after needing a moment to collect himself, he struggled to his feet. Feeling as if he would pass out from the sun's heat and the whiskey, Jackson cursed himself for drinking as much as he did. Somewhat regaining his composure, Jackson pulled out his pocket watch. He groaned inward as it was nearing noon. Replacing his watch back into his pocket, Jackson stumbled to the door. He leaned against the door briefly before slowly pulling it open. Jackson took two steps out of the door and fell to his knees. Last night's dinner spewed from his mouth. Jackson crawled a short distance away from the slave quarter before collapsing in the grass. He felt himself being lifted to his feet and led to the house. Lucas escorted Jackson through the back door and up the stairs to his bedroom. Lucas assisted Jackson to his bed and left him alone to sleep off his drunken stupor.

    Hialeah woke up bright and early. She had baked an apple pie the day before to share with Jackson after they had finished their fishing. She had never been so excited to go fishing. For the first time, she would have someone to talk to. She knew that since Jackson hadn't been fishing in a long time that he wouldn't have a pole, so she set out to make him one of his own. She gathered her pole and Jackson's new pole, their sweet treat and her bait and loaded it onto her wagon. She styled her long black hair into two braids and had sewn whatever holes she could find in her fishing dress. On any other fishing day, she wouldn't have cared about her appearance, but today, she wanted to look somewhat pretty. She wasn't exactly sure why she wanted to make herself look decent for Jackson. It was no secret that he would be marrying Sara Williams. Their upcoming nuptials were all the talk in town. Hialeah decided to clear her head of anything that would ruin her day. She was always cautious around white folk, especially white men, and Jackson Harding would be no different. She didn't trust the lot of them, but he was nice to her, and that's all that mattered for now.

Jackson woke up in the dead of night. His stomach was at ease and his head was now clear. A wave of guilt washed over him as he realized that he had missed his fishing venture with Hialeah in a futile attempt to drink his misery away. He would make it up to her. Jackson sat up in his bed. His mouth was dry and his clothes were sticking to his skin. It was too late to request warm water to be brought up for a bath. Jackson remembered the small pond on his family's land that the slave women would use to do the wash and the children would swim on hot days. He was not accustomed to taking cold baths, but it would have to do for now.

Hialeah waited patiently for Jackson to meet her at Milliner's Pond. She set out their poles at her favorite spot and set the apple pie on a small blanket. The fish were jumping and she was anxious to get started. With every approaching horse she heard, her excitement grew only to be disappointed time and again. The day was moving on and Jackson still had not arrived. Hialeah watched as fish after fish were caught by others enjoying the fine fishing weather. She had sat and waited for nearly two hours when it dawned on her. Jackson Harding was not being nice to her, he pitied her. He was a wealthy man. His food was served to him on the finest china. He wouldn't dare be seen catching his dinner with some poor half-breed. He pitied her indeed. The very thought of a white man pitying her like she was some helpless dog upset Hialeah tremendously. She gathered her fishing pole and her, her apple pie and tiny blanket and set them back in her wagon. She hadn't needed anyone for as long as she could remember. For all she cared, Jackson Harding could go to hell.

Jackson went into town everyday searching for Hialeah, but she was nowhere to be found. Jackson woke up early everyday for nearly a week hoping they would cross paths, but each day was just as disappointing as the day before. Jackson had no idea where Hialeah lived and he refused to ask Sheriff Willard for his assistance. The man was nothing but a gossip and trouble for Hialeah. Word was already spreading around town that his wedding to Sara Williams had been called off and the loose tongues of the town were blaming Hialeah for coming in between him and Sara. The rumors didn't bother Jackson. He heard the whispers behind his back. He knew folks had branded him a nigger lover. Yet none of that mattered to him. His only concern was finding Hialeah.

Hialeah, on the other hand, had no intention in going into town. She had enough to do around her small home to keep herself occupied. She was still very much upset with Jackson. She didn't expect the white folks in town to treat her descent. They never had, but he pretended to care, and that, to Hialeah was the worst kind of person. No matter, Hialeah thought to herself as she pounded her fists into the dough she was preparing to make fresh bread. She had about had it with this town anyway. She had been thinking about selling her small home and land and starting over somewhere new. She deserved better than this. She deserved to be happy. Unable to bear the sorrow swelling inside of her, Hialeah buried her face in her hands and sobbed.

It had been nearly two weeks since Jackson had seen Hialeah and he feared the worst. He hardly knew her yet she consumed his every thought. He kept conversations with his mother and father to a minimum. The tension between them still lingered. Jackson spent most of his time in his bedroom pacing the floor. He had to find her, even if it meant looking to Sheriff Willard for answers. Jackson raced out of his bedroom and ran to the stable. He saddled his horse and quickly rode toward the town. As Jackson rode in the burning heat, he remembered Hialeah's favorite place; Milliner's Pond. He slowed his horse and changed direction.

Hialeah had spent so much time in her home, she felt as if she would lose her mind from boredom. It was extremely hot out and she desperately needed to cool off a bit. The small creek on her land wouldn't do. She was sure the fish in Milliner's Pond wouldn't mind if she joined them for a swim. Hialeah gathered what she needed for her swim. She climbed onto her wagon and set about on her way to enjoy a peaceful swim.

Jackson rode the length of Milliner's Pond. He spotted a wagon parked underneath a massive oak tree. As he rode closer, he recognized Hialeah's wagon and a huge smile came across his lips. Jackson released a long held breath as he dismounted his horse and walked it the short distance to where Hialeah's wagon was parked. Jackson tied his horse's reins to Hialeah's wagon. He leaned against the oak tree just as Hialeah emerged from underneath the water unaware that Jackson was watching her from the small hill. She wiped at her face with her hands before swimming to the edge of the pond. Hialeah climbed out of the pond refreshed and started up the small hill. As she made it to the top, she was met by Jackson. Hialeah didn't take another step. "Hello." Jackson said. "What you doin' here?" Hialeah replied upset that Jackson had intruded on her swim. Jackson noticed the tone in her voice but her agitation with him was overshadowed by what Hialeah had chosen to swim in. The thin white dress clung to every inch of her wet skin. Jackson took in the sight of her. Her full breasts and sensuous nipples were visible from the cold waters of the pond. The silhouette of her body was mesmerizing and Jackson was captivated by her beauty. "What you here for?" Hialeah asked as she walked passed Jackson. "I was concerned about you." Jackson replied. "No need to concern yourself bout me." Hialeah remarked stubbornly as she began to dress. "I owe you an apology." Jackson said. "No need for that neither." Hialeah replied sternly. "Miss Nokosi…" Jackson began. Hialeah spun on her heel to face Jackson. "Don't you Miss Nokosi me none." Hialeah replied angrily. "I handle myself just fine. Don't need your pity." Hialeah remarked defensively. "Pity?" Jackson said confused. "That's what I say." Hialeah replied sternly. "I assure you, I don't pity you." Jackson said. "Then what you here for?" Hialeah demanded. "I'm here because I thought we were friends." Jackson replied. "You just as much a friend to me as them white folks in town." Hialeah spat as she climbed onto her wagon. "You know nothin' bout me." Hialeah replied angrily. Jackson wasn't about to let her get away. He rushed over to Hialeah's wagon, grabbed her by her tiny waist, and effortlessly brought her back down before him to finish their conversation. "Then tell me about you." Jackson said. His deep voice sent chills through Hialeah. "Don't matter none." Hialeah replied defiantly trying to break away from Jackson's hold. "Tell me." Jackson said sternly refusing to let her go, his hazel eyes piercing through hers. Unable to bear the intensity of his gaze, Hialeah exploded. "I leavin' this place." Hialeah burst out fighting back tears. Taken aback by her words, Jackson released his hold on her waist. "I goin' up north. I gone find me a good man to care for me; love me. Treat me good." Hialeah said allowing her tears to fall freely. Jackson could hear the pain in her voice. He ached to comfort her, but he somehow knew she would resist his touch. "When will you go?" Jackson asked. "Don't know yet. Soon. Maybe." Hialeah replied wiping at her fallen tears. "This is your home." Jackson said. "Ain't my home." Hialeah replied defensively. Jackson frowned at her response. "How so?" Jackson asked curiously. Hialeah shook her head slowly. "This here my mama's home. She run away from here. She escape her master and go to Florida." Hialeah said. "Where she met your father?" Jackson asked. "He find her while he huntin'. He bring her back to his people. Mama said he cared for her but good and she love him. He married her and I come along some summers ago. As soon as I was able, mama learned me to read and write best she could. Daddy didn't like that too good." Hialeah said. "He taught you his tongue?" Jackson replied. "Says I shouldn't learn white man's words." Hialeah remarked. "And their names?" Jackson replied. "My mama, she called Annie, and my daddy called Nokosi." Hialeah said. "Nokosi?" Jackson replied. "Mama say she Annie Nokosi and she call me Hialeah Nokosi." Hialeah said. "Your father's given name became your surname." Jackson replied. "Mama say no white man would ever call her by her master's name." Hialeah said. "Hialeah Nokosi." Jackson replied absentmindedly. "What does it mean?" Jackson asked. "My name, it mean 'Pretty Prairie' and my daddy's name, it mean 'Bear'." Hialeah said. "Where are they?" Jackson asked. Hialeah lowered her gaze. "They stay behind. I disappoint my daddy. He turn me away." Hialeah replied sadly returning her gaze to meet Jackson's. "They're alive?" Jackson asked. Hialeah hunched her shoulders. "Ain't got no letter from 'em never." Hialeah replied. "I am sorry." Jackson remarked. "No need to be. My daddy real strong. He went off to fight the white man with colored soldiers during the war. He say his troops made it all the way to union lines in Kansas. Me and mama was so proud of him. Then I go and break his heart and I ain't wantin' to talk bout it." Hialeah said her tears swelling up in her again. She wiped at her eyes before any tears could fall. Hialeah turned to face her wagon. "You came here because this is your mother's home?" Jackson asked. Hialeah kept her back to Jackson and nodded her head. "Do you know the name of the man who enslaved her? Did she ever tell you?" Jackson asked. "Don't matter no more. She far away safe." Hialeah replied. "Who enslaved her?" Jackson demanded. Hialeah turned around to face Jackson. "You ought to know. You fixin' to marry his daughter." Hialeah replied defensively. "Mr. Williams? Judge Harland Williams?" Jackson said incredulously. "That be him." Hialeah replied. Hearing Hialeah's confession sent Jackson into a rage. He raced around Hialeah's wagon to get to his horse. Hialeah immediately followed after him. "Where you goin'?" Hialeah asked confused. Jackson ignored her question. He furiously tried to untie his horse from Hialeah's wagon. "What you fixin' to do?" Hialeah rushed out. "I'm going to kill that bloody son-of-a-bitch!" Jackson exploded. Hialeah quickly grabbed the reins from Jackson's hand. "You can't do that." Hialeah rushed out. "Oh believe me, I can." Jackson replied heatedly. "What good it gone do?" Hialeah asked. "It'll do a lot of good trust me." Jackson replied. "Will it erase the years of pain she suffered? You kill that man, and they gone hang you dead." Hialeah said. "So what." Jackson spat in disgust. "So I ain't gone let you do it." Hialeah remarked. "Give me the reins." Jackson ordered. "I ain't gone let them hang you on account of my mama's pain." Hialeah replied. "Give me the goddamn bloody reins!" Jackson yelled snatching his horse's reins with so much force that Hialeah fell to the ground. "Please don't do it!" Hialeah screamed after Jackson as he prepared to mount his horse. "Master please!" Hialeah pleaded. Jackson's blood went cold at Hialeah's plea. He angrily marched over to her and roughly grabbed her by her arms bringing her to her feet. Jackson stared daggers into Hialeah's eyes. "Don't ever call me master." Jackson spat viciously. Hialeah was truly terrified. "I am master over no man. Do you understand?" Jackson said deeply. Hialeah was too frightened to speak. "Answer me! Do you understand?" Jackson yelled. Jackson's grip was excruciating against her arms. "Henka (Hinga)." Hialeah mustered out. "In English." Jackson demanded sternly. "Yes." Hialeah rushed out. Jackson abruptly released his hold on Hialeah and took a few steps away from her to calm himself. Hialeah couldn't move. She trembled where she stood. She watched as Jackson furiously ran his hands through his short hair. "I so sorry." Hialeah said. Jackson turned around to face her. "I was beaten mercilessly by my father when I was a boy for playing with the slave children. He beat me for refusing to believe that my skin color made me better than them; for refusing to be their master and when he and my mother could no longer bear the scandalous gossip brought on by their nigger loving son, they sent me away to a school in England where I was beaten even more for being rebellious." Jackson replied heatedly. For the first time, Hialeah's heart went out to Jackson. She had never been a slave. She never knew what it was like to have someone beat her. "How old were you?" Hialeah asked softly. "Seven." Jackson replied. "Were you scared?" Hialeah asked. "Of course I was, but it didn't matter." Jackson replied. "Is that why you talk funny? I mean, you don't speak like folks around here. You talk right proper." Hialeah said innocently. "I'm sure after many years living amongst the English I've acquired their way of speaking." Jackson replied. "This England, they got slaves there?" Hialeah asked. "They did once, a long time ago." Jackson replied. "That why you talk to me?" Hialeah asked. "You're no different than I am." Jackson replied. "Folks around here think so. They think colored folks aren't the same as them. They call me names. Treat me lower than a dog cause I got indian blood in me and that Sheriff Willard, he the worst. He says I ain't nothin' but a filthy wretched savage and I only good for whorin' for the white man." Hialeah said. "Do you believe that?" Jackson asked. "I tell myself it ain't true, but it hard some time not to believe it." Hialeah replied. "That's why I leave this place. Ain't nothin' or nobody for me here." Hialeah said walking toward her wagon. "And if I asked you to stay?" Jackson said. Hialeah climbed onto her seat with Jackson's assistance. "Why you do that?" Hialeah replied. Jackson smiled. "Well as you stated, I've taken a liking to you." Jackson remarked lightly. "And I also need my coat repaired. I recall on our first meeting that you stated you could mend it good as new." Jackson said teasingly. "Can too, but it gone cost you." Hialeah said smiling. She was relieved that their dark conversation had taken on a lighter tone. "Name your price." Jackson replied. Hialeah continued smiling as she pretended to think of a price to charge Jackson for her services. "Hmm, well since you was kind enough to get Mrs. Nesbit to let me into her store, and I ain't never thank you, this time it free of charge." Hialeah said. Jackson laughed. "Can I ask you a question?" Hialeah said. "Depends on the question." Jackson replied teasingly. "What that mean, Justice of the High Court?" Hialeah asked. "It's what I am in England. The same as a judge here." Jackson said. "So I should respectfully call you Justice of the High Court Jackson Harding?" Hialeah said. Jackson chuckled. "That's a bit much wouldn't you say? Besides, I'm addressed as Your Lordship." Jackson replied smiling. "Your Lordship Jackson Harding." Hialeah remarked. "How about simply calling me Jackson as we've already established?" Jackson said teasingly. "That ain't too proper." Hialeah replied. "I'd presume not to be proper whilst on holiday." Jackson remarked smiling. "Alright, Jackson it is." Hialeah said. "Perfect. Now have you anymore questions?" Jackson asked chuckling. "I'll let you know if one comes up." Hialeah replied. Jackson laughed at Hialeah's response. "I have no doubt that you will." Jackson remarked. "Alright then, come on." Jackson said mounting his horse. "Where we goin'?" Hialeah asked. "My mother has a sewing room. You can repair it there." Jackson replied. Hialeah's smile instantly faded from her lips at the thought of going to Jackson's home. Jackson noticed the worried look on her face. "Not to worry, my mother is on an outing. She won't be back for hours." Jackson remarked. "You sure?" Hialeah replied nervously. "I am." Jackson replied as he gave his horse a nudge. Hialeah followed Jackson away from Milliner's Pond.

Jackson rode up the dirt road that led to his home followed by Hialeah. When they reached the house, Jackson dismounted his horse and ran over to assist Hialeah down from her wagon. For the first time, Hialeah noticed his strength. She also truly noticed him. He was dressed in all black and his clothes looked as if they were molded to his tall and muscled physique. His presence was definitely intimidating. Jackson handed Lucas the reins of his horse. "Lucas, Miss Nokosi." Jackson said formally introducing the pair. Lucas nodded his head in greeting and Hialeah returned Lucas's nod with a nervous smile. Jackson escorted Hialeah up the stairs and into his home. Hialeah gazed in awe at the size of Jackson's home. She had never been inside of a white person's home. It was breathtaking. Hialeah thought that if she ever had a house this magnificent that she would never leave it. "Shall I show you around?" Jackson said. Hialeah nervously shook her head. She didn't dare go any further. "Then I'll show you to the sewing room." Jackson said simply and led the way to his mother's sewing room. He opened the door to the sewing and ushered for Hialeah to enter. She slowly walked into the room and Jackson closed the door behind him. Hialeah jumped at the sound of the door closing and Jackson chuckled. "Relax." Jackson said smoothly. He walked over to the drapes and opened them wide to let the sunlight into the room. He returned to Hialeah's side and reached for his coat that lay on the chaise. Jackson showed Hialeah where his coat needed repair. "So what do you think? Is it repairable?" Jackson asked. "I do my best." Hialeah replied. "Perfect." Jackson said smiling. Hialeah took a seat on the chaise and readied her sewing utensils. "You get started and I'll see what Mama Lilly has prepared in the kitchen." Jackson said before exiting the sewing room.

Jackson returned a short while later with a tray of chocolate chip cookies and two glasses of milk. He set the tray on a small table in front of the chaise and reached for a cookie. "Fresh baked. Would you care for one? Mama Lilly always made the best cookies." Jackson asked offering Hialeah a cookie. "What is it?" Hialeah asked. "You've never had a chocolate chip cookie?" Jackson said. Hialeah lowered her eyes in embarrassment. Jackson felt like a fool humiliating her in such a thoughtless manner. "Forgive my arrogance." Jackson said. "Please." Jackson said offering the treat to Hialeah. Hialeah accepted the cookie and bit into it. She had never tasted anything like it. She took another bite and Jackson smiled. "Delicious?" Jackson said. Hialeah nodded her head. She didn't want to speak with her mouth full. Jackson handed her a glass of milk. "Tastes even better with milk, trust me." Jackson said. Hialeah accepted the glass and drank the cold milk. When she returned her empty glass to the tray, Jackson chuckled at the line of milk that creased her top lip. Jackson tapped his top lip and Hialeah quickly wiped her mouth with the back of her hand garnering another chuckle from Jackson. "There's plenty more in the kitchen. I'll wrap these up for you." Jackson said. Jackson stood and retrieved the tray of cookies and left Hialeah alone to continue her mending.

Hialeah busied herself with the task of repairing Jackson's coat. She made sure to pay attention to every detail and every stitch as she worked. Jackson's coat was indeed quite fine. It was clearly evident to Hialeah that a man of his caliber only desired the best. Her fingers worked their sewing magic. Hialeah was somewhat relieved that Jackson had left alone. His presence made her nervous. When Jackson finally returned to the sewing room after nearly an hour, Hialeah was practically finished with her mending. Jackson entered with a knapsack of cookies for her to take home. He smiled at her as he showed her his sweet gift before placing them inside of her sewing bag. "To enjoy later." Jackson said as he once again took his seat across from her. "Thank you." Hialeah said never looking up from her work. Jackson was amazed at how diligently she handled a needle. Hialeah could feel his eyes upon her and her body reacted to his glare. She felt herself blushing. Jackson leaned in closer to get a better view of her work. Hialeah swallowed hard at his nearness. "I've never seen anyone's hands move so quickly with a needle." Jackson said. Hialeah fought back an appreciative smile. "You always watch your garments bein' mended?" Hialeah asked lightly. "Never, but it is fascinating to observe your skill." Jackson replied. "You got my mama to thank for that. She learned me." Hialeah said. "An excellent teacher." Jackson remarked. Hialeah smiled as she continued to work. They both sat in silence until Hialeah was unable to bear the quiet. "I didn't mean it that way." Hialeah said. "You didn't mean what what way?" Jackson replied. "When I say that you talk funny." Hialeah remarked. Jackson smiled at her attempt to rectify what she thought was an insult to his person. "Then you like the way I speak?" Jackson asked teasingly. Hialeah kept her eyes on finishing up her work as she nodded. "I like it just fine. Better than the folks around here." Hialeah said. "And had I never left here, would you still like the way that I speak?" Jackson asked. Hialeah hunched her shoulders. "Can't say." Hialeah replied. "Why can't you say?" Jackson said. "Cause then you'd be like the rest of the folks around here." Hialeah replied. "What do you mean?" Jackson said. "I mean you wouldn't speak to me like the other white folks here. They don't speak to me." Hialeah said. "Then I suppose I should thank my parents for abandoning me." Jackson replied. "Why's that?" Hialeah asked. "Otherwise, I'd be just another bigoted fool."

Jackson replied. "Mr. Harding..." Hialeah began. "Jackson, remember?" Jackson replied smiling. "Jackson." Hialeah said. "Yes, Miss Nokosi?" Jackson said teasingly. "Hialeah, remember?" Hialeah replied returning the jest. "Pretty Prairie." Jackson said to which Hialeah laughed. She liked how he spoke her name's meaning. She could feel herself blushing as she finished Jackson's coat. "All done." Hialeah said. Jackson stood. Hialeah handed him his coat and Jackson tried it on. "What do you think?" Jackson asked smiling. "You look right fine." Hialeah replied. "You are indeed a master at your craft." Jackson remarked. "Thank you." Hialeah said. "Brilliant." Jackson replied before taking off his coat. He placed it on the sofa next to him and sat back down. "Are you always this way?" Hialeah said. "What, giddy as a school girl over a coat?" Jackson replied lightly. Hialeah smiled. "Charming." Hialeah said using Sara Williams' description of Jackson. "I mean charming to women...to...colored women." Hialeah stammered out. "Doesn't matter the skin color." Jackson replied. "Then you charm talk colored women back in England?" Hialeah asked. "I generally try to be kind to all women." Jackson replied. "That ain't what I mean." Hialeah remarked. "Then what is it you mean?" Jackson replied casually. "I mean do you charm talk colored women cause you like them?" Hialeah remarked. "Perhaps I would have were I given the opportunity." Jackson replied. "The opportunity?" Hialeah repeated. "I spend most days in court. My time is very limited." Jackson replied. "You have time to share your bed with white women? I'm sure there's been plenty." Hialeah said. Jackson leaned back in his seat thoroughly enjoying where this conversation was headed. "Then you wish to know the number of women I've shared my bed with?" Jackson replied. "Ain't my place to know your personal affairs." Hialeah said standing to gather her things. "Yet you question them?" Jackson replied. "No sir, besides, I been here long enough to know how white men like you truly feel about colored folk; especially colored women." Hialeah said matter-of-factly as she made her way to the door of the sewing room. Jackson stood to his feet. "And what, pray tell, do you know of my feelings for colored women?" Jackson asked upset by Hialeah's presumption of him. "That they good for sharin' your bed; nothin' more. Not for lovin', not for kissin'..." Hialeah began her tirade but her words failed her as Jackson took what seemed like two long strides to reach her. He grabbed her unceremoniously by her arms bringing her closer to him. Hialeah could see in his eyes that he was seething with anger. "What do you accuse me of Miss Nokosi?" Jackson spat. "Do you believe me to be some bloody bigot incapable of loving a woman whose skin doesn't match my own?" Jackson replied heatedly as he stared fiercely into Hialeah's eyes. Her voice was stuck in her throat. "Say it!" Jackson demanded. Hialeah opened her mouth to speak but her lips were captured by Jackson's unexpected kiss. Taken aback by his boldness, Hialeah broke their kiss and struck Jackson across his face. The shocking realization of what she had done startled Hialeah. She quickly reached for the door handle. In one swift motion, Jackson grabbed her hand and spun her around to face him. Hialeah was terrified at what Jackson would do. She had struck one of the wealthiest men in town; a Justice of the High Court no less. Jackson pressed Hialeah against the door and without a word took her lips in yet another unyielding kiss. Jackson marveled at the fullness of her pouty lips. He wanted to taste more of her. Jackson parted Hialeah's lips with his tongue. Innocent to a man's kiss, Hialeah gasped and pulled away. Jackson's eyes pierced through Hialeah's. "There's your answer." Jackson said low. Afraid to utter a sound, Hialeah hastily raced from the sewing room.

As Hialeah frantically ran from Jackson's presence, Jackson strode over to the sofa to retrieve his coat. He stopped momentarily at the sounds of yelling coming from the hall. Jackson's heart skipped several beats. The shrill voice of his mother chilled his blood. Jackson quickly grabbed his coat and ran out of the sewing room. He stopped dead in his tracks as his mother and father barred Hialeah's exit. Mrs. Harding turned on her son as he entered the hall. "Jackson Andrew Harding, I'll have the reason why this savage nigger is in my home!" Georgina Harding demanded. "You will not address her in such a manner!" Jackson fired back. "I will address this filthy good for nothing trash in any manner I see fit!" Georgina Harding screeched. Devastated, Hialeah ran out of the front door nearly knocking Mrs. Harding down in her haste to get away from the woman's vicious tongue. "Hialeah!" Jackson called out. He dropped his coat and raced after her. Hialeah kept running; refusing to look back. "Miss Nokosi!"

Jackson yelled. Hialeah frantically tried to climb onto her wagon. Her foot caught in the folds of her dress, her hurried escape was futile. Jackson caught her just as she managed to free her boot from her dress. Jackson grabbed her arm and Hialeah angrily slapped his hand away. "Miss Nokosi wait." Jackson pleaded. "Why you bring me here!" Hialeah yelled fighting back angry tears. "You leave me be, you hear? You leave me be!" Hialeah demanded her chest heaving with anger and hurt. Jackson took a step back and Hialeah climbed onto her wagon. Jackson furiously watched as Hialeah rode away. He paid none of the servants who had stopped their work any mind.

Jackson stormed into the house and slammed the front door just as his mother was preparing to go up the stairs. "You had no right to speak to her so cruelly!" Jackson exploded. "And you had no right to bring that vile woman into our home." Georgina spat. Jackson strode over to his coat and snatched it from the floor. "I hired her to repair my coat." Jackson replied through gritted teeth. "I'm sure she was here for more reasons other than your coat." Georgina Harding replied sarcastically. Jackson scoffed at his mother's assumption. He had heard enough. Jackson turned to walk away. "Do you have any idea what's being said in town?" Georgina asked. "No, and I don't care to hear idle nonsense from…" Jackson began. "It's being said that she's carrying your child." Georgina said. Jackson slowly turned to face his mother. "And if it were true mother, would you turn your back on my child as you did your own?" Jackson asked coldly. "I will not have a half-breed heathen for a grandchild." Georgina said matching her son's cold tone. "For God's sake Jackson, you speak as if you care for this woman." Georgina said. "Because I do care for her, mother! I care for her more than anyone in this room!" Jackson exploded. "Jackson!" Georgina rushed out. "Don't fret mother, she'll not be sharing my bed." Jackson replied icily as he walked out of the door slamming it hard behind him.

Henry Harding entered the hall holding a glass of brandy but said nothing to his wife. Georgina focused her outrage on her husband. "This is your doing." Georgina spat at her husband. "Do you think for one moment that he never saw you entering the quarters of our slaves? Pleasuring yourself in their beds whenever you saw fit." Georgina said menacingly. "You're a disgrace. The only difference is our slaves despised your touch." Georgina spat. "Go to hell." Henry replied calmly. "I live there." Georgina remarked disgustedly before climbing the stairs.

Chapter 5

Hialeah barreled up the path to her home; Georgina Harding's cruel words ringing in her ears. She jumped from her wagon and bolted inside of her small home and slammed the door collapsing against it. She despised Georgina Harding, she despised everything that South Carolina stood for, and she despised Jackson Harding as well. Jackson Harding, Hialeah thought to herself. Her hand instinctively touched her lips where his had just been. Her first kiss and her last. She could not allow herself to be swept away by his words. That is all that they were. He was a man of many privileges. Privileges that she were not afforded. He was also a man that would soon be wedded to Sara Williams. She is the woman who held his heart. Hialeah promised herself to never forget that truth. Jackson Harding no longer existed in her world.

Jackson walked the length of the family's dirt road to calm himself after another intense argument with his mother. In his angst to separate himself from his mother, he was unaware of the encounter that had taken place between his parents. Jackson continued to walk absentmindedly down the road when the sound of approaching hooves from behind him caught his attention. "Jackson." Miss Lilly called out. Jackson stopped walking and waited for Miss Lilly to slow her wagon down. When Miss Lilly came to a complete stop, Jackson walked over toward her wagon. "Jackson, I so glad I caught you." Miss Lilly said. "Is there a problem?" Jackson asked. "No problem, but I wanted to show you these here." Miss Lilly replied. Jackson watched as she produced three spools of thread from her lap. "Your mother asked me to clean the sewin' room and I found these on the chaise." Miss Lilly said. "I'm sure they belong to Miss Nokosi. I can take them to her if you like." Miss Lilly remarked. "You know where to find her?" Jackson asked curiously. "I ain't never been to her place but she comes to hear the preachin' on Sundays. Trouble is, as soon as the preachin' over, she gets right on up and leave. Don't give nobody a chance to greet her. But tomorrow we have our own celebration for Independence Day." Miss Lilly said. "We colored folk get together every year for a celebration." Miss Lilly said. "And she'll be there?" Jackson asked. "Well she ain't miss one yet." Miss Lilly replied. "Are outsiders permitted to attend this celebration?" Jackson asked. "If you's askin' if white folk allowed at colored folk festivities, we don't turn no good Christian away. Besides, don't you go actin' like you ain't never been around us before." Miss Lilly replied. Jackson smiled at her invitation. Miss Lilly handed Jackson the spools of thread and his smile faded. Miss Lilly noticed his waning smile. "Jackson, it might not be my place to say, but I ain't ever bit my tongue where you was concern and I ain't gone start to now." Miss Lilly said. "Of course." Jackson replied feeling very much the boy of his youth in Miss Lilly's presence. "It ain't right that you and your mama hollerin' at one another like you both ain't got no home trainin'. But a man with no eyes can see that you done took a likin' to that woman." Miss Lilly said. "You think it's wrong?" Jackson replied. "Now I didn't say that. You hush up and let me finish." Miss Lilly said. Jackson nodded his head at her command. "You's a privileged man. You always have been and you's always gone be, but that woman ain't got nothin' and nobody. How she as strong as she is, I don't know. Folks walk on by that girl like she every bit of nothin' all cause she got that injun blood in her. Some folks don't appreciate her remindin' them that those injuns helped colored folks defeat them white soldiers to free us. She a painful reminder of that battle." Miss Lilly said. "I'll stake my life on it that she isn't the only colored person with indian blood walking around here." Jackson replied. "That's sure true, but most colored folks, injun blood or not, we keep to our own kind." Miss Lilly remarked. "I understand. I do, but she had nothing to do with the war." Jackson replied heatedly. "I knows that and you's know that, but some folks are just miserable and they just full of hate and ain't nothin' you or I can do to change it; that includes your mama and your daddy." Miss Lilly remarked. "I never should have come home." Jackson said. "That just it, Jackson. This here your home for a short time. But that girl, she gone be here when you get back on that ship, and go on back to livin' your privileged life, and it gone be even worse for her; especially with folks thinkin' you chose a colored girl over a white girl." Miss Lilly replied. "Miss Nokosi has nothing to do with my refusal to marry Sara Williams. I would have defended any colored woman had they been reduced to a mere nothing by Sara's cruelty." Jackson remarked defensively. "I knows that to be true. You've been that way since you was a little boy. But you ain't no child no more, and that girl wants to be seen by somebody, anybody. You get what I'm tellin' you?" Miss Lilly said. "I understand." Jackson replied. "Good. Now you get on up in that house and stop wanderin' round here like you's done lost your mind." Miss Lilly ordered in her motherly tone. Jackson smiled. "Besides, I got your supper waitin' for you." Miss Lilly said. "Yes ma'am." Jackson replied. "We get started tomorrow evenin' right at nine." Miss Lilly said. "I'll be there." Jackson replied. "Goodnight, Mama Lilly." Jackson said. "I sure hope so." Miss Lilly replied before continuing her way down the road. Jackson looked at the spools of thread in his hands momentarily then stuffed them into his pockets.

Hialeah was overjoyed that she had finished her dress in time for the celebration with the fabric given to her by Mr. Nesbit. She saved some of the fabric to make a ribbon for her hair. She was extremely grateful for Mr. Nesbit's kindness. She was also grateful that she had produced a hearty crop of vegetables this year. She had picked and shucked two huge baskets of corn to take to the celebration. Hialeah was certain that this year's batch of corn would be better than last year's. She found herself humming delightfully as she placed the corn into her wagon. She wanted to get to the celebration early so that her corn would have time to cook in the big pots. With her corn secure in the back of her wagon, Hialeah started off to the Independence Day celebration.

When Hialeah arrived at the celebration site, she was assisted from her wagon by one of the male partygoers. Two younger men at the request of Miss Lilly grabbed the two baskets of corn from Hialeah's wagon. Miss Lilly waited until the two young men were out of earshot before she introduced herself as the Harding family's cook and Jackson's former nanny. Hialeah was surprised by the introduction. She complimented Miss Lilly on her delicious homemade cookies. They continued their conversation over by the cooking pot and Miss Lilly helped Hialeah prepare her corn. Hialeah enjoyed talking to Miss Lilly. She usually watched the fireworks and ate alone. This was the first time that she had even spoken to any of the partygoers. Miss Lilly didn't mention to Hialeah that Jackson would be attending the celebration nor did she tell her how Jackson felt about her or that he wouldn't be marrying Sara Williams. She didn't feel that was her place to mention his personal affairs. She did, however, inform Hialeah that Jackson would be returning to his home in England very soon. Hialeah kept her emotions calm hearing the news. She didn't want Miss Lilly to see how upset that bit of news made her feel. Hialeah felt disgusted inside. How dare he pretend to care about her when all along he would be leaving and taking Sara Williams with him? Hialeah could feel the anger boiling inside of her. She hoped that she never laid eyes on Jackson Harding again.

    Jackson rode up on his horse just as the festivities were beginning. The smell of fried fish and chicken along with roast pig and other delicious aromas filled his nostrils and the sound of glorious music and laughter filled the air. Lanterns were hung throughout the church yard. Jackson dismounted his horse and tied him to a fence post. He tapped his pocket to make sure that Hialeah's spools of thread were still there. He wore his black coat that Hialeah had repaired, a white shirt, black trousers and a pair of black riding boots. After how his mother had treated her, Jackson thought it fitting to purchase a gift for Hialeah in hopes that she would accept his apology. Jackson walked through the partygoers and spotted Miss Lilly serving apple pie to several children. He walked over to her and by the stares that he received; it was quite obvious that he was the only white person in attendance. Jackson didn't mind the looks. He nodded his head in greeting and went on about his way. "May I?" Jackson said smiling as he reached for a piece of apple pie. Miss Lilly looked up from her pie cutting. Seeing Jackson's smiling face, she playfully taped him on his arm. "Of course you may and while you're at it, how bout you take a slice of pie over that way." Miss Lilly said nodding her head in Hialeah's direction. Jackson looked in the direction to where Miss Lilly nodded. Hialeah sat alone on a bench tapping her foot to the music being played watching as others danced nearby. Jackson took the two plates of pie that Miss Lilly held out for him. He thanked her with a kiss on her cheek and walked over towards Hialeah.

Hialeah sat smiling as people danced and twirled around by her. She had never been asked to dance and for some strange reason she wondered what it would be like to have Jackson twirling her around in a dance. She quickly dismissed the vision from her mind just as Jackson approached her. Jackson set the two plates down. Hialeah didn't pay the stranger any mind. She just assumed it was someone needing a place to sit. Jackson followed her gazed before returning his attention back to her. "Would you mind if I joined you?" Jackson asked. Hialeah looked up to where the familiar voice had come from. Seeing Jackson standing next to her, she bolted from her seat and ran toward her waiting wagon. Jackson hurried after her. "Miss Nokosi, wait!" Jackson yelled out over the loud music. Hialeah kept running but Jackson easily caught up with her. He grabbed her arm only to have Hialeah angrily pull away from him. She turned on him like a vicious dog. "You ain't welcomed here." Hialeah said angrily. "Miss Nokosi…" Jackson began. "Why you come here?" Hialeah demanded. "Ain't you white folks got your own fancy party to sit around and talk bout us colored folks?" Hialeah replied heatedly. "Mama Lilly invited me. She told me you'd be here." Jackson said. "Why she talkin' bout me to you for?" Hialeah demanded. Jackson dug into his pocket and pulled out the three spools of thread and showed them to Hialeah. "She found these in my mother's sewing room." Jackson replied calmly. Hialeah snatched her threads and dumped them into her sewing bag. "If that's all you here for, you can go now." Hialeah remarked angrily as she started to walk off. Jackson continued to follow her and Hialeah stopped mid stride but kept her back to Jackson. "I don't want you followin' me none either." Hialeah said sternly. Jackson hurried his steps around Hialeah until he was directly facing her. "Miss Nokosi, you have every right to be upset after how my mother treated you and with me for kissing you without permission. I took liberties that I shouldn't have." Jackson said. Hialeah didn't wish to hear any more. She side stepped Jackson to continue on her way. "At least accept my gift." Jackson said. Hialeah stopped. Jackson walked over to her. Hialeah watched as Jackson opened his coat and reached into his inner coat pocket. Jackson pulled out a black rectangular box with a red bow on it and held it out for Hialeah. Hialeah looked at the gift but kept her hands to her sides. "What is it?" Hialeah asked suspiciously. "You'll have to open it." Jackson replied casually; fighting the urge to smile. Hialeah took the box and Jackson nonchalantly walked away. He returned to the bench where he had set their plates of pie and sat down. He watched from his seat as Hialeah opened her gift.

    Hialeah removed the small red bow from the box and opened her gift. Jackson took a bite of his dessert as he watched Hialeah pull out the blue fan that he had gifted her. Hialeah spread the fan open and admired the butterfly crafted on it. She had never received such a beautiful gift. Hialeah closed the fan and looked over in Jackson's direction. Jackson pretended that he didn't notice Hialeah slowly making her way back toward him. He casually kept eating his pie. Hialeah sat down beside Jackson and placed her gift on her lap. "It's beautiful." Hialeah said softly. "I was hoping you'd like it and accept my apology." Jackson replied. "I ain't never had anything like it." Hialeah said. "And I have never had anything like this. Well actually I have but it's been years since I've had Mama Lilly's apple pie." Jackson said teasingly taking another bite of pie. He stuck his fork into the last bit of apple pie and held it for Hialeah to taste. Hialeah ate the small piece of pie from Jackson's fork and Jackson smiled. "May I ask you a question?" Hialeah asked. "Depends on the question." Jackson replied grinning. "Why you call her Mama Lilly? Most folks call her Miss Lilly." Hialeah said. "She was a mother to me the short time I was here. I adore her." Jackson replied. "She got a kind spot for you too." Hialeah remarked. Jackson chuckled. "Ahh but her kind spot came with a swift hand to my rear when I needed it." Jackson replied. Hialeah giggled at Jackson's fond memory. "Am I forgiven?" Jackson asked. "I'll think about it Your Lordship." Hialeah replied teasingly. Jackson burst into laughter at Hialeah's teasing. Hialeah liked very much the sound of his deep laughter. "May I ask you another question?" Hialeah said. Jackson chuckled and nodded his head. "Why did you kiss me?" Hialeah asked. Jackson looked longingly into Hialeah's eyes and gently caressed her bottom lip with his thumb. His touch sent chills over Hialeah. "I kissed you because your lips are perfectly made to be kissed." Jackson replied deeply. Hialeah felt her cheeks warming. "I ain't never been kissed before." Hialeah said softly. "May I?" Jackson said. Hialeah lowered her eyes as Jackson took her lips in a tender and gentle kiss. Hialeah thought she had imagined it.

Fully aware of their surroundings, Jackson shortened his kiss. He couldn't risk anyone in attendance at the party speaking harshly about Hialeah being kissed by a white man. Jackson abruptly stood up and held his hand out. "Will you dance with me?" Jackson asked smoothly. Hialeah looked up at Jackson. "Folks gone stare." Hialeah said worriedly. "I'd stare too if I weren't dancing with the prettiest girl at the party." Jackson replied. Hialeah smiled and took Jackson's hand. He led her to where the other guests were dancing.

Hialeah danced four dances with Jackson; laughing and smiling through every step, twirl, and spin. Their dancing caught the attention of the other dancers. Some moved out of the way so that Jackson and Hialeah could take over the dance floor. Their dancing moves even had Miss Lilly clapping and smiling. Hialeah's contagious laughter soon had Jackson laughing. He had never seen her so beautiful in the lanterns' light. She was mesmerizing. Hialeah was so entranced by Jackson that for a brief moment, she had forgotten the conversation that she had had previously with Miss Lilly. Nothing mattered but how she felt at that very moment in his arms. He was dashing and witty and handsome and she never wanted the night to end. Even when Jackson needed to rest, Hialeah took on other dance partners, several of whom asked if they could come calling on her. Hialeah simply laughed their question off and continued dancing. Jackson sat at their little bench and watched joyously as Hialeah continued enjoying herself. Although Hialeah was being whisked around by her other dance partners, she didn't feel as enthused in their arms as she had been in Jackson's. While dancing with another gentleman, she glanced over at Jackson and the all true realization hit her, that this night would not last forever, that she could not be in Jackson's arms forever, and that she had best get used to being in the arms of another man.

Hialeah suddenly felt as if she had been punched in the stomach. She abruptly stopped dancing and ran from her partner much to the surprise of Jackson. Jackson jumped up from the bench and hurried after Hialeah as she bee-lined her way toward Miss Lilly in search of her corn baskets. Jackson reached Hialeah's side as she frantically continued to search for her baskets. "What happened?" Jackson rushed out. Hialeah ignored his question and moved to another spot where she thought her baskets could be. Hialeah found her baskets set aside in a corner. She quickly grabbed them and brushed by Jackson. Jackson quickly made his way to her side keeping up with Hialeah's pace. Hialeah tossed her baskets into the back of her wagon. Jackson stepped in her way to block her from taking another step. "What happened?" Jackson asked sternly. "Ain't nothin' happened. I just goin' home is all." Hialeah replied. "Home?" Jackson remarked. "That's what I say." Hialeah replied stubbornly. "Why? We were having a great time." Jackson said. "Well you keep on havin' a great time Mr. Harding, I goin' home." Hialeah replied. "Alright, then I'll see you home." Jackson said. "I don't need you to see me home. I get there just fine." Hialeah remarked defensively. "I'll not have you travel alone in the dark. If you insist on leaving, I can't stop you, but I will see you home." Jackson replied adamantly. Hialeah decided not to argue with Jackson any further. Satisfied with her acceptance to see her home, Jackson walked toward his horse and mounted him just as Hialeah rode by him in her wagon.

Jackson kept up with the pace of Hialeah's driving. Hialeah couldn't help but to notice Jackson's position on his horse. She slyly took side glances at him as he rode protectively next to her. She noticed how the muscles in his thighs flexed with every stride his horse took. He was an impressive rider and an gentle kisser. Hialeah could feel her cheeks warming once again as she thought of their shared kiss. The wind swept through his opened coat and the moonlight shone on his revolver. "It's loaded." Jackson said. Hialeah inhaled a breath, cursing herself at having been caught watching Jackson. She straightened up in her seat and focused on her driving. Jackson smiled at her attempt to hide the fact that she had been watching him. They rode the rest of their short trip in silence.

Hialeah led Jackson up the small road that led to her home. Jackson noticed that they had passed two grave markers. He was curious as to who was buried there. Hialeah's parents never returned to

South Carolina. Hialeah stopped her wagon by the entrance to her barn. Jackson dismounted from his horse and assisted Hialeah from her wagon and immediately released her before he could receive one of her tongue lashings. Hialeah placed her hands on her hips. "Alright you can go now." Hialeah said sternly. It was Jackson's turn to ignore her. "Who was that; buried?" Jackson asked. Hialeah walked away from Jackson and began to undo her horse's harness. Jackson waited patiently as Hialeah walked her horse into his stall. She returned within seconds and closed the barn door. Hialeah then retrieved her two baskets from the back of the wagon and made her way toward the front of her home. "Miss Nokosi." Jackson said agitated. Hialeah stopped and spun on her heel to face Jackson. "You think I killed those people?" Hialeah replied sarcastically. Her tone received a look of annoyance from Jackson. Hialeah caught the look. He was in no mood for games. "Alright, I'll tell you, but first, I need to get outta this here dress." Hialeah replied. Hialeah continued toward the front of her home and Jackson was close on her heels. Hialeah set the two baskets down in the corner of the porch and picked up her lantern and the small box of matches. She lit the candle inside and entered her home. Hialeah set the lantern on the table and with the use of its light lit another lantern. She took one of the lanterns with her and disappeared into her tiny bedroom.

While Hialeah changed, Jackson picked up the remaining lantern and illuminated Hialeah's home. The room held Hialeah's small kitchen, two rocking chairs that set in the corner, and a small table with three chairs around it. Hialeah had decorated her home with several pieces of Seminole artwork. Jackson was impressed that she had chosen to stay true to her father's people with her décor. On the table set a vase with fresh flowers in it. Jackson noticed that on top of the fireplace was a framed picture. He walked over to the frame and glanced at the picture. In the picture were a young white man in a tuxedo and his wife dressed in her wedding gown. Jackson set the picture down just as Hialeah emerged from her bedroom wearing a shear white robe. Her long black hair was loose and covered her breasts. The very sight of her in the lantern's light aroused Jackson immediately. He took her in completely. From her bare feet to the crown of her head, she was breathtaking. Hialeah felt her body warming at his intense glare. She could feel her heart pounding away in her chest. She prayed she could find her voice to break the silence in the room. She quietly cleared her throat. "The people in that picture and in those there graves were called Malcolm and Miss Lydia Hastings." Hialeah said softly. "They were good people. They were the only folks that helped me when I first come here. I walked around town lookin' for work and Mr. Hastings and his wife were in town purchasin' supplies. Other folks ignored me like I wasn't even there, but not Mr. Hastings. He called me over to his wagon and asked me what skills I had. He hired me right there in the middle of town. I tell him that my daddy was an Indian and he didn't care none. He said I could live in their extra bedroom but that he couldn't pay much. He tell me he too old to work his crops like he used to and that his Missus was ill. I looked after her and helped out around the house, cookin' and cleanin' and tendin' to the animals and the gardenin'. We sit here, Mr. Hastings and me and we talk bout their children and grandchildren after Mrs. Hastings retired to her bed. He said talkin' bout their children upset her. They never come for a visit not once. Three years I help out here. Five children and ten grandchildren and not one visit. Mr. Hastings say, their children wanted money, but they didn't have a lot, so they couldn't be bothered to come down and see their own mama and daddy. Mrs. Hastings took real ill one day and she never recovered. Doctor say she died from fever. I think, cause her heart was broken. Their own children didn't even come to her funeral. Poor Mr. Hastings, why he was beside himself with grief. He loved Miss Lydia more than anything. Then one day, he got real low. He wouldn't eat and he barely slept none. I hear him from my room walkin' around late at night talkin' to his wife like she here with him. I hear him say that they gone be together real soon. Scared me somethin' fierce to hear him talkin' like that. I send word to his eldest boy, Oliver. He doin' real fine for himself. I tell him that his daddy ain't well; talkin' strange and he should come quick. Oliver, he live in Connecticut. He arrive too late. Mr. Hastings dead before Oliver make it here." Hialeah said. "What happened to him?" Jackson asked. "I wake up one mornin' to fix his breakfast. I call for him, but he didn't say anything. I go to his room and nobody there. I find a letter on the bed. It said 'My dearest Lydia, it's time for us to be together.' I got so worried that I run outta the house callin' for him. I go into the barn, and I find him, hangin' from the rafter, dead. All I could do was scream 'til I couldn't scream no more. I run into town pleadin' for somebody to help me. Sheriff Willard come and the doctor. I tell them what happened and Sheriff Willard, he says I kill him." Hialeah said. "He accused you of murdering a man?" Jackson asked incredulously. "He says that I wanted this here land for myself. Said he would see me hang for murder, but the good doctor, he stop him. He tell Sheriff Willard that Mr. Hastings come to see him, ask him for some pills that would help him die while he sleepin', but the doctor refused to give him any. Doctor tell us that Mr. Hastings say that he was gone be with his wife one way or the other. When Oliver get here, I had my things packed. Wasn't sure where I was fixin' to go. I knew for sure he gone sell his daddy's land and everything on it cause it all go to him. Oliver, he take one look at this place and turn his nose up. He say ain't no way he could make a profit on account the land bein' small and the house run down. He say I was more family to his mama and daddy then any of them and he wanted to do right by me. He let me stay here as long as I want but he rightfully own the place. Sheriff Willard try and talk him into sellin' the place to him but Oliver already give his word to me. Say he wouldn't go back on it. Sheriff Willard ain't take too kindly to bein' bested by a savage. He tell Oliver, whatever happen to this place is outta his hands. Oliver, he threatened the sheriff. Say he see him hang if any foul dealin' come to his parents' home. Sheriff Willard ride off fumin'. I thank Oliver for his kindness and just like that, he take a train back to Connecticut." Hialeah said. "And Sheriff Willard's been harassing you ever since?" Jackson said. "He says this land is white folk land and a heathen savage nigger whore like me ain't got no right to it." Hialeah replied. "Son-of-a-bitch." Jackson remarked heatedly. "I get so scared he gone come after me. I worry he gone set my house on fire just to get rid of me. This here is all I got." Hialeah said softly. "You shouldn't be here alone." Jackson said. "I ain't exactly got a husband to look after me, Mr. Jackson." Hialeah replied sarcastically. "Then, I'll stay with you." Jackson said sternly. "That ain't needed. I can take care of myself." Hialeah replied. "We will not debate this. I'm staying." Jackson remarked firmly. Hialeah nodded her head in agreement. This clearly was one debate she would not win.

Hialeah watched with concern as Jackson pulled his revolver from his coat and gave it a going over. "What're you fixin' to do?" Hialeah asked curiously. Jackson returned his gun to its holster. "I'm going to make sure that if anyone's here, they won't come back." Jackson replied his tone was as dark as his mood. Hialeah swallowed nervously. "I'll make some coffee." Hialeah said. Jackson nodded and stormed out of the door. Hialeah waited until Jackson had left the house and ran to her bedroom. She peered out of the window just as Jackson walked by. She watched him grab his horse's reins and led him to the barn. Hialeah took off quickly to her kitchen to prepare their coffee. Jackson secured his horse in the barn. Before he exited the barn, Jackson stopped and looked up at the rafters. He didn't know Malcolm Hastings, but he thought it only fitting to have a drink in honor of the good man's memory. Jackson opened his coat and pulled out his flask. He raised the flask in the air, opened the bottle and took a long swig before returning it to his coat pocket. "To you Mr. Hastings." Jackson said before exiting the barn.

Jackson walked the grounds of Hialeah's home enjoying a few more sips of his drink as he did so. The night was quiet and Jackson's thoughts turned to Hialeah. She was indeed the challenge that he had been wanting. She was fiery, strong-willed, and beautiful. Jackson found himself craving everything about her. Her light brown eyes, her full lips, her hips, and her round breasts drove him to the brink of insanity. Even when she cursed him in her father's tongue, he wanted her. Jackson found himself smiling in the moonlight. She was indeed a handful. Jackson's thoughts were interrupted by the sound of his name being called out. He raced back to Hialeah's door but slowed his paced when he saw her standing on the front porch. Jackson walked onto the porch. "Are you alright?" Jackson asked. "Where were you?" Hialeah asked. "Securing your property." Jackson replied. Hialeah smelled the alcohol on his breath and walked inside of the house. Jackson followed her and closed the door behind him. He noticed two cups of coffee setting on the table. Hialeah turned around to face Jackson. "You been drinkin'?" Hialeah said. "A little." Jackson said simply. He pulled his flask from his coat and set it on the table. Hialeah took a seat and Jackson did the same, sitting across from her. Hialeah couldn't help but to gaze at the silver flask setting between them. Jackson followed her gaze. She was clearly curious about its content. He was feeling quite relaxed from the contents. Jackson leaned back in his chair a playful grin coming over his lips. Hialeah picked up her cup of coffee and took a sip. Jackson burst into laughter. Hialeah frowned over her cup. "What's so funny?" Hialeah asked offended. "Miss Nokosi, I'd be more than willing to offer you a drink." Jackson replied teasingly. "No thank you. I ain't never had that stuff before." Hialeah said. "No worries." Jackson said as he reached for the flask to return it back to his coat. "What is it?" Hialeah rushed out. Her curiosity brought a chuckle from Jackson. "Gin." Jackson replied. Jackson grinned as Hialeah pursed her lips together contemplating whether or not to try the gin. "What it taste like?" Hialeah innocently asked. "I can't explain the taste to you." Jackson replied laughing. "You like it?" Hialeah asked. "I do." Jackson replied. Hialeah motioned for Jackson to slide the flask her way. Jackson handed the flask to Hialeah. She removed the cap and smelled its contents. Jackson laughed as she frowned from the smell. Hialeah smelled the contents again, and again frowned from the odor. Jackson continued to laugh. "Miss Nokosi, I assure you, it'll smell the same no matter how many times you sniff it." Jackson teased. His teasing received a 'be quiet' expression from Hialeah. Jackson threw his hands in the air in surrender. He knew what that look meant. Hialeah placed her lips around the flask and threw her head back taking in a large amount of the gin. Jackson jumped from the table and hurried to Hialeah when she began coughing uncontrollably. "Miss Nokosi!" Jackson rushed out frantically. Hialeah couldn't speak. Her eyes were filling with tears as she continued to cough. Jackson took the flask from her hand and set it on the table. Hialeah continued to wheeze and gasp. Jackson quickly left her side and went to her cupboard to retrieve a cup. Jackson pumped water into the small cup and returned to Hialeah's side handing her the cup. "Here, have some water." Jackson said. Hialeah downed the cold water and Jackson took the cup from her hand. "Are you okay?" Jackson asked. Hialeah nodded her head and wiped at her eyes. "What's in that?" Hialeah wheezed out. "I don't know…gin." Jackson replied. "It's horrible." Hialeah said. "For the love of God, what on earth possessed you to drink such a large amount?" Jackson asked. "That's how the women at the tavern drink. They laugh with their gentlemen friends and toss their heads back. I saw them do it plenty of times." Hialeah replied. Jackson laughed at her innocent explanation. "Well I did." Hialeah remarked. "Oh I don't doubt you, but I assure you, those women are quite seasoned in their drinking." Jackson replied. "However, a lady doesn't toss her head back and swallow such an ungodly amount of liquor." Jackson remarked. "You sayin' I ain't no lady?" Hialeah asked offended. "Not at all, but those women in the tavern do not qualify as such." Jackson replied. "Well no matter, I won't be havin' no more of that." Hialeah remarked. "I think you'd best stick to coffee." Jackson replied teasingly.

After fully catching her breath, Hialeah sat back down to finish her coffee. Jackson took his seat once more across from her. To further his teasing of Hialeah's inability to handle alcohol, Jackson took a long swig of his gin without coughing and cocked a playful brow in Hialeah's direction. Hialeah responded by sticking her tongue out at Jackson, who burst into laughter at her childish gesture. Jackson leaned back in his chair once more truly feeling the effect of the gin. Hialeah took another sip of her now warm coffee. She placed the cup back on the table and began tapping on the side of it with her fingers. "Is there something you'd like to ask me?" Jackson said. "Your home in England, what's it like?" Hialeah asked. "It's a home like any other." Jackson replied. "That ain't true." Hialeah remarked. "Speaking of my home will appear as if I'm boasting." Jackson replied. "Is it as fine a home as your parents?" Hialeah asked. Jackson smiled. She was not one to give in. "If you must ask, then I'll tell you. In truth, my home is bigger than one person needs. It is quite grand to say the least." Jackson said. "Like royalty?" Hialeah asked. Jackson chuckled. "I assure you, it's not that grand." Jackson replied smiling. "Are there colored folks like me in England?" Hialeah asked. "Like you?" Jackson replied. "Well, I mean, I know there's colored folks, but are there any with um..." Hialeah began. "You're referring to mulattoes with indian blood?" Jackson said. "Yes." Hialeah replied. "I don't know, possibly." Jackson said. "No matter what them white folks say bout me in town, I ain't ashamed of who I am." Hialeah replied. She stood as did Jackson. "Nor should you be." Jackson said as he reached for Hialeah's hand. He looked into her eyes as he caressed her hand. "You're absolutely beautiful." Jackson said as he looked into Hialeah's eyes. Feeling her body warm to Jackson's touch, Hialeah slid her hand away from Jackson's and lowered her eyes. "You shouldn't say such things." Hialeah said softly. "Why not, if it's the truth?" Jackson replied. Hialeah raised her eyes to meet Jackson's gaze. Jackson closed the small gap between them and began caressing Hialeah's face. Hialeah closed her eyes at his gentle touch. She had never felt such emotion from anyone.

Jackson leaned in and placed a soft kiss on Hialeah's lips as he continued to gently stroke her cheek. "Miss Nokosi, I'd be a liar if I said that I didn't desire to have you." Jackson said his deep voice sending chills through Hialeah's body. Hialeah opened her eyes just as Jackson captured her lips in a kiss that mesmerized her very being. Jackson deepened their kiss as he lifted Hialeah into his arms. Hialeah could think of nothing as Jackson carried her into her bedroom where he gently laid her onto her awaiting bed. Jackson began to undress in the moon's light and Hialeah couldn't take her eyes off him as the moonlight played on the features of his muscled body. Hialeah's heart raced as Jackson approached her completely naked. Jackson undid the two tiny buttons that held Hialeah's thin robe together revealing her soft brown skin. Jackson began placing soft, feather-like kisses along the side of Hialeah's neck. She inhaled a breath as Jackson made his way to her shoulder teasing her body with his lips. Jackson's sexual pleasure continued as he focused his attention on Hialeah's full breasts; cupping them in his hands as his tongue tickled her now piqued nipples. Jackson sucked on one tantalizing nipple after the other sending Hialeah into a whirlwind of emotions.

Hialeah's hands trembled in the light of the moon as she reached out to touch Jackson's chiseled chest. She slid her hands down the length of his chest marveling at his extremely toned flesh. Jackson leaned toward her and blew gently on her flat stomach before leaving a trail of kisses back to her waiting sensuous lips. Hialeah longed for his kiss. She parted her lips to invite his probing tongue. A soft moan escaped Hialeah's lips that excited Jackson. He plunged his tongue deeper moaning his pleasure of her sweetness. Jackson could feel his body awakening with every touch. He wanted her ready to receive him. Her soft moans and silky skin were driving him mad.

Jackson refused to release Hialeah from his sultry kiss as he slid his hand between her thighs; caressing her sweet spot delicately. Hialeah broke their kiss as her back arched and her breathing quickened from Jackson's teasing of her body. Hialeah's heart raced. She had never felt such a sensation coursing through her body. She felt as if she were about to explode from his sexual torture. Jackson continued his teasing relishing the tremors that had overtaken Hialeah's body. He also relished the sound of her once pleas in English now being spoken in her true tongue. He wasn't sure if she were aware that she had ceased speaking in English, but no matter, he reveled in her moans. Hialeah could take no more. She climaxed from Jackson's touch and fell back breathless onto her bed. Jackson took her lips in another passionate kiss. Watching her explode from his touch sent him past the brink of control. She was his and he would have her. Jackson broke their kiss and stared down into Hialeah's eyes. Her chest was still heaving from her own release. "Name your price." Jackson said. He could wait no longer. "My price?" Hialeah asked breathless. "Whatever the amount, will be worth your pleasures." Jackson replied no longer able to control his desire to have her. He captured her lips once more in a savage kiss as he entered her like a crazed animal. Hialeah cried out in pain as Jackson took her uncontrollably. Jackson moaned with pleasure from every thrust inside of her. Unable to take the size of Jackson's erected staff inside of her, tears of pain welled in Hialeah's eyes and fell down her cheeks. As Jackson held onto their kiss, her tears began to dampen his face. Jackson broke their kiss momentarily and wiped gently at Hialeah's fallen tears. "Tears of pleasure I hope." Jackson said unable to see the hurt on Hialeah's face. Hialeah said nothing. She winced in pain as he continued to thrust his throbbing staff deeper inside of her moaning ferociously as he felt his own climax arising. Hialeah dug her nails into Jackson's back as his onslaught of her body continued. She struggled against his powerful thrusts unable to find her voice. Jackson reached his climax just as Hialeah cried out his name. His body erupted as he released his seed deep inside of her. His intense moan of satisfaction as he climaxed took over his whole body. Jackson collapsed from their lovemaking. Hialeah rolled onto her side. She quickly wiped at her tears as Jackson wrapped his arm around her pulling her closer to him. "My God, you're perfect." Jackson said breathlessly. He kissed Hialeah on her shoulder, but she remained silent and closed her eyes.

Chapter 6

Jackson awoke the next morning with the sun beaming on his face. He rolled over and stretched his arm out finding no one there. He opened his eyes to discover that he was alone in Hialeah's bed. A confused look furrowed his brow. He had no idea what time it was or how long he'd slept. What he did know was that he had made love to the most beautiful woman he had ever laid his eyes on. Jackson found himself smiling as he sat up in Hialeah's bed. Still very much naked, Jackson stood up and walked over to the water basin on Hialeah's small table and splashed water on his face. He reached for the towel that set next to the basin and dried his face. He then tossed the towel aside and turned back toward the bed. His smile faded as he noticed a red stain peering from the white sheet on Hialeah's bed. Jackson hurried over to the bed and ripped the sheet from it. His heart sank at the sight of blood on the bed. She couldn't have been Jackson thought to himself. Their night of lovemaking came flooding back in his mind. The tears on Hialeah's cheeks, and the cries that he had heard coming from her. Jackson felt as if someone had punched him in the stomach. He had taken her like some untamed beast. She said nothing. Why? Jackson wondered to himself. His curiosity was getting the best of him as well as his anger. Jackson hurried to get dress and bolted from Hialeah's front door.

Jackson raced off the front porch yelling Hialeah's name but he received no response. Jackson continued to yell for Hialeah as he headed toward her opened barn. When he heard his horse whinny, he ran inside the barn and stopped short as he saw Hialeah inside the barn with her back to him brushing her horse. Hialeah ignored his presence as she kept busy at what she was doing. "Why didn't you answer when I called?" Jackson asked gruffly. "You think you own me now cause you had me?" Hialeah said with calm sarcasm. Jackson ignored her question. He wanted answers to his. "Why didn't you tell me?" Jackson asked his temper beginning to rise. "Don't know what you mean." Hialeah replied nonchalantly. "You know damn bloody well what I mean!" Jackson exploded as he strode over to Hialeah grabbing her arm and turning her around to face him. He angrily snatched the horse's brush from her hand and threw it out of the barn. "Why didn't you tell me you were a virgin? That you had never known a man!" Jackson yelled. Tears of betrayal began to fill Hialeah's eyes. "Answer me!" Jackson yelled. Hialeah angrily yanked her arm from Jackson's grasp. "You believe what that Sheriff Willard say bout me; that I'm a whore!" Hialeah fired back. "That is a bloody lie!" Jackson yelled. "It's the truth!" Hialeah fired back again. "Besides, why it matter to you?" Hialeah demanded. "It matters to me because I hurt you!" Jackson shouted. "You got what you wanted from me." Hialeah spat. "What I wanted from you?" Jackson asked incredulously. "Rich and mighty white man fuckin' his poor little heathen colored whore!" Hialeah yelled. Her heated words brought an explosion from Jackson. He roughly grabbed her by both of her arms and brought her mere inches from his icy glare. "Do not ever speak to me in such a disgusting manner." Jackson said menacingly. His tight hold of Hialeah's arms made her wince in pain. She was beside herself and hurt. "You just like the rest of them savage men." Hialeah said sobbing. Jackson released her and took a few steps back to collect himself. He had never known a woman aside from his mother that could enrage him. "I am nothing like them." Jackson spat. "Then why you ask my price to have me?" Hialeah shouted. "Because that is what you commanded!" Jackson replied heatedly. "Any white man who wanted you would have to pay you for your pleasure! Is that not what you said to me?" Jackson fired. Hialeah stood speechless as Jackson threw her words back at her. Jackson was livid. He thought it best to leave before any more harsh words were said. He angrily strode by Hialeah and unlocked the door to his horse's stall. Hialeah stood by as he saddled his horse and led him from the barn. Jackson mounted his horse and Hialeah ran after him. "You think I don't know that you're leavin' here? That you're goin' back to your grand house in England. That you're fixin' to marry that Miss Sara and take her with you?" Hialeah spat. Jackson looked down on Hialeah from atop his horse. "That's why you wanted to leave the celebration? You believe I am to wed Miss Williams?" Jackson replied. "Well ain't you?" Hialeah asked. "I assure you, Miss Nokosi, that I have no intention of marrying Miss Williams." Jackson replied heatedly. "That ain't what folks say in town." Hialeah remarked. "I don't give a bloody damn what's being said in town." Jackson said harshly. "Since when you decide you ain't fixin' to marry her then?" Hialeah asked. "From the moment I met you. Or is it foolish of me to have fallen in love with a woman whose skin doesn't match my own?" Jackson replied angrily leaving Hialeah speechless once more. He loved her. Jackson nudged his horse and took off. "Jackson!" Hialeah called out as she ran after Jackson. Her woman's spot was still very much sore from Jackson's unyielding and savage love making. Jackson stopped his horse and waited for Hialeah to catch up to him. Hialeah looked up at Jackson. She had no right to say such harsh words to him when all he ever did was show her compassion. "I sorry." Hialeah said. "Don't be." Jackson said as he gestured with his head to the side of Hialeah's barn where they were being watched. Hialeah followed his gaze. "It appears you have caught more than just my eye." Jackson said his anger evident in his tone. He nudged his horse once again and took off down the dirt road away from Hialeah.

One of the gentlemen who had danced with Hialeah at the Independence Day Celebration stood by the side of Hialeah's barn. Heart-broken, Hialeah watched as Jackson disappeared from her sight. Hialeah kept her back to the strange man who had no doubt heard their outbursts. "What you doin' here?" Hialeah asked. "Forgive me for not askin' your permission to come calling, but I wanted to come by and introduce myself formal like. We danced last night at the party, but I ain't never get your name. My name's Isaac Leonard." Isaac said walking toward Hialeah with a bouquet of flowers. "These here for you." Isaac remarked holding the flowers out to Hialeah. Hialeah slowly turned around. "Thank you." Hialeah said somberly accepting the gift, her mind still very much on Jackson. Isaac smiled and removed his wide brimmed hat as Hialeah took the flowers.

Hialeah looked Isaac up and down, but said nothing. He was a tall, well-built man with dark brown skin and dark brown eyes. His white shirt was somewhat faded, his brown trousers were slightly worn, and his black boots were covered in dust from the road. Hialeah noticed that he had rolled his sleeves up to his elbows and had two buttons on his shirt undone to keep cool in the sun's heat. She glanced down at his hand and saw no ring on his finger. Isaac bent over and picked up the horse brush that Jackson had thrown from the barn and handed it to her. "You eavesdroppin' on what's goin' on here?" Hialeah asked curiously. "Not at all." Isaac replied. "You got family around here?" Hialeah asked. "Yes ma'am I do. I got a brother, two sisters, and my mama, we all live not too far from the church." Isaac replied. "No children? No wife?" Hialeah asked. "None of either…yet." Isaac replied smiling. "I hope to find me a wife someday, have a family of my own." Isaac remarked. "That why you come here, to find a wife?" Hialeah said. "Uh…no ma'am, well not exactly. I wanted to come and meet you in person. I mean I seen in church, but you don't stick around too long for me to make your acquaintance. I was right happy to have a dance with you last night, and then I see you leave with Mr. Harding…" Isaac began. "How you know his name?" Hialeah asked suspiciously. "I meant Mr. Harding's son. Mr. Henry Harding." Isaac stammered out. "You know Henry Harding?" Hialeah asked. "Yes ma'am. Well not exactly like that. I mean I work for him in his tobacco field." Isaac said. "You his slave?" Hialeah asked curiously. "I ain't nobody's slave no more, but I use to be before the war." Isaac replied. "You know his boy then?" Hialeah asked. "I seen him around the tobacco field since he come home. Mrs. Harding, why that's all she talk about, but I ain't ever seen him as a youngin'." Isaac replied. "How long you Mr. Harding slave?" Hialeah asked. "Mr. Harding buy me when I was about ten years old. They done shipped they son away when I get there." Isaac replied. "Weren't allowed to speak his name neither. Kind of like they was ashamed of him or something." Isaac remarked. Hialeah looked off down the road that Jackson had taken as he left. "Cause he a nigger lover." Hialeah whispered. "Excuse me?" Isaac said. Hialeah turned to face him. She simply shook her head to dismiss their conversation. "Oh, well I don't wanna keep you, but I would, if it's alright with you, I'd like to call on you sometime. Get to know you." Isaac said. "I suppose that be fine." Hialeah said. Hialeah's response brought a smile to Isaac's face. He put his hat back on and touched the brim before he turned to walk away. Realizing that he hadn't asked Hialeah her name, Isaac stopped mid-step and turned around with a boyish grin on his face. "I feel right foolish talkin' to you all this time and still not know your name." Isaac said. "My name's Hialeah. Hialeah Nokosi." Hialeah replied. "Well I hope you don't mind my sayin' so Miss Nokosi, but you were the prettiest girl at the party and I sure look forward to callin' on you." Isaac said. "Thank you again for the flowers Mr. Leonard." Hialeah replied. Isaac smiled and went on his way up the road. He had work to do and Henry Harding didn't take kindly to his employees being late to the tobacco field.

Seething with absolute rage, Jackson rode with break neck speed to clear his head after his heated argument with Hialeah. He felt it was time for him to return back to his life in England. The time he had spent in his hometown had disgusted him. His mother was still cold hearted and cared for nothing but her socialite life, his relationship with his father would no doubt forever be strained, the woman his mother thought would be the perfect wife was a spoiled and cruel bigot, and the only person who brought him the slightest bit of joy on this miserable holiday couldn't see passed the differences of their skin. His life in England was far from perfect, but it wasn't engulfed in turmoil. He had dear friends in England and a very profitable law career. Perhaps that is how he was meant to spend his life; defending the law, spending his wealth any way he saw fit, and sharing the beds of the many women who lusted after him. Perhaps he wasn't meant to settle down and have a family of his own like so many of his gentlemen friends hoped for. He was, however almost certain that Hialeah would have loved England and she would have made him extremely happy as his wife and mother to his children Jackson thought. Yet, as quickly as that pleasing thought entered his mind, Jackson just as quickly dismissed it. She was clearly incapable of love and he would no longer waste his time chasing after a woman who didn't wish to be caught.

With that very thought in mind, Jackson stopped in town and inquired about the next passenger liner going back to England. His brow furrowed after hearing that he would have to wait another nine days before he could return home. The only question left to answer was, what on earth would he do to occupy his time for those nine days? Well first off, Jackson thought, he needed to get home and soak in a long bath, and then he would decide what to do with what was left of his ruined holiday.

Jackson entered his home and approached a servant dusting. He asked if she would be so kindly as to draw him a bath. "Of course, Mr. Jackson." The servant replied. Georgina heard her son as she sipped on her tea in the dining room. "Jackson darling, where on earth were you last night? You missed all of the festivities." Georgina called out from the dining room. "I'm sure they were lovely." Jackson replied somberly. "Well are you going to tell me where you were?" Georgina asked. Jackson rolled his eyes as he stood on the bottom step. "Drinking mother. I spent the night drinking with a few blokes I met in the tavern." Jackson said. "And where did you sleep? You certainly weren't home when your father and I arrived." Georgina remarked. "Of course not mother, as I am just returning home." Jackson replied annoyed at their conversation. "Well I dare hope you didn't spend the evening with that woman." Georgina remarked. His mother's condescending tone reminded Jackson of the conversation that he had shared with Miss Lilly. He recalled Miss Lilly telling him how Hialeah wanted to be seen and not treated as if she didn't exist in the eyes of white people. "As a matter of fact mother, I did spend the evening with Miss Nokosi; a wonderful evening indeed. I dare say, that I pray our wonderful evening produces a son or a daughter. Either would be splendid wouldn't you say mother?" Jackson asked sarcastically. He waited for his mother to respond. Her response was better than Jackson could have ever hoped for. Georgina Harding fainted and the sound of her body hitting the floor brought a devilish grin to Jackson's face as he walked up the stairs.

A soothing bath was precisely what Jackson needed. As he soaked in the warm water he thought of the malicious joke he played on his mother. He found himself chuckling and smiling. His humorous jest led to a more serious thought. What if he had indeed gotten Hialeah with child? Would she love their child or see it as a burden being half white and half mulatto? If he asked her to come back to England with him, would she accept or demand to be left alone to raise their child without him? Surely she wouldn't keep him from his child. Jackson shook his head to dismiss the thought. She wasn't with child.

Besides, Jackson thought, she had another man to share her affections with now. He was never in the habit of chasing women and he wouldn't start now. She was the challenge that he couldn't win and he would have to accept it. There were plenty of women in England to occupy his time. Jackson convinced himself that Hialeah no longer mattered and finished his bath. As he stepped out of the tub, the smell of Miss Lilly's cooking teased his nostrils. He had missed dinner chasing after Hialeah the night of the party. His growling stomach reminded him that he was starving. Jackson quickly dressed and hurried downstairs to have his breakfast. He was met at the bottom of the stairs by Miss Lilly. Her look of displeasure on her face could always turn him into that young boy. "Don't you look at me with that innocent face. I knows you done did somethin' to upset your mother." Miss Lilly said accusingly. "No ma'am, I've just had a warm bath." Jackson replied. "Then you tell me why I find your mother on the floor in the dinin' room mutterin' some nonsense bout a mulatto grandchild?" Miss Lilly remarked sternly. Jackson tried to stifle his laugh. "It was a jest Mama Lilly, really it was." Jackson said smiling. "Well you just jest yourself right on into that kitchen and have your breakfast before you send your mother into another fit." Miss Lilly said in her mother-like tone. "Yes ma'am." Jackson replied chuckling as he headed toward the kitchen. "How's it between you and Miss Nokosi anyway?" Miss Lilly asked. Jackson stopped walking but kept his back to Miss Lilly. Her question immediately reminded him of his horrendous morning with Hialeah. "It's done." Jackson replied somberly. "Well, I'm sorry to hear that." Miss Lilly said. Jackson didn't offer a response to her remark. Miss Lilly noticed his head drop slightly as he continued silently into the kitchen.

As soon as Isaac disappeared from view, Hialeah returned to her chores. She walked back into the barn and set the flowers down on a stool and busied herself with tending to her horse once more. She was able to finish brushing his coat and tend to the rest of the animals on her small farm. She fed her chickens, her pig and one cow and made her way to her garden. Hialeah gathered some tomatoes, a few onions and potatoes and corn from her garden. As she walked into her front door, she noticed something shiny underneath her table. She set the basket with her vegetables in it on the table and knelt down onto the floor. Hialeah's heart fluttered briefly as she reached for Jackson's flask. She assumed that it must have fallen from his jacket in his haste to confront her. Hialeah stood and held the flask in her hands. She hadn't noticed the night before, but she saw on the flask that on it was inscribed a J and an H for Jackson Harding. Hialeah found herself sitting in her chair. She began to relive their night together and how it all started so wonderfully and ended with Jackson riding away from her livid. Hialeah rubbed her hand along the flask. She was sure he would come back for it or maybe, he left it as something to remember him by. Perhaps, she thought, that he had had enough of trying to win her over. With that thought in mind, Hialeah decided she would have to erase her mind of Jackson Harding no matter how difficult a task it may be. Besides, Isaac Leonard was a man of color as were she. He was also a very attractive man, clearly a gentleman, and a hard worker. He was, after all, employed by Henry Harding, one of the richest men in town. Hialeah decided to give Isaac a chance, after all, Jackson would be leaving soon whether he married Sara Williams or not, he would be returning back to his life in England. Hialeah thought it best to leave the flask at her home. If Jackson did miss it, he would know where to find it.

Jackson finished his breakfast deep in thought. He didn't hear Miss Lilly enter the kitchen. He sat frozen in his chair with a scowl on his face. Miss Lilly took Jackson's empty plate and noticed the dark look on his face. Miss Lilly stood back with her arms crossed while leaning against the counter. Jackson kept his eyes fixated on the spot where his plate once set in front of him. "You are a troubled man." Miss Lilly said. Jackson looked up slowly hearing Miss Lilly's voice. "How so?" Jackson replied. "You wanted so desperately for that girl in a matter of weeks to fall in love with a man whose very own people treat her so harshly." Miss Lilly said. "I never once treated her harshly." Jackson replied sternly. "That makes no difference. But herein lays the trouble. That girl ain't ever been in love and you, aside from me lovin' you all those years ago, why you ain't ever felt loved; not even by your own folks. So how two people ignorant of love gone connect with each other's heart?" Miss Lilly asked. "I'll not chase after a woman who insists on running." Jackson replied. "Then you were never the man she needed and deserved." Miss Lilly remarked matter-of-factly. The truth in Miss Lilly's words stung Jackson's ego and he angrily stood from his chair and strode from the kitchen.

Miss Lilly's words flooded Jackson's mind as he walked through the tobacco fields amongst the workers. He knew she was correct but he had his pride. A good walk through the tobacco field would surely clear his head. It was one of his favorite places to play as a child. He loved to help the slaves pick the huge leaves and get them ready for selling at his father's factory. Jackson rolled up his sleeves and joined in a group of colored employees picking the ripened tobacco leaves and gathering them into a pile to be hauled for curing. Jackson worked diligently alongside the others. The longer he worked, the more he remembered just how the tobacco picking was done. He also remembered hiding in the huge leaves from his father to avoid a whipping when he wasn't supposed to be assisting the slaves. The tobacco fields held some fond memories as well as cruel memories for Jackson. Nonetheless, he was an adult now, and being out in the heat toiling in the hot sun was just what he needed.

Jackson had put in a full day's work pulling tobacco leaves. When one of his father's field hands rang the bell alerting the workers that their day of work was done, Jackson found himself covered in dirt and sweat. He was exhausted yet invigorated. Jackson carried his load of collected leaves and followed the others to the tobacco barn where the leaves would be stored until they were shipped to his father's factory for curing. Jackson walked behind a worker who had set his load of leaves down in the. When the man turned around to exit the barn, he slightly bumped Jackson, who immediately recognized the man. He didn't know his name, but Jackson was quite certain that the man was the same fellow who had danced with Hialeah at the Independence Day Celebration as well as the man who had been standing alongside her barn just hours earlier. Jackson felt his blood freeze in his veins. His calm mood was now becoming dark. Jackson stared glaringly at Isaac. Visions of Hialeah wrapped lovingly in the man's arms flooded his mind. Isaac didn't miss the heated glare and grinned nervously knowing all too well that the man he had bumped was the boss's son and the man who had followed Hialeah home last night and had left her home that very morning. "Sorry sir." Isaac said nodding his head before exiting the barn. He didn't want to give his boss's son any reason to fire him. He and his family depended on the good wages that Mr. Harding paid him.

Jackson unceremoniously dropped his leaves and turned to walk out of the barn. He was so blinded with impending rage that he nearly collided with his father who had been standing at the barn's entrance. Henry Harding grabbed his son's arm. "What are you doing?" Henry asked. Recognizing his father's voice, Jackson snapped out of his angered daze. "What?" Jackson replied. Henry released Jackson's arm. "I asked you what are you doing?" Henry said. "I needed to clear my head." Jackson replied. "I pay these men good money to work the fields…" Henry began. Jackson strode off toward the bathing house to wash off the sweat and dirt from his face. He was in no mood to hear his father's scolding. As Jackson washed himself clean his mother tapped on the opened door to get his attention. Jackson turned around at the sound. Seeing his mother standing in the doorway, Jackson turned his attention back to what he was doing. "I see you've been out in the fields." Georgina said lightly. "If you're going to reprimand me like some child, don't. Father already tried that." Jackson replied annoyed at the intrusion. "That wasn't my intention. I merely came to invite you to Sylvia Cunningham's engagement party she's throwing for her daughter Katherine. Although I haven't the faintest notion why I should after that awful joke you played which nearly sent me to my grave." Georgina remarked. Jackson tossed his wash cloth aside and faced his mother. "Why not? I could use some entertainment." Jackson replied dryly brushing passed his mother. "Do hurry and get changed. They'll be some lovely young ladies attending." Georgina called out after Jackson.

After finishing her daily chores, Hialeah washed the blood stained sheet from her night with Jackson and hung it out to dry on the line. Since the house was quiet she opted to do a little knitting before she prepared herself a little dinner. Hialeah sat in the corner in one of the rocking chairs once owned by the Hastings and peacefully began to hum a little tune her mother would hum to her as a child as she knitted with the yarn that had belonged to Lydia Hastings. As Hialeah knitted, lost in her own world, she would find her mind wondering. She found herself thinking of Jackson and how he had befriended her from the very moment he arrived in town until their magical night of dancing at the Independence Day Celebration and even her horrible yet amusing drinking lesson. How he had protected her against Sara Williams, Sheriff Willard, convinced Mr. Grisby to pay her what he owed her, how he convinced Mrs. Nesbit to allow her to shop in her store, and even the way he stood up for her to his own mother. He was a perfect stranger to her and she allowed her mistrust in the only person who showed an ounce of decency toward her ride out of her life. Hialeah scolded herself mentally for being such a fool. After the way she spoke to him, accusing him of being like Sheriff Willard and the rest of the evil white folks in town, she was sure he would never forgive her. She was even more sure that she would never feel his lips on hers again.

The sound of a horse approaching her home snapped Hialeah from scolding herself. She fought back the tears that threatened to fall from her eyes as the sound of the horse's hooves got closer to her home. Hialeah set her knitting aside and hurried to her feet. She dared hoped it was Jackson returning to retrieve his flask. Hialeah thought of a quick apology as she grabbed Jackson's flask from her table. She rushed to the door and swung it open praying that Jackson would at least hear her out before giving her a well deserved tongue lashing. Hialeah's hopes of seeing Jackson and make amends with him were dashed as Isaac dismounted his horse. Hialeah casually slid the flask into the pockets of her dress and forced a smile on her face as Isaac approached her front porch with a full smile on his face. "It appears, I have forgotten my manners yet again." Isaac said. "I know it ain't proper to come callin' unannounced but I wanted to get here before you had a chance to have your supper." Isaac said. "You ain't had your supper just yet have you?" Isaac asked. "No, I was just catchin' up on some knittin." Hialeah replied. "Well if it can wait a bit longer, I'd be right pleased if you'll agree to havin' supper with my family tonight." Isaac said. "Don't you think it a might early for me to be meetin' your family?" Hialeah asked. "Oh it's just a simple supper. My mama fixed a real good meal. Besides, a pretty woman like you shouldn't be eatin' alone." Isaac replied. "Done it plenty times before, but since you came all this way, I suppose I could accept your invitation." Hialeah said. Isaac's smile widened even further. "That's swell, right swell. I'll saddle your horse for you." Isaac said excitedly before running off toward Hialeah's barn. Hialeah quickly ran into her house, retrieved Jackson's flask from her dress pocket and set it back on her table. She hurried back to the porch and waited for Isaac to return with her horse. She was getting rather hungry and it would be nice for once to have someone to talk to over dinner. Besides, she thought to herself, having dinner with Isaac's family would definitely take her mind off of Jackson, if only momentarily.

Isaac returned with her saddled horse still smiling. Hialeah allowed Isaac to assist her onto her horse. She decided to ride side saddle like a proper lady, although she preferred to ride astride. Isaac mounted his horse and clicked his tongue for his horse to get moving and Hialeah did the same as she followed Isaac down the road.

Georgina, Henry and Jackson arrived at the Cunningham residence and were greeted by footmen who held onto the horses' reins while Lucas climbed down to assist Georgina from the carriage. Henry and Jackson exited the carriage and Henry took his wife's hand and escorted her to the entrance of the Cunningham home while Jackson strolled nonchalantly behind his parents groaning inward at what he assumed would be a disaster of an evening. Georgina looked over her shoulder and noticed the visible scowl on her son's face. "Do try not to scowl so Jackson. It isn't becoming of a gentleman of your status." Georgina said. Jackson ignored his mother's reprimand and continued to scowl at the partygoers. Sara Williams and her father, Judge Williams, walked a few feet away from Jackson. Sara fought the urge to look in Jackson's direction. Jackson caught her watching him and gave her an impromptu wink and Sara turned her head quickly insulted at Jackson's gesture. Jackson smiled, amused that he was able to irritate the spoiled bitch.

Jackson entered the Cunningham residence behind his parents and welcomed the sight of the servants carrying trays of champagne. He signaled for one of the female servants to come his way and Jackson helped himself to two glasses of the champagne and made his way to a corner to avoid the other guests. He was strictly there for the entertainment, the food and of course, the liquor. Jackson was content in his corner watching the other guests gossip and laugh and share in the merriment of the occasion. He did, however, catch several young women in a group glancing his way and giggle to one another when he raised his glass in their direction in acknowledgment. Sara Williams was not impressed with Jackson's flirtatious manner. She had caught the exchange while pretending to be interested in a conversation with a young gentleman. She excused herself from the young man's company and made her way to the corner where Jackson stood. Jackson had summoned another servant over and again helped himself to yet two more glasses of champagne. He was rather pleased with the hostess's selection of drink. Jackson smiled and nodded his head in appreciation at the servant. The young servant blushed and walked away. Unaware that Sara Williams was standing next to him with a smug look on her face, Jackson took a sizable amount of champagne to his lips. Sara tapped him on the shoulder and Jackson turned to face the unwelcomed intrusion. "You think you're pretty clever don't you?" Sara asked smugly. Jackson gulped down the wine and began choking uncontrollably. Sara annoyingly crossed her arms while Jackson continued to choke. "Are you quite done?" Sara asked impatiently. Jackson shook his head and Sara stormed away in a huff. Jackson immediately stopped choking and watched as Sara returned to her gentleman friend all the while staring daggers at him. Pleased with his performance and his ability to get rid of Sara, Jackson felt the need to antagonize her further. He held his other glass of champagne to her and downed it casually. He grinned in Sara's direction and her eyes widened in utter disbelief. Why his mother thought such a brat would be the perfect wife for him was laughable at best.

   Hialeah and Isaac rode up to his family's home. His two younger sisters were bringing in the wash while his brother, who also appeared to be younger than Isaac, was sitting on the front steps playing a harmonica. When their brother rode up with Hialeah alongside him, Isaac's family immediately stopped what they were doing and made their way towards their older brother and his guest. Isaac hopped down from his horse and assisted Hialeah down from her own. "Who is this?" Isaac's brother asked curiously. Isaac laughed. "Well if you let me make my introductions, I can tell you all." Isaac replied. Isaac's mother walked out onto the porch just as he was about to make his introductions. Isaac turned to Hialeah. "That there's my mama." Isaac said. Hialeah just grinned but said nothing. "Mama." Isaac called out ushering his mama to come closer. "This here is Miss Nokosi." Isaac said. Isaac's mother approached him and Hialeah. Mrs. Leonard was a dark skinned heavy set woman with black and gray hair hidden underneath a brown scarf. Her eyes were brown and sunken in from the years of being a slave wearing on her. Hialeah could tell that she was once a very beautiful woman but life had not been kind to her. Life had not been kind to any of her mother's people. Hialeah forced a nervous smile on her face. "Miss Nokosi, this is my mama, Louise Leonard, my brother George, my sister Ruby, and my youngest sister, Rosie." Isaac said. "It's nice to meet you all." Hialeah said. "What she doin' here?" George asked. "I invited her for supper." Isaac replied. "You sweet on my brother?" Ruby asked smiling. "We only met last night." Hialeah replied. Rosie whispered to her sister and they both start giggling. "Mama make them stop with all the whisperin'." Isaac said. "You two mind your manners now." Louise replied sternly. "I only said that she's the girl Isaac danced with last night at the party." Rosie remarked. "She also danced with that white man, too." George replied offended that his brother would bring home a colored girl that fancied being in a white man's arms. "What you bring that white man to a colored folk party for anyway? You know his daddy owned us before the war?" George asked. "Now you hush up and mind your business." Louise ordered. "That was a long time ago." Louise said. "I didn't invite Jack…Mr. Harding to the party. His maid told him where to find me." Hialeah replied. "Why she do that? Don't she know white folks and colored folks ain't supposed to be together?" George said. "George, you go on and set the table. I'm sure Miss Nokosi don't appreciate all them questions." Louise said. "You two go on and help your brother." Louise said addressing Isaac's two sisters. Ruby and Rosie followed George into the house. "Don't be too long. I don't want my good supper gettin' cold now." Louise said as she followed her children into the house. Isaac turned to Hialeah. "I'm sorry bout my brother. He knows better than to misbehave in front of guests." Isaac said. "It's alright." Hialeah replied. "Well we best get inside. Mama don't take too kindly to her good cookin' gettin' cold." Isaac said as he escorted Hialeah into his home for dinner.

When Isaac and Hialeah entered his home, George was already seated while Ruby and Rosie assisted Louise with the food. Isaac pulled out a chair for Hialeah to be seated next to him. George sat across from Hialeah frowning in her direction. Hialeah pretended not to notice George's rude expression. Isaac went around the table and poured everyone a glass of his mother's cold lemonade before seating himself next to Hialeah. Louise had prepared a nice roast with potatoes, fresh green beans, corn on the cob and homemade bread. Hialeah couldn't wait to taste the appetizing meal. Isaac said grace before the family dug into their meal. Hialeah watched as each dish was passed around the table and everyone helped themselves to a generous helping of the roast. Isaac offered Hialeah a slice of buttered bread and corn on the cob to wit she graciously accepted. Isaac and his siblings tore into their dinner before their mother finished filling her plate with the dinner that she had prepared. Hialeah waited until Louise's plate was filled and she had taken a bite of her dinner before she took a bite of her own meal. It was a rule her mother always enforced. Hialeah started with a forkful of roast. It was one of the best meals she had ever tasted. Louise glanced at Hialeah. She took a sip of her lemonade to wash down her meal before addressing Hialeah. "So how is it?" Louise asked. Hialeah wiped her mouth before on her napkin before speaking. "Very good, thank you." Hialeah replied smiling shyly.

Ruby sat next to Hialeah and couldn't resist the urge to touch Hialeah's hair. Hialeah turned to face Ruby. "You got really pretty hair." Ruby said. "Leave that woman's hair be so's she can finish her dinner." Louise remarked sternly. "It's so fine." Rosie said. Hialeah grinned. "You'd have fine hair too if you were a half-breed." George scoffed. "You watch your mouth." Isaac warned. "It's true and everybody knows it." George replied. "Your daddy white?" Rosie asked. "No you big dummy. Her daddy one of them injuns." George replied. "George, now that's enough outta you." Louise remarked angrily. "You speak injun?" Ruby asked. "Creek. I speak Creek." Hialeah replied. "Can you speak some?" Ruby said. "If you want me to." Hialeah replied. "Can you say, 'Hello, how are you'?" Ruby asked. "Of course. Hensci (Hins-cha), Estonko (Is-don-go)?" Hialeah said. Ruby and Rosie clapped as they smiled. Their applause of appreciation brought a smile to Hialeah's face. She had never received applause for something so natural to her. "Now you leave that woman to her supper." Louise said. Ruby disobeyed her mother's order to let Hialeah alone. She found Hialeah fascinating and wanted to know more. "If I may, how is it that your daddy an injun? Most mulattoes around here came from their massuhs?" Ruby said. "I might have too if my mama hadn't run away when she did." Hialeah replied. Ruby became even more fascinated by Hialeah. She was aching to know even more about her. "Where she go; your mama?" Ruby asked. "She go to Florida." Hialeah replied. She looked at Isaac's family. They all had the same look of interest on their faces; even George. It was quite evident they were anxious to hear her mother's story.

Hialeah took a sip of her lemonade and began retelling Isaac's family the story that she had told Jackson of her mama and how she had escaped Judge Williams' family and made her way to Florida. She told them of how her father demanded that she speak his tongue and how he went off to the war. Hialeah's story held everyone's attention. Isaac's family went from tearing into their dinner to barely touching a single morsel on their plates. Hialeah finished her story of how and why she returned to her mother's home and how she acquired the Hastings' place. Ruby was so entranced by Hialeah's story, that she had wiped several tears from her eyes. Hialeah reassured Ruby that her mother lives a happy life amongst her father's people and she a free woman and there were no need for tears on her mother's behalf. George sat back in his chair; a smug look forming on his face. He had listened intensely to Hialeah's story but his own curiosity was getting the best of him. "I got a question." George said arrogantly. "No more questions. Eat." Louise demanded. "If my brother gone be courtin' her, I got a right to know bout his woman ain't I?" George replied. "You ain't got no right to be askin' her nothin' less I says you do." Isaac said sternly. "You may be my brother, but you ain't my daddy." George fired back. "You best mind your manners." Isaac warned. George ignored his brother's threat and leaned over his plate. "If my brother courtin' you, and your own mama ran away from her massuh, why you bring that white man to a colored folk celebration, huh? You his girl or somethin'? You openin' your legs to a white man and my brother too?" George said harshly. His rude questioning earned him a slap across the face from Louise that startled everyone at the table. Louise stood up angrily. "You take yourself right on outta here." Louise said heatedly. Humiliated, George too stood up angrily and stormed out of the room. Hialeah jumped at the sound of his door slamming closed. Louise slowly sat back down. "I so sorry. I just don't know what done came over that boy." Louise said. Hialeah nodded her head slightly in forgiveness; embarrassed by George's barrage of malicious questions toward her. She lowered her eyes as did Ruby and Rosie. The rest of the meal was eaten in silence after several attempts by Isaac to lighten the mood with uplifting conversation. Hialeah never wanted to disappear so badly in her life. She fought the urge to run out of the Leonard's home, but didn't wish to upset Louise by wasting her food. Hialeah finished her supper yet passed on dessert. The chocolate cake that Louise presented looked tantalizing but Hialeah wanted nothing more than to get home. She could somewhat bear the insults from white folks. It was expected of them to turn their snobbish noses up at colored folks but to hear such vile talk against her by one of her own, was gut-wrenching.

    Ruby collected the empty plates and Hialeah thanked Louise for a delicious dinner. Louise offered another apology on George's behalf and Hialeah accepted it with a faint smile on her lips. Isaac walked Hialeah outside to her horse and offered to escort her home to wit Hialeah graciously turned down. Isaac nodded his head in understanding. He too, apologized for his brother's behavior and leaned in to give Hialeah a soft kiss on the lips. Hialeah turned her head away slightly; refusing Isaac's kiss. Hialeah could see the disappointed look in Isaac's eyes and he recognized the hurt in her eyes due to his brother's cruel treatment of her at dinner. Isaac assisted Hialeah onto her horse and asked if he would see her tomorrow at church. Hialeah had never missed a Sunday sermon and she wasn't about to allow George's comments keep her from her Sunday routine. Unable to console Hialeah any further, Isaac tapped her horse gently and watched as Hialeah rode off into the night.

    Isaac turned around to find his mother standing in the doorway. Louise walked down the wooden steps of her front porch and approached her son. She didn't want Ruby and Rosie to hear what she had to say to her eldest child. She placed a gentle hand on her son's arm to calm him down. Her sons had fought many times before as young boys, but she wouldn't have any fighting in her home over a woman. Isaac looked down at his mother and smiled faintly. Louise could see in her son's eyes that he wanted to tear into his younger brother. "We need to talk." Louise said. Isaac knew that tone but was in mood to converse with anyone. "Not now mama." Isaac replied softly but Louise wouldn't be put off. She had something to say and her son was going to hear it. "Is it true what your brother said?" Louise asked concerned. "What truth?" Isaac replied offended at his mother's question. "I saw her just like everybody else at the party; dancing and carryin' on with Mr. Harding's son." Louise said. "So what? Colored folks and white folks can't dance together?" Isaac said sarcastically. "Don't you dare take that tone with me Isaac Leonard." Louise replied sternly. "Mr. Harding pay you good money to work on his tobacco field. If that girl belong to his son, I don't want you mixed up in that." Louise said. "Belong? Mama we ain't slaves no more, and Hialeah, she ain't never been no slave." Isaac replied offensively. "That may well be true, but he has an eye for her." Louise remarked. "I got an eye for her too, and ain't no white man gonna keep me from her, and I ain't gone lose my job over it neither." Isaac said matter-of-factly. "Isaac, there are other girls." Louise replied. "I don't want no other girl, mama. If I have to go away from here, make my own way to be with her, then that's just what I'll do." Isaac replied heatedly before storming away from his mother's side. He marched into the house and slammed his door shut.

Jackson had spent the majority of the evening mocking the guests at the party, drinking glass after glass of champagne and trying to avoid Sara Williams. He found it quite amusing that no matter how hard he tried to keep away from the vile woman, she made it a point to inch her way closer and closer to him. He was running out of ways to upset her. His mother had reprimanded him several times for being intoxicated and not paying any attention to the hostess or the bride-to-be. Jackson hardly heard a word his mother said to him. The effects of the champagne had him feeling at ease. He had filled his plate numerous times with fresh fruit and cheeses and other assorted treats being served. He had refused several offers to dance. He was quite content walking aimlessly around the ballroom eavesdropping on any conversation that caught his interest. He flirted with every female servant in attendance and even took the time to have a friendly smoke outside with the Cunningham's butlers.

Jackson surrounded himself with the male staff laughing and enjoying their company. He thought he'd amuse the men with a joke that he had heard many times. When none of the men laughed at his joke, Jackson began to explain it to them. He frowned as he noticed their eyes were fixated on whatever it was behind him. Jackson turned around and groaned inward at the cause of their distraction. Sara Williams was standing behind him with her arms crossed and a telling look on her face. The staff excused themselves and left Jackson alone with the one woman he had desperately wanted to be far from. Sara waited until the Cunningham's staff was out of earshot before she proceeded. "Mr. Harding." Sara said. Jackson cringed at the sound of her voice. Her southern drawl made his skin crawl. She was indeed a pretty woman but Jackson pitied the man who found her claws stuck in him. "Miss Williams." Jackson said mockingly. "Surely you can find more suitable company to spend your time with instead of the servants?" Sara replied smugly. "Too much color for your liking?" Jackson remarked sarcastically. Sara smirked at his sarcastic tone. "Surely you prefer the company of a gentleman who shares your beliefs regarding coloreds." Jackson said dryly. "I assumed that gentleman would be you the way your mother carried on about you." Sara replied. "I'm afraid my mother misled you or have you conveniently forgotten how you referred to me as a nigger lover for forbidding you to strike Miss Nokosi?" Jackson remarked his annoyance with Sara's presence evident in his tone. "So you'd reject a woman of my high caliber for a destitute simpleton?" Sara said. Jackson's temper began to flare. Sara caught the icy glare of his hazel eyes. "Forgive me, please. That was inexcusable and unbecoming of a lady to speak in such a vicious manner." Sara rushed out. "A lady?" Jackson scoffed before walking by Sara. "Jackson, do let's start over shall we?" Sara said pleadingly. Jackson kept walking. "I am sorry." Sara called out. Jackson stopped and turned around. "You're sorry?" Jackson replied mockingly. Sara took several steps toward Jackson and stopped mere inches from his tall frame. Sara lowered her eyes in an attempt to play on Jackson's sympathies. "I'm sorry and quite honestly, ashamed of my behavior." Sara said softly. "Ashamed?" Jackson replied cocking a suspicious brow. Sara raised her eyes to meet Jackson's gaze. "Can you forgive me?" Sara asked. Before Jackson could reply, Sara stood on tip toe and wrapped her arms around Jackson's neck and kissed him. Surprised by Sara's abrupt kiss, Jackson pulled away. "What are you doing?" Jackson said. "Apologizing." Sara replied sweetly with a smile on her lips before walking casually away from Jackson. Jackson stood dumbfounded; unsure as to what had just transpired.

After returning home from her horrible evening with Isaac's family, Hialeah threw herself onto her bed. Her thoughts quickly turned to Jackson. She truly did care for him; loved him even, but it was too late. Hialeah was most certain that Jackson would not want anything more to do with her. Scolding herself for being so foolish, she burst into tears and cried herself to sleep.

Chapter 7

Jackson had awakened with a huge victorious smile on his face. He had survived his treacherous holiday in his childhood home. He had waited a whole nine days for this glorious day to arrive. The passenger liner to take him home would be arriving today and he was most eager to return to his life in England. He had kept true to his word. He had not thought about Hialeah nor sought her out. He was most certain that her time was well spent in the arms of her new beau. He did, however, receive several visits from Sara and joined her for lunch and strolls through the park on several occasions. They had even exchanged several pleasantries across the table during their luncheons together and shared a few kisses as they walked through the park but not even complimentary lunch outings and mere kisses were enough to keep him in South Carolina.

Jackson practically hopped out of his bed. He found himself humming as he strolled over to the window and threw the curtains back. He let the sun's rays heat his face and chest before going to the water basin to wash his face. He was indeed in good spirits as he pulled his luggage from beneath his bed and playfully tossed them onto it. Still humming aloud, Jackson walked over to his closet to retrieve his clothing and like a child, tossed them into the air and watched as they fell to the bed atop his luggage. With not a care in the world, he then casually strolled over to his desk where his coat that Hialeah had repaired hung on the back of his chair. Jackson grabbed his coat and folded it over in his arms. His smile faded as a look of confusion came over his face. Jackson laid his coat on the bed and opened it wide. He investigated the pockets in search of his silver flask. Jackson groaned. It dawned on him that the last place he had had his flask was the night he had spent with Hialeah. He had been in such a rush to leave her home after their heated argument; it had no doubt fallen from his pocket somewhere along the road. His cherished gift; gone. No doubt picked up by some vagabond and sold at a pawn shop for booze.

Jackson hated that he had lost such a valuable gift, but there was nothing he could do about it now. He continued packing in silence.

Hialeah continued to see Isaac and even allowed him to sit next to her in church. She welcomed the company as they listened to the preacher's sermon. She hadn't returned back to visit Isaac at his home after her terrible experience with George, however she had extended an invitation to Isaac to her home for dinner. She liked having Isaac around to talk to, especially during their picnic and fishing outings. However, Hialeah still shied away from Isaac when he attempted to kiss her. Jackson had been the only man to ever kiss her, and she feared such intimacy with Isaac. She liked Isaac a lot and could see the frustration on his face, but when he wasn't around, her thoughts always crept back to Jackson.

On one of their outings, Hialeah asked Isaac what it had been like for him and his family to be enslaved by Jackson's family. She had heard the stories that her mother had shared with her, but she wanted to hear it from someone who wasn't close to her. Isaac told Hialeah his life as someone's property and how there were days when Henry Harding was kind to his slaves and the days when he was brutal. Isaac's words sent chills over Hialeah's skin. Her heart ached to hear such cruelty. She wondered if Jackson even knew his father had owned Isaac's family. She sobbed just imagining how difficult it must have been for slaves like Isaac's family and her mother. Hialeah wanted to hate Jackson for how his father treated her people, but she knew he had nothing to do with his father's merciless acts. She remembered how horribly Jackson was treated himself at the hands of his father.

Jackson had finished packing and was preparing to carry his luggage downstairs when the faint sound of moaning caught his attention. Jackson set his luggage down in the hall and crept down the hall following the sounds of the moaning. The moans led him to his father's door. Jackson placed his ear against the door and tapped lightly on it. When his father didn't respond, Jackson slowly opened the door and peeked inside. "Father?" Jackson said suspiciously. Henry let out an agonizing moan and Jackson rushed inside of his parent's bedroom. He ran over to the window and flung the curtains open before turning to his father. Jackson's blood drained from his face from father's appearance. Henry was drenched in sweat and his face was ghostly white. Jackson rushed to his father's side and ripped his nightshirt down the middle. Henry's chest was covered in rose colored rashes. His eyes were shut and his lips were dry. "Father!" Jackson said frantically. With no response from his father, Jackson hurried from the room and ran to the top of the stairs. "Mama Lilly!" Jackson yelled. Miss Lilly quickly appeared from the kitchen. "What is it, Jackson?" Miss Lilly rushed out. "Send for the doctor! It's my father. Hurry!" Jackson replied frantically. Miss Lilly ran from the front door in search of Lucas.

Jackson and Georgina nervously paced outside of Henry's door while the doctor assessed Henry. Georgina sobbed uncontrollably waiting on word from the doctor regarding her husband's condition. Jackson tried to keep his emotions intact. He didn't want his mother to suffer a breakdown if he weren't able to keep it together. He wasn't overly fond of his father, but he didn't wish to see him dead. His mother would be lost without her husband. Jackson went over to his mother and pulled her into his arms. Georgina collapsed in her son's arms and continued to sob hysterically. Jackson stroked his mother's hair and she looked up into her son's eyes. "I just don't know what I'll do if he dies." Georgina cried. "He'll be fine mother. The doctor will see to his care." Jackson replied in an effort to reassure his mother. Jackson pulled out his pocket watch. It seemed as if the doctor had been with his father for hours instead of minutes. He was growing inpatient. "Jackson, I know you're eager to return home, but..." Georgina began. "I'll not leave you while father is ill." Jackson said. "The business..." Georgina said. "I'll take care of it." Jackson replied. Georgina squeezed Jackson's hand just as the door to her bedroom opened. The doctor walked out and closed the door behind him. "Is he alright?" Georgina rushed out. "Your husband has Typhoid fever." The doctor said. "Oh my God." Georgina cried hysterically. "I've given him some medicine to fight the infection. He's very weak and his fever is quite high. See to it that he's looked after constantly and send for me immediately if his condition worsens." The doctor said. "Thank you doctor." Jackson replied. The doctor nodded his head and left Georgina and Jackson in the hall.

Georgina moved to another bedroom in the house at the instruction of the doctor to avoid being infected by Henry's Typhoid fever. Georgina hired a live-in nurse to care for her husband. Her staff feared catching the infection and bringing it home to their families. Word spread like wildfire of Henry's illness and that Jackson would be taking on the family responsibilities. Hialeah heard the terrifying news from Isaac while he joined her at her home for dinner. She pretended that the news of Jackson stay in South Carolina held no interest to her and changed the subject while they dined together. She didn't want to offend Isaac. He had been a wonderful companion and she truly valued their time spent together. Jackson worked the tobacco fields alongside the workers as well as traveled in to town to visit his father's warehouse to go over the books. He wanted to make sure that his father's lawyers were doing their job properly and that his father's workers were being paid fairly and that the tobacco buyers were receiving their payments as well. Jackson returned home most nights extremely exhausted. Some nights he slept in his office. He would stop home periodically throughout the day to see to his father's well-being before returning back to the warehouse to finish his work.

The Harding home was like a madhouse while Henry was ill. Georgina's friends and many of Henry's as well came to visit to see how Henry was faring and if Georgina needed anything and to thank Jackson for being there in his mother's time of need. Sara Williams took this opportunity to spend time with Georgina in an attempt to get closer to Jackson in hopes that he would see her as the woman he could depend on in such terrible times as a friend and hopefully as a wife. Sara visited Georgina everyday and often brought some sort of treats with her to share as they had their tea. She even accompanied Georgina on several outings when Georgina was feeling up to going into town. Sara came by Harding Tobacco, Henry's warehouse, where Jackson spent most of his mornings, to bring him lunch while he oversaw the running of the business. Some afternoons, they dined for lunch at one of Sara's favorite restaurants. Sara explained her reasoning as wanting to get Jackson away from the office. He agreed with her. Stepping out of the office on occasion to have lunch would indeed do him some good.

Hialeah traveled into town to do some shopping at the street markets. It was a gorgeous Saturday afternoon and she loved walking the streets when the vendors carted their goods for the passersby to admire and purchase. Hialeah carried a small basket to hold the fresh flowers she intended on purchasing. Her money was scarce but she loved fresh flowers in her vase that set on her table. The streets were filled with white and colored folks alike browsing the carts of the vendors. Sheriff Willard was also out with his deputies perusing the streets in search of pickpocketers and other petty thieves and trouble makers. Hialeah shuddered when she saw Sheriff Willard. She kept her distance from him and continued on with her browsing. Hialeah was in search of daffodils. She loved the flower and thought they would look perfect on her dinner table. She walked by cart after cart until she spotted her flowers being sold by a vendor across the street. Hialeah could hardly contain her excitement as she crossed the road to get to the vendor. There were a few customers ahead of her and she crossed her fingers and said a silent prayer that the shoppers in front of her would at least leave her two daffodils to take home.

Hialeah dug into her sewing back and gathered her money. She didn't want to keep the vendor waiting when it was her turn in line. Hialeah smelled the flowers as she stood in line. She knew exactly which ones to choose. When it was finally her turn, Hialeah greeted the vendor and chose her five daffodils. She paid for her flowers and laid them carefully in her flower basket before thanking the man and going on about her way. She had a little money left and considered browsing a bit more but thought against it. She had housework to tend to before she could relax and enjoy the rest of her Saturday in peace.

Hialeah strolled happily down the street on her way back to her wagon. When she reached her waiting wagon, she stroked her horse gently on the nose before setting her basket on the seat. Just as she stepped one foot onto her wagon, she was roughly grabbed around the waist by Deputy Blake and swung back down to the ground. She quickly turned around and was met by Sheriff Willard. Hialeah's eyes widened as she struggled against Deputy Blake who had a tight grip on her. "Well well well." Sheriff Willard said smirking. "Looks like we caught ourselves a little heathen thief." Sheriff Willard said mockingly his deputies laughing at Hialeah's expense. "I ain't no thief." Hialeah spat struggling to free herself. "I purchased these flowers." Hialeah said defensively. "Oh it's not the flowers I'm talking about. I'm talking about the money you stole from a one Terell Grisby after you assaulted him." Sheriff Willard replied. "I don't know what you talkin' bout. I ain't steal nothin' from that man." Hialeah spat. "Well, that's not what he says. Terell just got his memory back after being hit something fierce on the head. Why he come right to my office just moments ago and named you as his attacker. Says he got witnesses to back his claim." Sheriff Willard replied. "He's lyin'. I ain't attack him and I ain't stole from him neither." Hialeah said heatedly. Willie had had enough of the disrespect toward his sheriff. He took it upon himself to strike Hialeah across the face with the back of his hand surprising even Sheriff Willard. The slap was so forceful that Hialeah's hair swung into her face. When she angrily swung her head to remove the hair that had fallen out of place, her stinging face revealed a now busted lip. She stared daggers of pure hate in Willie's direction. "That's for sassin' our good sheriff. Maybe now, you'll learn some respect." Willie replied smugly as Hialeah continued to stare viciously at Willie. "Well it's his word against yours and I'm inclined to believe an honest businessman over a dirty mutt any day." Sheriff Willard replied smirking. "Lock her up on the charges of assault and robbery." Sheriff Willard said. Both deputies grabbed Hialeah by the arms. She struggled to break free as Sheriff Willard led the way to the jail followed by his deputies. Stunned faces and gasps of surprise could be heard as Sheriff Willard and his deputies led Hialeah to her waiting cell.

Jackson chose to sleep in. The warehouse was closed for business and the tobacco fields were not worked on the weekends. Jackson had slept a good portion of the morning well into the afternoon cocooned in his bed covers. When he finally awakened he felt as if he had slept 1,000 years. He was well rested and ready to get his day started before he was left with no Saturday to enjoy at all. After dressing and mentally preparing himself for the day, Jackson walked down the stairs. He heard voices coming from the dining room. His mother was having company. Jackson wasn't interested in seeing anyone before he had his coffee and a bite to eat. When he reached the bottom step he couldn't help but to over-hear his mother's guest mentioning the excitement that had just transpired in the town market. His mother's guest gossiped on and on about how she had rushed over to share the news. Jackson's curiosity was piqued. He remained on the bottom landing of the staircase and listened with a scowl on his face. He couldn't make out the voice of whom his mother was entertaining but she was quite thrilled to be spreading her juicy tidbit of gossip. Between her nibbles of cookie chewing and tea slurping, Jackson was ready to shout for the woman to get on with it. He rolled his eyes impatiently; annoyed that he had allowed himself to be taken in by idle chatter.

Jackson had had enough of waiting. He started for the kitchen when mention of Sheriff Willard's name stopped him dead in his tracks. He listened as his mother's friend vividly explained how she had been shopping at the market and how right before her very eyes, Sheriff Willard apprehended that bothersome colored girl who harassed decent white folk begging for work. When his mother gasped and questioned as to the reasoning of the arrest, Jackson listened for a response. His mother's friend simply declared that she hadn't the faintest idea why, but that all she knew was that she saw that miserable half-breed being dragged down the street by the sheriff's deputies and Sheriff Willard leading the way.

Hearing his mother's friend's story, Jackson became enraged. He knew all too well whom his mother's friend spoke of. His blood began to boil at the thought of Sheriff Willard hurting Hialeah. He was well aware of how the sheriff felt about Hialeah. Jackson bolted out of the front door hollering for Lucas to bring him his horse. Georgina and her friend hastily ran to the window at the sound of Jackson's boisterous yelling. They stared at each other dumbfounded as Jackson sped off down the road.

A million thoughts ran through Jackson's mind as he raced to town to get his hands on Sheriff Willard. Jackson rode fiercely through the market causing shoppers to dash quickly out of his way. Jackson practically jumped from his horse and stormed into the jail where Sheriff Willard was sitting in his chair with his feet casually propped up on his desk. Jackson had burst into the jail with such fury that the door slammed against the wall startling Willie and James. Hialeah sat on her cot and as if in a daze stood up and walked slowly toward the cell bars. She had never seen Jackson looking as sinister and menacing as he did at that moment. He was dressed in all black, his body was rigid and his eyes were like a hazel fire. Hialeah found herself afraid to breathe as Jackson strode up to Sheriff Willard, his eyes fixated on the man. Sheriff Willard promptly removed his feet from his desk as Jackson approached him. Willie and James stood a short distance behind Sheriff Willard; in an awkward attempt to appear fearless. Jackson stopped mere inches from Sheriff Willard's desk ignoring Willie and James. "Well look it here. The Honorable Judge Harding. I was wondering if you were going to show up to rescue your fair maiden." Sheriff Willard said tauntingly. Willie and James chuckled at their boss's joke but Jackson remained stone faced. "Sheriff, I demand to know what charges are against this woman to have her arrested." Jackson said sternly. Sheriff Willard smirked and leaned back in his chair. "Is that right?" Sheriff Willard replied mockingly. "Indeed sir." Jackson remarked coldly. "Well since I am the sheriff and I am obligated to divulge your request, I'll do just that." Sheriff Willard said before taking out a cigar from his vest pocket and lighting it. Sheriff Willard took a puff of his cigar, exhaled the smoke and leaned forward on his desk. "I arrested this...whatever the hell you insist on calling her, on the charges of assault and robbery." Sheriff Willard said lightly. "And who has made these charges?" Jackson replied gruffly. "A one Terell Grisby. Says he's got witnesses too." Sheriff Willard remarked. "Witnesses?" Jackson replied. "That's right. Said this pitiful half-breed squaw assaulted him and stole some monies from his coat." Sheriff Willard remarked matter-of-factly. "Well, I'd hate to make an upstanding man such as yourself look foolish or incompetent in front of your equally upstanding deputies, but it appears to me that you've arrested the wrong individual." Jackson said taunting the sheriff in return. Despising Jackson's tone, Willie erupted. "Now you wait just one god..." Willie began heatedly. "Do not speak in my direction!" Jackson fired glaring at Willie. His tone startled Hialeah. Sheriff Willard held up a hand to silence Willie's futile tirade. "Now what say you about this so-called mistake?" Sheriff Willard said. "Well let me first start off with informing you, sheriff, that I was there in the tavern on the night in question." Jackson began. Hialeah's brows rose curiously as Jackson began to speak. "You were there?" Sheriff Willard replied doubtfully. "Absolutely. What I and every patron in the tavern witnessed that night was a very heated argument between Miss Nokosi and Mr. Grisby." Jackson said sternly. "An argument about what?" Sheriff Willard interrupted. "Mr. Grisby's refusal to pay what was owed Miss Nokosi for her services. She demanded her pay and he mocked her outright in her face and threatened to have her arrested if she refused to vacate his property." Jackson spat. "What does that have to do with her taking what don't belong to her?" Sheriff Willard said. "Miss Nokosi left the property and did not return." Jackson replied heatedly. "Just how do you know she didn't return later, assault Mr. Grisby and steal his money?" Sheriff Willard said smugly. "She had no need." Jackson replied. "And why is that?" Sheriff Willard replied sarcastically. "It's very simple sheriff, even for you. Maybe not so much for your hired fools, so I'll go slowly." Jackson replied with his own sarcastic tone. "You're walking a mighty fine line judge or no judge." James said threateningly. Jackson smirked. "Whatever you say, James." Jackson replied mockingly. "Never mind them. I'd like to hear more of this fairy tale." Sheriff Willard said smiling. "I'm glad I can amuse you, sheriff. Perhaps you'll also find it amusing to know that after Miss Nokosi was thrown out of the tavern by Grisby, I followed him to his office, bashed his face quite swiftly, watched his body fall limp to the floor and retrieved Miss Nokosi's wages from Grisby's coat pocket. After a brief moment of searching the streets for Miss Nokosi, I located her and handed her what was owed her." Jackson said calmly. Hialeah inhaled an astonished breath hearing Jackson's confession. All four men turned to face her but she kept her eyes on Jackson. "You tell me Mr. Grisby give it to you." Hialeah said in disbelief. "No. I told you it was something like that." Jackson replied. "Now wait just one damn minute. You're telling me, that you, the son of one of the wealthiest men in South Carolina, an esteemed judge no less, not only assaulted a man that you've never met, but robbed him of his money only to give it to a woman you know nothing about?" Sheriff Willard said incredulously. "Hardly a complicated confession, sheriff." Jackson replied sarcastically. "Confession or not, I think you're full of shit, Your Honor." Sheriff Willard remarked annoyed at Jackson' smugness. "Of course you do, but may I ask, did Grisby tell you how much were missing from his coat pocket?" Jackson asked. "Of course he did. Said everything was all there except..." Sheriff Willard began. "Four dollars." Jackson replied before Sheriff Willard could finish his statement. Sheriff Willard's eyes nearly protruded from his head. "How did you know the amount that was missing?" Sheriff Willard asked curiously. "Incredible isn't it?" Jackson replied mockingly.

Sheriff Willard turned to James. If it was one thing he hated, it was to be made a fool of. "You get her out of that cage and bring her here." Sheriff Willard said through gritted teeth. James hurried over to Hialeah's cell and opened it. Hialeah walked hesitantly toward Jackson. She found herself quite nervous in his presence. It had been some time since she had saw him last. She was sure she looked a sight with her hair disheveled. Sheriff Willard had grown impatient with Hialeah's slow approach to his desk. "You tell me how much it was that Mr. Harding handed you?" Sheriff Willard demanded. Hialeah kept her eyes on Jackson. She took her hand and absentmindedly removed her hair from her face before she spoke. "It was four dollars like Mr. Harding here said." Hialeah muttered softly. Her lip was sore from Willie's strike to her face. Jackson immediately noticed the dried blood from Hialeah's busted lip. Jackson completely lost his composure as he grabbed a startled Hialeah by the arm bringing her quickly to him. Jackson pushed Hialeah's hair aside and assessed her face. Her swollen lip enraged him. "Who struck you?" Jackson demanded fiercely glaring into Hialeah's eyes. Hialeah could feel her entire body begin to tremble. "Answer me." Jackson said angrily. "That's what happens when you step outta line." Willie said smugly. Jackson turned to face Willie. "You put your hands on her?" Jackson spat angrily. "I don't take no sass from no coloreds; especially savage coloreds." Willie replied continuing with his smug tone.

Disgusted by Willie's arrogance and willingness to strike a woman, Jackson snapped. Before another word could be uttered from anyone in the room, Jackson caught James off guard and forcefully shoved him out of his way before thrashing Willie's face with his fist.

Hialeah stood frozen in fear as Jackson stood over Willie pummeling his face again and again and again until blood spewed from his nose and mouth. Sheriff Willard nearly fell out of his chair in a mad rush to avoid being Jackson's target. Hialeah screamed for Jackson to stop when she noticed Willie's spilled blood. She ran over to Jackson and grabbed his arm before he could strike Willie again. Jackson angrily turned toward Hialeah unaware that it was her stopping him from continuing his attack on Willie. Hialeah's eyes were widened in terror. She could only manage to quickly shake her head no. Jackson roughly released Willie's shirt front and backed away from Willie's limp body. Sheriff Willard was even momentarily shaken up from what he had just witnessed. He cleared his throat and the moment he found his voice, after Jackson was calmed by Hialeah, he ordered James to arrest Jackson for assaulting an officer of the law and for the confession of assault and robbery against Terell Grisby. James pulled out his gun and angrily pointed it at Jackson. "Who the hell do you think you are? That was my partner!" James yelled. "That's what happens when you step out of line like a bloody coward and strike a woman." Jackson replied menacingly using Willie's words against him.

Isaac and his family had gone to the street market and had witnessed Sheriff Willard arresting Hialeah. Isaac insisted on intervening but Louise wouldn't hear of it. She refused to allow her son to get into any trouble that didn't concern him. Isaac jumped from the family wagon and stormed away angry at his mother's refusal to allow him to see about Hialeah. He walked through the market cursing his mother. When Jackson rode by him on his horse, Isaac knew exactly where he was headed. He wasn't about to let anyone come to the aid of his woman. Isaac dashed down several streets in an effort to reach the jail. He had gotten so angry with his mother that he hadn't realized how far he had walked off. Isaac disregarded Louise's order and burst into the jail just as James had pulled his gun out and pointed it at Jackson. All eyes turned toward Isaac, whose attention was focused solely on Hialeah. "Miss Nokosi?" Isaac said breathless. "Isaac, what you doin' here?" Hialeah replied surprised by Isaac's presence. "I saw you get taken away. I was worried bout you." Isaac remarked taking the liberty to embrace Hialeah. Jackson tensed up as Isaac held Hialeah in his arms. Isaac also took the celebratory moment of Hialeah's release to capture a gentle yet lingering and unexpected kiss on Hialeah's lips. Hialeah was surprised by Isaac's kiss, Jackson was angered by it but said nothing. He didn't want to give Sheriff Willard any more cause to harass Hialeah or use his anger against Isaac to spread any new rumors about himself and Hialeah.

Sheriff Willard smirked devilishly as he witnessed the scene before his eyes. He hadn't failed to notice Jackson's hands clench into fists when Isaac embraced and kissed Hialeah. Sheriff Willard would not allow this tempting moment to go untouched. It was quite evident, that Jackson Harding was in love with a colored woman. He would enjoy this, but he didn't dare test the man until he was behind bars. Sheriff Willard ordered James to bring Terell Grisby to his office before nodding his head at James to take Jackson to his cell. He wanted to clear this whole mess up right away. "Let's go Mr. Harding." James ordered heatedly. "Deputy Blake." Sheriff Willard said. "Yes sir." James replied. "For Pete's sake get Willie to a damn doctor." Sheriff Willard remarked annoyed that Willie were still lying on the ground. "Right away sir." James said. Jackson didn't hesitate to make his way to his cell. The sooner he was locked up, the sooner he could erase Hialeah from his mind once more.

Hialeah couldn't bear the thought of Jackson being locked up for helping her. She walked toward Jackson before he entered his cell and reached for his arm. Hialeah looked up into Jackson's hardened hazel eyes. Her face was etched with worry. Hialeah briefly looked over her shoulder at James hoping he was out of earshot before returning her attention back to Jackson. "What they gone do to you?" Hialeah whispered worriedly. "Don't concern yourself. Your beau is waiting." Jackson replied coldly before continuing on to his cell. "Mr. Harding..." Hialeah said. "Go home Miss Nokosi." Jackson replied harshly keeping his back turned. Stunned by Jackson's harsh tone, Hialeah ran out of the jail followed by Isaac. James locked the cell door once Jackson was inside and quickly hurried over to a moaning Willie and helped him to his feet. A bloodied face Willie was practically dragged from the jail.

Hialeah was on the verge of tears as she ran down the street toward her wagon. Isaac chased after her calling her name. Hialeah kept on running until she made it to her wagon. Isaac grabbed her arm and turned Hialeah around to face him before she had a chance to climb onto the seat. He was baffled as to the tears that were visible in Hialeah's eyes. Isaac released Hialeah's arm and she wipes at her tears. "I'd like to be alone if you don't mind." Hialeah said as calm as she could hoping that Isaac wouldn't question her. "Of course. I'll come by later, make sure you're fine." Isaac replied. He assisted Hialeah onto her wagon and took a step back. "Walk on." Hialeah said ordering her horse to take her home.

Once the jail was free of its occupants aside from Jackson, Sheriff Willard casually strolled over to Jackson's cell and leaned against the bars. He pulled out a cigar from his vest pocket and lit it. Jackson sat on his small bed with his head against the wall and closed his eyes. He scolded himself for coming to Hialeah's rescue. If he had have known that Isaac were going to be her savior, he would have remained home, and had his lunch. Being behind bars wasn't an issue for Jackson. He had been there before in his youth. In truth, Jackson was envious of Isaac. Not a single scandal could come from a colored man courting a colored woman. His caring for Hialeah, on the other hand, would set the town's tongues wagging even more than they already were. Hialeah didn't deserve to be ostracized anymore than she has been on his account. Jackson decided to concede defeat to Isaac and allow Hialeah to move on from him. Isaac was clearly the better man for her.

Jackson could smell the cigar smoke that Sheriff Willard was purposely exhaling into his cell. He kept his eyes closed and head pressed against the jail wall but felt the need to indulge the sheriff in whatever game he insisted on playing. "Is there a problem sheriff?" Jackson asked casually. Sheriff Willard exhaled once more before speaking. "Oh no, Mr. Harding. No problem at all." Sheriff Willard replied tauntingly. "That is good to know. I do hope you're not sore at me for thrashing good ol' Willie's face." Jackson remarked sarcastically. "Trust me Mr. Harding, it's not Willie's face that concerns me." Sheriff Willard said. "I am relieved." Jackson replied continuing his tone of sarcasm. "You see it's your face that I found most amusing. I mean the look on your face when that colored stormed in here and ran off with your girl. Now that…that was a face that just tickled me." Sheriff Willard teased. "My girl?" Jackson replied in mock confusion. "You can deny it if you'd like, but I've seen you in town chasing after that black squaw. You know, the embraces you two have shared, the smiles and the like, why Mr. Harding you even came to that whore's rescue your first day in town." Sheriff Willard remarked tauntingly. "Merely being a gentleman, sheriff." Jackson replied calmly. "A gentleman you say?" Sheriff Willard said sarcastically. "Nothing more." Jackson replied. "Well, tell me, just how much of a gentleman were you when you spread that savage's colored thighs? Ohh, I bet you were a real gentleman then, yes sir." Sheriff Willard replied mockingly. "You assume I've shared Miss Nokosi's bed, sheriff?" Jackson asked remaining calm. "Oh come now Mr. Harding, I'm sure she gave herself to you in gratitude for being her white knight." Sheriff Willard said. Jackson opened his eyes. He wanted to see the angry reaction he was sure to receive from his next statement to the sheriff. "Do go on sheriff. I'm almost certain that you've entertained a colored woman or two in your bed. You have that 'nigger lover' look written all over your face." Jackson teased. Sheriff Willard didn't appreciate Jackson's tone. "You go straight to hell you European trash! I am happily married to my Sadie going on thirty-five years. Ain't no colored woman ever gone come between us." Sheriff Willard replied angrily before tossing his cigar end into Jackson's cell. Jackson smirked victorious but he was just getting started with Sheriff Willard.

Sheriff Willard angrily returned to his chair and began to riffle through some papers on his desk. Jackson stood up and nonchalantly walked over to the cell bars and leaned against them; imitating Sheriff Willard. "Dear sweet sheriff, there's no one here but us." Jackson said teasingly. Sheriff Willard ignored Jackson's taunt. "You're telling me that you've never had the burning desire to bury your head betwixt the ample chocolate bosom of a colored woman? Take her so ravenously that she screams your name in absolute ecstasy?" Jackson said deeply in an attempt to rile Sheriff Willard. Sheriff Willard slammed his papers to his desk. "I have never and I would never." Sheriff Willard spat offended by Jackson's accusation. Jackson smirked devilishly.

"Pity. The pleasures that come from a colored woman are like none other. Silken chocolate colored thighs, tantalizing curves that lustfully haunt your every waking moment, full luscious lips, made to be kissed and the sweetest nectar that could weaken the strongest of men the very instant you enter her." Jackson continued in his deep tone. His words were having the desired effect on Sheriff Willard. Jackson fought the urge to break his taunting character and burst into laughter as Sheriff Willard pursed his lips together. "And then there is the lovemaking itself..." Jackson began in the same deep tone. Sheriff Willard refused to listen to anymore. He hastily stood up in his chair and faced Jackson. "That's enough damn it all." Sheriff Willard spat. "That's the devil's talk. You keep that up and I just may lose my way. Might just be tempted to pay a late night visit to your little colored whore. Find out if what you say has any truth to it." Sheriff Willard said smirking. Jackson didn't take too kindly to Sheriff Willard's threat against Hialeah. Jackson began sadistically tapping his fingers against his cell bars; a menacing smirk of his own creased his lips. "You go near her, sheriff, and your dear Sadie will be known throughout the town as the Widow Willard." Jackson replied smoothly. Sheriff Willard quickly whipped out his gun and pointed it at Jackson. "Don't you threaten me you son-of-a-bitch!" Sheriff Willard shouted nervously at Jackson. "Promise sheriff. It's a promise." Jackson replied coolly.

Before Sheriff Willard could utter another word, James walked into the jail with an annoyed Terell Grisby in tow. "I brought you Grisby just like you asked sheriff. Would have been here sooner but Willie was in a lot of pain and Terell here was causing a fuss down at the Gentleman's Club." James began. "I weren't causing no fuss neither. I was in the middle of acquiring my membership." Terell replied defensively. "Shit. You were being tossed on your ass. Everyone in town knows that only men of high social standing are permitted, and that sure as hell ain't your cheating ass." James remarked mockingly. Terell chose to ignore James's poor attempt at an insult against his person. "Just what am I doing here anyway? You catch that thieving whore yet?" Terell asked annoyed. "Shut up, the both of you." Sheriff Willard replied heatedly. "And that thieving whore is innocent." Sheriff Willard said disgustedly. "That's impossible. I was attacked and robbed of my monies just like I told you and that trouble making trollop is guilty of said crimes." Terell replied matter-of-factly. "Well unless my eyes are deceiving me, that don't look like no colored woman." Sheriff Willard yelled pointing in Jackson's direction. Jackson burst into laughter at Sheriff Willard's declaration. Terell scowled confused at what Sheriff Willard was getting at. "I ain't ever seen that fellow before." Terell said. "Well let me introduce you to the fellow what assaulted and robbed you." Sheriff Willard replied sarcastically. "That there is the Honorable Judge Jackson Harding." Sheriff Willard said. "And just what in the hell does that mean to me?" Terell said. "Henry Harding, the owner of the Gentleman's Club, is my father." Jackson interjected casually. Terell's eyes widened in surprise at Jackson's statement. He had all but forgotten about Sheriff Willard's admission of Jackson's guilt. "You really Henry Harding's boy?" Terell asked suspiciously. "Indeed I am, and it just so happens that any distinguished member of my father's prestigious club are permitted to request admittance to any fine gentleman they so choose." Jackson replied casually. Terell knew precisely where Jackson was going with their little conversation. "You get me full membership and all what comes with it at no cost to me and I'll drop all charges." Terell said. Jackson nodded his head in agreement. "Welcome to the Gentleman's Club, Mr. Grisby." Jackson replied smoothly. Terell's eyes lit up as he hurried over to shake Jackson's hand. "Thank you, Your Honor." Terell replied happily. "Now wait just one goddamn minute!" Sheriff Willard exploded. Terell turned on his heel to face Sheriff Willard. "No sir sheriff! I got all the right to drop the charges against the Honorable Judge here and I'm doing just that." Terell replied sternly. Sheriff Willard angrily turned his attention to James. "Don't you have a town to see after? Get out of here!" Sheriff Willard yelled. "Yes sir." James rushed out and hurried from the jail.

Sheriff Willard waited until James had left the jail before making his plea. "Now that just isn't fair. Your father promised me years ago when I won the election and re-election to become sheriff of this town that he'd grant me membership. I've been waiting five years and not a word." Sheriff Willard said heatedly. Jackson was thoroughly enjoying the sheriff's tantrum. "Well seeing as how my father has taken ill, and has entrusted me to run all of his businesses, including his fine club, I fear what the other members would think if they ever learned that a Justice of the High Court is being held on charges of assault against your deputy." Jackson replied grinning. Sheriff Willard caught Jackson's drift just as quickly as Terell did. He rushed to his desk to retrieve the key to Jackson's cell. Sheriff Willard fumbled with the keys and Jackson reached out and grabbed a hold of his wrist. Jackson stared coldly into Sheriff Willard's eyes. "I trust Miss Nokosi will have no more issues." Jackson warned. "Never heard of her." Sheriff Willard said in agreement as he unlocked Jackson's cell door. Jackson strolled by Sheriff Willard and Terell. "Enjoy the club gentlemen." Jackson said smoothly as he left the two men alone to celebrate their admittance into his father's club.

Hialeah was glad to be away from Sheriff Willard and that awful jail. Her lip was sore and she was hurt by Jackson's harsh tone. Hialeah was in tears as she made her way home. She furiously wiped at her tears as she tried to convince herself that Jackson still cared for her. Why else would he come to her rescue, and nearly beat a man to death for hurting her? Hialeah drove her wagon up to her barn but her thoughts of Jackson kept her from climbing from her seat. She played the entire scene over in her head. Jackson had protected her. He hadn't spoken harshly to her until Isaac kissed her. Hialeah absentmindedly touched her lip. She inhaled a breath as it dawned on her that Jackson was jealous of her relationship with Isaac. He had even angrily referred to Isaac as her beau. Hialeah decided that she would simply return to town, enter the jail and explain to Jackson that Isaac was merely a good friend. Surely he wouldn't be opposed to her having any friends. Hialeah smiled and giggled over the absurdity of it all as she reached for her reins. Her smile quickly faded. Jackson would no doubt still be upset and Sheriff Willard would most certainly be cross after having to release her. She would have to wait until Sheriff Willard was out patrolling the streets, before she paid a visit to Jackson and explain things. Sheriff Willard didn't allow visitors on the Lord's Day.

Hialeah climbed down from her wagon and unharnessed her horse before leading him into the barn. She walked out of the barn just as Isaac was approaching her home on horseback. Hialeah grabbed her basket of daffodils and walked toward Isaac. The closer she got to him;

Hialeah could see the worried look on Isaac's face. Isaac remained on his horse. Hialeah stopped a short distance from him. "I know you said you wanted some time to yourself, but I couldn't stop myself from thinkin' bout you." Isaac said. "I appreciate your concern for me, but I just fine. A little tired is all." Hialeah replied. "I think it's best if I stay over for the night and tomorrow we can attend the preachin' together." Isaac remarked. "Ain't no need for you to trouble yourself." Hialeah said. "It's my duty as a man to look after my woman." Isaac replied adamantly. "I can get myself to the preachin' like I always done and until I've been asked proper to be courted, you just be on your way Isaac Leonard." Hialeah said sternly. She turned on her heel and stormed away from Isaac. Hialeah slammed her door shut leaving Isaac alone in the scorching heat.

Jackson mounted his horse and rode through the shoppers. He had wasted enough time dealing with Sheriff Willard and Terell Grisby. Jackson scolded himself for taunting Sheriff Willard the way he had. His words were coming back to haunt him. For days he had cleared his mind of Hialeah and in an instant, she captured his thoughts. Thoughts that he cursed himself for having. She was sharing her bed with another man; a truth that he would do well to remember.

Chapter 8

Jackson had tossed numerous times during the night in his effort to get some sleep. He woke the next morning in a foul mood. Sleep deprived and still very much upset over seeing Hialeah, he dressed dreading the day. As Jackson climbed down the stairs, he cringed at the multitude of voices that wafted in the air. His mother was no doubt, having guests over for breakfast. Jackson wanted no part of being trapped in a room with so many cackling hens. Jackson gestured for their butler to close the doors to the dining room so that he could slip by unnoticed. Forgoing his breakfast, Jackson crept out of the front door. He placed his wide brimmed hat on his head and mounted the first available horse that his footman brought. Jackson rode off to town. He had some documents of his father's that needed his attention. Jackson figured he could get more work done in quiet warehouse instead of hearing obnoxious laughter from his mother's chatty friends.

Hialeah woke still stewing over Isaac's brazen attempt to force himself in her home in the name of chivalry. She said a silent prayer asking for forgiveness for deciding to miss the preaching. It wouldn't be proper for her to go being so riled up at Isaac. Hialeah figured on going into town to cause some sort of trouble hoping that Sheriff Willard would toss her into the cell next to Jackson. Then he'd be forced to listen to her. Hialeah bathed and got herself dressed. She hadn't decided on just what sort of trouble she'd cause. She would think of something along the way. Hialeah grabbed her sewing bag and headed to town. She drove her wagon through the crowded streets. The closer she got to the jail, the more nervous she became. She tried to convince herself that Jackson still loved her. He only needed reminding. She drove by Harding Tobacco and noticed a man standing at the entrance. Hialeah frowned, curious as to who would be trying to gain entrance on a Sunday. Everyone in town knew that the warehouse was closed on Sundays.

Jackson removed his hat briefly to wipe at his brow before returning his hat to his head. Hialeah's heart nearly stopped beating as she recognized Jackson from across the street. She was relieved that she wouldn't have to get herself arrested to speak to him, but her nervousness was full on seeing Jackson standing there. Hialeah exhaled a breath and put on her parking brake to keep her horse from riding off. She quickly climbed down from her seat and darted across the street before Jackson could disappear into the warehouse. Hialeah said another quick prayer. This time hoping that Jackson would not be cross with her. She stopped a short distance behind Jackson and slowly exhaled. "Hensci (Hins-cha)." Hialeah said nervously. Jackson heard the soft voice coming from behind him. He turned around, a brooding look on his face. Hialeah stood behind him with her hands clasped nervously in front of her. "Shouldn't you be in church?" Jackson said dryly reminded of Miss Lilly's statement that Hialeah had never missed preaching. Hialeah smiled faintly. "I decided not to go today." Hialeah replied. Jackson turned his attention back to unlocking the warehouse door. Hialeah walked slowly up to Jackson. "I heard bout your daddy takin' ill and all." Hialeah said trying to calm herself. "What do you know of my father's illness? Did your beau tell you that?" Jackson replied coldly. "The whole town knows bout it." Hialeah said softly. "My father is doing much better and the very moment he's able to resume his responsibilities, I'll be forever grateful to leave this place behind me." Jackson replied harshly. Hialeah could hear the anger in Jackson's tone. She swallowed before daring to ask her next question. "Cause of me?" Hialeah asked her voice quivering. Jackson caught the hurt in her question. He didn't want to admit that he needed to be away from her before he lost his sanity. "Miss Nokosi, I have a lot of work to do." Jackson replied sternly. Hialeah was taken aback by Jackson's tone. "Go on then, do your work. Just you know that when you leave here, you'll be leavin' somethin' behind." Hialeah said matter-of-factly. Jackson was in no mood for riddles. He was quite certain that she was referring to herself. He did, however catch her reference of something instead of someone. He turned to face Hialeah. "And what would that 'something' be?" Jackson asked cocking a curious brow. "Could be your fancy silver drinkin' cup." Hialeah replied stubbornly. "My flask? You have it?" Jackson asked curiously. "Maybe I give it to you, maybe

I don't." Hialeah replied nonchalantly. "You think to just keep what belongs to me?" Jackson remarked. "You tell me what it mean to you, and I just might return it." Hialeah replied. "I'll not pay for what belongs to me." Jackson said sternly. Hialeah defiantly crossed her arms. "Ain't said you had to, Your Lordship." Hialeah replied. Jackson conceded and chuckled at her use of his title. "If I tell you what it means to me, you'll return it?" Jackson asked. "A girl give it to you no doubt." Hialeah said. "It wasn't a gift from a girl." Jackson replied. "Then why you want it back so bad?" Hialeah asked. "First off, it's mine and second, it was a gift from a dear law professor who has since passed on. Now I'll have it back." Jackson replied. "Is that true?" Hialeah asked suspiciously pleased to have made Jackson laugh. "I assure you, it is very much true." Jackson replied. "Fine. I believe you." Hialeah remarked. "Thank you for your trust in me." Jackson replied sarcastically. "Now return it." Jackson said holding his hand out. "If you want your fancy cup back, then you'll have to come get it." Hialeah rushed out teasingly before quickly removing Jackson's hat from his head and taking off running. "Bloody hell." Jackson said.

Jackson chased Hialeah as she led him down several streets and alleys. Jackson was amazed by her speed, but he refused to be outdone by a girl. Hialeah ran into a dead end alley. Her game of cat and mouse was ended by a brick wall. She turned around as Jackson came around the corner panting heavily. Jackson stopped several feet away from Hialeah and bent over to catch his breath. "Bloody hell woman, have you gone mad?" Jackson asked breathlessly. "Of course not, I perfectly happy." Hialeah replied. "I don't mean mad as in angry. I mean crazy; insane." Jackson said. "You just upset that you can't catch a girl." Hialeah replied teasingly. "I've caught you." Jackson said. Hialeah tapped the wall behind her. "This here wall catch me." Hialeah replied. "Nevertheless, you're caught. Now return my things." Jackson said. Hialeah playfully placed Jackson's hat on her head and pressed it down snugly exposing only her nose and lips. She then clasped her hands behind her back. Jackson burst into laughter at the sight of her. "What kind of hat is this?" Hialeah asked. "It's called a Gambler." Jackson replied. "Well how I see it, you took my doll and I took your here Gambler." Hialeah remarked simply. Jackson was instantly reminded of the day they had spent at the fair when he had stolen Hialeah's doll in order to get her to stay at the fair. "Ah the art of revenge." Jackson replied smiling.

    Hialeah remained perfectly still. Jackson smirked as he slowly approached her. He would be prepared to catch her if she decided to take off again. Hialeah listened to Jackson's footsteps coming closer to her but she held her position and fought desperately not to smile. Jackson was mere inches from Hialeah's face. He slowly reached his hand up to remove his hat from Hialeah's head. Hialeah remained frozen as Jackson removed his hat. She smiled and quickly threw her arms around his neck. Standing on tiptoe, Hialeah kissed Jackson. Jackson was surprised by her awkward kiss and took over; forcing her lips apart allowing his tongue to invade her mouth deepening their kiss. Hialeah let a soft moan escape her lips as she surrendered to Jackson's kiss. She missed his touch, his scent, she simply missed him and she would tell him as much. Jackson lifted Hialeah from the ground and she broke their kiss laughing as her feet dangled in the air. Jackson returned Hialeah to the ground and she nervously lowered her eyes as she still clung to his neck. She had never told a man how she felt about him. She mustered up the courage and looked up into Jackson's hazel eyes. "I've missed you something terrible." Hialeah said her voice quivering. Jackson could hear the nervousness in her voice once more. "Have you now?" Jackson replied smiling. Hialeah relaxed at Jackson's playful tone. She nodded her head. "Henka (Hinga)." Hialeah said. "What of Isaac?" Jackson asked. "Isaac's a good man, but I don't...I don't love him." Hialeah replied. She found herself trembling and once again lowered her eyes from Jackson's intense gaze. "Ecenokecvyet os (Ih-chih-no-kih-chuh-yeet ose). I love you." Hialeah stammered out. "You love me yet you can't look at me? Why is that?" Jackson replied calmly. "Cause I ain't ever said those words before. Cause I feared you'd hate me." Hialeah said softly. "Hialeah, I don't hate you. I will admit that I was jealous of Isaac; being so free to escort you around town without any scrutiny, and when he kissed you, it enraged me." Jackson replied. "Miss Nokosi, I meant it then when I said that I had fallen in love with you, but after chasing you through the streets like a mad man, I'm not too sure now." Jackson replied teasingly. Hialeah looked up at Jackson's smiling face and she smiled and laughed. Jackson shared in her laughter before lowering his head to kiss Hialeah once again.

Hialeah was relieved beyond belief to hear Jackson admit to still loving her. She was, however, now concerned about their conversation before she stole Jackson's hat. He was still leaving. Hialeah was unsure what that meant for her. Her smile faded to a confused frown. Jackson noticed her facial expression. "What is it?" Jackson asked. Hialeah's heart began to sink. Hialeah felt the stinging of tears burning her eyes. She released Jackson's neck and turned away from Jackson who gently took her chin and turned her to face him. "What's upsetting you?" Jackson asked confused. "I don't...I don't want you to go." Hialeah replied and gave way to her tears. Jackson embraced Hialeah and stroked her hair to comfort her. "My life, my home is in England." Jackson said gently. He released Hialeah from his embrace and looked down into her eyes. "Our home will be in England." Jackson said. Hialeah tried to smile through her tears. She was overcome with emotions as Jackson shared his plan to take her with him to his home. "You'll take me with you?" Hialeah asked surprised. "If you'd like." Jackson replied. Hialeah nodded her head and quickly wrapped her arms around Jackson. Hialeah was overjoyed but her joy was quickly replaced with a frown and she hastily released Jackson. Hialeah was moving so fast, Jackson couldn't keep up with her whirl of emotions. "I best go pack." Hialeah rushed out excitedly. "Now?" Jackson replied laughing. "I want to be ready for the boat and..." Hialeah replied anxiously. "Miss Nokosi, they'll be plenty of time to board the ship." Jackson said smiling. "My father is still not well. Besides, I haven't had my breakfast just yet." Jackson replied lightly. Hialeah's eyes widened. "Breakfast. I'll make us breakfast." Hialeah rushed out. "Miss Nokosi, if you don't calm yourself, I fear you'll burst." Jackson teased. Hialeah pressed her lips together to calm herself. Jackson laughed at her overzealous mood. "How about I get some work done, you go hear your preaching, and perhaps around noon, you join me at your favorite spot and we'll have a quiet lunch just the two of us. Yes?" Jackson said. Hialeah nodded her head. "I'd like that." Hialeah replied. "Good." Jackson said. "Til later, Your Lordship." Hialeah said smiling before turning to run away from the alley. "I beg you, no more running." Jackson called out pleadingly.

Hialeah stopped quickly and began to speed walk from the alley. She could hear Jackson laughing from behind her.

Hialeah could hardly contain her excitement as she made her way back to her wagon. She was so overjoyed that she wanted to run and shout through the streets but reminded herself that Jackson and his family were well respected in town. Jackson was a gentleman of a high social caliber so she had best behave like a lady. Hialeah glanced around and took notice of the other women walking down the street. Their shoulders were straight, their heads were held high and they walked tall and proper. Several of the women had their hands clasped in front of them. She would do the same. Hialeah straightened her shoulders and lifted her head to what she thought was the proper height. She stood tall and clasped her hands in front of her as she continued walking along the street. Hialeah was unaware that Jackson was following several feet behind her observing her imitation of the women she passed on the street. Jackson was thoroughly enjoying her desire to be seen as a proper woman.

Hialeah found herself frowning from the slight pain that was starting in her lower back. It wasn't easy to walk prim and proper but she was determined to carry on through the pain of her back. None of the other women were in a hurry and she would take her time as well. Besides, she thought to herself, any one of the Harding's high society associates could be watching her and it would be most humiliating for Jackson if one of them were to mention that they saw her carrying on unruly like in public. Hialeah continued to mentally remind herself to keep her head up and shoulders straight and walk tall as she finally made it to her wagon. She wanted to breathe a long held sigh of relief. Just as Hialeah was preparing to climb onto her wagon, Jackson walked up behind her. "I am impressed." Jackson said. Hialeah quickly spun around startled by Jackson. "Mr. Harding." Hialeah replied in shock. "How long you been standin' there?" Hialeah asked. "I was following you." Jackson replied smiling. Hialeah could feel her cheeks warming from sheer embarrassment. Jackson had no doubt thought she looked foolish imitating those other women. Jackson could see in Hialeah's eyes that he had embarrassed her. He took Hialeah's hand and raised it to his lips. "Beautiful and proper. Every man should be so lucky."

Jackson said smoothly before kissing the back of Hialeah's hand. Hialeah blushed as Jackson assisted her onto her wagon. Hialeah smiled down at Jackson. "Noon." Jackson said. "Noon." Hialeah replied still blushing as she released the brake from her wheel. Jackson tapped her horse on the hind quarters and watched as Hialeah rode off.

Hialeah rode away from town ecstatic. The air between her and Jackson had been cleared. They were both very much in love with one another and she would be leaving with him when he returned home. The very thought of traveling by such a huge boat was exciting and frightening at the same time. Hialeah found herself beaming with happiness. A feeling that quickly faded as she was reminded of Isaac and how he felt about her. Oh how would she tell him that they could not be together? Hialeah cherished the time that they had spent but her heart had been swept by Jackson. She would have to think of something. She couldn't very well tell him that she was in love with a white man. She would be ostracized within their community and Isaac would be humiliated. He didn't deserve that. Yes, she would have to think of a way to tell Isaac that she cared for him but that she was not the woman for him.

Hialeah could hear the preaching taking place as she got closer to the church. She was pleased that she hadn't missed very much of the sermon and grateful that the church doors were open. It was rather embarrassing walking into the church late and have everyone turn around to see just who it is interrupting the preacher. Hialeah was also a bundle of nerves where Isaac was concerned. Hialeah parked her wagon in its usual spot away from the other members. She had more than once practically bolted from the church as soon as the preaching was over to avoid being spoken to. Hialeah had always feared that even though she was colored, she wouldn't be accepted by the other members of the church simply because of her father's Indian blood.

Hialeah quickly hopped down from her seat and hurried toward the church. She slowed her pace, straightened her dress out and walked calmly inside. Her usual seat in the back was unoccupied. Hialeah avoided eye contact with the preacher but when he gave a slight pause and smile at her presence, several of the members turned around in their seats; including Isaac and his family. Hialeah hastily took her seat in the pew just as the preacher called for a song selection from the choir. As the choir was preparing to sing, Isaac took the opportunity to hurry to the back of the church to take a seat next to Hialeah. The church's piano player began playing and Isaac leaned in to whisper into Hialeah's ear. "You alright? Ain't ever known you to not be on time for preachin'." Isaac said. Hialeah kept her eyes on the choir. "I fine. I slept a little longer than planned is all." Hialeah replied in a whisper. "Well, you look right pretty." Isaac said low. Hialeah replied with a simple grin. Isaac sat back in the pew and reached for Hialeah's hand. Hialeah allowed Isaac to take her hand as she tried to keep her focus on the song being sung. Isaac began to caress Hialeah's hand with his thumb. Hialeah could feel beads of sweat forming on her brow. She sat up straight and slid her hand away from Isaac and reached into her sewing back. Hialeah pulled out the fan that Jackson had given her as a gift. To avoid Isaac's caress, she placed the fan in the hand that Isaac had held and began fanning herself. Isaac took notice of the extravagant fan, but said nothing. He was well aware of where the gift came from and he didn't appreciate having it flaunted in his face. Isaac sat stone faced for the rest of the sermon. Hialeah never took notice.

It was noon when the church services ended and Hialeah was quite anxious to meet with Jackson for lunch. She was practically starving after having foregone breakfast. Isaac still sat frozen in his seat as the other members were exiting the church. It was custom that after every service, the members of the congregation gathered for lunch prepared by the wives and other women. Hialeah had never taken part of the Sunday meal. She had always felt she would be unwelcomed. Hialeah turned to face Isaac with a smile on her face. She always felt uplifted after hearing the preaching. "Wonderful preachin'." Hialeah said. Isaac offered no response. "Hialeah, come on, us women folk gotta set the tables." Ruby said. Hialeah turned around to find Isaac's sister standing near them with her hand extended to assist Hialeah from her seat. Ruby noticed her brother's somber expression. "Isaac, you comin'?" Ruby asked. Isaac offered no response to his sister. Ruby simply hunched her shoulders indifferent to her brother's foul mood. "Come on Hialeah, we best get goin'." Ruby said. Hialeah folded her fan and returned it back to her sewing bag. She then took Ruby's hand and both women left Isaac sitting alone in the church.

Hialeah worked quickly alongside Ruby to help with the luncheon preparations. She didn't want to keep Jackson waiting any longer than she had to but she also didn't want to be rude to the members of the congregation. Hialeah explained her haste to Ruby in little detail; simply stating that she had sewing work to do and couldn't be late. Ruby didn't question Hialeah's explanation, she was grateful for the assistance. Ruby nodded her head in her sister Rosie's direction. Ruby frowned as her sister was busy carrying on in laughter with a young man instead of helping prepare for the lunch. Hialeah laughed at Ruby's annoyance of her sister. Hialeah and Ruby continued setting up the tables in the heat while other women moved on to setting the food on the tables. Fed up with her sister's lack of assistance, Ruby marched over to the couple followed by Hialeah and pulled Rosie away. All three women gathered pies, and baskets of fried fish and fruits and whatever else they could carry on set it on the tables while the men stood around talking. After each table was filled with food and assorted desserts, Hialeah hugged both of the sisters and hurried to her wagon. Isaac stood brooding in the doorway of the church watching Hialeah. He looked around to make sure no one was near before storming his way over to her. Just as Hialeah was preparing to step onto her wagon, Isaac roughly grabbed her wrist. "What you in such a hurry for? You too good to eat with the rest of us colored folks or maybe you hurryin' off to spread your legs for that white man?" Isaac said heatedly. Isaac squeezed Hialeah's wrist and she grimaced in pain. "You take your hands off me, Isaac Leonard." Hialeah spat. Isaac responded by squeezing Hialeah's wrist even harder as he glared menacingly into her eyes. A wave of fear washed over Hialeah as the pain from Isaac's tight grip on her wrist nearly brought tears to her eyes. Hialeah swallowed fearfully before gaining the courage to strike Isaac across his face. Isaac released Hialeah's wrist, stunned by her retaliation. Hialeah hastily took a few steps back fearful of what Isaac might do next. She stared daggers at him all the while her chest was heaving profusely. "How dare you Isaac Leonard? How dare you." Hialeah spat angrily. "You think I don't know who give you that fancy ol' fan you so proud to wave in my face?" Isaac replied heatedly. "Don't make no never mind who give it to me. Don't give you the right to hurt me so." Hialeah spat. "My brother was right bout you. You ain't nothin' but a whore for that white man." Isaac replied disgustedly. "I ain't no whore." Hialeah remarked gritting her teeth. "Then what you call a colored woman who give herself freely to a white man?" Isaac demanded. "I call it my business." Hialeah replied defensively. "Besides, Jackson, he loves me. He tell me so." Hialeah said. Isaac scoffed. "You think he gonna parade you around town in front of all his uppity white friends, huh? You think his white mama and daddy gonna welcome a colored girl with injun blood into they family? You can't marry him even if he does love you. White folk and colored folk ain't allowed to be wed." Isaac spat mockingly. "That's why we leavin' here soon as his daddy fit to work again. He goin' back to England, and he takin' me with him. He gone marry me there and I ain't never comin' back here. Not never." Hialeah fired back before climbing onto her wagon seat. "You go off with that white man, and I'll tell everybody in church just what kind of woman you really are. What you think they gonna say when they hear bout you sharin' your bed willingly with the massuh? You ain't gonna be welcomed here no more that's for sure." Isaac threatened. "You tell folks whatever it is you wanna tell 'em, but you keep your distance from me, you hear?" Hialeah warned. "Walk on." Hialeah commanded her horse.

 Hialeah was fed up with Isaac. She was fed up with anyone who condemned her for having indian blood. Her mother loved her father. He was a proud Seminole Indian and she was no longer going to hide the fact that she too, was proud of the blood that flowed through her veins. Hialeah stopped at her home. She was already late for her lunch outing with Jackson. She hoped he wouldn't be too upset with her. She was determined from that day forward, to walk and live as a proud Seminole woman.

 Hialeah marched into her home and bee-lined toward her bedroom. She began fervently stripping off her clothes and tossed them aside. Hialeah knelt down in front of the massive trunk at the foot of her bed. She opened the trunk and pulled out one of her native dresses and a pair of buckskin moccasins. The dresses meant everything to Hialeah. They were the dresses her mother had worn when she became a member of the Seminole tribe after marrying Hialeah's father. In a small bag held her glass bead necklaces. Hialeah adorned herself in her Seminole dress. The multi-colored dress had bands of intricate designs on it. The skirt was very full and floor-length. It gathered at her waist with knee-length ruffles. Her blouse was long sleeved with an attached cape which was also trimmed with a ruffle and came only to her shoulders. Her very short blouse barely covered her breasts which exposed some of her midriff. Hialeah placed her beaded glass necklace around her neck before slipping on her moccasins. She walked over to her dresser and grabbed her brush and comb and pulled her hair into a tight bun on top of her head leaving a few strands of hair down to wisp around her face. Once finished with her hair, Hialeah looked herself over in her floor-length mirror. Overjoyed with her true self reflecting back at her, Hialeah walked proudly with her head held high out of her home.

Jackson waited for Hialeah underneath the tree of her favorite spot. Their lunch of assorted fruits and cheeses, and sliced tomatoes and cucumbers, and smoked meats were spread out on a blanket. Jackson looked at his watch, curious as to what could be keeping Hialeah. She was nearly an hour late. Jackson found himself chuckling, wondering if Hialeah was getting him back for not showing up for their fishing outing several weeks ago. He leaned back against the tree and pulled his hat over his eyes. He would wait a few minutes longer and call it even if she failed to show. Just as Jackson was beginning to find some comfort against the tree, his relaxing position was disturbed by the sound of horse hooves quickly approaching. Hialeah quickened her horse's steps hoping that Jackson hadn't already left for home. She breathed a sigh of relief at the sight of Jackson's horse tied to a nearby tree. Hialeah suddenly began to feel quite nervous about her appearance. She hadn't worn her native clothes since she arrived in town and been ridiculed by Sheriff Willard and several other angry white folks for doing so. Jackson had stated many times that he was nothing like the other folks in town. Hialeah prayed that he would stay true to his words after seeing her in her native dress.

Hialeah pulled her wagon next to Jackson's horse and applied the brake. She couldn't see Jackson from the distance she had parked and she was sure that since he hadn't met her at her wagon to assist her, he was surely upset with her tardiness. Hialeah climbed down from her wagon and straightened her dress before hurrying over to meet Jackson. Jackson smiled at the sound of Hialeah's hurried steps. "You're late." Jackson said. His deep voice halted Hialeah's steps. "Are you angry?" Hialeah replied nervously. "Angry? No. Famished? Yes." Jackson replied teasingly. Hialeah breathed another sigh of relief before walking the rest of the way to meet Jackson. She was utterly awestruck at the sight of the delicious food Jackson had brought for their outing. Hialeah stifled a laugh as Jackson still sat with his eyes covered by his hat. "Hensci (Hins-cha)." Hialeah said smiling. "Hensci? Does that mean Jackson Harding is a most handsome bloke?" Jackson replied teasingly. "I'm afraid it only means 'hello', however, you are a most handsome bloke, whatever that is." Hialeah said lightly. Jackson smiled. "Well then…" Jackson began as he lifted his hat from his eyes. His mouth nearly dropped to the ground and his eyes practically popped from his head at the surprising sight of Hialeah. "Hello." Jackson said astonished. Hialeah nervously clasped her hands in front of her when Jackson rose to his feet. She found herself lowering her gaze as he approached her.

Jackson walked a full circle admiring Hialeah's dress. Hialeah stood trembling as Jackson assessed her. He stopped in front of Hialeah as she kept her eyes cast down. All of the confidence that she had in herself as she dressed began to wane; unsure of what Jackson would say. "You don't like it?" Hialeah asked her voice quivering. "You are mad aren't you?" Jackson said teasingly. Hialeah lifted her eyes to meet Jackson's. "I've never seen anything like it. Can you make one for me?" Jackson said jokingly. Hialeah threw her arms around Jackson's waist. "Although, I'm quite positive I won't be able to pull it off as well as you." Jackson continued. Hialeah laughed at Jackson's jest. "You look beautiful." Jackson said. "Mvto (Muh-doe). Thank you." Hialeah whispered in Jackson's ear. She released him from her embrace and Jackson kissed her gently on her lips. "It belonged to my mama. I was afraid you would be put off to see me dressed as the women in my father's tribe." Hialeah said. "I could never be put off by who you are. I'm sure your father was just as enchanted by your mother's beauty as I am yours." Jackson replied.

Hialeah smiled at Jackson's truth. Jackson took Hialeah's hand and led her to their waiting lunch. Hialeah took a seat on the blanket and Jackson took a seat across from her. Hialeah folded her legs behind her and Jackson noticed her buckskin moccasins on her feet. "I must insist that you dress like this more often." Jackson said smiling. Hialeah nodded her head smiling. "Henka (Hinga). Yes." Hialeah replied. "Perfect." Jackson said. Hialeah was thrilled to hear Jackson insist upon her native dress. She watched as he retrieved a bottle of wine and two glasses from the basket. Jackson laughed as Hialeah's smile turned into a frown at the sight of the wine. He was sure she was thinking of their night at her home and her incident with the gin. "It's not gin. It's a more suitable drink for a lady." Jackson said. "What is it?" Hialeah asked curiously. "Wine." Jackson replied. He poured Hialeah just a bit to taste and handed her the glass. "It looks almost like water." Hialeah said. "It's a white wine made from grapes." Jackson replied. "Grapes?" Hialeah said suspiciously. Jackson poured himself a glass and reached for a strawberry. Hialeah watched as Jackson bit into the strawberry and washed it down with the wine. She copied Jackson's every move and was quite surprised by the taste. Hialeah reached for three more strawberries and held her glass to Jackson to fill. "Not bad?" Jackson said. Hialeah bit into another strawberry and washed it down with more wine. "I like it." Hialeah replied licking her lips. Jackson chuckled. He handed Hialeah a plate and they both added more fruit and cheeses and several pieces of smoked meats along with slices of tomatoes and cucumbers to go along with their wine.

Jackson and Hialeah barely left any food untouched. Hialeah was feeling the effect of the three glasses of wine she had consumed. She pleaded teasingly for Jackson to allow her to have one more glass, but Jackson refused. Hialeah pouted and Jackson laughed, unable to resist kissing her full lips. Jackson leaned against the tree and pulled Hialeah close. He had unbuttoned his shirt to cool off from the sun's heat. Hialeah removed her shoes, released her hair from its bun, and rested her head on Jackson's massive chest. Jackson listened lightheartedly as Hialeah rambled on questioning the whiteness of the clouds to giggling uncontrollably as she wiggled her toes. Jackson was most positive that Hialeah was intoxicated. He resisted his urge to laugh as Hialeah's rambling went from Creek to English. Jackson stroked Hialeah's hair smiling as he agreed with everything she uttered. He even agreed with her when she spoke in Creek. From time to time, Hialeah would look up at Jackson and ask him in Creek if he was listening to her. Jackson simply smiled and nodded his head clueless as to what Hialeah was saying. Satisfied with Jackson's head nod, Hialeah continued rambling in Creek. When Jackson couldn't contain his laughter, Hialeah pinched his side causing Jackson to laugh even harder.

Jackson adored hearing Hialeah speak, but he welcomed the silence. After spending several hours under the shade of the tree, Jackson closed his eyes and listened to the sounds surrounding them. Within mere minutes, Jackson had drifted off to sleep. Hialeah was quiet and relaxed, content with Jackson's arm around her. She breathed in the scent of him and smiled as her head moved slightly up and down to the rhythm of Jackson's breathing. Hialeah looked up at Jackson's sleeping face. She was feeling quite playful in her intoxicated state and enamored with Jackson's toned and tanned body. Hialeah looked up once more at Jackson to reassure herself that he was still sleeping before she slowly slid her hand beneath his shirt in search of his nipple. She pressed her lips together to keep from giggling as she began to caress Jackson's nipple. Hialeah inhaled a silent breath of surprise when Jackson's nipple became a small peak. She circled Jackson's nipple with her finger and bit down on her bottom lip when a soft moan escaped Jackson's lips. Her curiosity even more piqued, Hialeah's hand traveled slowly down Jackson's chest and over his firm stomach stopping right before she reached the tip of his trousers. She circled his bellybutton and rested her hand on Jackson's stomach. The very thought of going any further made Hialeah blush. She was reminded of how sore she was after their last encounter. Jackson hadn't stirred. Hialeah gazed up at Jackson and inhaled in shock to find Jackson's hazel eyes peering back at her. Jackson grinned. "Naughty aren't we?" Jackson said smoothly. Hialeah's cheeks were on fire. Jackson laughed. "We should go." Jackson said still chuckling at Hialeah's blushing face.

Jackson stood and properly done his shirt while Hialeah put her moccasins back on her feet. "I'll prepare the horses." Jackson said.

"Alright." Hialeah replied. While Jackson walked toward his horse and Hialeah's wagon, Hialeah gathered the dirtied dishes and glasses and stacked them into the basket before picking up the blanket. She shook off any debris and folded it neatly and placed it on top of the plates. Jackson had tied his horse to the back of Hialeah's wagon. He thought in her state, it would be best if he drove her home. Jackson strode over to a waiting Hialeah and escorted her back to the wagon. Jackson retrieved the basket from Hialeah and placed it in the back of the wagon before returning to her side to assist her onto her seat. Jackson climbed up next to Hialeah and took the reins. Hialeah leaned her head against Jackson's shoulder as they made their way from Milliner's Pond. She had had a wonderful afternoon with Jackson and wished it would never end. Hialeah wanted to be with him always.

Jackson pulled up at Hialeah's door and hopped down from the wagon. He grabbed a hold of Hialeah's waist and lifted her from her seat. Hialeah walked to the back of the wagon and picked up the basket as Jackson untied his horse. He handed Hialeah his horse's reins before climbing back onto his seat of the wagon. Hialeah watched as Jackson drove her wagon toward the barn and unharnessed her horse before leading him into the barn. Jackson emerged from the barn and hurried back to Hialeah. Hialeah greeted him with a warm smile. "Today was nice." Hialeah said. "Very nice." Jackson replied. "If you'd like, I'll clean the dishes for you and bring them to town tomorrow after I finish my chores." Hialeah said. "I think Mama Lilly would appreciate that." Jackson replied smiling. "I suppose you have to get goin'." Hialeah said softly. "I think that I should." Jackson replied. Hialeah forced a faint smile to her lips as she handed Jackson the reins. A whirlwind of emotions began to wash over Hialeah. Isaac's stinging words ran rampant through her mind. He had accused her of being Jackson's whore. His harsh accusation was tearing at Hialeah's very being. She struggled to dismiss Isaac's jealous cruelty from her mind. Jackson loved her and above all else, she loved him and she would not allow Isaac or anyone else take that love from her.

Hialeah calmly removed the reins from Jackson's hand and tied his horse to the post next to her porch. She returned to her spot and stood very close to Jackson and placed her hands against his broad chest. She rose up on tiptoe and captured his lips in a brazen kiss. Hialeah mimicked Jackson's boldness by pressing her tongue against his lips. She nearly collapsed with pure satisfaction when Jackson parted his lips to accept the mating of their tongues and moaned deeply in his chest. Feeling most courageous, Hialeah began to undo the tiny buttons of Jackson's shirt as she deepened their kiss. All too aware that Hialeah had had more than enough wine, Jackson broke their kiss and took a hold of both of Hialeah's wrists before what she was hinting at could go any further. "What are you doing?" Jackson said sternly. Hialeah avoided Jackson's glare. She quietly, yet calmly, slid her wrists down to release herself from Jackson's hold. Hialeah then took a step away from Jackson before briefly meeting his gaze. She walked up the three steps and stood on her porch. Hialeah turned to face Jackson and proceeded to remove her moccasins from her feet as she stood. Jackson intensely watched Hialeah's every move. Now having captured Jackson's full attention, Hialeah slowly began to remove her native shirt and cape, exposing her full breasts. Jackson was more than aware of Hialeah's intentions. He practically ripped his coat off and rushed over to Hialeah and threw it around her shoulders. Jackson looked around to ensure that Hialeah's little tease wasn't witnessed by any passersby before returning his attention back to her. "Miss Nokosi, you have had quite a bit of wine. Your thinking is not clear." Jackson said holding his coat around Hialeah's small frame. "My thinkin' is just fine." Hialeah replied matter-of-factly. "I'll take you inside." Jackson remarked sternly.

Jackson gathered Hialeah's shoes and shirt, picked up the basket of dirtied dishes, and opened the door to Hialeah's home. Feeling humiliated over Jackson's rejection, Hialeah bolted inside and tossed Jackson's coat from her shoulders. Jackson quickly set Hialeah's things on the table and ran after her. Hialeah hurried to her room and slammed the door locking it before Jackson could catch her. "Hialeah, open the door." Jackson said. "I don't wanna see you." Hialeah cried from the other side of the door. "Hialeah." Jackson said. "Leave me be, please." Hialeah replied pleadingly. "Alright. I'll go." Jackson remarked. He didn't want to upset Hialeah any further. Jackson turned to leave and stopped in his tracks when he noticed his flask setting on top of the fireplace mantle next to Hialeah's vase of daffodils. Jackson walked over to the fireplace and picked up his flask. He grinned and returned it back to its spot before walking out of Hialeah's home. Hialeah leaned against her bedroom door with her eyes closed and listened as Jackson rode off.

Hialeah took to her bed early and woke the next morning with an unsettling feeling in her stomach. She was still quite upset over Jackson's refusal to share her bed but she could not allow that incident to interrupt her day. She had told him that she would wash their lunch plates and return them to him and that's precisely what she set out to do. Hialeah all but rolled herself from bed. She washed her face and put on one of her dresses that were perfect for doing chores. Hialeah had put off several tasks around her house that needed her attention. She started her morning with her gardening. She picked baskets of corn and tomatoes and carrots before gathering eggs and brought them into the house. Her next task was to tend to her animals followed by doing the laundry and cleaning the Harding's plates. Hialeah loved her little home but she was exhausted and sweaty and craved a bath. She worked well into the afternoon and sorely needed a break. She gathered her scented soaps and prepared herself a bath. While her water cooled, Hialeah went into her trunk and brought out all of her native dresses and laid them across her bed. She would give those snooty folks in town something to talk about and she would do it with her head held high.

After finishing her bath, Hialeah took special care as she dressed. She parted her hair down the middle and styled it into two ponytails. She then braided each ponytail and coiled them around her head and secured them with hairpins. Pleased with the appearance of her braided crown, Hialeah then finished off her look with more beaded glass necklaces. She decorated her neck with blue and green necklaces to go with the patterns of her full skirt and caped shirt. Hialeah adored her appearance. She left her room and quickly grabbed the basket of her and Jackson's lunch plates and hurried out of the door. Hialeah was thankful that the Hastings had built their home somewhat close to town yet still secluded from passersby.

Hialeah found herself humming a tune that her mother sang to her when she was a child as she rode into town. She caught the attention of everyone she rode by in town adorned in her mother's dress. She simply smiled and nodded her greeting at the shocked on-lookers. The streets were already busy as Hialeah continued on toward Harding Tobacco. Tobacco filled wagons lined the street and Hialeah was forced to park across from the warehouse as Jackson's employees were unloading in front of the warehouse. It was well past lunch time. Hialeah climbed from her wagon and reached for the basket that set next to her on the seat. Hialeah made sure to straighten her skirt before starting across the street. Hialeah took several steps just as Sara Williams' carriage pulled in front of the warehouse. Her heart nearly stopped beating as Sara sat in her carriage accompanied by Jackson. Hialeah watched in utter shock as Sara wrapped her arms around Jackson's neck and kissed him. Caught off guard by Sara's actions, Jackson removed Sara's arms from around his neck and broke her kiss. Sara smiled sweetly at Jackson. "I do believe I have forgotten my manners." Sara said teasingly. "So it appears you have." Jackson replied forcing a smile to his lips. "I do, however, thank you for lunch." Jackson said. "We simply must do it again." Sara replied smiling. "Of course." Jackson said dryly as he opened the door to the carriage and exited. "Jackson, you know I'd just love it if you come to call on me sometime." Sara said. "I'll give it some thought." Jackson replied. Thrilled by Jackson's consideration of calling on her, Sara waved goodbye before requesting her driver to take her home.

As Sara's carriage rode away, Jackson immediately noticed Hialeah standing across the street. Hialeah absentmindedly released the basket from her hand. The crashing of the plates as they hit the street snapped Hialeah out of her shock. She hastily turned away from Jackson and scrambled to climb back onto her wagon; leaving the broken plates and basket where they lie. In her haste to avoid Jackson, Hialeah's skirt caught onto her wagon and she fell into the street. Jackson ran over to assist Hialeah to her feet only to have her angrily fight him off. "Let me help you." Jackson said. "Leave me alone." Hialeah said angrily pushing Jackson's hands away. Jackson ignored Hialeah's command and took a hold of her arm and lifted her to her feet. Hialeah angrily pulled away from Jackson. "You're a liar."

Hialeah said heatedly drawing attention to herself and Jackson. "And what precisely have I lied about?" Jackson replied sternly. "You think I don't see you with her? With that Sara Williams." Hialeah spat. "I see you kiss her." Hialeah continued. Jackson roughly grabbed Hialeah's arm bringing her close. He didn't take kindly to being called a liar or that their exchange was being witnessed by passersby whom had stopped to get an ear full of whatever it was that was transpiring. "It is quite evident that you're upset, but I will not discuss this publicly." Jackson replied sternly. He released Hialeah's arm and turned to walk away. Jackson grabbed the basket on his way back to his office. He was grateful that Alice, his father's secretary, hadn't come into the office just yet. She was known to have a loose tongue and relished on spilling any kind of gossip. Hialeah watched Jackson disappear into the adjoining office of the warehouse.

Hialeah squared her shoulders and took a deep breath before gaining the nerve to confront Jackson as she marched across the street. She would not be made the villain. She was not the one gallivanting around town and she would tell Jackson just that. Hialeah opened the door to Jackson's office and was met by a flight of stairs. She climbed the stairs, and walked down the long corridor that dead ended to Jackson's office. Jackson sat on the edge of his desk with his arms crossed in anticipation of Hialeah's confrontation. Hialeah walked into Jackson's office and gave the door a slight push behind her. She opted to stand mere inches from the closed door. Hialeah placed her hands on her hips in opposition to Jackson's defensive crossed arms. Hialeah's legs felt as if they would give out at any minute seeing Jackson's calm demeanor and intense hazel eyes glaring at her but she would stand her ground. Jackson fought hard to keep his stern face in Hialeah's presence. He found everything about her mesmerizing. In truth, he wanted nothing more than to strip her clothes from her body and ravish her. Hialeah cocked an eyebrow. "Alright, I'm here." Hialeah said boldly. "So you are, and looking quite tempting." Jackson replied coolly. Hialeah scoffed at Jackson's attempt to be charming. "You think I here to listen to your sweet talk?" Hialeah said offensively. "No ma'am. Just being truthful." Jackson replied. "The only truth I wanna hear is if you got feelings for Miss Sara." Hialeah said. "None at all." Jackson replied simply. "You think I believe that?" Hialeah said. "You asked for the truth and I gave it to you. If you'd like more truth, then I'll happily oblige you that. Sara has visited my mother every day since my father took ill; a rather generous gesture." Jackson replied. "Still don't explain none why you with her and why you kiss her like you did." Hialeah said defensively. "Alright, you want an explanation, I'll give you one. Miss Williams invited me for lunch and I didn't kiss her, Miss Nokosi, Sara kissed me." Jackson replied. "You know, I'm curious. Are you upset that Sara kissed me or that I didn't share your bed?" Jackson said curtly regretting his question the moment it escaped his lips. Stunned by Jackson's tone, Hialeah turned on her heel to leave Jackson's office. Jackson was behind Hialeah with both hands pressed against the door before Hialeah could make her way out.

    Hialeah stood frozen with her back erect. Her chest was heaving. "I didn't mean that." Jackson said. "You let me go." Hialeah demanded. "Not until you look at me." Jackson replied. Hialeah kept her back to Jackson. Jackson lowered his head and kissed the right side of Hialeah's neck. Hialeah angrily spun around. "Don't you dare touch me." Hialeah said heatedly. Her eyes stared daggers into Jackson's piercing hazel eyes. "I am sorely tempted." Jackson replied deeply. Hialeah pressed her hands against Jackson's chest. Jackson swiftly grabbed both of Hialeah's hands and brought them over her head as he pressed her against the door with his massive frame. Hialeah struggled against Jackson's hold, her heart was pounding in her heaving chest as she continued to glare at Jackson. "You gone force me, Mr. Harding?" Hialeah spat. "Barbaric." Jackson replied smoothly. Hialeah tried to break Jackson's hold once more only to have Jackson prove his strength by holding both her wrists together with one hand. Hialeah's attempts were futile and she was out of breath. Jackson released his hold on Hialeah and returned to the edge of his desk and crossed his arms once again. Hialeah shook her head. "I ain't never wanna see you again." Hialeah said trying to catch her breath. "If that is what you want." Jackson replied calmly. Hialeah kept her eyes on Jackson as she reached behind her in search of the door knob. Jackson remained in his spot. Hialeah cautiously opened the door and hastily made her way out of Jackson's office.

Hialeah left Jackson's office devastated by his words. She wanted nothing more than to go home and never see him again. Hialeah tried to convince herself on the ride back home that Sara was welcomed to have him. Hialeah's mental encouragement of being free of Jackson and her urge to keep from bursting into tears were cut short as she pulled up to her home to a waiting Jackson leaning against her porch frame smoking a cigar. Jackson's horse was tied to her hitching post drinking water from her trough. Hialeah was in utter shock at Jackson's cool disposition. If she had the strength to ring his neck, she would surely do it. Hialeah stopped her wagon in front of her home. Jackson exhaled a puff of cigar smoke into the air with a devilish grin on his face. He was rather amused by the angry glare that Hialeah was shooting his way. "It's a lot easier to maneuver a single horse through crowded streets." Jackson said teasingly. "What're you doin' here?" Hialeah demanded. "Having a bit of a smoke." Jackson replied coolly. Hialeah furiously climbed down from her wagon. Jackson noticed that she was barefoot as she marched toward him. Hialeah looked Jackson in the eyes. "I told you I ain't ever wanna see you again." Hialeah said matter-of-factly before walking by Jackson. Jackson followed closely behind Hialeah. "I believe I've heard that before." Jackson replied teasingly. "Well, this time, I mean it." Hialeah remarked sternly. Jackson tossed his cigar just as Hialeah opened the door to her home. Before Hialeah could take a step further, Jackson swiftly grabbed Hialeah's arm and tossed her over his shoulder as if she weighed next to nothing. Hialeah gasped in surprise; kicking her feet as she cursed Jackson in her father's tongue. Jackson struck Hialeah's backside with his hand as he strode into her room and dumped her onto her bed. Hialeah scurried to the top of her bed in utter disbelief. "Have you gone mad?" Hialeah said astonished using Jackson's words against him. "You a far cry from a gentleman." Hialeah said. Jackson laughed. "A gentleman?" Jackson replied smiling. "This coming from the lady who not only steals my hat, but races through town with it." Jackson said teasingly. "I see you still upset you couldn't catch me." Hialeah replied mockingly. Jackson grinned devilishly at Hialeah. "Perhaps." Jackson said undoing the buttons of his shirt. "But I've caught you now." Jackson replied his voice low and seductive. Hialeah's eyes widened as Jackson approached her. Jackson removed his shirt and tossed it onto the floor. Hialeah bolted from her bed, trapping herself in a corner. Jackson smirked and cocked a brow. "Caught by yet another wall Miss Nokosi." Jackson said. Hialeah stood in the corner and raised her chin defiantly as she watched Jackson. She was unsure where to place her gaze; Jackson's captivating hazel eyes or his muscled chest.

Jackson stood mere inches from Hialeah. She placed her hands on her hips in an attempt to appear unbothered by Jackson's closeness. "Ah, defiant ecstasy. I live for it." Jackson said low. "You best keep your distance." Hialeah replied. "Or?" Jackson said smirking. "Or…or I'll have you arrested." Hialeah rushed out. Jackson burst into laughter. "And what would you accuse me of?" Jackson said mockingly. "Trespassin'." Hialeah replied matter-of-factly. "Trespassing?" Jackson said smiling. "That's right." Hialeah replied. Jackson inched his way even closer to Hialeah. He leaned in so that their lips nearly touched. "I'll take my chances." Jackson said deeply. Hialeah opened her mouth to speak but her lips were taken savagely. Jackson growled deep in his chest as he forced Hialeah's lips apart with his invading tongue. Hialeah's hands fell from her hips from the passion of Jackson's kiss. Jackson deepened their kiss as he moved Hialeah from the corner and guided her toward her bed. He gently laid her back and covered her body with his own. Hialeah abruptly broke their kiss. Jackson looked down into Hialeah's eyes. He was not amiss of what her body was telling him. Her breathing had quickened, her lips quivered, her hands were gripping the sides of her bed, and her eyes displayed a sign of nervous fear.

The very sight of her trembling body immediately gave Jackson pause. She had been a virgin before their shared night. The night he had assumed she was experienced with men. The night he had hurt her; taking her with no regard except his own satisfaction. She had only boldly touched him in the park after the wine had taken over her thoughts and actions. Jackson caressed Hialeah's face. He would not make the same mistake while possessing her body. Hialeah closed her eyes at his soft touch. "What do you want, Miss Nokosi?" Jackson said calmly. Hialeah opened her eyes and swallowed; struggling to find the right words. "What is it?" Jackson asked. It was evident in Hialeah's eyes that she was worried. "I see the way the women in town look at you. They all want you." Hialeah replied softly. "None of them matter to me." Jackson said. Hialeah lowered her eyes. "I ain't...experienced like they are. I'm afraid..." Hialeah replied. "What are you afraid of?" Jackson remarked gently. "Not pleasin' you none." Hialeah replied in a soft whisper. Jackson took Hialeah's hand. "Look at me." Jackson said. Hialeah raised her eyes to meet Jackson's. Jackson slid Hialeah's hand down the front of his trousers and guided it along his swollen shaft. Hialeah could feel her cheeks warming as she stroked Jackson's growing erection. Jackson let out a satisfying moan. He leaned into Hialeah's ear. "That, Miss Nokosi, pleases me." Jackson said low. Feeling rather bold, Hialeah stroked Jackson's shaft a bit faster. She was rewarded with a slew of profane words mingled with more deep moans. Jackson took Hialeah's lips in a passionate kiss; growling deep in his throat as Hialeah's sexual play of his staff was driving him mad.

Jackson slid his hand underneath Hialeah's shirt and began teasing her breasts. Still locked in their fervent kiss, Hialeah's nipples responded to Jackson's touch. Jackson circled the peaks of her nipples with his fingertip before breaking their kiss. Jackson removed Hialeah's hand from his trousers to slide her shirt over her head. He lowered his head to Hialeah's bare breasts and took one then the other breast into his mouth teasing each of her nipples with his tongue. As Jackson continued his tease game with Hialeah's breasts, Hialeah reached for Jackson's staff. Jackson took Hialeah's hand. It was his turn to command her body. Jackson slid his hand beneath the layers of Hialeah's skirt. He parted her legs and found her women's spot. Hialeah inhaled a breath as Jackson caressed her softly. Hialeah arched her back as she whispered Jackson's name. Jackson marveled at the way her body responded to his touch. Jackson teased and tormented Hialeah's sweet spot. He wanted her ready to accept his throbbing staff. Hialeah's breathing quickened as Jackson continued his sexual onslaught of her body. Hialeah couldn't contain her moans of erotic pleasure as she climaxed from Jackson's seductive teasing. Jackson was fueled by Hialeah's climactic outburst. The sultry look in her eyes assured Jackson that she was indeed ready to receive him. Jackson took Hialeah's lips in a quick and sensuous kiss. He placed more kisses on her breasts before completely removing Hialeah's skirt.

Hialeah's body was still reeling from Jackson's naughty play as she laid naked on her bed. She watched in fascinating fear as Jackson began to undress in front of her. Hialeah kept her eyes locked on Jackson's, daring not to allow her eyes to travel any further down his masculine and well defined body. Jackson insisted that Hialeah look at his full on erection. He wanted Hialeah to see not just feel what her body did to him. Hialeah blushed from the sight and size of his member. Jackson returned to Hialeah's waiting beside and took her hand once more and guided it along his shaft. He kissed her luscious lips while caressing her woman's spot once more. Hialeah responded to Jackson's touch by slowly breaking his kiss. She gazed into Jackson's eyes with a look of wanton desire. Hialeah's gaze aroused Jackson. She was ready to have him and he would not refuse her his pleasures. Jackson parted Hialeah's legs and positioned her for his taking. He brought Hialeah's parted knees toward her chest and entered her gently. Hialeah was unable to stifle her cry of immense pleasure as Jackson entered her softness. She found herself wrapping her arms around Jackson's neck as he began to thrust himself in and out of her. With every thrust of Jackson's hardened staff, Hialeah cried out in ecstasy. Jackson intensified his love making. He parted Hialeah's thighs further and thrust himself deeper into her woman's cove. Hialeah inhaled a sharp breath. Her hands fell from Jackson's neck to his back where she raked her nails across his skin. Jackson continued his powerful strokes. The fierce rhythm of his body brought moan after pleasured moan from Hialeah's lips. She breathlessly called out Jackson's name against his ear as she wrapped her legs around his waist; pulling him further inside of her. Jackson took Hialeah with such a fervent passion. Hialeah's hands fell from Jackson's back to grip the sides of her bed. "You're mine." Jackson growled out. Hialeah could feel her body begging for release. Her legs began to tremble and she arched her back to Jackson. Jackson relished the way Hialeah's body responded to his love making. He thrust himself ferociously inside of her and Hialeah dug her nails into Jackson's back as she gave way to her climax. Feeling Hialeah's nails painfully dig into his flesh and the erotic moan that escaped her body, Jackson erupted inside of her. His chest was heaving as he filled Hialeah with his secd.

After their sensuous love making, Jackson rolled over onto his back and pulled Hialeah next to him massive frame. She draped her arm over his chest and her leg across his. Using Jackson's chest as a pillow, Hialeah closed her eyes and listened to the sound of Jackson's heart beating. She absentmindedly ran her fingers down his chest to his stomach. Jackson smiled and kissed the top of Hialeah's head. She had never felt so safe and content. She loved being in Jackson's arms. If he never left her bed, that would be just fine with her.

Chapter 9

Jackson was awakened from his sleep by the sound of Hialeah's front door opening. Alarmed that Hialeah was not in bed next to him, he quickly reached for his gun that set on Hialeah's nightstand table. From the other side of Hialeah's bedroom door, Jackson could hear the familiar sound of Hialeah humming. He exhaled and set his gun back on the nightstand table. Jackson stood and wrapped Hialeah's bed sheet around his waist and headed toward the door. He opened the bedroom door and made his way to Hialeah's front porch. He smiled as he watched Hialeah busying herself with loading the last of her baskets of fresh vegetables and fruits from her garden onto her wagon. Hialeah hadn't noticed Jackson standing in her doorway. Jackson listened to her peaceful humming before deciding to alert her to his presence by joining in on her tune. Hialeah laughed at Jackson's attempt to join her. "You know that tune?" Hialeah asked. "Not at all." Jackson replied laughing. "Did I wake you?" Hialeah said. "I don't mind being awakened to beautiful music; especially if it's coming from beautiful lips." Jackson replied. "So you would mind if I had horrid looks and horrid lips?" Hialeah said teasingly. "Very much so." Jackson replied smiling. "What is all this?" Jackson asked. "Isn't it wonderful? The Earth has blessed me with such a bountiful crop." Hialeah replied proudly. "It is wonderful indeed." Jackson said. He loved the exuberant smile on Hialeah's face. "Where are you taking it all?" Jackson asked. "Into town to sell at Mr. Nesbit's store. He'll surely give me a good price don't you think?" Hialeah asked. Jackson walked off the porch to inspect Hialeah's baskets of fruits and vegetables. Jackson twisted his lips and frowned at Hialeah's crops. "I don't think these will do at all. Mr. Nesbit would never accept such a crop." Jackson said. "Of course he would. I have eggs too." Hialeah replied. "Eggs? Well that changes everything. Alright then, twenty-five dollars." Jackson said simply. "Twenty-five dollars?" Hialeah replied frowning unsure of Jackson's meaning. "My purchase price for the lot." Jackson said casually as he walked back into Hialeah's home.

Hialeah followed after Jackson as he made his way into her bedroom. "Your purchase price?" Hialeah replied confused. "It'll save Mama Lilly a great deal of time of having to go into town and purchase food for my employees." Jackson said. Hialeah's eyes widened. She had never had so much money. She squealed like a happy child before pouncing on Jackson knocking them both onto her bed. Jackson held Hialeah in his arms and rolled them over. He looked down into Hialeah's eyes and arched his brow playfully. "Careful Miss Nokosi, it's against the law to harm a judge." Jackson said teasingly before taking Hialeah's lips in a lingering kiss.

After having made love once more, Jackson and Hialeah bathed in the creek that ran alongside Hialeah's house. Jackson dressed and requested that Hialeah bring his newly purchased crops to the north gate entrance of his home. The north entrance was the closest to the cook house. Hialeah worried about returning to Jackson's home after her last encounter with his mother. Jackson assured Hialeah that he would be awaiting her arrival and the harsh treatment she had received previously from his mother would never happen again. Jackson insisted that Hialeah trust him and she nodded her head smiling faintly. Jackson placed a gentle kiss on Hialeah's lips before leaving her.

Hialeah had never gone to Jackson's home unescorted by him. After having two unfavorable encounters with Georgina Harding, Hialeah was feeling ill at ease. She opted not to wear her native dress; preferring to wear one of her self-made dresses instead. She didn't want to bring any unwanted attention to herself. Hialeah tried to keep her nerve up by relishing Jackson's love making. The very thought of Jackson's touch made her blush and smile as she rode to the Harding home. Everything about Jackson Harding made her heart skip several beats. His dress, his demeanor, his voice, his commanding presence, and especially his…Hialeah laughed to herself feeling quite naughty as she thought about Jackson's member. She now knew how her mother felt when she looked at her father with such adoration in her eyes. Hialeah's happy memories of her mother and father and their shared love were short lived. She frowned as she thought of her mother and father in that moment. She found herself wondering if they would have approved of her loving a man whose people had done so much harm to colored and indian folks. She hated to think of them being disappointed in her. Her mother and father meant everything to her and she prided herself on being the product of their love.

Hialeah had to dismiss her thoughts as she arrived at Jackson's home. She could feel a lump forming in her throat. As Hialeah rode her wagon up the long dirt road that led to Jackson's home, her mouth opened wide. She had no idea just how many people the Harding's employed on their tobacco field. Unsure of the exact location of the cook house, Hialeah stopped to ask a worker and was pointed in the direction of where Jackson would be. She continued on the road but didn't have long to wait before her presence drew the attention of an over-weight white man on a horse. Mr. Warner, Henry Harding's foreman, approached Hialeah's wagon with a disgruntled look on his face. He was dressed in tan colored trousers held up by suspenders and a green shirt stained with his sweat. His boots were dusty and covered with dirt. His red hair was greasy and slicked back on his head. Hialeah remained seated on her wagon as Mr. Warner rode directly next to her wagon. Hialeah kept driving as Mr. Warner spit on the side of the road. Failing to wipe his mouth, Mr. Warner's saliva lingered on his bushy red beard. Hialeah nearly gagged in disgust. As if he could read Hialeah's thoughts, Mr. Warner wiped at his beard with the back of his hand before running his hand along his trousers. He eyed Hialeah suspiciously. "You lost girl?" Mr. Warner said. "No sir, I ain't lost." Hialeah replied nervously. "Then what's your business here?" Mr. Warner said suspiciously. "My business is with Mr. Harding." Hialeah replied. "Mr. Harding took ill." Mr. Warner remarked. "I mean Jack...the other Mr. Harding." Hialeah said hastily correcting herself. She knew all too well that some white folks didn't appreciate a colored forgetting their place; being brazen enough to address their 'betters' by their first name. "He's expectin' me." Hialeah said. "Mr. Harding didn't mention anything to me about it." Mr. Warner replied. "Well if you'd kindly tell him I'm here..." Hialeah began. "You think to tell me what to do girl?" Mr. Warner said heatedly cutting Hialeah's request short. "I ain't none of your girl." Hialeah spat. Angered by Hialeah's tone, Mr. Warner reached over in an attempt to grab Hialeah's reins from her hand. Hialeah furiously slapped his hand away. She yelled at the filthy man to keep his hands from what was hers.

Jackson stood in the hot sun waiting for Hialeah. The north gate entrance was lined with tall trees and their shade obscured Jackson's view of the road. Jackson decided to head down the road to meet Hialeah. Before he could take a step, he recognized the angry voice of Hialeah and he took off racing down the road. Jackson's temper began to flare as he watched his father's foreman grabbing in Hialeah's direction. "Hey!" Jackson yelled as he ran the short distance to meet Hialeah. Startled by Jackson's booming voice, his father's foreman stopped his horse. Hialeah stopped her wagon and waited for Jackson to reach her. The presence of their boss gave the field workers pause. "What's going on here?" Jackson asked sternly. "This uppity nig…" Mr. Warner began accusingly. Hearing what he knew was to be a harsh insult against Hialeah; Jackson swiftly pulled his father's foreman from his horse by the front of his shirt startling Hialeah and the other workers. Jackson held tightly onto Mr. Warner's shirt and glared menacingly down into his eyes. "I suggest the next words that come from your haggard lips best be an apology to the lady." Jackson spat venomously before releasing Mr. Warner roughly. The obese foreman straightened his clothing and swallowed hard before turning to face Hialeah. Mr. Warner's hesitance to apologize to Hialeah caused Jackson to lose his patience. "Mr. Warner, how long have you been in service to my family?" Jackson asked. "I've worked for your father going on three years." Mr. Warner replied. "Well, I would hate to terminate your employment with my family's business, Mr. Warner, but I trust I'll no doubt be able to fill your position rather quickly." Jackson said casually. "I ain't never apologized to no colored before." Mr. Warner replied defensively. "Well I've never had to fire a bloody fat fuck before either, but I'll get over it." Jackson remarked heatedly. "Alright alright alright." Mr. Warner said before turning his attention to Hialeah again.

Every colored worker in ear shot in the Harding tobacco field waited anxiously to hear the slovenly foreman apologize. Some of the workers even walked closer to the road so that they could get a better view of the spectacle. Mr. Warner wiped at the sweat that had fallen from his brow with his forearm. "My…my apologies ma'am." Mr. Warner stammered out. The tobacco workers who had the pleasure of witnessing Mr. Warner's displeasure broke into laughter. "Perfect."

Jackson said mockingly before his mood darkened. "Now take whatever it is that you came here with and get the hell off of my property." Jackson spat. The eyes of the workers as well as Hialeah's widen in utter shock of hearing Jackson fire a white man before their eyes. "What?" Mr. Warner replied in disbelief. Jackson ignored Mr. Warner's question. He instead scanned the field of workers. "You there." Jackson said pointing to an older colored man who appeared to be in his fifties. His muscular stature for a man his age impressed Jackson. The man stood next to his wife, whom clinched a hold of her husband's arm worriedly. "Me sir?" The older man asked. "How long have you worked here?" Jackson asked. "All my life sir." The older man replied. Jackson knew very well what that meant. The older man had been one of his father's slaves. "What's your name, sir?" Jackson asked. "Joseph...Joseph, sir." Joseph replied nervously. "Is that your wife, Mr. Joseph?" Jackson asked. "Yes sir, Mr. Harding, sir. This my Violet." Joseph replied. "She's a lucky woman, sir." Jackson remarked. "No sir, I'm the lucky one." Joseph replied. "Of course, sir." Jackson remarked smiling. "Well, Miss Violet, I trust you'll prepare a fine supper this evening in honor of my new foreman." Jackson said.

Joseph and Violet stood in a state of momentary shock as Jackson's words sunk in. Hialeah smiled. "Congratulations, sir." Jackson said. A roar of celebratory cheers went up through the field. Violet squealed happily and threw her arms around Joseph's neck as she kissed her husband. "Now you just wait one goddamn minute!" Mr. Warner yelled drawing everyone's attention. Jackson took a step toward his former foreman. He towered over Mr. Warner, his hazel eyes shooting daggers at the pathetic man. "Get off my property." Jackson growled out. Mr. Warner backed away fearfully from Jackson. He turned to mount his horse. Jackson quickly grabbed the reins before Mr. Warner could mount the horse. Jackson waved Joseph over to his side. Joseph proudly walked over to Jackson. All eyes were on the three men. Jackson handed Joseph the horse's reins. "Mr. Joseph, your first duty as my new foreman is to escort Mr. Warner to gather his belongings and see him off my property." Jackson said sternly. Joseph nodded his head. "Yes sir." Joseph replied before mounting the horse. "Your father's gonna hear about this. Everyone in town is gonna hear about this." Mr. Warner said threateningly. "Get him out of here."

Jackson said to Joseph. "Yes sir." Joseph replied. "You heard the man, get movin'." Joseph said addressing Mr. Warner. Mr. Warner angrily wiped at his brow before stubbornly making his way up the road. Jackson turned his attention to Hialeah whose face still beamed with adoration at what she had just witnessed. "May I?" Jackson said. Hialeah nodded her head and slid over on her seat as Jackson climbed up next to her. Jackson looked at Violet and the swarm of ladies who had encircled her to share in her proud moment. Jackson nodded his head at the ladies before commanding Hialeah's horse in the direction of the cook house.

It was a short ride to the Harding's cook house. Jackson stopped the wagon and was immediately met by one of his footmen. Jackson handed over the reins and hopped down. He assisted Hialeah from the wagon and they both walked toward the rear of the wagon. Jackson hailed a colored female worker over to him and Hialeah and requested that she fetch Miss Lilly and the cook staff to unload Hialeah's crops. As the woman ran off, Hialeah smiled up at Jackson. Jackson cocked a brow teasingly at Hialeah. "What?" Jackson said smiling. "What you did for Mr. Joseph was mighty special." Hialeah replied. "He was the better man for the job." Jackson remarked simply. Their conversation was interrupted by Miss Lilly and six other women. Miss Lilly smiled in Hialeah's direction. Hialeah blushed fully aware that Miss Lilly knew that Jackson had stayed the night in her home. Jackson caught the exchange. "What are you two going on about?" Jackson asked curiously. Miss Lilly waited until the cook staff had grabbed a basket and disappeared into the cook house before responding. "Oh nothin' at all. It's just that you weren't here for last night's supper." Miss Lilly replied teasingly. Jackson caught the humor in her statement and he too blushed at Miss Lilly's bluntness. "Come with me, Miss Nokosi." Jackson said.

Hialeah followed Jackson through the door of the cook house. He led her to his father's study and closed the door behind them. Hialeah remained by the door as Jackson took a seat behind his father's desk. Hialeah watched as Jackson unlocked one of the drawers and pulled out the money he had offered her for the crops he had purchased. Jackson looked over at Hialeah who had her lips pressed together in an attempt to stifle a laugh. Jackson smiled. "What is it?" Jackson asked. "I don't know. I mean I ain't ever seen you dressed like a field worker before." Hialeah replied. Jackson smiled as he stood up and turned around so that Hialeah could take in his full attire. He was dressed in black boots and trousers that were also held up by suspenders and a dark blue button up shirt. "You like it?" Jackson asked. "It's quite nice." Hialeah replied chuckling as she walked over to Jackson. Jackson made no reference to the fact that Hialeah wasn't wearing her native dress. He knew the reason without even having to mention it. Jackson slid the money in Hialeah's direction. "Per our agreement." Jackson said. Hialeah didn't pick up the money in front of her. She was instantly distracted by watch she saw out of the window. Jackson's brows furrowed as he followed Hialeah's gaze. Hialeah was amazed at the multitude of colored women that Jackson had working in his tobacco field. "What are you looking at?" Jackson asked curiously. Hialeah kept her focus on the women outside. "You gotta lot of women workin' for you." Hialeah replied. "Why wouldn't there be? The women here work just as hard as the men." Jackson remarked. Hialeah turned to face Jackson. "I could do that." Hialeah said. "Work in the tobacco field?" Jackson replied. "I'd like a job." Hialeah said. "No." Jackson replied simply. Hialeah was taken aback by Jackson's reply. "I can do it Jackson. I'll work just as hard as those women out there." Hialeah remarked. "Those women need the money to care for their families. I am more than capable of providing for what's mine." Jackson replied sternly. "What's yours?" Hialeah said incredulously. "I'll not have you toiling for hours in this dreadful heat. Besides, you've earned quite a hefty profit from your crops." Jackson replied. "You know how I got them crops?" Hialeah began heatedly. She angrily snatched her money from Jackson's desk. "From toiling for hours in the dreadful heat." Hialeah said matter-of-factly before turning on her heel to exit Jackson's study. "Hialeah." Jackson called out but Hialeah ignored him. She slammed the door. Jackson quickly locked the desk drawer and hurried after Hialeah.

Upset by Jackson's refusal to allow her employment in the tobacco field, Hialeah hastily made her way through the cook house with her money in her hand. She quickened her steps as she went through the tobacco plants. Jackson hurried after Hialeah, but the moment he stepped out of the cook house into the tobacco field, his name was called by one of his foremen, who was carrying an arm-load of tobacco. Jackson scanned the tobacco field in search of Hialeah but she had disappeared. Jackson was annoyed by his foreman's intrusion but turned his attention to the man nonetheless.

Hialeah stormed her way toward the footman who tended to her wagon. She stopped mid-stride before the footman noticed her and made a bee-line toward the road where she had entered through the north gate. She would show Jackson just how good of a worker she was. Hialeah hastily made her way toward Joseph's wife Violet and the other group of ladies who were working on the northern side of the tobacco field. Hialeah knew all there was to know about growing and harvesting tobacco. Her mother had told her as a slave enough stories about the plant. Hialeah jumped right in alongside the other women. None of them paid Hialeah any attention. They simply assumed she was a new hire and kept to their work. Hialeah carried arm load after arm load of tobacco and tossed her bundles into an empty cart. She worked diligently for hours filling up cart after cart all the while humming child hood tunes that her mother had sang to her as a young girl. Joseph made his rounds in his new position as foreman and was impressed with Hialeah's stamina and speed. He was sure that Jackson would want to hear about the 'new girl' was coming along.

Joseph dismounted his horse just as the lunch bell rang. He found Jackson on the other side of the tobacco field making his way toward one of the tables set up by Miss Lilly and her cook staff. Joseph was eager to report on Hialeah's hard work. Jackson's brow furrowed. He was confused as to whom Joseph was speaking of. Joseph described Hialeah and boasted to Jackson of how Hialeah had filled several carts of tobacco with no assistance. Jackson was upset that Hialeah had openly defied him. He thanked Joseph for the report. Joseph walked away to join his wife for lunch.

Violet and the other women heard the lunch bell ring and immediately stopped their work to make their way toward the food. Hialeah was clueless as to what the bell meant but she decided to follow the other women. Her nostrils were instantly struck by the aroma of food. She was starving, thirsty and exhausted from the time she had spent in the tobacco field. Hialeah followed closely behind the other women in hopes of blending in. She was determined to avoid Jackson. Many of the workers were already in one of the lines being served and taking their seats at one of the many tables set up. Hialeah glanced at one of the worker's plate as he walked by. She was curious as to what was being served. Her mouth started to water at the sight of beef stew and cornbread.

Jackson immediately spotted Hialeah in the lunch line. He made his way toward Miss Lilly and her cook staff. Jackson stood behind Miss Lilly with his hands clasped behind his back as she continued to dish out plates of her beef stew. He stood patiently as worker after worker was served. Hialeah's stomach was grumbling uncontrollably. When it was her turn to be served, Jackson made it a point to personally serve her. Hialeah's eyes widened and her stomach sank as Jackson held her plate of stew. The scowl on his tanned face was enough for Hialeah to suddenly lose her appetite. Hialeah reluctantly took her plate as she was holding up the line. She avoided Jackson's glare and calmly walked toward a table that hadn't quite filled up with workers. Jackson followed Hialeah with two cups of cold water. Hialeah sat at the end of the table and kept her eyes cast down on her plate. Jackson stood over her until Hialeah caught on and slid down the bench a tad. Jackson set the two cups of water on the table before taking a seat next to Hialeah. Jackson hadn't said a word yet Hialeah was hesitant to pick up her fork. She could feel his heated glare upon her. Hialeah swallowed in an attempt to find her voice. Jackson still hadn't spoken and she could no longer bear his silence. "You angry?" Hialeah said low as she did not wish anyone to hear their conversation. "Very." Jackson replied heatedly his voice deep. Hialeah stood to leave but her arm was quickly grabbed by Jackson who unceremoniously pulled her back down to her seat. "Have your lunch. You've earned it." Jackson growled out. "Jackson..." Hialeah began. "When you've finished your meal, Joseph will see you off the property." Jackson interrupted harshly. "I don't understand what you so mad for. I only wanted to help." Hialeah said. Before Jackson could answer, Sara Williams' carriage pulled up and she is escorted from her carriage by her driver. Dressed in a light blue sun dress, Sara walked by several tables filled with workers having their lunch. "Jackson. Jackson, are you here?" Sara called out sweetly in her deep southern drawl.

All eyes followed Sara as she continued to walk by in her search for Jackson. Jackson stood and left Hialeah to her lunch before Sara could catch him sitting next to her. Hialeah watched as Jackson approached Sara. Hialeah frowned at Sara's big toothy smile. Jackson took Sara's arm and walked her away from the workers and out of earshot from Hialeah. "Sara, what are you doing here?" Jackson asked. "Why I've come to have lunch with your mother and I thought it'd be nice to have you join us." Sara replied smiling. "I was just about to have my lunch." Jackson remarked. "With the hired help?" Sara replied frowning. "We work together; I see no problem eating together." Jackson remarked. "Why Jackson, they're the help." Sara scoffed teasingly and placed her hand on Jackson's arm. Upset by Sara's gesture, Hialeah angrily stands up from the table and bumps into Isaac. She briefly glanced at him but said nothing before running for her wagon. Jackson walked Sara around the front entrance of his home just as Hialeah rode hastily by in her wagon. Overjoyed that Jackson has his arm around her waist, Sara doesn't notice Hialeah leaving. Jackson felt his stomach tie up in a knot. He knew all too well that Hialeah would give him an ear full about this and in Creek no less. Jackson thought it best to give Hialeah time to settle down before going for a visit.

Jackson escorted Sara into the dining room. Georgina was seated at the table and frowned her displeasure at her son's appearance. Jackson was covered in dirt and sweat from his morning in the field. Before he could take a seat, Georgina raised her hand in objection. "Jackson, you simply will not be joining us looking as if you've rolled in the dirt." Georgina said. "Of course mother." Jackson replied. He turned to face Sara, who had taken her seat across from Georgina. "My apologies, Sara. Another time perhaps?" Jackson said. "Absolutely." Sara replied smiling. Jackson nodded his head at the ladies and left them to have their lunch. Relieved, Jackson returned to the lunch tables outside and joined his workers.

Hialeah was beside herself with anger. She despised Sara Williams and Jackson's harsh treatment of her wasn't sitting too well with her either. Hialeah decided to take her mind off of Jackson by doing a little shopping in town. She didn't care that she looked an absolute sight. She had money and she would enjoy her alone time.

Sheriff Willard walked the streets keeping order in town as folks went about their daily affairs. Hialeah parked her wagon and climbed down. Her attention was instantly caught by beautiful baskets displayed in a store front window. Hialeah stood in awe in front of the window. Her heart began to race as Sheriff Willard's reflection cast through the glass as he approached her. Hialeah quickly turned around to face the sheriff. She feared the worst and Jackson was nowhere to aid her. Before she could utter a word, Sheriff Willard tipped his hat. "Ma'am." Sheriff Willard said simply as he went on his way. Hialeah felt as if she would faint. She nervously watched as Sheriff Willard walked on. Hialeah looked around for the sheriff's two deputies. They were always close by. Relieved that they were nowhere in sight, Hialeah hurried into the store.

Hialeah was barely able to breathe a sigh of relief from her confusing encounter with Sheriff Willard when the shop's door was opened and she was roughly pushed from behind. Hialeah fell to the ground. Shoppers in the store gasped in shock. A colored woman rushed to Hialeah's aid and assisted her to her feet. Hialeah was shaken up by the ordeal and turned to face her attacker. Willie Calhoun stood smug face in front of the door. He was dressed in filthy clothes and his hair was a greasy mess atop his head. He held a bottle of whiskey in his hand and his face was grimy. Willie took a long swig of his whiskey and wiped his mouth with the back of his hand. Hialeah's eyes widened nervously. "Well, look what we have here. A goddamn savage nigger whore." Willie spat. "Deputy Calhoun, you're drunk, and I won't have such talk in my store." The Gentleman Store Owner said. "Don't call me deputy! I ain't no goddamn deputy anymore and it's all thanks to this black trash here!" Willie yelled. Hialeah swallowed hard. She could see by the look of Willie's face that Jackson did a number on him. Willie's nose was crooked and he was missing a tooth. "Now you listen here. I've got law-abiding customers coming in here to spend their hard earned money and if you don't leave, I'll be forced to send for the sheriff." The Gentleman Store Owner replied. "Hang your law-abiding customers and to hell with the sheriff!" Willie fired. "That son-of-a-bitch sheriff sold me out and it's all because of her!" Willie spat heatedly. He slammed his bottle on the counter and marched up to Hialeah and forcefully grabbed her arm. Hialeah winced in agonizing pain from Willie's tight grip of her arm. Willie stared daggers into Hialeah's eyes. "Now you tell these good people in here just what kind of wretched whore you are! You tell them how you went and spread your legs to that nigger lovin' Jackson Harding. You tell them how Sheriff Willard made himself a deal with that bastard Harding to gain entrance to the Harding Gentleman's Club. You tell them!" Willie spat. Hialeah looked around the store and found all eyes were on her. Her heart was pounding mercilessly in her chest. "I...I don't know what you talkin' bout." Hialeah stammered out. "Liar!" Willie yelled as he squeezed Hialeah's arm even tighter. Hialeah cried out as she fell to her knees. The store owner bolted from his store in a frantic search for Sheriff Willard. Hialeah dug her nails into Willie's hand in an effort to free herself from his grasp. Willie screamed out and struck Hialeah with a back hand to her face causing several of the women to gasp in horror. Hialeah scurried away from Willie as he advanced on her. Terrified of what Willie would do to her, Hialeah kicked Willie between his legs and fearfully jumped to her feet as Willie doubled over in pain. Hialeah's act of defense received applause from the women. Hialeah raced from the store hysterically and ran to her wagon. Sheriff Willard and the store owner dashed down the sidewalk. Hialeah was too frightened to wait around. She ushered her horse to go and sped off down the road.

    Hialeah's face was burning from Willie's strike. She hurried home to put something cold to her face before any bruising could show. She knew all too well that if Jackson found out, he would go after Willie again and then the whole town would hear of it. The scandalous rumors of her being Jackson's whore would be on everyone's lips. Hialeah prayed that Jackson was still angry with her for working in his tobacco field and that his anger would keep him away until her face healed. After having reached her home, Hialeah burst through her front door and raced to her room to gather her scented soaps. She practically threw her clothes from her body and headed straight for the little creek that ran alongside her home to bathe the dirt and sweat from her body and hair.

Sheriff Willard rode with break neck speed to the Harding Estate. He cursed Willie's name the entire ride. It had taken him years to become a member of the distinguished Gentlemen's Club and he wasn't about to be tossed on his ass due to Willie's drunken attack on the woman that he was sure that Jackson Harding loved. He still found it sickening that a man of Jackson's caliber would dare love a colored woman, but as long as he was in good standing with Jackson and the members of the club, he would hold his tongue and treat Jackson's lover like any other citizen.

Jackson had returned to his duties in the tobacco field after his lunch. The sun was beating ferociously down on his back. He found himself humming one of Hialeah's familiar tunes. Jackson laughed to himself as the tune was pretty catchy. Just as he wiped the sweat from his brow, Jackson was approached by Joseph whom had noticed Sheriff Willard racing toward the house. "Mr. Jackson, sir." Joseph said. Jackson stopped his work and turned to face his new foreman. "How goes it Joseph?" Jackson replied. "Sheriff Willard's here. He come racing up the road." Joseph remarked pointing in the sheriff's direction. Jackson's heart began to pound in his chest. If Sheriff Willard was at his home, the news could not be pleasant. Jackson immediately thought of Hialeah and bolted through the tobacco. His workers stopped their work, confused as to their boss's strange behavior. Sheriff Willard dismounted his horse when he recognized Jackson's massive frame heading toward him. He hadn't the slightest notion of what he would say to Jackson but the younger Harding didn't look at all pleased to have him on his property. Sheriff Willard rushed to the other side of the road and Jackson hastily followed him. He didn't want to have their conversation overheard by anyone. "Where is she?" Jackson growled out. Sheriff Willard raised his hands in front of him in an attempt to calm Jackson down. "I want you to know, I personally handled the situation." Sheriff Willard replied quickly. "I won't repeat myself." Jackson spat. "There was an incident in town..." Sheriff Willard began. "What bloody incident?" Jackson replied through gritted teeth. He was seething with rage. "My deputy...um former deputy Willie...you're familiar with..." Sheriff Willard stammered out. "Get on with it." Jackson said menacingly. "Well, um he was drunk, you see, and he followed your friend, the young lady into a shop..." Sheriff Willard began once again, but Jackson had heard enough. "Where is Willie?" Jackson demanded. "I arrested him." Sheriff Willard replied. Without a word of warning, Jackson marched over to Sheriff Willard's horse and mounted it. He sped off down the dirt road leaving Sheriff Willard alone.

Jackson rode with a mad haste to Hialeah's home. Sheriff Willard's horse kicked up clouds of smoke with every stride he took. Jackson hungered to give Willie another much needed pummeling as well as shake the stubbornness from Hialeah's body. The thundering of hooves approaching her home caused Hialeah to stop her reading. She had decided to sit on her front porch and calm herself with one of her favorite books. Jackson all but jumped from Sheriff Willard's horse. Hialeah's poised and calm demeanor instantaneously infuriated Jackson. He could think of only one thing, that Hialeah was hell bent on driving him insane. Hialeah paid no attention to the menacing scowl on Jackson's face. She had grown accustomed to his brooding look when he was near her. She did, however, recognize Sheriff Willard's horse. Hialeah gasped. Jackson's dark scowl wasn't on account of her. He had clearly done something vicious to the sheriff. Hialeah sprang to her feet just as Jackson furiously climbed the three steps to her porch and none too politely grabbed her by both of her arms. "Why didn't you come to me after what happened in town?" Jackson demanded. His eyes pierced through Hialeah's. "What you do to the sheriff?" Hialeah replied in a hushed whisper. Jackson furrowed his brow; confused by Hialeah's question. "What?" Jackson remarked. "That horse. That horse belongs to the sheriff. They hang horse thieves around here." Hialeah said. Jackson released his hold on Hialeah's arms and took a step back. He was in total disbelief that Hialeah was more concerned about the sheriff's horse than her own well-being. There was absolutely no doubt at this point, that Hialeah was definitely trying to make him insane. Near his wit's end, Jackson ran his hand down the length of his face to calm himself. "I didn't ride all the way over here to discuss the goddamn sheriff or his bloody fucking horse."

Jackson said as calmly as he could. "All I want to hear is what happened in town." Jackson said. Hialeah crossed her arms. "Seems to me you already know what happened." Hialeah replied. "What on earth is that supposed to mean?" Jackson remarked annoyed. "It means just what I say." Hialeah replied stubbornly. "Miss Nokosi…" Jackson began his voice deep. "You didn't just happen by the sheriff's horse." Hialeah said. "Enough with the fucking horse!" Jackson exploded. His outburst startled Hialeah. Her hand flew to her mouth.

Seeing the reaction on Hialeah's face, Jackson left the porch to collect himself. He paced back and forth several times then suddenly stopped. Jackson turned to face Hialeah but kept his distance from her. He took in a few deep breaths. "I love you, I swear it, but as the good Lord is my witness, I will turn you over my knee if you don't tell me what that bastard did to you." Jackson said. Hialeah huffed and marched off her porch and stood toe to toe in front of Jackson. She tilted her head slightly to meet Jackson's eyes. She balled both fists to her sides. "You wanna know what he did to me?" Hialeah replied heatedly before giving Jackson a shove in his chest with all the power she could muster. Jackson was caught off guard by Hialeah's push but he could see the fire and hurt in her eyes. "Hialeah." Jackson said calmly. "I'll tell you what he did to me." Hialeah spat as she gave Jackson another shove to the chest. "Miss Nokosi." Jackson said calmly in an attempt to ease Hialeah's pain but she was far too upset to be taken in by soothing words. "He did to me what every cowardly white man done to me since I come here." Hialeah spat angrily and tearfully as she continued to shove Jackson against his chest. Jackson thwarted Hialeah's next impending shove and grabbed her from behind trapping her body against his. Hialeah struggled aimlessly against Jackson's hold; spewing heated words in her father's tongue. "Enough." Jackson said sternly. Jackson held Hialeah firmly until the fight had left her and she was reduced to a mass of tears. "It all cause of you." Hialeah replied tearfully. Jackson released Hialeah hearing her tearful accusation. Hialeah turned to face Jackson. "I am sorry this happened to you but I am not to blame for your disobedience." Jackson remarked. "Disobedience?" Hialeah replied incredulously. "That son-of-a-bitch never would have hurt you had you gone home after our discussion." Jackson said. "He never would have hurt me if you let me stay with you." Hialeah replied heatedly. "I gave you my answer. That should have been the end of it." Jackson spat. "Why? Cause you say so?" Hialeah fired back. "Yes!" Jackson yelled. "Ain't I got a right to go into town like white folks and not get beat on by cowards?" Hialeah said. "Of course you do." Jackson replied. "I pull up to that store and Sheriff Willard come by and greet me all nice like. He ain't ever been kind to me." Hialeah said. "Sheriff Willard was there?" Jackson replied. "He go on bout his business and I go on bout mine. I step right inside and Willie follow after me. I ain't never seen him lookin' the way he did." Hialeah said. "What do you mean?" Jackson replied. "He smelled right awful; dirty, holdin' a bottle. He start causin' a fuss. Said I was your whore in front of everyone listenin'. Said he ain't work for the sheriff no more on account he sold him out. Said you to blame cause you let the sheriff in your gentlemen's club." Hialeah replied. "Is that what he said?" Jackson remarked. "Is it true? You pay the sheriff off?" Hialeah said. "I paid him nothing. I did, however, allow him entrance to my father's club." Jackson replied. "If he leave me be?" Hialeah remarked. "Yes." Jackson replied. "You think that Willie gone leave me be now?" Hialeah spat as she marched back toward her porch. "No job. No money. He gone come for me again and again." Hialeah said heatedly as she gathered her book.

Jackson followed behind Hialeah and grabbed her arm. He looked sternly into her eyes. "I'll kill him if he comes near you again." Jackson said menacingly. "And then what? The whole town gone know you killed a white man to defend your nigger squaw." Hialeah replied. "The whole town will know that I defended a woman that I intend to make my wife and do not ever degrade yourself to me again. You have been warned before. Is that clear?" Jackson spat. His low tone sent chills through Hialeah's body. She was at a loss for words. "I want an answer in English or your father's tongue but you will answer me." Jackson growled out. Hialeah swallowed and nodded her head. "Yes." Hialeah replied. Jackson released her arm and stormed off the porch. He mounted Sheriff Willard's horse. "Go inside and lock the door. Answer it for no one." Jackson demanded. Hialeah raised a stubborn chin to Jackson's demand. "Is that an order Mr. Harding?" Hialeah said. "Do not test me Miss Nokosi." Jackson replied heatedly before riding off. Hialeah marched inside her home and slammed the door. She was furious that Jackson had dared order her to confinement to her home. She was even more furious with herself for doing as she was told.

Jackson rode up to the main entrance of his family's home and dismounted from Sheriff Willard's horse. One of his footmen took a hold of the reins and Jackson hurried into the house. He could hear his mother, Sheriff Willard and Sara conversing and laughing in the parlor. Jackson opened the door to the parlor and was greeted with a smile from his mother. "Why Jackson, do come join us." Georgina said happily. Jackson was in no mood for pleasantries after his heated discussion with Hialeah. "Not now mother. I need to speak to the sheriff alone." Jackson replied calmly. "Why, whatever for?" Georgina remarked. "Mother." Jackson sternly said. "Well, alright." Georgina replied. Sheriff Willard reached for Georgina's hand and placed a kiss on the back of it before doing the same to Sara. He grabbed his hat and placed it on his head. "Ladies, it was a pleasure." Sheriff Willard said. "Give my best to your husband." Sheriff Willard said. "I surely will." Georgina replied. Sheriff Willard exited the parlor followed by Jackson. The two stepped outside and Jackson led Sheriff Willard a few feet away from the house. He wanted to make sure his mother couldn't over hear their discussion.

Jackson turned to Sheriff Willard. His expression was dark. "Did you find her?" Sheriff Willard said. "Why did you fire Willie?" Jackson replied sternly. "I had no choice. Besides, he had it coming." Sheriff Willard remarked. "Why is that?" Jackson replied. "Willie is quite fond of the bottle. So much so that he confronted me one night as I was coming out of your daddy's club. He knew that I had longed to be a member but with what I'm paid for keeping order in this town, I couldn't afford it. He had been drinking and started making a huge spectacle in the street. He wanted everyone in earshot to hear him declare how I was Jackson Harding's puppet. Well, to put it in his words, that nigger lover's puppet. He started crying at how I sold him out and that he would see to it that no one in town voted for me in the upcoming election on account that I support nigger lovers. I fired him right there in the street." Sheriff Willard remarked. "What about Blake?" Jackson said. "You'll have no problems out of Blake." Sheriff

Willard replied. "Rest assured sheriff, this town will be missing one of its citizens if he harms her again." Jackson remarked angrily. He didn't wait for a response from Sheriff Willard. Jackson nodded his head toward his footman. He had nothing more to say to the sheriff. Sheriff Willard watched Jackson retreat into his home. The footman brought Sheriff Willard his horse and went on about his way leaving Sheriff Willard alone.

Jackson had had enough of this day. He wanted nothing more than to be alone. He walked quietly by the parlor, choosing his father's study to relax and have him a drink. Jackson was grateful that Sara was entertaining his mother yet again. He made himself comfortable in his father's chair and opened a desk drawer. Jackson retrieved a bottle of his father's favorite scotch and opened it. He didn't bother to use a glass. Jackson placed the bottle to his lips and downed a rather generous amount of the liquor. He leaned back in the chair and closed his eyes and thought of nothing. Jackson reveled in the serene and calmness of the room. No sooner than he exhaled a sigh of peace, he heard the footsteps of an impending nuisance approaching and a soft tap on the door. Jackson had enough time to grab the bottle from the desk and set it on the floor next to his chair before Sara entered the room without being invited to do so. Jackson groaned inward as he forced a smile to his lips. "Miss Williams." Jackson said nonchalantly. "Jackson, you don't have to be so formal. Sara is just fine." Sara replied smiling. "Of course." Jackson remarked. "Is there a problem?" Jackson asked. "Not at all. I just wanted to tell you good night." Sara replied. "You're leaving so soon?" Jackson remarked. Sara blushed. "Why Jackson, I've been here most of the day. I declare, I think you've taken in too much of the sun." Sara replied teasingly. "I think you may be right." Jackson remarked. "You know, a man of your stature ought not to be working so hard in the fields. I mean you do have hired help for that." Sara replied. "That I do." Jackson remarked. "Well..." Sara said as she started to walk toward Jackson. Jackson practically bolted from his seat to Sara's surprise. He didn't want her to see the bottle setting next to him on the floor. Sara stopped short as Jackson met her near the door. "Do have a good night, Sara." Jackson rushed out. He took her hand and placed a kiss on the back of it. "I surely will. You try to do the same." Sara replied. Jackson nodded with a grin.

"Jackson. You are going to walk me to my carriage?" Sara said. "Of course. Forgive me." Jackson replied. Sara giggled. "I'm telling you, you've just had way too much sun." Sara remarked as Jackson led her out of the study to her awaiting carriage.

Away from his mother's prying ears, Jackson found this moment to be perfect to question Sara about Hialeah's confession of truth regarding Sara's father. He was completely sober and they were alone, unlike their previous encounters. Jackson reached for Sara's arm and led her away from her carriage and her driver's ears. Sara was confused as to Jackson's action. "Jackson, what are you doing?" Sara asked. "I have something to ask you." Jackson replied calmly. "Alright." Sara remarked. Safe away from any potential eavesdroppers, Jackson released Sara's arm and turned to face her. "Do you despise all coloreds or is there some particular reason for your deep seeded hatred of Miss Nokosi?" Jackson asked. "Miss Nokosi?" Sara replied confused. The expression on Sara's face was evident to Jackson that Sara thought so little of Hialeah that she hadn't even cared to remember her name. "I believe you referred to her as a destitute simpleton." Jackson remarked. "Of course, but I also apologized for my crudeness." Sara replied. "That you did." Jackson remarked. "Jackson, just what are you asking me?" Sara asked. "What has she done to you?" Jackson replied. "Done? Well, she's done nothing personally to me. I just don't care to believe that coloreds are my equal." Sara remarked. "Her mother, Anna. What do you know of her?" Jackson replied. "Why would I know anything about that heath…that woman's mother?" Sara remarked. "Your father owned her did he not?" Jackson asked. "Why does any of that matter? It was a long time ago." Sara replied. "Did he own her?" Jackson remarked sternly. "Yes. Yes father owned her. He owned a lot of slaves, Jackson, but I don't know anything about her except that she was a trouble maker and that father lost a dear friend on account of him having to sell her." Sara replied. Jackson's brow furrowed. "What do you mean?" Jackson asked. "Father said that she would run away constantly and when she was returned, she was punished time and time again." Sara replied. "Punished? Beaten?" Jackson remarked. "I'm not exactly sure. I wasn't born." Sara remarked. "All I know is that father paid run-away slave hunters tons of money to catch her each and every time until he finally had enough and decided to sell her. However, according to father, she somehow found out that she was going to be sold off and decided to run away again. Unfortunately, for my father and his dear friend, Mr. Croswell, they had signed the bill of sell one night and by the morning, she was gone. Mr. Croswell came to collect his property and she was nowhere to be found." Sara said. "Why didn't this Croswell collect her that night?" Jackson asked. "Why he and father had been drinking and he was in no position to transport her to his home." Sara replied. "No one could find her the next morning and father kept the five hundred dollars. He insisted that since the papers had already been signed, that she was Croswell's problem. Why they even fought about it in court, but seeing as how father is a judge himself and a pillar in this society, he was granted favor." Sara said. "Your father sold her for five hundred dollars?" Jackson asked incredulously. "Said she was good breeding stock. Treated her like a prize winning thoroughbred. A home-wrecking harlot if you ask me. Thank God mother forgave him or else I might not have been born." Sara replied matter-of-factly. "Just how did your father know she was good breeding stock?" Jackson remarked. "It is unbefitting of a lady to speak of other's marital misconducts." Sara replied. "Yet, you find it so simple to condemn Miss Nokosi's mother as a harlot." Jackson remarked smoothly. "Those women have no shame when it comes to sticking their claws into good God-fearing Christian white men such as my father." Sara replied. "Are you implying that Miss Nokosi's mother welcomed your father into her bed?" Jackson remarked. "Precisely." Sara replied.

Jackson couldn't fathom what he was hearing. Surely Sara could not be so naïve as to think her father was not guilty of forcing himself on his slaves. "Those women were property, nothing more. You know as well as I they had no say in whether or not their masters could visit their beds." Jackson said. "Are you now implying that there were slaves who couldn't have possibly fallen in love with their masters or their masters for them?" Sara replied. "Of course it is possible." Jackson remarked. "Well, thank you for that because I assure you, I have seen it with my own eyes. Just as I have seen the way she looks at you and you look at her." Sara replied. "I also know that you have shared her bed by invitation, have you not?" Sara asked simply. "Sara." Jackson replied. "So you see it is quite possible that her mother did willfully invite my father into hers. Of course, unlike my father, you're not foolish enough to conceive a half-breed bastard son with her and sell him off to the highest bidder to save your marriage." Sara said nonchalantly. Jackson stood dumbfounded. It took a moment to gather his bearings. "I've heard mother and father argue quite passionately about it over the years." Sara said. "You share a brother with Miss Nokosi?" Jackson replied. "Shared. He died three years before I was born." Sara remarked. "And you know for sure he's dead?" Jackson asked. "Of course, I'm sure. People love to talk." Sara replied. "His mother ran away some days later." Sara said. "I've never heard of this." Jackson replied. "Of course not. You weren't here Jackson. It was such a common thing. One moment, it's the most scandalous news in town and then, it's simply forgotten." Sara remarked before slinking her arm through Jackson's. "And Miss Nokosi? Does she know any of this?" Jackson asked curiously. "Well I'm sure I don't know. I've never spoken to her about it." Sara replied. "I do hope father's sordid past doesn't come between us. I simply couldn't bear it." Sara said hopeful that Jackson would agree. Jackson took a moment to answer Sara's request. "Jackson?" Sara said. "Of course not." Jackson replied as if in a daze. His mind was reeling hearing Sara's truth as he led her toward her carriage.

Jackson opened the door to the carriage and assisted Sara inside. "Your mother is an absolute treasure." Sara said sweetly. "Yes." Jackson replied absentmindedly. Sara opened her parasol. "I'll send an invitation for dinner." Sara remarked smiling. Jackson tapped on the carriage for Sara's driver to move along. He was curious if Hialeah knew any of this. He would speak to her about it after he was able to let it sink in himself.

Chapter 10

Jackson was awakened by the sound of footsteps stampeding up the stairs and pounding on his bedroom door. He had been unable to sleep for several days after his discussion with Sara. The thought of how he would even begin to have such a conversation with Hialeah tortured him. "Mr. Jackson, you better come quick! There's trouble in the tobacco field!" Miss Lilly rushed out. Jackson darted from his bed. He had nothing on and scrambled for his trousers and boots. His issue with Hialeah would have to wait until the tobacco matter was dealt with. Jackson dressed in a hurry and raced down the stairs. He ran through the cook house and out the door where Joseph was waiting for him. "Joseph, what is it?" Jackson rushed out. "Mr. Jackson, you gotta come see this." Joseph replied worriedly. Jackson nodded his head and followed Joseph to the north side of the tobacco field. Joseph led Jackson to the very spot where Hialeah had secretly been working several days before. Violet and the other female workers stopped their work once Jackson arrived to assess the issue with the tobacco. Jackson's brow furrowed at the sight of the small patch of rotted tobacco leaves. They were dried out and had a brownish hue to them. He looked around the field only to find that the rest of the leaves appeared to be undamaged by whatever it was that had caused this bunch of leaves to rot out.

Jackson rubbed his fingers along the leaves and turned to face Joseph. "What happened here?" Jackson asked. "Not sure, sir." Joseph replied. "Have you checked the rest of the fields?" Jackson remarked. "Yes, sir. Good bunch of crop everywhere else." Joseph replied. "What do you think caused it? Too much water, perhaps?" Jackson asked. "No sir. Been waterin' the same since I was a boy here. Never had a problem before." Joseph replied. Jackson knelt down and scooped up a handful of soil and rubbed his hands together allowing the soil to slide through his fingers. He stood up and brushed his hands on his trousers. "And you've never seen this before?" Jackson asked.

"Never, sir." Joseph replied. "What do you propose we do?" Jackson asked. "I think it best if we maybe wait a tad to see if it could be the waterin'." Joseph replied. "Alright then. We'll do that." Jackson remarked. "I have work to do on my father's books. Send for me if there are any more issues." Jackson said. "Yes sir." Joseph replied.

Hialeah had finished her breakfast and chores and had just sat down with a cup of tea. She was nearly finished with her book when she heard the sound of footsteps on her porch followed by a gentle rapping on her door. Fearful as to who could be calling on her, Hialeah cautiously walked toward the window and pulled the curtains back. She smiled and opened the door to a waiting Ruby. Hialeah hadn't seen her friend since the church luncheon and her horrid encounter with Isaac. Ruby greeted Hialeah with a smile of her own. "Hello." Ruby said. "Hello." Hialeah replied before embracing Ruby. "I hope I ain't intrudin' on you. I brought somethin' for you." Ruby said. She presented Hialeah with a small basket of assorted preserves. Hialeah was overjoyed with Ruby's generous gift. "Mvto. (Muh-doe) Thank you." Hialeah said. "You're welcome. I made it myself. I hope you like them." Ruby replied. "I'm sure I'll love them. Would you like to come in? I was just bout to have a cup of tea. I baked some fresh biscuits just this mornin'. I bet your preserves will be perfect on them." Hialeah remarked. "I'd like to join you." Ruby replied. Hialeah moved aside as Ruby entered her home. She set the basket of preserves on the table and hurried to fetch Ruby a cup of tea and a plate of her fresh baked biscuits.

Hialeah was beyond happy to have a lady guest in her home. "Please make yourself at home." Hialeah said. Ruby took a seat at the table and Hialeah sat across from her. Hialeah was anxious to taste the sweet preserves. "There's apple, peach and blackberry." Ruby said. "They all look so wonderful; I don't know which to choose." Hialeah replied. "Blackberry's my favorite." Ruby said. "Alright. I'll have the blackberry." Hialeah replied. She dug her knife into the jar of blackberry preserves and spread a more than generous amount onto her biscuit. Hialeah took a bite of her biscuit and closed her eyes at the wondrous taste of the preserve. "I ain't ever tasted anything so good." Hialeah said. "I'm glad you like it. I can show you how to make it if you like." Ruby replied. "Yes, please." Hialeah replied smiling before taking another bite of her biscuit. Ruby was pleased that her new friend found her preserves to be tasty. She helped herself to one of Hialeah's biscuits and preserves. "I'm glad you're here." Hialeah said. "Me too." Ruby replied. "I didn't think Isaac would allow you over for a visit." Hialeah said. Ruby frowned. "Isaac's my brother, not my daddy." Ruby replied. "He was right sore with me after the preachin'. He didn't take too kindly to my rejectin' him." Hialeah remarked. "Don't you fret none over Isaac. I'm not." Ruby replied. "Besides, anyone with eyes can see that you in love with Mr. Jackson." Ruby said. "That don't bother you none; that I love a white man?" Hialeah asked. "I mean, his daddy bein' your former master and all?" Hialeah said. "We free now. That's all that matters." Ruby replied. Hialeah nodded her head in agreement. "Besides, he pay good for workin' his daddy's tobacco field." Ruby said. "You work for him?" Hialeah asked. "Well, not at first. I go over there yesterday to pick up Isaac and he offered me a job. Says I can start tomorrow if I like." Ruby replied. Hialeah smiled faintly. "That was really nice of him to do that." Hialeah remarked somberly. "Perfect timin' too. I lose my job a few days ago. I was workin' for the Widow Webster and she just outright tell me she don't need me no more. Says she just sold her house and movin' up north with her sister. Just like that, I'm right out of a job." Ruby said. "She did pay me what she owed me for the week though." Ruby said. "I thank the good Lord for that, cause I outta money." Ruby replied. Hialeah picked up her cup and brought it to her lips. She felt so ashamed of herself. Here she was fuming and upset with Jackson for not allowing her to work when all along he was justified in hiring folks who really needed the money. Ruby noticed the somber look on Hialeah's face. "You alright?" Ruby asked. "Of course. Just lost in thought is all." Hialeah replied. "Well, I best be goin'. Thank you for the tea and biscuits." Ruby said. "Thank you for the preserves." Hialeah replied. Both women stood and embraced one another. Hialeah led Ruby to the door. "Bye now." Ruby said. "Cehecvres (Zee-hee-zah-les). It means, I'll see you again." Hialeah replied smiling.

Jackson's tobacco issue had taken its toll on him. It had been nearly two weeks since Joseph had shown him the rotted tobacco leaves and since then, matters had only gotten worse. A good portion of the north field had begun to rot. Jackson and his workers had tried everything imaginable to halt whatever it was that was causing the tobacco to die out. Jackson was beside himself. The smudge pots that were placed in the soil did nothing to solve the problem. To make matters worse, Jackson had received a letter from his father's investors that an anonymous letter alerting them that they were aware of the rotted tobacco and would be making a visit by the end of the month to inspect it. The letter also made mention that it had been brought to their attention that he had been seen in the company with a mulatto mixed with Indian blood, and such relationships with coloreds of any sort were severely frowned upon and they would have to cut ties with the Harding Tobacco Company if said accusations were found true. Aggravated beyond belief, Jackson thought to tear up the letter, but decided against it. Instead he folded up the letter and placed it inside of his coat pocket and hurried out to the field to meet with Joseph.

Joseph was in a panic in his attempt to cure the tobacco. Jackson hailed him over. "Any luck?" Jackson asked. "No sir." Joseph replied. "Bloody hell." Jackson remarked heatedly. "Not much we can do 'xcept burn it and start fresh." Joseph replied. "We can't do that. My father's investors are coming to inspect the tobacco." Jackson remarked. "Well, if we don't figure out somethin' soon, you won't have a choice." Joseph replied. "What do you mean?" Jackson asked. "Words got around that somethin's killin' your tobacco. Your fellow tobacco growers are worried that whatever it is that's causin' it is gonna come their way. Said they's gonna burn it for you if you don't get a handle on it." Joseph replied. "Son-of-bitch." Jackson remarked. "Alright. Do you remember who worked that area when the tobacco began to rot?" Jackson asked. "Yes sir. It was the new girl you hired. The mulatto girl; that half injun girl." Joseph replied. "Are you sure?" Jackson asked. "Yes sir. She was workin' right alongside my Violet. She was downright mad when I escorted her off the property. Those types ain't good to anger." Joseph said. "What do you mean those types?" Jackson replied curiously. "I mean it ain't no secret that them injuns, why they'll curse you if wronged." Joseph remarked. "A curse?" Jackson replied. "I didn't believe it at first, but durin' the war, I fought alongside some of them. The chantin' and the way they prayed;

scared me somethin' awful." Joseph remarked. "If she did curse your land, she did a right fine job of it." Joseph said. Jackson nodded his head. "Thank you." Jackson replied before leaving Joseph to his work.

Jackson made his way back to the main house. He thought to himself, surely Hialeah wasn't so angry with him that she would or could curse his tobacco. Jackson hated to believe in such superstitious nonsense, but if Hialeah were capable of such magic, he'd put a stop to it.

Joseph's words ran through Jackson's mind as he called for one of his footmen to bring his horse. Jackson hastily mounted his horse and sped off down the road. He rode thunderously up the small road that led to Hialeah's home just as she had finished picking the last apple from her tree that she would need to make her pie. Jackson spotted Hialeah and rode near her. He dismounted quickly and turned to face her. "We need to talk." Jackson said sternly. Hialeah knew that icy glare and that demanding tone all too well. "You havin' trouble with your tobacco? I hear folks in town sayin' so." Hialeah replied. Hearing Hialeah speak so calmly about the rotted tobacco, infuriated Jackson. "You're bloody right I'm having trouble with my tobacco and whatever dark magic you've used to curse it, I want it stopped now." Jackson spat. Hialeah's eyes widened. She was more than offended that Jackson would accuse her of witchcraft. "I ain't did nothin' wrong to your tobacco and I won't be accused of it neither." Hialeah fired back. "Joseph informed me that the tobacco rotted precisely where you were working it. He said that he fought alongside your father's kind and they would chant or such nonsense." Jackson replied. "Hang that Joseph and hang anyone else that think like him. That goes for that prissy Miss Sara, too." Hialeah spat. "Hialeah." Jackson said warningly. "He accuse me of bein' a Stikini (Stee-kee-nee)." Hialeah said. "What?" Jackson replied confusedly. "An Owl spirit. A monster. An evil witch who could turn into owl-like creatures. In the morning time, they look like regular people of the Seminole, but at night, they was said to vomit up their very souls and everything inside of them. They'd become these owl-like creatures that would feed on the hearts of humans. Our elders told us youngins just speakin' their name could possibly turn you into one of them." Hialeah said. "Is that what you think of me, Jackson Harding?" Hialeah asked accusingly. Jackson disregarded Hialeah's question. He was in no mood to go down that road with her. "All I know is that something that Joseph has never seen in all the years that he's worked my father's tobacco, is destroying it, and nothing we've tried thus far, can stop it. Not only that, my father's investors has received word regarding my tobacco matter and are due here by the end of the month to inspect it. If I can't stop this cur...this disease of some sort, my family could lose everything. I am bloody well aware that you care nothing for my mother or Sara..." Jackson began. "I don't think nothin' of either one of them, but there's good hard-workin' folks who depend on your wages. No matter what they say bout me, I wouldn't hurt them so. I wouldn't hurt you none either." Hialeah said. Jackson mounted his horse and looked intensely down on Hialeah. "God, I hope not." Jackson replied. He turned his horse and sped away toward his home.

Hialeah watched Jackson ride away until he disappeared from her sight. She hurried inside with her basket of apples and set them on the table. She had to see for herself just what kind of trouble Jackson's tobacco was in. Hialeah wasted no time in hitching up her wagon or even placing a saddle on her horse. Her father had taught her how to ride bareback when she was a young girl. She looped her war bridle around her horse's lower jaw, mounted him, and rode out of her barn.

When Hialeah arrived at the Harding Estate, she rode to the north side of the tobacco field where she had briefly worked. Her mouth fell open at the horrendous sight of the rotted tobacco leaves. Still sitting atop her horse, Hialeah scanned the infected area in search of Jackson. Unsure of where he could be, Hialeah dismounted her horse before Violet and the other ladies that surrounded her. Their eyes nearly protruded from their heads as they watched Hialeah tie her horse to the fence. Hialeah hopped over the fence and approached them. One of the ladies, at the order of Violet, ran off toward the main house in search of Jackson, while the other ladies took a few steps back as Hialeah made her way toward the rotted tobacco leaves. Hialeah paid the astonished women no mind as she knelt down to inspect one of the tobacco plants. Confident in what the problem is, Hialeah pulled the plant out of the ground. Hialeah could hear the gasps from the stunned women as she began pulling up plant after rotted plant and tossed them aside.

It didn't take long for Jackson to arrive with Joseph and the three other foremen. Jackson marched toward Hialeah, who kept at her task of pulling up the tobacco plants. "Miss Nokosi!" Jackson yelled out. Before she could respond, Jackson grabbed a hold of Hialeah's arm and hastily led her a short distance away from the workers. Jackson released Hialeah's arm and crossed his in annoyance. He glared down at Hialeah. "What are you doing?" Jackson asked sternly. "What I doin' is stoppin' them diseased plants from infectin' the rest of them." Hialeah replied. "And if you don't want your fellow tobacco growers to burn this here all down, you'd best tell them to start pullin' them plants up." Hialeah said sternly. Jackson's brows rose in curiosity. "You know what's causing the tobacco to rot?" Jackson asked. Hialeah nodded her head. "I sure that tobacco is disease ridden with Black Shank." Hialeah replied. "Black Shank? What the hell is that?" Jackson asked. "It's a disease, a fungus that kills tobacco. I've seen it before. Not sure what causes it though." Hialeah replied. Jackson looked over his shoulder and hailed his four foremen over to hear his and Hialeah's discussion. The four men hurried over. Jackson turned to face the men. "Black Shank. Have any of you heard of it?" Jackson asked. All four men shook their heads. "Miss Nokosi here says that's what's killing the tobacco." Jackson said. One of the white foremen arrogantly crossed his arms in doubt of Hialeah's knowledge. "How do you know it's Black Shank?" The foreman asked. Hialeah placed her hands on her hips and faced Jackson's foreman. "Cause I do." Hialeah replied matter-of-factly. Jackson cocked an impressive brow in Hialeah's direction. Satisfied that she put the arrogant man in his place, Hialeah turned back to face Jackson. "You want my help or don't you?" Hialeah asked. "Can you stop it?" Jackson asked. "Henka." Hialeah replied. "Henka? What the hell is henka?" The white foreman demanded. "It means yes in her language." Jackson replied. "Then why in the hell didn't she just say yes?" The white foreman asked. "Cause I can speak whatever the hell I want when I want." Hialeah remarked heatedly. Jackson tried to stifle a laugh. He found Hialeah's fiery demeanor amusing and very much a turn-on. "What do you need?" Jackson asked; regaining his composure. "We gone need a big pot, lots of ladles and buckets, and as many chrysanthemum petals and soap as you can find." Hialeah replied. "Chrysanthemums and soap?" Jackson asked confused. "That's what I said. Time's a-wastin' Mr. Harding." Hialeah replied. "You're that half-breed squaw that robbed Terrell Grisby." The foreman said accusingly. "You'd best stop your tongue right there and apologize to the lady if you want to keep your job." Jackson replied threateningly. "Yes sir. My apologies, ma'am." The foreman remarked. Hialeah squinted her eyes at the man in disgust. Jackson lowered his head briefly in an effort to keep himself from laughing before clearing his throat and returning his attention to his foremen. "You heard the lady. Get moving." Jackson said. Jackson's four foremen dispersed to do what they were told. Hialeah turned to Jackson. "I don't like him none." Hialeah said. Jackson chuckled at Hialeah's simple truth. "Clearly." Jackson replied laughing.

Joseph and the other three foremen instructed the workers to start pulling up the diseased tobacco and to gather the other items needed that Hialeah requested. Jackson turned back to face Hialeah. She raised her hand to stop him from speaking. "Don't care to hear your apologies." Hialeah said. Jackson grinned. "If this works, I'll be in your debt." Jackson replied. "When this works, I'll expect you to allow me to help out." Hialeah remarked. "Help? No wages?" Jackson asked curiously. "Like you said, there's folks here that need the money for their families." Hialeah replied. Jackson smiled before leading Hialeah back toward the others and the tobacco that needed their attention. He glanced over toward the fence and noticed Hialeah's horse tied up without a saddle. Jackson turned to Hialeah. "You rode here bareback?" Jackson asked surprised. "You impressed, Mr. Harding?" Hialeah replied teasingly. "Very much. Now get to saving my tobacco, Miss Nokosi." Jackson remarked smiling.

Jackson had ordered that every Chrysanthemum petal in the garden to be brought to Hialeah, along with every bar of soap. When there was no more soap and petals to be found, Jackson sent Violet and her group of women into town to purchase every Chrysanthemum from every vendor on the street and every bar of soap in each shop keeper's store. A massive black pot was brought to Hialeah and set up where bucket after bucket of water was poured into it until the pot was full. Once the fire was lit underneath the pot and the water had begun to boil, Hialeah and several of the other women workers went to task by shaving the soap and dumping every Chrysanthemum petal in the boiling water, while Jackson led the men in pulling up the rotted tobacco leaves. Jackson looked over his shoulder at Hialeah and nodded his head in appreciation. Hialeah offered a slight smile as to not raise any suspicious eyebrows of those who weren't aware of their relationship.

While Hialeah sat on a stool stirring up her soap and Chrysanthemum mixture, Jackson set the rotted tobacco leaves on fire. Jackson lowered his head in defeat at the size of the gaping hole that was left once the burned leaves had been carried away. He turned toward Hialeah and wiped his brow as he made his way to her. Hialeah noticed the concerned look in Jackson's eyes. "Don't worry." Hialeah said. "My father's investors." Jackson replied. "You've got plenty of tobacco to keep them happy and this here is gone stop the Black Shank from spreadin'." Hialeah remarked. Jackson nodded his head. "I trust you." Jackson said. "Good. Now let's get this to the rest of the plants." Hialeah replied. "Yes ma'am." Jackson remarked teasingly. Hialeah was happy to see the worry leave Jackson's eyes as he ordered for the buckets to be filled with her cure.

Joseph's crew watered the tobacco leaves on the north side of the field with Hialeah's mixture while the other three foremen went back to their respective sides of the fields to continue overseeing their workers. Hialeah continued to sit on her stool to distribute the proper amount of mixture to every bucket that was presented to her. Jackson worked diligently with Joseph and his crew. He returned several times to Hialeah for a refill and playfully teased her with little winks before returning back to the field. Hialeah found herself blushing at Jackson's naughty antics.

It didn't take Hialeah long to catch on that several of the workers that approached her for a refill were setting their buckets down and taking several steps back away from her before quickly retrieving their buckets once they were filled; making sure to avoid eye contact with her when she smiled at them. Hialeah wanted to be certain that she wasn't reading too much into what some of the workers were doing. She continued to stir her mixture patiently waiting for another one of Jackson's employees to approach her. Hialeah was all too ready when Violet and another woman came her way with their buckets in tow. Violet set her bucket down as did the other woman and both women took steps back and waited for their buckets to be filled. Hialeah calmly rose from her stool instead of refilling the buckets from her seat with her own ladle like she had done previously. She grabbed both ladles from the buckets that Violet and her friend had been using to water the tobacco leaves and dipped them continuously into her mixture until both buckets were full. Both ladies' eyes widened as Hialeah then returned their ladles to their buckets and knelt down to pick up both buckets by their handles. Glaring at both women, Hialeah inched her way toward them holding both buckets in her hands waiting for either Violet or her friend to retrieve their buckets of mixture.

    Hialeah's bold stance was met by Violet's bold stance. Violet crossed her arms in defiant refusal. Violet's friend caught both heated glares between the women and wanted no part of whatever was about to transpire. She frantically raced through the tobacco field in search of Jackson. Hialeah felt her arms beginning to wane from the weight of the buckets but dared not show weakness. "You gone do your job or ain't you?" Hialeah asked curtly. "I do my job when I get a bucket that ain't been touched by your cursed hands." Violet spat. "My hands ain't no more cursed than yours." Hialeah remarked heatedly. "Don't make no never mind what you say. I work for Mr. Harding." Violet replied. "Then you best take this here bucket and do what Mr. Harding pay you for." Hialeah remarked. "You worry bout your pay and I worry bout mine." Violet replied. Fed up with Violet's temperament, Hialeah dropped both buckets to the ground. "I ain't gettin' no pay. Mr. Harding came to me for help so you miserable cows can keep food on your tables! The whole lot of you would've been tossed on your prissy asses if it weren't for me!" Hialeah fired out. "Well I ain't fixin' to bow down to no half-breed mutt, whose mama would stoop so low and open her legs to one of them stankin' injuns!" Violet fired back.

Jackson could hear the explosive exchange between Violet and Hialeah as he and Joseph hastily made their way through the tobacco. A crowd of on-lookers had circled the women. Jackson broke through the chaotic crowd just as Hialeah landed a punch square against Violet's face knocking her to the crowd. Hialeah wasted no time. She pounced on Violet and wrapped her hands around her neck. "Violet!" Joseph yelled frantically, running toward his fallen wife. "Miss Nokosi!" Jackson yelled. Hialeah was oblivious to anyone around her. She was determined to choke the living soul from Violet's body. Jackson rushed over to Hialeah and with one swoop lifted her from her fallen victim. Jackson carried Hialeah like a rag doll a few feet away kicking and screaming and voicing her outrage in Creek. Jackson tightened his grip on Hialeah's waist in an attempt to break the fight in her. "You take your hands off of me!" Hialeah screamed. "Not until you've calmed down!" Jackson yelled. Hialeah continued to wrestle against Jackson's hold on her; her feet swinging through the air. "Bloody hell, Miss Nokosi, enough!" Jackson yelled. Instantaneously, Hialeah stopped her fight. Her chest was heaving fiercely and her hair was now a tousled mess. Jackson was reluctant to release his hold on Hialeah, but did so cautiously. He stood in between Hialeah and Violet.

Joseph nestled Violet's crumpled body in his arms. "That crazy witch attacked my wife!" Joseph yelled. Hearing Joseph insult her fueled the fire once again in Hialeah. She attempted a mad dash in Violet's direction only to be caught swiftly by the waist once more by Jackson's iron-clad grip. "And I'll pound her face again and again she talk bad bout my mama!" Hialeah fired back. "That goes for the rest of you too!" Hialeah warned angrily. "You're all just jealous cause my mama was stronger than the lot of you! She was smart enough to run away from her master; get herself free from bein' a slave, while you all cowered like mice, scared of your master's whip!" Hialeah yelled angrily. "Miss Nokosi, stop it!" Jackson yelled but his order fell on deaf ears. "And you hate me cause I ain't never been no slave and ain't never gone be one neither!" Hialeah screamed.

Jackson had had enough. "Joseph, have one of the women comfort Violet and get everyone back to work!" Jackson ordered. Joseph scooped Violet in his arms and carried her away. The rest of the workers continued on with their work. Assured that they were now alone, Jackson released Hialeah but quickly grabbed her arms in a rough hold. He glared menacingly down at her. "What in the bloody hell are you doing?" Jackson demanded. "I defendin' my mama against that evil woman." Hialeah spat; tears welling in her eyes. "You attacked her." Jackson replied angrily. "And I'll do it again to any one of them!" Hialeah yelled uncontrollably. "So you just go right on ahead and take her side!" Hialeah fired out. "This has nothing to do with taking sides." Jackson growled out low. "Why ain't it, huh? Why ain't you takin' my side? You my Jackson or ain't you?" Hialeah replied heatedly. She broke free of Jackson's hold and marched furiously toward the direction of her horse. "Where are you going?" Jackson asked; matching Hialeah's stride, step for step. "Home, before you get that big ol' fool, Joseph, to throw me off your property like before." Hialeah replied, keeping her back to Jackson and not breaking her stride. Jackson swiftly reached out and grabbed Hialeah by the arm. He turned her to face him. Hialeah lowered her head to hide the frustrated tears that threatened to fall from her eyes. Jackson caressed Hialeah's cheek gently. "Stay, please." Jackson said calmly. Hialeah gave way to her tears at the soothing caress of Jackson's touch and the deepness of his voice. She burst into tears and buried her head against Jackson's chest. Jackson wrapped his arms around Hialeah. He could feel her body go limp against his frame as Hialeah began muttering in Creek. "English." Jackson said soothingly. Hialeah wiped at her eyes. "She said I was cursed; that I this half-breed mutt; that my mama stooped real low openin' her legs to a stankin' injun." Hialeah said pitifully through her tears. "I couldn't bear it no more. I so sorry if I humiliated you." Hialeah said. "You defended your mother and your family's honor. There's nothing humiliating about that." Jackson replied. Hialeah looked up at Jackson. "And yes, I am your Jackson and yes I'm taking your side, but just to be certain that you're not tempted to strike any more of my workers, I think it'll be best if you work with me." Jackson said teasingly. "There's still a lot to be done before my father's investors arrive." Jackson said. "Yes sir, Your Lordship." Hialeah replied grinning. Jackson chuckled. "You're not going to let that go are you?" Jackson asked smiling. "Ain't plan on it.

It makes you blush." Hialeah replied teasingly. "Come on." Jackson remarked.

Hialeah and Jackson walked back to the black pot that contained the plant mixture. Hialeah picked up Violet's bucket of mixture and followed Jackson to the tobacco plants that still needed watering. Hialeah kept her eyes focused on Jackson's back as she followed him through the tobacco field; ignoring the icy and shocked stares she received from the women she passed. Jackson led Hialeah to the secluded spot in the field where he had been working before the altercation between her and Violet began. He picked up his bucket and instructed Hialeah where to water. Hialeah nodded her head in understanding. She walked off a short distance to water the rotted tobacco while Jackson picked up his bucket and headed in another direction. Jackson briefly kept a watchful eye on Hialeah. He could hear her humming as she worked alone. Satisfied that there would be no more trouble, Jackson returned to his watering. He dipped his ladle in his bucket and poured what remained of his mixture onto one of the plants. Jackson peered over his shoulder. Hialeah was still watering. He needed to refill his bucket and walked through the tobacco leaves.

Hialeah continued humming as she worked. She was so caught up in making sure that each plant was thoroughly watered, she wandered away from where she and Jackson had started. The sun was beaming down on her. Hialeah wiped the sweat from her face and momentarily looked up toward the sky. When she returned her attention to her work, she was standing next to a familiar face. Hialeah's face lit up. She smiled from ear to ear. "Ruby. Hensci (Hins-cha) Hello." Hialeah said excitedly; her joyous greeting was ignored. Ruby quickly picked up her bucket and began walking the way she had come. Hialeah frowned and hastily began to follow after Ruby. Ruby stopped short and kept her back to Hialeah. "Please don't follow me." Ruby said softly. "What's the matter?" Hialeah replied concerned by her friend's tone. "I can't talk to you." Ruby remarked. "I'm sure Mr. Harding won't mind if we talk a spell." Hialeah replied. Ruby turned to face Hialeah. "It ain't got nothin' to do with Mr. Harding." Ruby said. "Then what is it?" Hialeah asked. "Word done spread all around here that you attacked Miss Violet." Ruby replied.

"She tell you not to speak to me?" Hialeah asked. "I've known Miss Violet since I was a girl. If folks see me talkin' to you…" Ruby began. "I thought we were friends." Hialeah replied. Ruby simply shook her head and walked away. Hialeah watched Ruby walk away before somberly returning to her place in the tobacco field.

From where he stood, Jackson witnessed the brief exchange. He watched as Hialeah walked slowly back to her bucket. Jackson walked the short distance back to Hialeah. She quickly turned her back and continued with her watering when she noticed Jackson heading her way. Jackson was not amiss to Hialeah's sudden gesture. "How's it coming?" Jackson asked. Hialeah took a moment to clear her throat before she answered. "It's coming just fine." Hialeah replied, her throat slightly raspy. Jackson's brow furrowed at the saddened tone of Hialeah's voice. "A friend of yours?" Jackson asked curiously. Hialeah kept watering with her back towards Jackson. "It's awful hot out." Hialeah replied ignoring Jackson's question. "Hialeah, your bucket is empty, now answer me please." Jackson said sternly. "I don't wanna talk." Hialeah replied softly. Jackson set his bucket down and turned Hialeah to face him. Her eyes had filled with tears. "What happened?" Jackson asked. "She wasn't truly my friend." Hialeah replied. "Of course she was." Jackson remarked. "You don't always have to put on a façade of toughness." Jackson said. "I don't know what that mean. But I am tough; strong too; just like my mama and daddy taught me to be." Hialeah replied defensively. "That you are, but we all need someone there for us." Jackson remarked. "I got you ain't I?" Hialeah asked. Jackson grinned and nodded his head. "That you do." Jackson replied. "Then I don't need nobody else." Hialeah remarked matter-of-factly. Before Jackson could respond, the bell for the workers to break for lunch rang. Jackson smiled. "Alright then my tough girl, let's have lunch." Jackson said.

Hialeah welcomed the break. She was practically starving from the hours of work that she had put in. They both left their buckets and pails in the tobacco field. There would surely be more work to do after lunch. Hialeah walked closely next to Jackson as they headed to the lunch line. They crossed paths with Ruby on their way. Hialeah avoided making contact with her now former friend. If her altercation with Violet could so easily come between her friendship with Ruby, then she would let Ruby have her way. She refused to beg anyone to remain friends with her.

Jackson quickened his pace to a near run. Confused as to why Jackson had begun to run, Hialeah followed. "What you runnin' for?" Hialeah asked curiously. "Look around." Jackson replied. Hialeah glanced around her. Practically all of the workers were trying to get to the line in a hurry. "Mama Lilly's prepared chicken and dumplings for lunch. The best you've ever tasted." Jackson rushed out smiling. He and Hialeah were two of the first to reach the line. Out of breath, Jackson doubled over laughing. "I thought you said runnin' wasn't lady-like." Hialeah replied. Jackson looked over at Hialeah. "When Mama Lilly prepares chicken and dumplings, all manners go out the window." Jackson remarked lightly. Finally able to catch his breath, Jackson stood to his full height. Miss Lilly spotted Jackson in the line and was none too pleased about him standing in line for food that he paid for. "Jackson, what do you think you're doin'?" Miss Lilly asked sternly. "I'm waiting for some of your chicken and dumplings." Jackson replied smiling. "Well you just take yourself right on inside. I have your lunch prepared for you in the dinin' room." Miss Lilly remarked. Jackson thought this would be the perfect time to have some fun with Miss Lilly. "Can't I stay out a little longer with my good mates?" Jackson asked mockingly. His child-like questioning received laughter from his workers. "On'ry is what you are. Just downright on'ry." Miss Lilly replied. Jackson joined in on the laughter. He loved getting a rise out of Miss Lilly. "Well you suit yourself, you hear? You take yourself right on and sit down. I'll bring your lunch to you." Miss Lilly demanded. "Yes ma'am." Jackson replied smiling. "Why you anger her like that?" Hialeah asked. "I can't help but to get her goat up. I love her dearly." Jackson replied. "Well if you weren't so big, I think she'd tan your behind." Hialeah remarked. "She tanned it plenty, I assure you." Jackson replied smiling rubbing on his behind. "The way you just riled her, she fixin' to give you another lickin'." Hialeah remarked. Jackson chuckled. "I think you're right. We best take our seats." Jackson replied. He walked off to take a seat at one of the benches. Hialeah remained in the line. When Jackson realized that Hialeah was not by his side, he turned around and walked back toward her. "Aren't you coming?" Jackson asked. Hialeah glanced around at the other workers before returning her attention back to Jackson. "I think it best if I stay put. I don't want no one thinkin' you favorin' me. I ain't taken too kindly round here." Hialeah replied in a whisper. Jackson nodded his head in agreement. "I'll save you a seat." Jackson replied. Hialeah nodded her head and Jackson returned to the benches set up for lunch.

Miss Lilly made a plate of chicken and dumplings for Jackson just as Hialeah reached the front of the line. Hialeah always felt a tad timid around the older woman. She was highly respected in the colored community. Hialeah could feel her stomach growling as Miss Lilly served her. She lowered her eyes in Miss Lilly's presence. "Lord child, you need fattenin' up." Miss Lilly said smiling as she served Hialeah an extra helping of her chicken and dumplings. Hialeah looked up and grinned nervously. Miss Lilly nodded her head in the direction of where Jackson sat. Hialeah followed Jackson and sat down across from him. Miss Lilly set Jackson's lunch in front of him and poured him and Hialeah a glass of sweet tea. Jackson could barely wait to stick his fork into the meal. He cut a small piece of chicken and popped it into his mouth just as Miss Lilly leaned in close to Hialeah. "I heard what you did to Violet." Miss Lilly whispered. Jackson stopped chewing in fear that Miss Lilly was preparing to reprimand Hialeah for her behavior. "I ain't never liked that woman and I just laughed and laughed." Miss Lilly said lightly. Jackson and Hialeah's eyes nearly jumped from their sockets hearing Miss Lilly's confession. "Mama Lilly, I beg you, don't encourage her." Jackson said. Miss Lilly waved Jackson off. "Oh don't you Mama Lilly me. I said what I said and I meant what I said, you hear?" Miss Lilly replied. "Yes ma'am." Jackson remarked smiling. Miss Lilly then focused her attention on Hialeah. "And you, you keep makin' my boy happy and keep your head up. Stop all this lowerin' of your eyes. You got just as much right to be here as anyone." Miss Lilly said. "And next time that Violet step outta line, you sock her twice. One for you and me." Miss Lilly said matter-of-factly. "Yes ma'am." Hialeah replied. "Honestly, Mama Lilly." Jackson remarked feigning shock. "Shush." Miss Lilly replied walking away from the table. "I said what I said Jackson Harding, I said what I said." Miss Lilly bellowed as she made her way back to the serving line. "I like her." Hialeah said. Jackson laughed.

There was much work to be done after lunch. Hialeah was more than eager to get her hands dirty alongside Jackson and the other women. Even though word had spread about the curse on the tobacco and her attack on Violet, Hialeah was fascinated by the women who worked in the tobacco fields; including the women she had threatened earlier. The chrysanthemum mixture had all been used to water the diseased tobacco. Jackson worked closely with Hialeah. He instructed her to fill carts with tobacco so they could be moved to the curing barn. Hialeah worked diligently. She had filled four carts of tobacco while most of the men were only on their second cart. Jackson had been told by Joseph how proficient Hialeah was in the field but to witness her speed with his own eyes was impressive to say the least. Sweat poured from Jackson's face as he tried to keep up with Hialeah's pace. Many of the men who worked next to Hialeah were taken aback by her ability to fill cartloads of tobacco. Jackson couldn't help but to smile as the grunts from the men were replaced with profane words. Hialeah found the men's obscene words amusing. She laughed to herself as to not offend anyone. It was evident that the men hated being outdone by a woman. Jackson needed a moment. He had no issue in admitting to himself that Hialeah bested him in the field. He stopped to stretch his body after hours of nonstop grueling work.

Hialeah looked over at Jackson and smiled. She mimicked Jackson's stretch and he burst out laughing. They exchanged playful smiles and winks at one another. Their flirtatious glances were unknowingly witnessed by several of the women in the field. Hialeah recognized some of the women from church and she waved in their direction. When the women turned their heads as if they didn't recognize her, Hialeah dismissed their snub with a hunch of her shoulders and continued with her work. Jackson witnessed the women's dismissal and was proud that Hialeah refused to allow it to bother her.

Jackson's admiration of Hialeah was short lived. Georgina was being escorted by Lucas over to where Jackson stood. Jackson could hear his mother's voice as she walked by the workers thanking them for their hard work and dedication. "Mother." Jackson said. Hialeah heard Jackson and followed his gaze. She immediately became terrified and knelt down in the tobacco leaves to hide from Jackson's mother. Jackson noticed Hialeah the fear on Hialeah's face. His mother had not been kind to her but he would not stand by and allow Hialeah to be humiliated by his mother in front of his workers. He took what seemed like two giant steps over to Hialeah. His shadow completely covered Hialeah. Hialeah gazed up and saw that Jackson held his hand out for her to take. She was reluctant to take it. "Remember what Mama Lilly said. Head and eyes up." Jackson said reassuringly. "Jackson." Georgina called out. "Come on." Jackson said. Hialeah, still somewhat nervous, nodded her head and accepted Jackson's hand. Jackson assisted Hialeah to her feet. Hialeah removed her hand slowly from Jackson's and clasped both her hands behind her back as Jackson walked over a few feet to greet his mother.

Georgina smiled brightly as Jackson approached her. Lucas had left her side and returned to the waiting carriage. "Mother, you're looking well rested." Jackson said; placing a loving kiss on his mother's cheek. "My gentleman of a son flattering his mother." Georgina replied lightly. "I meant every word." Jackson remarked. Georgina playfully tapped Jackson on the arm. Their mother and son exchange was interrupted by a worker who brought an empty cart over to Hialeah. The squeal of the cart's wheels caught Georgina's attention. She turned toward the annoying sound and inhaled a shocked breath at the sight of Hialeah standing on her property. Georgina quickly turned her attention back to Jackson. "What is that woman doing here?" Georgina demanded. She hastily marched over to Hialeah with Jackson on her heels. Georgina stopped directly in front of Hialeah. "I asked you a question. What are you doing on my property?" Georgina demanded once more. Jackson stepped in between his mother and Hialeah. "I invited her here." Jackson replied. "How dare you bring that…that filth to my home?" Georgina remarked outraged. Hialeah nervously reached out and took a hold of the bottom of Jackson's untucked shirt. Jackson felt Hialeah holding on to him. He was sure that her hold on him was a sign of fear. Jackson kept his focus on his mother. "Mother, do mind your words." Jackson said. Georgina gasped, stunned at her son's simple warning. "Miss Nokosi is here because I needed her assistance." Jackson said. "Her assistance?" Georgina replied confused. "Come with me please." Jackson remarked. Hialeah released Jackson's shirt as Jackson escorted his mother over to where the rotted tobacco had been pulled up. Hialeah remained where she stood.

Jackson led his mother to the massive circle that was once filled with tobacco. Georgina gasped. "What is all this?" Georgina asked surprised. "My word, what is happening here?" Georgina replied. "We had an issue, a severe issue with the tobacco." Jackson remarked. "What sort of an issue?" Georgina replied worriedly. "Miss Nokosi referred to it as Black Shank. It's a disease and it attacked a good portion of the tobacco." Jackson remarked. "Well couldn't Joseph handle it?" Georgina asked. "He had never seen anything like it. None of the men had. Miss Nokosi recognized the disease immediately and was prepared to stop it from spreading to the rest of the field. You should be grateful for her assistance and knowledge. Our family would have been in grave peril if it were not for her." Jackson said. "What do you mean?" Georgina asked. "Unfortunately, if the disease had not been stopped, our neighbors and fellow tobacco growers were threatening to burn our crop to the ground to save their own." Jackson replied. Georgina inhaled yet another shocked breath. "We would have lost everything." Jackson said. "Why didn't you tell me sooner?" Georgina asked. "I thought to spare you any more stress. You have enough to deal with concerning father." Jackson replied. "That poor man." Georgina remarked somberly. "I expect, being the upstanding lady that you are, will no doubt express your gratitude to Miss Nokosi." Jackson replied. Georgina pressed her lips together briefly and exhaled. She forced a smile to her lips. "You are…correct." Georgina forced out. She refused to hear any more praise of that woman and her heroic feats. The sooner she got her apology over with, the better.

Hialeah went back to her work putting little effort into her task. She was filled with curiosity as to what Jackson could be telling his mother about her. Hialeah could hear the faint sound of Jackson's voice coming from behind her. "Miss Nokosi." Jackson called out. His booming voice startled Hialeah. She stood upright and clasped her hands in front of her waiting for Jackson and his mother to close the distance between them. Hialeah quickly wiped the sweat from her face and ran her hand down the length of her dress before clasping her hands together again. She could see from where she stood that Jackson's mother was scowling. Hialeah briefly closed her eyes and encouraged herself to not be put off by anything that could possibly come out of the vile woman's mouth. Hialeah caught the attention of some of the other workers. She glanced in their direction and they immediately returned back to their duties. "Miss Nokosi." Jackson said as he and his mother were now standing directly in front of Hialeah. "Yes sir, Mr. Harding." Hialeah replied. "I'd like to formally introduce you to my mother, Georgina Harding." Jackson remarked. "Ma'am." Hialeah said with a nod of her head. She kept her hands clasped as they were covered with dirt. Hialeah immediately felt uneasy as Georgina looked her up and down smugly. She knew she must look an absolute sight compared to Georgina's lavish dress. Jackson could see the nervousness on Hialeah's face. "Mother." Jackson said dryly. His tone was met with a slight huff from Georgina. "My son tells me that you are the one responsible for possibly saving our tobacco." Georgina said. "Yes ma'am." Hialeah replied. "A skill you no doubt acquired from your former master." Georgina remarked. "No ma'am. I'm sure your son here done told you that I ain't ever been no white man's slave. My mama made sure of that." Hialeah remarked. "Well, you are a lucky one, I suppose." Georgina replied. "No ma'am, you're the lucky one." Hialeah remarked. "Indeed I am. Thank you." Georgina replied smugly and left Jackson and Hialeah in the field. Jackson closed his eyes. "Bloody hell." Jackson said. He opened his eyes to a smiling Hialeah. "You're smiling?" Jackson said. "Of course I am." Hialeah replied. "I surely thought you'd be upset." Jackson remarked. "Not upset. Disappointed." Hialeah replied. "Then I should apologize for my mother's rudeness." Jackson remarked. "I ain't disappointed in your mother. I disappointed in you." Hialeah replied grinning. Jackson raised a curious brow. "Alright, what sort of riddle is this?" Jackson asked. "Ain't no riddle." Hialeah replied. "Then tell me, Miss Nokosi, why are you disappointed in me?" Jackson remarked. Hialeah placed her hands on her hips and twisted her lips at Jackson. "Did you really believe for one moment that your mother would thank a nobody like me for savin' her tobacco?" Hialeah asked. Jackson chuckled at the truth of Hialeah's question. "I had hoped." Jackson replied lightly. "Believe you me, Jackson Harding, that's the most gratitude your mama ever gone show me." Hialeah remarked teasingly. Jackson smiled and leaned in toward Hialeah's ear. "I love you." Jackson whispered. "That true?" Hialeah replied. "Absolutely." Jackson remarked. "Then how bout you go and ask Miss Lilly for her recipe for chicken and dumplings." Hialeah replied playfully. Jackson burst into laughter. "Alright. I'll do just that." Jackson remarked.

The bell clang once more for the workers to end their work day. Jackson escorted Hialeah back to her horse. Hialeah climbed over the fence and frowned regrettably at what she had just done. She turned to face a grinning Jackson. "I suppose ladies don't climb over fences." Hialeah said. Jackson couldn't hold back his laughter. "What you laughin' for?" Hialeah asked pouting. "Miss Nokosi, you rode here bareback, punched one of my employees and threatened several others." Jackson replied teasingly. Hialeah frowned. "You saved my tobacco and you're incredible." Jackson remarked before jumping over the fence. Hialeah grinned girlishly. Jackson untied Hialeah's horse's war bridle from the fence and handed it to her. He was still very much impressed that she was able to ride in such a fashion. Hialeah held the war bridle in her hands and started to climb on the fence for assistance onto her horse. Jackson playfully rolled his eyes and took a hold of Hialeah's waist and lifted her onto her horse. "No more climbing fences." Jackson said mockingly. Hialeah twisted her lips in annoyance. Jackson's assistance on her horse forced her to sit side saddle. Jackson knew Hialeah was about to object to his choice of her riding style. "Side saddle, Miss Nokosi. Gentle ladies ride side saddle." Jackson said. "Then side saddle it is, Mr. Harding." Hialeah replied.

Several wagon loads of Jackson's employees drove down the road passing Jackson and Hialeah on their way from the Harding property. Their little meeting turned the heads of every worker as they rode by. Violet glared daggers at her attacker as she and Joseph drove by. Once their wagon was out of sight, Hialeah burst into laughter. "Miss Nokosi." Jackson said with an arch of his brow. Hialeah straightened up hastily and wiped the smile from her lips. Her immediate change of demeanor caused Jackson to chuckle. He took a hold of Hialeah's war bridle and glanced up at her with a devilish smirk on his face. Jackson began to toy with the bottom hem of Hialeah's dress while keeping his eyes fixed on Hialeah's. He slowly slid the hem up revealing a good portion of Hialeah's leg before she playfully slapped his hand away. "I do wonder, Miss Nokosi, if you've had enough of me." Jackson said his voice seductively low. Hialeah pressed her lips together. The seducing gaze of Jackson's hazel eyes had her loss for any words. "I have some work that will keep me here for a time." Jackson said. Hialeah decided to play her own game. She sat upright on her horse. "Maybe I ain't up to receivin' visitors, Mr. Harding." Hialeah replied casually. Her reply brought yet another sinister smirk to Jackson's lips. "I assure you, Miss Nokosi, you'll receive me over and over until there's no more of me to give." Jackson remarked. Hialeah's voice had momentarily left her. Jackson's deep vow of total control over her body sent tingles of sensation throughout Hialeah's body. "It ain't proper like for you to speak that way, Mr. Harding." Hialeah replied mockingly. "I assure you Miss Nokosi; I don't plan on being proper. It's been far too long since I have felt you beneath me. I plan on making you scream my name in utter and absolute ecstasy." Jackson remarked. Hialeah could feel her body burning with intensity as she turned her horse for home. "Miss Nokosi." Jackson said. Hialeah looked over her shoulder at Jackson. "I am a man of my word." Jackson remarked. Hialeah turned away from Jackson and smiled as she rode away.

Hialeah was relieved and excited to have made it home. After a soothing and much needed bath, she was exhausted. She had slipped on a light night gown to keep cool and nestled in her bed as the sun began to set. Hialeah half-heartedly prayed that Jackson's work would keep him occupied for the night. She hadn't the strength to take him on yet his vow to make her scream his name after several weeks of not having him touch her excited her body beyond belief. Grateful for her simple prayer as the day faded away into night, Hialeah fell asleep alone in her bed only to be awakened a few hours later by the sound of footsteps on the other side of her bedroom door. Hialeah hastily sat upright in her bed and inhaled sharply. The glowing light from the other room allowed her to see the shadowy figure walking around. Hialeah remained frozen in her bed until she heard the footsteps stop and the sound of a chair scraping against her floor. She cautiously threw the covers from her body and crept from the bed. Hialeah took two steps and groaned inward as the floor beneath her creaked under her weight. Hastily making her way to her dresser, Hialeah quickly retrieved her dagger and pressed herself against the wall.

She could hear the sound of her heart racing as the footsteps came closer to her door. Hialeah held her dagger tightly. The sound of her doorknob turning sent chills of terror through her skin. She had never killed anyone before but any intruder was fair game in her eyes. Her bedroom door was opened slightly. Hialeah held her breath and watched as the unwelcomed guest stepped into her room. Hialeah nervously bit into her bottom lip. The silhouette of the man was enormous in stature. Hialeah watched anxiously as the man walked further into her bedroom. She gathered her wits about her waiting for the precise moment to strike. "Miss..." Jackson began. Hialeah leaped from the shadows screeching the war cry her father had taught her and charged after her would be attacker pouncing on him like a wild cat. She wrapped her legs around his waist toppling them onto her bed. Hialeah straddled the man and pressed her dagger against his throat. "You make one move mister and I'll run this here knife straight through and cut off your wretched member and feed it to my pigs." Hialeah said threateningly. "Then I wager you don't want children is what you're saying?" Jackson replied teasingly. "Jackson!" Hialeah remarked shocked that she nearly killed the man she loved. "You are indeed a brutal hell cat." Jackson replied. "What you doin' here this hour?" Hialeah remarked. "Being absolutely still as to not have my throat ran through and my member cut off." Jackson replied teasingly. Hialeah leaned over and placed her dagger on the small night stand. Out of imminent danger, Jackson placed his hands around Hialeah's waist and lifted her from his body. Hialeah twisted her lips in the semi darkness of her room as Jackson held her in the air. "Miss Lilly right bout you." Hialeah said. "How's that?" Jackson replied. "You just downright on'ry." Hialeah remarked. Jackson lowered Hialeah to meet his lips with a soft kiss. "Amongst other things." Jackson replied low. "Jackson Harding, you gone put me down or ain't you?" Hialeah asked.

Jackson placed Hialeah against his chest and rose from the bed. Hialeah wrapped her legs around Jackson's midsection and her arms around his neck. He carried her from the bedroom into her small living area where a half eaten slice of apple pie set on the table. Hialeah looked up at Jackson. He smiled and gave her a flirtatious wink before sitting down in the chair with Hialeah nestled on his lap. Jackson picked up the fork and resumed eating his sweet treat. Hialeah grinned. "I think you got it bad for apple pie." Hialeah said. "I honestly can't help but to have it when Mama Lilly prepares it." Jackson replied smiling. Hialeah broke off a piece of the crust and popped it into her mouth. "Good isn't it?" Jackson said. "Mmm hmm." Hialeah replied. "You know you really ought to lock your door. Some apple pie obsessed mad man might find his way to your door." Jackson said. "I right sure one just did." Hialeah replied smiling. She leaned against Jackson's chest and the sound of crushing paper slightly startled her. Hialeah rose up and frowned curiously at Jackson before taking it upon herself to open his coat. She retrieved the letter from his father's investors and moved away quickly before Jackson could take it from her. "What's this?" Hialeah asked curiously. "The letter from my father's investors that I told you about." Jackson replied. Hialeah began to read the letter. Jackson stood up hastily dreading for Hialeah to reach the bottom of the letter. "Hialeah, please return it." Jackson said. Hialeah moved away from Jackson's grasp. She used her table as a barrier to keep Jackson at bay. "Hialeah, I beg you to not read it, please." Jackson remarked. Hialeah looked at Jackson in utter devastation. Jackson exhaled and briefly closed his eyes. Hialeah placed the letter on the table and walked slowly toward her bedroom. "Wait." Jackson said. Hialeah stopped walking but kept her back toward Jackson. "Why you ain't tell me the truth?" Hialeah asked softly. "I thought to spare your feelings." Jackson replied. "Spare my feelins' or save your daddy's business?" Hialeah remarked. "Forgive me." Jackson replied. "They say they don't want you with no colored woman." Hialeah remarked. "What they want doesn't matter to me." Jackson replied. "Then why you keep the truth from me?" Hialeah demanded. "What do you want me to say? I can't change the minds of foolish people who don't want us to be together. I can't make them see that you're more than the color of your skin." Jackson replied. "I don't expect you to change nothin' bout them folks. I expect you to tell me the truth." Hialeah remarked in frustration. Jackson walked over to Hialeah and embraced her from behind. Hialeah turned around in Jackson's arms and laid her head against his chest. "The truth is, I am hopelessly in love with you Hialeah Nokosi, and I pray you to know this." Jackson replied soothingly. Hialeah nodded her head slowly. "Nothing will keep me from you. Not my father, my mother or any one of my father's investors." Jackson remarked. Hialeah looked up at Jackson. "What bout that ol' Sara Williams?" Hialeah replied. Jackson smiled. "Do I even need to mention her?" Jackson asked teasingly. His question was answered by Hialeah twisting her lips and raising a cocked brow. Jackson chuckled at her gesture. "Not even that ol' Sara Williams." Jackson replied mockingly using Hialeah's words to describe Sara. Satisfied that Jackson had included Sara into his promise, Hialeah laid her head back against Jackson's chest. "This just business, huh?" Hialeah asked. "Nothing more." Jackson replied. "You gone keep company with her while those investors here?" Hialeah asked. "Would it upset you terribly if I were seen in her company?" Jackson replied. "Would it upset you terribly if I pulled her hair out and gave her a sound poundin'?" Hialeah remarked. Jackson burst into laughter. "Would it be proper of me to admit that I would pay handsomely to see such an event?" Jackson replied. "How handsomely?" Hialeah remarked. "You'll not fight her." Jackson replied lightly. Hialeah looked up at Jackson's smiling face. "No fighting." Jackson replied adamantly. Hialeah simply hunched her shoulders and returned to the table to finish off Jackson's pie.

Jackson remained standing by Hialeah's bedroom door. He dreaded questioning Hialeah about his discussion with Sara and her mother having bore a son to Judge Williams but if they were going to speak truths, then she would hear his. Hialeah looked over at Jackson. His face had gone from amusing to somber. "It's only right that you share you know." Hialeah said teasingly as she ate what was left of Jackson's pie. Jackson ran his hands down the length of his face and exhaled. Hialeah didn't like the look on Jackson's face. "What's wrong?" Hialeah asked curiously. Jackson was reluctant to speak. "Jackson?" Hialeah said. "There's something else I need to ask you." Jackson replied. "I don't like the way you sound." Hialeah remarked.

"I don't know where to begin." Jackson replied. Hialeah's brows furrowed. "Jackson, you scarin' me." Hialeah remarked. Jackson exhaled once more. "Please say somethin'." Hialeah replied. Jackson nodded his head. "Alright. Alright." Jackson said. Hialeah slid the empty pie plate away from her. She didn't like whatever it was that was eating at Jackson. "Maybe it best if you come sit down." Hialeah said calmly. "It won't make a difference." Jackson replied. Hialeah nodded her head. "Hialeah, did your mother ever speak to you about Judge Williams?" Jackson asked. "Why you askin' bout my mama, Jackson?" Hialeah replied. "Because I need to know." Jackson replied. "You don't need to know nothin' but what I've told you." Hialeah remarked adamantly. "You asked me moments ago to tell you the truth. I'm asking you to do the same." Jackson replied. "My mama livin' free. Don't make no never mind what Miss Sara say bout her." Hialeah remarked sternly. "I need to understand why you and Sara harbor such hatred for one another." Jackson replied. "Cause she evil." Hialeah spat. Jackson cocked a curious brow. "Evil? Then you do know?" Jackson asked. "What I know?" Hialeah demanded. "About the story of your mother. That your mother bore a child to Judge Williams three years before you or Sara was born." Jackson replied. Hialeah's eyes widened. "Who tell you that lie?" Hialeah fired out. "That Sara tell you that?" Hialeah demanded. "She did and it's the truth." Jackson replied calmly. "You go away from here with those lies!" Hialeah yelled. "I will go nowhere until you have heard the truth!" Jackson fired back. "What truth? Ain't no truth in what that woman say." Hialeah replied angrily. "Hialeah, could your mother have loved Judge Williams?" Jackson remarked sternly. "She would never love that vile man." Hialeah spat. "How do you know?" Jackson asked. "Cause I seen the markins' on her back. That monster raped my mama again and again and he whip her for runnin' away. That sound like love to you?" Hialeah demanded. "No." Jackson replied in utter disgust. "My mama ain't never lied to me bout nothin'." Hialeah said softly. "I no doubt believe that she wanted to protect you from the truth. Hialeah, she had a son and he was sold and died some time later." Jackson replied gently.

The devastated look on Hialeah's face tore at Jackson's very soul. Hialeah covered her face with her hands and burst into tears. Jackson was desperate to comfort Hialeah but thought it best to give her some time. "Why you tellin' me this?" Hialeah asked through her tears. "Sara informed me that she had never mentioned it to you." Jackson replied. Hialeah removed her hands from her tear soaked face and looked at Jackson. "She taunt me bout it when she first seen me." Hialeah remarked somberly. Jackson's brows furrowed in confusedly. "What do you mean?" Jackson asked. "I ain't never understand what she meant. Before you come here, I ask her for work one day when she out shoppin' with her daddy. He look at me strange like. Like he knew me. Then he ask me if I knew a woman named Annie. I tell him that my mama named Annie; that she from around here. He just nod his head and walk away from me. He leave Sara outside the tobacco store with me. She give me a smug look; start walkin' around me. She touch my hair then she ask me if I some sort of half-breed. I ain't want to upset her none cause I lookin' for work. I tell her bout my daddy and she turn her nose up at me. When Judge Williams come back out, I ask him how he know my mama. That when she laugh in my face and tell me my mama was her daddy's slave. I just run away. I was so scared. From then on, she would see me and tell me how my brother was better than me cause he had white man's blood in him and not savage blood like me." Hialeah replied. "She told you that?" Jackson asked. "I tell her that I ain't got no brother and she laugh at me all snide like. I ain't ever give it much thought but she stop her tauntin' when you arrive." Hialeah replied. "I'm sorry." Jackson remarked. "Did he kill my brother?" Hialeah asked softly. "No, but he is dead. Has been for some time now." Jackson replied. "What was his name?" Hialeah asked. "I don't know. He was sold as an infant. I'm not sure when he passed on." Jackson replied. Hialeah nodded her head slowly. She didn't wish to hear any more. Hialeah stood from the table. Defeated, she walked toward Jackson. Jackson took her hand and placed a gentle kiss on the back of it. "I'll leave you." Jackson said releasing her hand only to have his taken by Hialeah. "I don't want you to go." Hialeah replied. "Then I'll stay." Jackson remarked. "I'll be along shortly." Jackson remarked. Hialeah released Jackson's hand and entered her darkened bedroom. Jackson stepped onto Hialeah's porch and reached into his coat pocket and pulled out a cigar and matches. Jackson lit his cigar and puffed on it leisurely while contemplating his next move. Gazing into the night sky, Jackson's conversation with Hialeah ran through his mind. Hialeah's teary face and confession began to take its toll on Jackson. Hearing Hialeah admit that Sara had taunted her profusely regarding their brother stirred a fire inside of him. Sara lied to him and that was a treacherous mistake.

Jackson extinguished his cigar on the bottom of his boot and tossed it before returning to Hialeah's side. He sat at her small table and removed his coat, boots and socks. He could hear the soft sound of her breathing and didn't want to wake her. She had been through enough. Jackson stood and walked quietly into Hialeah's bedroom and removed his shirt and trousers placing them at the foot of her bed. The gentle light of the moon illuminated Hialeah's sleeping form. Jackson climbed into the bed and wrapped his arm around Hialeah, cradling her against the warmth of his body.

Chapter 11

Jackson awakened alone in Hialeah's bed. He tossed the covers aside and reached for his trousers leaving his shirt at the foot of the bed. Jackson dressed and refreshed himself before leaving the room. Hialeah's front door was wide open. Jackson's heart began to race. He bolted through the front door and scanned his surroundings. Hialeah's barn door was ajar and Jackson rushed toward it only to find it occupied with both of their horses. Fearing that Willie may have gotten to her, Jackson's blood began to boil. He dashed back toward the house and immediately stopped short. Jackson squinted his eyes and exhaled; relieved at the sight before him. He walked toward Hialeah as she sat peacefully uphill in a field of lavender wild flowers; her sleek black hair blowing gently in the morning breeze.

Jackson reached Hialeah and sat next to her. He noticed that she was still wearing her nightgown and was barefoot. Hialeah placed her head against Jackson's shoulder and he wrapped his arm around her. Jackson inhaled the fragrant scent of Hialeah's hair. Hialeah gazed up at Jackson and began to caress his chest. Her soft touch on his skin awakened Jackson's arousal and he took her lips in a kiss. Hialeah moaned faintly and Jackson gently laid her back into the lush field of wild flowers while deepening their kiss. His tongue invaded her mouth and Hialeah's gentle moan now echoed in Jackson's ears. He removed his trousers and slid his hand the length of her silken leg stopping at her woman's cove. Jackson began to tantalize Hialeah's sweet spot inserting two of his fingers deep inside of her. Hialeah's erratic moans of pleasure heightened Jackson's arousal. He could wait no longer to ravage her body. Jackson slowly entered Hialeah's haven and Hialeah arched her back to fully receive him. Jackson growled out a moan of absolute ecstasy as he thrust himself between her satiny folds. Jackson peered down in Hialeah's eyes. "My God, what you do to me." Jackson said placing his arms beneath Hialeah's legs to engage himself deeper inside of her. His hardened shaft and fervent thrusts released erotic moan after moan of pleasure from Hialeah's lips. Jackson took both her hands and placed them above her head holding them in place with his own as he took her savagely. "Jackson." Hialeah cried out arching her back even more to meet Jackson's fierce thrusts. "Are you mine?" Jackson said as he continued to ram his throbbing shaft ferociously inside of Hialeah. "Henka. Henka." Hialeah rushed out breathlessly. "Say it." Jackson demanded. Hialeah's words were lost to her. "Tell me you are mine." Jackson growled out low taking Hialeah mercilessly. Hialeah's cries of uncontrollable pleasure rang throughout the field. "I am only yours." Hialeah cried out. Her admittance to belonging to Jackson fueled him. He could feel his climax rising. Jackson swiftly rolled Hialeah on top of him. He would force her to accept his seed. Jackson wrapped his arms around Hialeah's back bringing her closer to him. He captured her lips in a sinister kiss and hammered his erection further into Hialeah. Every powerful thrust of his shaft Hialeah screamed out his name. "Louder." Jackson demanded. Hialeah obeyed Jackson's command. She screamed out Jackson's name until her own climax exploded through her body. She lied limp against his chest begging for Jackson's release. "Do you wish to receive me?" Jackson growled out before taking Hialeah's lips once more his climax heightening. Jackson tightened his hold on Hialeah and spilled his seed deep within her.

Saturated in sweat and exhausted from their love making, Jackson and Hialeah held each other as the cool breeze brushed over their skin. Hialeah rested her head on Jackson's bare chest and listened to soothing beat of his heart. She hadn't slept very well after their tumultuous conversation and her eyes felt heavy. She found it difficult to keep them open. Jackson gazed down on Hialeah's peaceful form and kissed the top of her head. A light sigh escaped her lips. Jackson rested quietly next to Hialeah while she slept in his arms. He reveled at her beauty and smiled to himself as she was quite the timid appearing mouse while she slept but a ferocious lioness when she was riled. The wind blew tendrils of Hialeah's hair across her face and only when she stirred from the cool air did Jackson carefully slide Hialeah's sleeping form from his chest. He quickly donned his trousers and lifted Hialeah into his arms. Hialeah instantaneously woke from her sleep and peered up at Jackson. "Jackson." Hialeah said quietly. "You need to sleep."

Jackson replied. "There's work to do." Hialeah remarked. "I'll see to it." Jackson replied. "You need me." Hialeah protested. "You won't be much help without rest." Jackson replied. Hialeah hadn't gotten much sleep and knew that Jackson was correct. She nodded her head. "I suppose you're right." Hialeah remarked. Jackson smiled; amused Hialeah had not the strength to fight him over the issue of her needing rest.

Jackson entered Hialeah's home and into her bedroom and placed her gently on her bed. Hialeah curled into a tiny ball and Jackson placed her bed sheet over her. "Promise you'll get some rest?" Jackson asked. With her eyes closed, Hialeah slightly nodded her head. Jackson cocked an amused brow. He knew very well that Hialeah would make an appearance sooner rather than later. Jackson desperately tried to stifle his laughter. He shook his head and left the bedroom. Hialeah waited anxiously for her front door to close. The moment she heard Jackson ride off, she sat up in her bed. She hadn't a moment to lose. Although after Jackson's fervent love making, she was famished. Tossing her bed covers and hurrying to her kitchen, Hialeah dined hastily on the fresh preserves gifted to her by Ruby and a few slices of bread. She poured herself a cup of milk and downed it before racing back to her bedroom to get refreshed and dressed for a day of working in the Harding's tobacco field.

Jackson immediately requested a bath the moment his foot entered the door. The enticing aroma of Miss Lilly's homemade biscuits wafted through his nostrils. One of the younger female maids was heading to the dining room carrying a breakfast tray for Georgina. Jackson stopped her and retrieved the tray to the maid's surprise. She watched stunned as Jackson carried the tray up the grand staircase. Jackson could hear from his bedroom as he undressed his mother ringing her bell to be served her breakfast. He rifled through his mother's tray and ate of its contents smiling and humming as he shoved smoked sausage and fresh baked buttery biscuits into his mouth. Devouring what he wanted of his mother's stolen breakfast and now standing completely naked, Jackson chose his work attire for the day and laid his garments out on the bed. He wrapped his tanned frame in a towel and exited his room nearly colliding with his father's nurse. Her blushing face brought a boyish grin to Jackson's lips. "Good morning." Jackson said sheepishly. "Morning, Mr. Harding." The nurse replied still fully blushing. "Your father is doing much better." The nurse said. "Thank you for your assistance." Jackson replied. The nurse nodded before making her way down the grand stair case while Jackson opted to take the servants stairs which would lead him to the kitchen.

Jackson cautiously stepped into the kitchen. He didn't wish to give Miss Lilly a fright coming through practically naked. Satisfied that the kitchen was empty, Jackson hurried through the door that led to the bathing house. The bathing house didn't offer much space and Jackson couldn't bear being confined to such tight quarters. He closed the thin curtains to allow in the sun yet left the door that led to the outside ajar to take in the fresh air before disrobing from his towel. The water had cooled just perfectly and Jackson stepped in the giant white tub. He let out a long held sigh and sunk beneath the water.

Sara arrived early to accompany Georgina to do some shopping and later to join with their friends for a card game. She hoped to catch Jackson before he began his work on the tobacco crops. Dressed in a light pink summer dress with a matching parasol, Sara was assisted from her carriage by her driver and walked up the steps to the Harding front door. Sara stood in the great hall and waited until she was announced to Georgina by the Harding's butler, Samuel. While she waited, one of the younger maids walked by and Sara inquired as to Jackson's where about. After being told that Jackson was indisposed at the moment, Sara frowned her displeasure prompting the maid to explain that Jackson was bathing. As soon as the maid disappeared to continue on with her duties, Sara hastily made a beeline for the back entrance before the Harding's butler could return.

Hialeah rode her horse back to the north side of the field and dismounted. She handed her reins to one of the footmen and hurried to join the mass of workers that stood around awaiting their instructions for the day's work. She styled her long black hair into two long braids and covered her head with a scarf to keep them in place. Making her way into the middle of the crowd, Hialeah half listened as Jackson's four foremen were giving out orders of what needed to be done. She immediately noticed Ruby standing next to Violet who sported a fresh black eye. Hialeah turned away without as much as a wave to her former friend. She heard a familiar voice coming from behind her and glanced over her shoulder to find Isaac standing a few feet behind her chatting with another worker. They locked eyes briefly. Isaac smirked in Hialeah's direction and whispered into the guy's ear. He raised his eyebrows in surprise and chuckled at whatever it was that Isaac had told him. Hialeah quickly returned her attention to the foremen but found herself unable to focus on what was being said. She glanced around the crowd in search of Jackson.

The workers were broken into four groups. Hialeah was placed into the group led by the snobby foreman who questioned her knowledge of Black Shank. Although she detested the man, she was grateful that she wasn't working alongside Violet. She would find it most difficult to work without laughing at the women's well deserved black eye. Hialeah walked along with the other workers to the east side of the field. Her skin began to crawl as Isaac's and his companion's voices wafted to her ears. She could hear both men laughing and she fought the urge to demand to know what was so amusing but she kept silent and stood tall and continued walking to her destination. She refused to allow Isaac's spiteful behavior ruin her day and no doubt humiliate her in front of complete strangers. Hialeah quickened her pace to separate herself from Isaac. Her attention was instantly drawn away from Isaac by the appearance of Sara. Hialeah furrowed her brows curious as to what Sara would be doing in the tobacco field. She intensely glared in Sara's direction and twisted her lips as Sara crept into the small room near the cook house.

Sara was pleasantly surprised to see Jackson in all his naked glory as he bathed. His eyes were closed and his face was covered with soap. Sara took great delight in the massive size of Jackson's toned and tanned chest. She was rather grateful that the Hardings kept up with the maintenance of their home. She was half expecting the door to squeal and give her away. Feeling quite naughty, Sara tiptoed quietly around the back of the tub and dropped to her knees behind Jackson. Hialeah quietly crept to the door and peeked inside. Sara smirked smugly in Hialeah's face as she ran her hands down Jackson's chest.

Startled by the intrusion, Jackson bolted up from the tub exposing his bare back side Sara. "Bloody hell!" Jackson rushed out to a laughing Sara. "My my Jackson. You are all man." Sara said seductively. She quickly stood to her feet and clapped. Hialeah angrily barged into the room and grabbed Jackson's towel that set on a chair near the tub and tossed it onto his head. Jackson hastily wiped the soap from his eyes and face. Hialeah glared daggers at him before racing from the bathing house.

He immediately turned his focus on Sara who stood near the door smiling. "What the fuck are you doing here?" Jackson exploded. Sara playfully pouted her lips. Jackson swiftly covered his member with the towel. "Why should she be the only one to get a glimpse of the mighty Jackson Harding?" Sara replied smirking. "Get the hell out of here." Jackson remarked heatedly. "It was a pleasure." Sara replied haughtily before taking her leave. Her wicked laughter as she left echoed in Jackson's ears. Jackson angrily threw his towel on the ground. "Fuck!" Jackson yelled.

Seething with utter rage, Jackson stepped out of the tub and quickly retrieved his towel. He furiously wrapped it around his body and burst through the door that led to the kitchen startling Miss Lilly and the other maids. "Where is she!" Jackson exploded. Not one to exercise patience, Jackson rushed through the kitchen door followed by Miss Lilly and her staff. Georgina stood wide eyed in the great hall next to a smirking Sara. "Jackson, where on Earth are your clothes?" Georgina said surprised to see her son in practically nothing. Jackson ignored his mother's question. His eyes stared icy daggers into Sara. Jackson's booming voice drew every servant in the house to the great hall. "Who in the bloody hell do you think you are!" Jackson yelled. "Jackson, do lower your voice." Georgina replied sternly. "How could you be so foolish as to believe I would ever consider marrying such a vicious and evil liar is beyond me." Jackson spat. "Jackson this is not the time or place..." Georgina began. "It is the perfect time, mother." Jackson growled out. "Miss Williams delights in humiliating others. Indeed this is the perfect time." Jackson spat angrily. "I do not have to stand here and be berated by the likes of you, Jackson Harding." Sara said arrogantly. She turned for the door only to have her escape barred by Samuel. Sara slowly turned around to face Jackson. "You took great pleasure in taunting Miss Nokosi about the death of her brother. A brother she knew nothing about." Jackson growled menacingly. Sara raised her chin in defiance. "So what if I did? That heathen whore is beneath me." Sara spat. "You, Miss Williams, will never be the woman that she is nor will you ever have my heart or share my bed." Jackson replied heatedly. "Jackson." Georgina remarked stunned. "Do not ever come to this house again. You are no longer welcomed here." Jackson said low. "My father will hear about this." Sara threatened. "To hell with you and your father. You should be grateful, Miss Williams. Hialeah wanted to rip your hair out and give you the sound pounding you so rightfully deserve. Go near her again, and I'll not stop her." Jackson replied. He nodded his head toward Samuel who opened the door for Sara. Sara scoffed and left the Harding home in a huff.

Georgina marched up to Jackson stunned and upset by her son's inappropriate behavior. "Jackson Harding, just what is going on here?" Georgina demanded looking around at her servants. "Get back to work. All of you." Georgina ordered. She waited until the servants had gone back to their respective duties before continuing. "How dare you mistreat a guest in this house in such a manner?" Georgina said. "She is not the innocent woman you claim her to be and I'll not have you in her company." Jackson replied sternly. "You will not tell me who I can and cannot keep as company." Georgina spat. "Father has placed me in charge of your well being and until he has recovered, I will do just that." Jackson replied harshly. Wanting no more to do with the horrendous ordeal, Jackson took his leave and made his way up the stairs. Georgina jumped at the slamming of Jackson's door.

Jackson angrily paced the length of his room. He needed a moment to calm himself before seeking out Hialeah. He barely caught a glimpse of her before she ran out of the bathing house. Jackson let out a yell of pure frustration. He was on the verge of going mad. He wanted nothing more than to leave South Carolina and all that it was behind him. He regretted allowing his father to talk him into running the house and the Harding business. What he regretted most of all was not being able to take Hialeah far away from the madness that surrounded her. Jackson sat on the edge of his bed and buried his head in his hands. He sat frozen in the same spot for nearly an hour cursing Sara's very existence. A knock on his door brought Jackson from his thoughts. "I do not wish to be disturbed." Jackson said sternly. "A message was just sent from the Williams' house." Samuel replied from the other side of the door. "Enter." Jackson remarked curious as to what new threat Judge Williams had issued upon him. Samuel entered Jackson bedroom and Jackson stood. He took the message and read it. Jackson angrily crumbled the letter. "Has my mother seen this?" Jackson asked. "No sir. I was instructed to give it to you straight away." Samuel replied. "Thank you." Jackson remarked. Samuel nodded and left Jackson alone.

Jackson hastily dressed and raced from his room and barreled down the main stairway yelling for his mother. Georgina hurried from the library and into the grand hall. "Jackson whatever are you carrying on about?" Georgina asked slightly annoyed at having been interrupted from her reading. "The bloody bastard has gone mad." Jackson replied handing his mother Judge Williams' note. Georgina gasped in horror after reading the letter from Judge Williams. "Surely he can't be serious." Georgina replied. "I fear he is. The fool has challenged me to a duel to the death in three days for insulting Sara." Jackson remarked. "I'll have Lucas drive me over. I'll speak with him." Georgina replied. "No. His battle is with me. I'll go." Jackson remarked. "You'll do no such thing. You're far too hot headed to speak rationally. Besides, he's a close neighbor and dear friend of your father's. I know I can reason with him." Georgina replied. "Someone had best reason with him. I'll not have the blood of an elder and fellow judge on my hands." Jackson remarked. "I'll simply tell him out of respect for your father and their long standing friendship, you have declined his challenge." Georgina remarked handing the message back to Jackson. Jackson stuck the message into his trouser pocket. "A moment, mother." Jackson said. He rushed into his father's study and grabbed a sheet of writing paper and his father's fountain pen. Jackson took a moment and sat down to write down his refusal to duel taking Judge Williams' age and his friendship with his father into consideration. He also sent his deepest apologies for his crass treatment of Sara and regret that he had no desire to wed her.

Jackson signed the letter and left his father's study. He handed the letter to his mother. "You do realize this is all happening on account of that woman you insist on parading around?" Georgina said matter-of-factly. Jackson resented his mother's words. "I am not parading Miss Nokosi around." Jackson spat. "If you would just marry Sara as everyone expects…" Georgina began. "No!" Jackson fired back. "What everyone expects means nothing to me." Jackson growled out. "I love Miss Nokosi. My heart and all that I am belongs to her." Jackson said low. Georgina scoffed. "You know nothing of this woman. How can you possibly love her?" Georgina replied incredulously. "Tell me mother. What do you believe me to know of Sara? A woman I had not seen since we were children. A woman who bores me to no end. A woman whose very presence sickens me and shares nothing in common with me aside from the color of our skin. That alone is not enough to make me love her or take her as my wife and I won't." Jackson remarked harshly. "Now please, let Judge Williams know I am most anxiously awaiting his response." Jackson said.

Georgina held her tongue after hearing her son's professed love of Hialeah. She huffed her objection of Jackson's truth and stormed from the house. Samuel closed the door behind Georgina and Jackson made a hasty retreat to his father's study once again. He was in dire need of a drink and some air. Jackson grabbed his father's bottle of gin and stormed out of the house toward the garden cursing Judge Williams and his arrogance and stupidity. He stormed by Hialeah without a glance.

Hialeah inhaled sharply at the sight of Jackson carrying the bottle. She peered over her shoulders hoping no one would notice her absence and hurried after Jackson whom had already removed the cork from the bottle and had taken a long swig of the liquor as he paced eagerly back and forth awaiting his mother's return. Hialeah crept into the garden and crossed her arms defensively before clearing her throat to gain Jackson's attention. Jackson spun around to face an obvious upset Hialeah. He knew by her disposition that he was in for a tirade. He took another swig of gin. "So is that what you meant by keepin' company with that ol' Miss Sara?" Hialeah demanded. "Miss Nokosi, I assure you you have every right to be sore with me but I am dealing with a most crucial matter." Jackson replied. "Your daddy's investors houndin' you again?" Hialeah remarked. "If it were only that simple." Jackson replied. Hialeah inched closer to Jackson. She could see in his face that whatever was troubling him was indeed serious. "Well it must be somethin' awful if it got you out here drinkin' like you doin'." Hialeah remarked. Jackson walked over to Hialeah and dug into his pocket. He handed Hialeah the message. Hialeah briefly looked into Jackson's disturbed eyes before turning her attention to the message. Her eyes widened in shock. "Is this true? A duel?" Hialeah said stunned. "Indeed it is. At Milliner's Pond." Jackson replied taking another drink from the bottle. Hialeah frowned her displeasure at Jackson's drinking. "Well that ain't gone help none." Hialeah remarked. "It helps plenty." Jackson replied. "I ain't got no care for the man on account of what he did to my mama but it ain't for me to judge him none either." Hialeah remarked. "What are you saying?" Jackson asked. "What I sayin' is you gotta stop this. Why that man ain't fit to duel someone your age." Hialeah replied. "He's a bloody fool." Jackson remarked. "Why ain't you over there puttin' a stop to this?" Hialeah asked. "My mother believes me to be hot headed and thought it best if she speaks in my stead." Jackson replied. "For once, I agree with her." Hialeah remarked. "What in bloody hell is taking so long?" Jackson said annoyed.

No sooner than the words left Jackson's lips, Samuel tapped on an upstairs window to catch Jackson's attention. Jackson and Hialeah both looked up as Samuel gestured for Jackson to come inside. Jackson groaned. Both his family and the Williams were close neighbors, however, his mother had not been gone long enough to have a conversation with Mr. Williams. "That was too quick. Stay here." Jackson said before handing Hialeah his bottle of gin. "And no, that is not what I meant by keeping company." Jackson replied before rushing off to learn the outcome of his letter. Hialeah sat on one of the benches in the garden to await Jackson's return. Inside the house, Georgina paced frantically in the main hall. When Jackson entered the house, she rushed to him. "You see what you've done by refusing Sara's hand? He wouldn't even see me." Georgina rushed out. "What do you mean he wouldn't see you?" Jackson asked. "Why Harland was standing right on his front porch when Lucas drove up. He didn't even give me a chance to step one foot out of the carriage. He practically threw me off his property without so much as reading your letter. Why I've never been so humiliated." Georgina replied. "Perhaps I should pay Harland a visit." Jackson remarked. "He was angrier than a swarm of bees." Georgina replied. "Oh I don't doubt it." Jackson remarked casually. "Jackson, do be careful." Georgina replied. Jackson nodded his head. He had some quick business to finish up with Hialeah before he would take his leave.

Jackson called out to Hialeah. She stood and waited for Jackson to enter the garden. Unbeknownst to either of them, Georgina stood gazing down on them from the upstairs window. "I need for you to go home and wait for me." Jackson said. "What for?" Hialeah replied. "I must pay a visit to Judge Williams." Jackson remarked. "What you gone do?" Hialeah asked worriedly. "Try to reason with the fool." Jackson replied. "Please wait for me." Jackson said. "Alright. You'll be careful won't you?" Hialeah replied. "I will." Jackson remarked. Georgina's heart nearly leapt from her chest as she watched her son embrace then gently place a kiss on Hialeah's lips.

Jackson rode the short distance to the Williams' property. He could hear the firing of gunshots as he rode up the entrance-way to the main house. He was surprised and yet somewhat relieved to find Sara sitting underneath a tree on a bench reading. Jackson dismounted his horse and Sara stood also surprised to see Jackson at her home. Jackson handed his reins to one of the Williams' footmen and approached Sara. "Mr. Harding, how very bold of you. You throw me from your property and trespass upon mine." Sara said arrogantly. "This isn't a social call." Jackson replied. "Isn't it?" Sara remarked. "No. I need to speak to your father. Where is he?" Jackson replied. Another gunshot rang out in the air. "Don't mind all the fuss. Father's engaged in his favorite activity." Sara remarked. "You don't know do you?" Jackson asked. "Know what?" Sara replied smiling. "That your father has challenged me to a duel to the death in three days." Jackson remarked. Sara's smile faded immediately from her lips. "You wouldn't dare hurt father." Sara replied stunned at Jackson's news. "Did you not hear what I said? This madness has gone beyond mere hurt feelings. Your father is out for blood; my blood, now take me to him." Jackson remarked sternly. "You'll not accept his challenge?" Sara asked hopeful. "My mother tried to decline the challenge on my behalf and he refused to see her." Jackson replied. "Come with me." Sara remarked quickly. Jackson followed Sara to Judge Williams' make-shift shooting range in the back of their home.

Judge Williams was joined by two of his colored male servants. He was in the middle of taking aim at empty bourbon bottles lined on a fence. Sara raced to him while Jackson stood some distance away. He watched as Sara pointed in his direction. Judge Williams handed his pistol to one of the servants and bee-lined his way toward Jackson with Sara on his heels. Jackson stood with his hands clasped behind his back. Judge Williams closed the distance between him and Jackson. Jackson could see from where he stood the look of displeasure on Judge Williams' face. "Get off my property!" Harland yelled. "Not until you cease this bloody foolishness and call off the duel." Jackson replied glaring heatedly at Judge Williams. "I'll call off nothing you arrogant bastard." Judge Williams spat. "You've humiliated my Sara for the last time. I'm going to send your European ass to hell where you belong." Judge Williams said heatedly. "You're doing this for my honor, father?" Sara asked. "Of course I am. I'll see this son-of-a-bitch six feet deep before I allow him to disgrace your good name any further." Judge Williams replied. "I came here to offer my sincerest apologies for my crude manners toward Miss Williams but I will not accept your challenge." Jackson remarked. "It appears that you have the guts to insult my daughter's good character, yet not the guts to fight a man." Harland remarked smugly. Jackson would not be drawn into a game of wits. "Will you or will you not accept my apology and my refusal to duel?" Jackson asked impatiently. "I will not." Harland rushed out angrily. Jackson turned toward Sara. "Do try and talk some sense into your father." Jackson said. "There is nothing that my daughter can say to change my mind." Harland replied. "Then you are a fool." Jackson remarked before turning on his heel and walking away. "If you do not accept my challenge, Judge Harding or shall I call you coward? I will smear the Harding name throughout this county and this state." Harland yelled out. Jackson stopped dead in his tracks and turned to face Harland. "My father is your closest friend and you would dare drag his name through the mud?" Jackson spat. "Maybe your father should have raised a decent son instead of a nigger loving and pathetic bastard." Harland replied smugly. "Perhaps once you're dead, that sweet little savage that you've chosen to replace my Sara with will warm my bed as did her mother." Harland remarked with a sinister smirk on his face. Jackson marched toward Harland and without warning punched him square in the jaw sending a stunned Harland to the ground. Sara's hand flew to her mouth as she hurried to her father's side. Harland's two servants remained in their spots with wide eyes. Jackson stood menacingly over Harland. "I tried to reason with you but no more. If you insist on this bloody madness then I will oblige you, sir. Your challenge is accepted." Jackson growled out. "My weapon of choice; pistols. To the death at first light." Jackson said menacingly. "Please don't do this either of you." Sara pleaded. She turned to her father. "Father." Sara urged. "It is done." Harland spat from his position on the ground. Devastated, Sara burst into tears before racing toward the main house screaming hysterically for her mother. Jackson didn't care much for Sara but even his heart went out to her. He turned to face Harland. "Look at what you're doing." Jackson said low. "What I'm doing is protecting my daughter from scum like you. Now get off my property and if you come back, I'll have you arrested." Harland replied heatedly. "Have it your way." Jackson remarked menacingly and turned to walk away. He stopped suddenly and turned to face Harland. "Tell me Judge Williams, is this madness truly about your daughter's honor or could it perhaps be that you're terribly sore that your former slave, Anna, fled from the forced comfort, if you will, of your bed to the arms of an Indian man and bore him a child out of love unlike the son she bore you from your vicious assault of her body?" Jackson asked smirking. Insulted by Jackson's cruel truth, Harland gritted his teeth. "Get off my property." Harland spat. Undaunted by Harland's tone, Jackson clasped his hands behind his back and thought to torment the older man a bit more. "Or could it perhaps be that you're livid because Anna's child, Miss Nokosi, welcomes me to her bed lovingly; a love that you could never share with her mother because she despised you horribly and cost you dearly when she ran away from your torture? Or could it be that I am correct on both of my theories?" Jackson said. "Get off my property you son-of-a-bitch." Harland spat once again. Jackson grinned and nodded his head sarcastically before leaving Harland with his servants.

Isaac's curiosity got the better of him. He watched Jackson leave in a hurry without Hialeah in tow. He waited until his foreman was occupied and left his position. He found Hialeah sitting on a bench loss in whatever thoughts were going through her mind. Isaac smirked. "You thinkin' bout that white man of yours?" Isaac said cockily. Hialeah jumped from the bench. "Don't you worry none bout what's on my mind." Hialeah replied annoyed by Isaac's intrusion. "You a fool girl if you thinkin' you ever gonna be one of them." Isaac remarked. "I don't wanna be anybody but who the good Lord made me." Hialeah replied adamantly. "Now you know that ain't true. You think cause you openin' your legs for that white man folks gonna start treatin' you like you some prissy white woman? Well it ain't ever gonna happen." Isaac replied mockingly. "How bout you leave me to my business?" Hialeah remarked. "Where you think he done run off to, huh? He gone chasin' after Miss Sara. He fixin' to marry her cause she white and rich, somethin' you ain't never gonna be." Isaac replied arrogantly. Hialeah marched up to Isaac and glared into his eyes. "Maybe it's you who wantin' to be a white man since you all the time talkin' bout 'em." Hialeah remarked smugly with a cocked brow before leaving Isaac alone in the garden. "Maybe you ought to get back to workin' in the white man's field." Hialeah yelled out as she kept on walking.

Hialeah went home as Jackson requested. She sat on her porch unable to hold a single thought. She was worried about Jackson's visit to Judge Williams. Every little sound brought her from her seat. When Jackson finally rode up the dirt road to her home, she bolted from her seat and ran to meet him before he could reach her house. Jackson dismounted quickly from his horse and took Hialeah's arm. Hialeah didn't like the dark scowl on his face. "What happen?" Hialeah asked worriedly. "I hit him." Jackson replied casually. "Jackson." Hialeah remarked surprised. "I want you to pack your things immediately." Jackson said sternly. "What for?" Hialeah replied. "I'm going to send you to my home in London. I've already made the arrangements. The ship leaves in two days time." Jackson remarked. "Monks (Mo-ngs).

No." Hialeah replied in a soft whimper. Jackson cupped her face with his hands. "I had no choice but to accept Judge Williams' challenge. I must know that you're safe." Jackson remarked. Hialeah threw herself into Jackson's arms and held him tight. She gave way to her tears. "Please don't send me away." Hialeah cried pleadingly. "I'll come as soon as all of this foolishness is over." Jackson replied. "I don't know nobody in London." Hialeah remarked sobbing. "You'll be well taken care of, I promise. My servants will see to your every need. Nothing is going to happen to me." Jackson replied reassuringly. "You can't know that." Hialeah remarked tearfully. "Look at me." Jackson replied. Hialeah reluctantly looked up to meet Jackson's hard hazel gaze. "He threatened my family's name and most importantly, he threatened to harm you." Jackson said. "I don't care none what he say. We can leave together." Hialeah replied. "I will not stand by like the coward he deemed me to be and allow any man think to do you harm." Jackson remarked. "I know you real fast with a gun but I just so worried bout you." Hialeah replied. "Don't be. This is a fight I will not lose." Jackson remarked. "Jackson…" Hialeah began. "Your father is a brave man, is he not?" Jackson asked. Hialeah nodded her head. "He would do whatever it takes to protect his family; to protect the woman he loves, your mother, yes?" Jackson said. "Henka." Hialeah replied softly. "Then I will do the same. Do you understand?" Jackson remarked. "I understand." Hialeah replied. "Then do as I have told you." Jackson remarked. Hialeah released her hold on Jackson and took a step back wiping her tears. "My mother would never leave the side of the man that she loves." Hialeah replied. "Hialeah." Jackson said. "If you can speak of the courage my daddy has for my mama then I can speak of the love my mama has for my daddy. She would never leave the man she was spoken for." Hialeah replied. "I beg you do not make this any more difficult for me." Jackson remarked. "Are you spoken for or ain't you, my Jackson?" Hialeah asked adamantly. "I am very much spoken for." Jackson replied. "Then please don't ask me to leave your side." Hialeah remarked. "I am not asking you. I am commanding you to leave." Jackson replied sternly.

Hialeah lowered her head and once more her tears fell. She cried uncontrollably and pleaded with Jackson through her tears; insisting that her place was with him. Jackson closed the short gap between them and wrapped his arms around Hialeah's tiny frame. Her body trembled as she bawled against Jackson massive chest. He could feel the wetness of Hialeah's tears as they soaked through his shirt. Jackson briefly closed his eyes. He prayed that he would not regret his decision. Jackson took Hialeah's hand and she raised her head to meet his now sympathetic gaze as he placed a soft kiss on the back of it. Her eyes were still wet with her tears. "Your place is indeed by my side, but say nothing to anyone and stay clear of Judge Williams. Do you understand?" Jackson asked sternly. Hialeah nodded.

Jackson was too preoccupied with the thought of his impending duel to sleep. After having made love to Hialeah, he cradled her in his arms while she slept. He thought of how his life would be once he and Hialeah left South Carolina and with the pleasant thought of having Hialeah as his wife, he was finally able to drift to sleep if only for a moment. Jackson awoke early. He wanted to get home and then to town to see to the goings on in the Harding warehouse. He left Hialeah a note proclaiming his love for her and made his way home to prepare for the day.

Jackson was surprised and somewhat bothered to find his mother taking an early breakfast on the front porch as he rode up. He dismounted his horse and gave his reins to a footman. He said a silent prayer in hopes that his father would soon be well enough to resume his role as head of his home and other affairs. Each lingering day that he was forced to spend in the company of those who had a disdain for colored people and their heir of superiority of anyone who looked differently than them made him more eager to return to his home in England.

Jackson walked up the steps with no intention of conversing with his mother. Georgina took a sip of her coffee and placed the cup back on the saucer. She waited for Jackson to put his hand on the door handle before she cleared her throat. Jackson straightened to his full height preparing himself for whatever it was his mother had on her mind. "You were with her again?" Georgina said calmly. "Yes, mother I was and I stand by what I said." Jackson replied dryly. "I saw you with her yesterday afternoon before you left for Judge Williams'. You kissed her." Georgina remarked. "Her, mother? She has a name. It's Hialeah, but if you prefer to be formal then by all means address her as Miss Nokosi." Jackson replied sternly. Jackson exhaled his aggravation. "Sit with me." Georgina said. "I am in no mood to match words with you." Jackson replied. "You truly love this Miss Nokosi?" Georgina asked simply. "I do mother and I am well aware of your feelings for Hialeah." Jackson replied. "The way you defended her against me is most honorable and clearly evident that she has indeed captured your heart. She makes you happy. I can see it in your eyes." Georgina remarked. Jackson cocked a curious brow; now interested as to where his mother was going with her assessment of Hialeah.

Jackson kept his back to his mother. "What are you saying, mother?" Jackson asked suspiciously. "I was wrong to assume to know your heart. Sara does not bring out the spark in your eyes as this Miss Nokosi." Georgina said. His curiosity absolutely piqued, Jackson released the door handle and took a seat across from his mother. He found her fruit dish tempting and slid it toward him and began to pick out the blueberries and pop them into his mouth. "Where is this coming from?" Jackson asked curiously. "From my heart." Georgina replied. "I was a fool and a horrible mother to send my precious boy away because you chose to see the beauty in those who did not look as we did or have what we had." Georgina said. "Why are you telling me this now?" Jackson asked. "Because it needs to be said. I have always considered myself a God fearing woman and I turned my back on the gift that the good Lord gave me out of shame and fear of the scandals your actions would have caused this family and here you are taking care of me in my time of need." Georgina replied. "You're my mother." Jackson remarked. "I am a rotten person. I cared more about my reputation than my own child. But I can change my ways starting today." Georgina replied. "How so?" Jackson asked curiously his brows furrowed. His facial expression brought a chuckle from Georgina. "Now don't look at me in such a manner. You go on and get to town and make sure you bring Miss Nokosi back with you after work." Georgina replied lightly. "Why would I do that?" Jackson asked. "Because I would like to have the woman who has stolen my son's heart over for a family dinner." Georgina replied. "Family?" Jackson said in disbelief. "Yes family. You are no doubt going to take her back to England with you and marry her. Or are you simply going to carry on like some uncultured creature?" Georgina replied teasingly. Jackson shook his head to clear his ears. He could not believe what he was hearing. "Who are you?" Jackson asked playfully. Georgina squealed with laughter. "Jackson I want you to be happy believe it or not and clearly Miss Nokosi makes you happy." Georgina replied. "She is a tad stubborn as are you but that she does." Jackson remarked reaching his hand in his mother's fruit dish. Georgina slapped Jackson's hand away playfully. "Go on to work." Georgina said. "If you stay here any longer, I won't have anything left to eat." Georgina replied. Jackson smiled at his mother. He had never heard her speak so affectionately. It was rather refreshing and very much needed. Jackson stood and genuinely desired to place a kiss on his mother's cheek. He leaned in and did just that before taking his leave. Georgina smiled and touched her cheek where Jackson kissed her.

After his unexpected yet heart-felt conversation with his mother, Jackson decided that he would after all dine with his mother for breakfast. Georgina was thoroughly surprised when Jackson returned to her table with a plate of his own. Jackson sat across from his mother and they spoke about his life in England. Georgina frowned when Jackson recanted the many times he had been in lovers' altercations over the multitude of women he had taken away from the men who vied for the attention of the young women that he had stolen away. Her expressions of disbelief brought several bouts of laughter from Jackson. Georgina hated to admit that hearing her son's skills with his fists and his capability with a gun brought her some sense of relief with his impending duel just two days away. She dismissed the horrid event and listened contently to Jackson's wild tales. Jackson entertained his mother until it dawned on him that he hadn't yet bathed or changed for work. He kissed his mother on the cheek once again and bolted upstairs to prepare for his hectic day.

Jackson had Lucas drive him to the office and had a message sent to Hialeah informing her of their dinner engagement later that evening. He made sure to leave out where the engagement would be and requested that she was to be dressed in her best and that Lucas would arrive around five to escort her. Hialeah had read Jackson's note that he had left for her on her table. She was now curious as to where he would be taking her. She busied herself with work around her home to occupy her mind from the thought of sharing an engagement with Jackson but her mind continued to wonder in utter fascination. She had never had a dinner engagement. She wanted to look her very best. Hialeah left her gardening undone and quickly ran inside her house to her bedroom. She hurriedly grabbed the money from her drawer that Jackson had paid her for her crops. She paced around her bedroom momentarily thinking about what she would need to look her best. Hialeah decided that the money would be best spent on new nylons and fresh scented soaps and whatever else she could think of on the way to town. She dreaded another run-in with Willie but put her fear to rest as she knew that Jackson would be in town. If Willie decided to give her any trouble, she was assured that Jackson would best him again.

Jackson stepped out of the carriage and entered his office. He was greeted by Alice, his father's secretary. Alice was a petite woman with brunette colored hair and brown eyes. She was the sister of General Bradford Stevens, one of many men who fought in the war and a very well respected man in the town. Alice was several years older than Jackson and unwed. She was absolutely smitten by Jackson and had a habit of knocking things over whenever Jackson was around. She wasn't much of a looker and Jackson paid her no mind. Jackson wasn't so much concerned about her looks but she was just like everyone else in the town. She had a disgusting habit of turning her nose up at colored folks much like Sara. That in itself was a complete turn-off. Jackson had thought of firing her but her father was very close to his and she was rather efficient at her job.

As soon as Jackson walked into the office, Alice stood and knocked over a small vase of flowers soaking her paper work. "Oh dear." Alice said hurrying to find something to wipe the water up. Jackson cocked an amused brow. "Good morning, Alice." Jackson said sarcastically. "Good morning, Mr. Harding." Alice rushed out nervously. "May I assist you?" Jackson replied. "Uh no. I can handle it. You have a guest waiting for you in your office." Alice remarked. Jackson furrowed his brows. "A guest?" Jackson replied curiously. "Miss Sara Williams." Alice remarked wiping at her soaked papers with a cloth she was able to find in her desk. Jackson took a peek out of the window. He hadn't even realized Sara's carriage was parked outside on the street. "Did she state her business?" Jackson asked. "No sir." Alice replied. "Thank you." Jackson remarked. He had a sinking feeling that his pleasant morning would no doubt be ruined by whatever it was that Sara had come by to discuss.

Jackson left Alice to her cleaning. He climbed the stairs to his office. If Sara was there to speak to him then that could only mean that her father had called off the duel and was sending Sara in his place to inform him. Jackson entered his office to find Sara staring out of the window. He cleared his throat and Sara turned to face him. "Miss Williams, to what do I owe this visit?" Jackson asked. "I want you to call off this nonsense." Sara replied. Jackson crossed his arms. "You're kidding?" Jackson remarked. "Why would I kid about something this serious?" Sara replied. "Sara, your father challenged me. You were there. You know this." Jackson remarked. "Then do the right thing and not show up." Sara replied. Jackson scoffed incredulously. "Not show up?" Jackson asked incredulously. "Yes." Sara replied. "Unbelievable. Did you not hear what your father threatened to do? My family's honor and name are on the line here. Two facts that your father doesn't give a bloody damn about." Jackson remarked. "My father is defending my honor." Sara replied. "He snubbed my mother and refused to accept my apology and my refusal to duel him." Jackson remarked. "He was angry." Sara replied. "Then perhaps you should speak to him." Jackson remarked. "I tried. He wouldn't hear of backing down." Sara replied. "Yet you come here and insist that I cower and have my name drug through the mud and give your father the satisfaction of labeling me a coward?" Jackson asked. "My father is a very important man in this town." Sara replied. "Then he would do well to remember that fact and accept my refusal." Jackson remarked. "I am trying to spare your mother the horrid image of seeing her only son killed right before her eyes. Your father is ill. How much more do you think she can bear?" Sara asked. "You speak as if your father has a chance against me." Jackson replied. "My father practices his shooting daily." Sara remarked. "I am an expert shot. I will not lose." Jackson replied matter-of-factly. "If your father insists on this insanity then I will oblige him. My hands are tied." Jackson replied. "You will not kill my father." Sara remarked adamantly. "Unless he calls this duel off, that is precisely what I'll do." Jackson replied. Sara scoffed and stormed out of Jackson's office slamming the door to add to her frustration.

Hialeah felt like a princess in the Nesbit's store. She purchased what she needed for her engagement with Jackson with no issues from anyone; including Mrs. Nesbit herself. Hialeah topped her shopping day off with a bag of licorice, some sour balls, a light blue parasol and handbag that she was eager to try out, and a new black Gambler hat for Jackson that she had Mrs. Nesbit place in a nice hat box. She couldn't wait for Jackson to open it. The shopping was a much needed distraction from the fact that Jackson would be dueling for his life in two days time. The very thought made Hialeah's shoulders slump. She quickly dismissed the thought and reminded herself that Jackson promised that he would come out of this foolishness alive and well. With her shoulders now straightened and her head held high, Hialeah opened her parasol to block out the sun and continued down the street.

It was such a lovely day that Hialeah chose to walk to the Harding Tobacco Company instead of driving her wagon the short distance to visit Jackson at his office. She was anxious to know just where they would be going for their dinner engagement. Hialeah rounded the corner just as Sara was being assisted into her carriage by her driver. Hialeah lowered her parasol to cover her face. Jackson had warned her to stay clear of Judge Williams. Although he didn't mention Sara in his warning, Hialeah thought it best to stay clear from her as well. As much as she wanted to pound Sara's smug face into the dirt, for Jackson's sake she would decided to hold her temper and refrain from fighting. She was, however curious as to why Sara would be going to meet up with Jackson after what her father was threatening to do.

Hialeah waited impatiently for Sara's carriage to pass her by before she quickened her steps and hurried into the Harding Tobacco office. Hialeah opened the door to Jackson's office and was caught off guard by Jackson's secretary. She had never seen the woman before. Hialeah stopped and quickly shuffled her packages so that she could close her parasol. Alice gasped at the sight of Hialeah and hastily stood. "May I help you?" Alice asked snobbishly as she looked Hialeah up and down. "I...I here to see Mr. Harding." Hialeah stammered out. "And just who are you?" Alice asked. "Miss Nokosi." Hialeah replied. "I don't recognize that name. Do you have an appointment?" Alice remarked smugly. "No ma'am I don't but he is expectin' me." Hialeah replied. "Well if you don't have an appointment just how is he expecting you?" Alice asked arrogantly. Hialeah didn't like the tone of Alice's voice. Whoever this woman is was getting her dander up. Hialeah squared her shoulders and looked Alice straight in the eyes. "He just is." Hialeah replied curtly. "Are you sassing me girl?" Alice remarked. Hialeah exhaled impatiently. "I tryin' to be courteous but you makin' it right hard, now are you goin' to tell Mr. Harding I here or ain't you?" Hialeah demanded. "He isn't here." Alice replied curtly matching Hialeah's equally curt tone. Hialeah hadn't noticed Jackson's horse out front. She wasn't for sure whether Jackson was there or not. Perhaps he stepped out and Sara had missed him too. However, Hialeah didn't trust the rude woman. "Well then I just go on up and see for myself." Hialeah remarked stubbornly. "You stay right there or I'll fetch the law!" Alice yelled. "You go right on ahead and do that." Hialeah spat. She turned on her heel and made her way toward the stairs with Alice following close behind screaming threateningly.

From upstairs in his office, Jackson could hear the ruckus and bolted for the door. He swung the door open and headed for the stairs. "What in bloody hell..." Jackson began yelling. He stopped short at the sight of Hialeah being trailed by Alice. "I tried to stop her, Mr. Harding." Alice replied. Hialeah turned around to face Alice her face livid. "You say he ain't here you lyin' ol' goat." Hialeah bit out. "How dare you speak to me in such a manner?" Alice remarked stunned. "Miss Nokosi." Jackson said in an attempt to direct Hialeah's attention away from Alice. "Cause you a liar is how." Hialeah spat. "You best remember your place girl." Alice warned. "My place?" Hialeah replied heatedly. Jackson exhaled impatiently before exploding. "Enough!" Jackson yelled. Both women jumped from Jackson's booming voice and looked up the stairs to face his glaring scowl. "Alice, I'll see Miss Nokosi." Jackson said calmly. "Yes, Mr. Harding." Alice remarked before leaving the stairwell and returning to her desk.

Jackson met Hialeah midway down the stairs and retrieved the items that she carried in her arms. His stone face weakened Hialeah's knees. He nodded his head toward his office and stepped aside for Hialeah to take the lead up the stairs as he followed behind. Hialeah quietly led the way. She entered Jackson's office and stood in front of the small sofa with her hands clasped in front of her. Jackson set her packages on the sofa and closed the door behind him. He crossed his arms and raised a brow as he stood directly in front of Hialeah. She felt as if she were about to be reprimanded by her father. The deafening silence was too much for Hialeah. She took it upon herself to take a seat on the small sofa next to her packages and began smoothing out the nonexistent wrinkles in her dress. Jackson playfully rolled his eyes. "Stop it. There isn't a wrinkle in sight." Jackson said lightly. "Of course there is." Hialeah replied avoiding Jackson's gaze. "Miss Nokosi." Jackson remarked. "Fine, but there could have been." Hialeah replied. "No." Jackson remarked. "Alright, then let me have it." Hialeah replied. "Let you have it?" Jackson asked teasingly. "The scoldin' for what I said." Hialeah replied. "Hialeah, you called the woman a lying old goat." Jackson remarked. "You heard how she speak to me. She tell me to remember my place like I some kind of nothin'. Like I suppose to just let her speak to me any kind of way and now here you are fumin' cause I stood up for myself." Hialeah replied. "I'm not angry with you." Jackson remarked. "Ain't you?" Hialeah replied. "Not one bit." Jackson remarked. "Then why you standin' there with your arms crossed glarin' at me like you do?" Hialeah asked still smoothing out her wrinkle free dress. Jackson chuckled. "Just how do you know how I'm looking at you when you haven't looked up once?" Jackson asked. "Cause I know you." Hialeah replied. Jackson's chuckle was replaced by full on laughter. "You're very observant, I'll give you that." Jackson said. Hialeah looked up at Jackson. "Well just so you know, I came here very much lady-like until she start speakin' down on me." Hialeah replied. "And I admire you for that." Jackson remarked. "I ain't never heard of needin' no appointment to see the man I spoken for." Hialeah replied. "Hialeah, Alice is not aware of our relationship and I'd like to keep it that way. You do understand?" Jackson asked. Hialeah nodded her head. "I remember. She one of those folks who turn her nose down at seein' my kind with someone like you." Hialeah replied. "A part from that, she's the sister of General Bradford Stevens and a horrible gossip." Jackson remarked. "The general fought for the Confederates." Jackson said. "They slave owners?" Hialeah asked. "Unfortunately. They were." Jackson replied. "Those times are over." Hialeah remarked. "Indeed they are, but for many, the sting is unbearable and they will never recognize coloreds as their equals." Jackson replied. "What you consider speaking up for yourself, there are some that will perceive your tone as uppity and they will not hesitate to attempt to do you harm or worse." Jackson said. "I just get so tired of folks lookin' down on me." Hialeah replied. "How you stand so tall when folks insult you like they do; callin' you nigger lover and such." Hialeah said. "The world's ignorance is of no consequence to me, Hialeah. I'm a white man who fell in love with a colored woman. I am no better than you." Jackson replied. "Well you can't run faster than me that's for sure." Hialeah remarked. Jackson threw his head back in laughter. "Is that a challenge, Miss Nokosi?" Jackson asked teasingly. "Ain't no need to challenge. I done best you once before." Hialeah replied matter-of-factly. "Yes, but you cheated." Jackson remarked. "That's what you say. If that wall ain't been there, I still be runnin' and you still be tryin' to catch me." Hialeah replied. "Then it's a challenge. Tonight, after dinner. We'll see who can best who." Jackson remarked.

Hialeah twisted her lips at Jackson's suggestion that they race. "I don't get you none. When I wanna run, you say that ain't lady-like." Hialeah said. "Tonight we race then we'll return to dignity and class. Deal?" Jackson said. "That right fine with me. Guess I fixin' to win twice." Hialeah replied nonchalantly. "That, Miss Nokosi, we shall see." Jackson remarked smiling. "Now what do you have in your packages?" Jackson asked. Hialeah's eyes lit up. She had nearly forgotten about her packages and Jackson's gift. She picked up the gift wrapped hat box and presented it to Jackson. "This here is something I picked up special for you." Hialeah replied. "A gift for me?" Jackson asked surprised. "I think you gone like it." Hialeah replied. Jackson took the present and walked toward his desk. He sat on the edge of it and began tearing off the wrapping paper. Hialeah smiled from ear to ear watching Jackson rip into the paper. She could hardly contain her excitement. When Jackson tore off the last bit of paper, Hialeah squealed like a young child.

Jackson opened the hat box with a surprised look on his face. "A new Gambler?" Jackson said smiling. Hialeah jumped to her feet ecstatically and rushed to Jackson. "You like it?" Hialeah asked proudly. Jackson frowned. "I don't know." Jackson replied. Hialeah's smile faded. "What you mean you don't know?" Hialeah asked curiously. "Well I guess it all depends on whether or not you're going to take it from me and run a mile down the street with it." Jackson replied laughing. Hialeah smiled and threw her arms around Jackson's neck. Jackson stood up and wrapped his arms around Hialeah's waist and spun her around. Hialeah burst into laughter. Jackson returned Hialeah back to the floor and kissed her softly on her lips. "I love it. It's the best gift I've ever received." Jackson said. "You really love it?" Hialeah asked hopefully. "I do indeed. Thank you." Jackson replied. "In fact, I love it so much, I shall wear it tonight. What do you think about that?" Jackson remarked. "I think you gone look right sharp. Of course, you always look right sharp." Hialeah replied matter-of-factly straightening Jackson's tie. "Is that so?" Jackson asked teasingly. "I mean that's one of the reasons why the women around here give you such wanton looks." Hialeah replied. "Do they now? I hadn't noticed." Jackson remarked lightly. "You most certainly have. You're tall, handsome, well-dressed, wealthy, and you talk real proper like. I hear what they say bout you." Hialeah replied. "Really? Maybe I ought to introduce myself." Jackson remarked teasingly heading toward the door. Hialeah quickly grabbed his arm and Jackson burst into laughter. He snapped his finger sarcastically as an after-thought. "Oh that's right, I'm spoken for." Jackson said smiling wrapping his arms around Hialeah once again.

Hialeah stood on tip toe and kissed Jackson tenderly. "Ecenokecvyet os. (Ih-Chih-No-Kih-Chuh-Yeet Ose)." Hialeah said softly. Jackson gazed down into Hialeah's eyes. "I love you too, Hialeah Nokosi." Jackson replied low. Hialeah was in awe that Jackson cared enough about her language to remember something so special. She smiled faintly but shied away from Jackson. Jackson reached out and took a hold of Hialeah's hand. He caught the saddened look in her eyes. "What's troubling you?" Jackson asked. "I don't wanna make a big fuss bout it, but I seen Miss Sara leavin' here before I come in." Hialeah replied. "What she want with you?" Hialeah asked. "She came here to ask me to forfeit the duel." Jackson replied. "Forfeit? What that mean?" Hialeah asked. "She asked me to not show up." Jackson replied. "What her daddy say bout it?" Hialeah asked. "According to her, he wouldn't hear anything about it. He's adamant about going through with it." Jackson replied. Hialeah let out a long sigh. "I ain't never think I would say this, but I agree with her. I think it best you just don't show up." Hialeah said. "I can't do that." Jackson replied. "Why can't you? What you got to prove?" Hialeah remarked. "I will not give that smug self-righteous bastard the satisfaction of thinking he bested me." Jackson replied harshly. "He don't matter none." Hialeah remarked. "Why can't you see my side of this? Do you think I take pleasure in killing a man?" Jackson asked. "For bloody fucking sake, Hialeah, my honor is on the line." Jackson said heatedly. "What honor is there in killin' an old fool?" Hialeah asked. Jackson slams his fist on his desk startling Hialeah. "He brought this fight to my door!" Jackson exploded. "I will not back down." Jackson yelled out. "Now leave me to my business." Jackson growled out.

Taken aback by Jackson's tone, Hialeah grabbed her packages and slammed the door on her way out. Jackson immediately felt guilty for taking his frustration out on Hialeah. He quickly opened the door to his office and called out to her. Hialeah stopped briefly on the stairs and turned around swiftly to face Jackson. "You tell me not to worry bout you. Well I am worried. I scared too." Hialeah said matter-of-factly before leaving Jackson in the stairway. She ran down the street tears stinging her eyes. Jackson stood in the stairway momentarily before returning back to his office. He threw himself into his chair behind his desk. Aggravated by what had just transpired between him and Hialeah, Jackson buried his face in his hands. Hearing their conversation from her desk, Alice raised a curious brow. She was unsure of what was going on between her boss and his colored lady guest but it was quite evident that whatever it was, their relationship was more than just business. Alice could barely sit still in her chair. She was eager to spread this bit of juicy gossip to the ladies in her social circle.

Jackson couldn't keep his mind on his work. Hours had passed since Hialeah had left upset over their quarrel. Jackson found himself going over the same line of numbers repeatedly in his father's ledger. The ticking of the clock on the wall amidst the silence in the room was driving him insane. Lucas wasn't due to arrive for another three hours to carry him home. Jackson thought to himself that if he stayed any longer he would surely snap. He slammed his father's ledger book closed and locked it away in the desk. He grabbed his new hat and placed it back in its box before leaving his office. Jackson called down to Alice. He rolled his eyes at the sound of glass breaking as he descended the stairs. After informing Alice that he was leaving for the day, he requested that she lock up.

Jackson stepped out of his office building and immediately felt the scorching heat from the sun beating down on his neck. He thought to himself that the long walk from town would be horrendous but worth it to clear his head. A wave of guilt washed over Jackson and he thought it best if he purchased some lovely roses for Hialeah. Crossing over several streets Jackson found a vendor selling a multitude of fresh flowers. The vendor was surrounded by colored women waiting in line to make their purchase. Amidst the women was Hialeah taking in the aroma of the vendor's flowers while she too waited in line. Jackson casually strolled up to the vendor pretending that he was not aware of Hialeah's presence. The eight colored women that were waiting in line stepped back to allow Jackson ahead of them. Lost in the scent of the various flowers, Hialeah was oblivious to Jackson standing near the group of women. Jackson nodded his head in greeting and smiled at the women. "Excuse me." Jackson began garnering the attention of the women. Hialeah jumped at the sound of Jackson's voice as he addressed the eight women all the while not making eye contact with her. "Would either of you enchanting women be able to assist me in a dire matter?" Jackson asked casually. The women simultaneously smiled and giggled; delighted by Jackson's compliment. "You see, I'm very much in love with an incredibly beautiful woman but I fear that I've upset her tremendously and I thought if I purchased her a lovely bouquet of roses she'd forgive me and join me this evening for dinner. The trouble is, I haven't the faintest notion of how to go about selecting the perfect flower." Jackson said innocently.

Like bees to honey, the women swarmed around the vendor's selection of roses and immediately began to choose the ones they thought would be perfect for Jackson. Jackson took a step back while the women busied themselves in creating his bouquet. Hialeah was lost in the shuffle as the women reached around her picking a rose here and there. Jackson was thoroughly amused and pleased by the women's careful selection and willingness to assist him.

After each woman handed Jackson what she thought was the best rose for his bouquet, they stood back and awaited his approval. Jackson looked the bouquet over and smiled. "Are you sure this will do?" Jackson asked in mock innocence. The women all agreed. Satisfied with their approval, Jackson took a single rose from his bouquet and to the ladies' surprise handed each of them their very own rose. Their smiles of disbelief melted Hialeah's heart. Jackson paid the vendor, nodded his head in appreciation to the ladies, and left the women in awe by his generosity before continuing his walk home with four roses for Hialeah. Curious as to where Jackson was headed, Hialeah hurried to her wagon. Jackson looked over his shoulder in time to see Hialeah making her way toward her wagon. He smiled to himself and quickened his pace. Hialeah climbed onto her wagon but was unable to move. The streets were crowded with passersby. She looked over her shoulder and furrowed her brows. Jackson had disappeared from her view. When she was finally able to proceed, Hialeah turned her wagon around in the middle of the street and headed in Jackson's direction.

Jackson ducked in an alley and watched as Hialeah drove by him. Hialeah scanned the crowd of people but Jackson was nowhere to be found. Disappointed that she had lost Jackson, Hialeah rode out of town in hopes of catching up with Jackson somewhere down the road. Satisfied that he had lost Hialeah, Jackson returned to the vendor and purchased eight more roses to replace the ones that he had given to the ladies for their assistance. After his business was concluded with the vendor, Jackson strolled casually to his father's Gentlemen's Club and caught a ride home with a fellow member.

Hialeah made her way home curious as to where Jackson had gone. She drove up the dirt road to her home just as Rose was walking off of her front porch. Hialeah furrowed her brows at the sight of Rose on her property. They hadn't spoken since the church luncheon. Hearing the sound of Hialeah's wagon approaching, Rose stopped and waited for Hialeah with a huge smile across her face. She was practically jumping up and down with excitement much to Hialeah's confusion. Hialeah noticed that Rose was waving a small piece of paper ushering her to hurry. Hialeah was eager to find out what brought Rose to her home. She hurried her wagon and stopped right in front of her porch. Rose let out an enthusiastic squeal as Hialeah climbed down from her wagon. Rose instantly rushed to Hialeah and embraced her tightly before releasing Hialeah, who nearly lost her footing from Rose's ecstatic embrace. "Hensci, my friend. Estonko? (Is-don-go) How are you?" Rose said happily. Hialeah's eyes widened with amazement that Rose had remembered her tongue. "Did I say that good?" Rose asked hopeful. "Henka. (Hinga) Yes. It's fine you remember." Hialeah replied. "But what bring you here?" Hialeah asked curiously. "Oh yes, this here for you." Rose replied giddy with joy holding the small piece of paper for Hialeah to take. Hialeah was reluctant but took the paper from Rose's hand.

Rose clasped her hands together tightly between her breasts smiling while Hialeah read the message. When Hialeah finished reading the card she looked up at Rose and joined in her merriment. "This true? You gettin' married?" Hialeah asked smiling. Rose squealed once again. "I gettin' married next month and I want you to come see me jump the broom." Rose replied. "You know what that mean?" Rose asked. "My mama told me bout it. I'm right happy for you but I ain't too sure why you want me there. Ruby don't care for me none no more and your brother Isaac, well he just plain mean to me cause he can't have me." Hialeah remarked. "Well it ain't their weddin', it's mine. We're still friends ain't we?" Rose asked. Hialeah nodded her head. "Then it's settled." Rose said. Hialeah smiled. "Alright. I'd like that." Hialeah replied.

Hialeah's acceptance of Rose's invitation brought forth another giddy squeal from Rose followed by another tight embrace. "I so happy but I scared just the same. " Rose said softly. Hialeah frowned, unsure of what her friend meant. "What you got to be scared for?" Hialeah replied. Rose felt her cheeks warming. "Ain't right sure how to say it." Rose confessed innocently. "Just say it right out." Hialeah remarked. "Well I ain't talk to my mama bout it and Ruby, why she just poke fun." Rose began. "You can tell me." Hialeah said reassuring her friend of her trust. Rose nodded her head in agreement before exhaling a nervous breath. Hialeah clasped her hands in front of her anticipating whatever it was Rose needed to confide in her. "Well, I...I don't know what to do after the weddin'. I mean when we in bed together. When he on top of me. I hear...well I hear that it hurt. That true?" Rose stammered out. "I mean you, well you...you had Mr. Harding on top of you. Did it hurt when he put himself in you?" Rose continued nervously. Hialeah was taken aback by Rose's inquiry of her relationship with Jackson. She had never spoken to anyone about their lovemaking before but she had to be honest with her friend. "I gone be right truthful with you. It hurt a bit the first time but then it feel like what you think heaven is when they lovin' you real good." Hialeah replied. "You gone be fine. If he love you then he gone love you good." Hialeah said. Rose pressed her lips together and nodded her head. She embraced Hialeah. "Thank you. I best be goin' now. I gotta lot to do yet." Rose said. "Goodbye." Hialeah replied. Rose leapt off the front porch waving goodbye to Hialeah until she disappeared from sight. Hialeah glanced back down at her invitation. She was happy that Rose found someone to love her. Rose's upcoming wedding suddenly brought out envious feelings in Hialeah. Jackson declared that he would marry her but with his father still being ill and now this mess of a duel coming about, Hialeah started to wonder if she would ever become Jackson's wife. Hialeah sank into her small chair on the front porch and began to sulk. It quickly dawned on her that she had a dinner to prepare for. There was no time for sulking. Jackson would be arriving soon and she looked a sight. Hialeah bolted from her chair and hurried back to her wagon. She hurried to the barn and unhitched her wagon and put her horse in his stall. Hialeah then gathered her purchases and ran toward her home cursing herself for spending so much time at the shops.

There was no time for her to take a heated bath. Jackson was a punctual man and he would not take too kind to having to wait. Hialeah internally scolded herself as she stripped down to her bare skin and gathered her bathing items. She wrapped herself in a large towel and raced toward the creek. She dreaded a cold bath on such an important evening. Hialeah hoped that the sun was kind and warmed the water just a tad. Reaching the edge of the creek bank, Hialeah dropped her towel. She said a quick prayer for warm water and dashed into the creek. The sun had not been generous and Hialeah screamed as the cold water touched her skin. She thought to make quick work of her bath before Jackson arrived and the revelation that she hadn't even decided on what to wear hurried Hialeah along.

Hialeah climbed from the creek and wrapped herself back into her towel and slid her feet into her moccasins as to not dirty them up on the walk back to her porch. Once inside her bedroom, Hialeah contemplated on what to wear. She hadn't a proper dress that resembled what the ladies in town wore and she hadn't the time to go back into town to purchase a new one with the money she had from her crop sell to Jackson. Somewhat annoyed over her decision, Hialeah paced her room. She didn't wish to embarrass Jackson in public by donning one of her mother's dresses. They were acceptable around her father's people but Hialeah wasn't too sure the white folks in town would appreciate her style of dress. Distressed over her decision, Hialeah plopped on her bed and tapped her chin absentmindedly with her finger tips. As she sat on her bed pondering her situation, time was slipping away from her.

It suddenly dawned on Hialeah that Jackson admired her greatly in her mother's dresses. She sprang from her bed and moved hastily to her trunk. With much haste, Hialeah looked through her mother's dresses in search of the perfect dress. A hint of blue and orange caught her eye and Hialeah pulled the dress up from the trunk. She smiled. "Perfect." Hialeah said. The blue and orange patterned dress would go well with her new parasol. Now for the appropriate glass necklace and moccasins to complete her ensemble.

Hialeah dressed and took extra care with her necklace and hair. She styled her sleek black hair in the traditional bun of the Seminole women; leaving a few strands of hair to cascade around her face. Jackson found the look extremely enticing. Hialeah adored everything about her look. She reminded herself that Jackson's opinion of her was the only opinion that mattered. She would ignore any smug faces that she was sure to receive. No sooner than Hialeah gave herself a quick glance, the approaching sound of hooves could be heard coming up the dirt road. Hialeah quickly grabbed her parasol and the fan that Jackson had gifted her at the Independence festival and hurried to the door. She could hardly contain her excitement at the sight of Jackson's lavish carriage driven by Lucas as it rolled towards her home. She recalled how regal the carriage looked the day Jackson arrived from London. It was truly magnificent.

Hialeah clasped her hands together in front of her as her parasol hung from her wrist. She held tightly to her fan and walked to the end of her porch a huge smile gracing her lips. A sudden burst of nervousness washed over Hialeah. She imagined what folks would say when they saw her riding with Jackson into town to enjoy their dinner engagement. Hialeah inhaled a proud breath seeing Lucas on top of the carriage. He looked so sharp in his uniform. His burgundy colored coat, white crisp shirt, black trousers and black riding boots gave him the appearance of a high class gentleman. Hialeah couldn't help but to wave at Lucas. He nodded his head as he stopped the carriage a short distance from her porch. Hialeah stepped off her porch and Lucas jumped down from the carriage. Hialeah's smile faded when she noticed that Jackson was not present. "Where Mr. Harding?" Hialeah asked. "Ain't he comin'?" Hialeah said. "Mr. Harding waiting for your arrival. He ask that I come carry you to dinner." Lucas replied. Lucas held the door open for Hialeah and assisted her into the carriage.

Lucas climbed back on top of the carriage. "Walk on." Lucas said as he led the horses back down the road. Hialeah sat quietly in the carriage. She felt somewhat offended that Jackson didn't accompany her to dinner. Hialeah wondered if Jackson didn't want to be seen arriving into town with her. Disappointed at the very thought, Hialeah's shoulders slumped forward. She was oblivious to the onlookers whose mouths hung open in surprise and shock at seeing a colored woman being driven by a colored man in such a fancy carriage. She took in the scenic view quietly with her hands placed in her lap. Lucas peered over his shoulder. "You mighty quiet. Reckon I would be too if I were fixin' to have dinner with that wicked old crow." Lucas said. Hialeah instantly perked up at Lucas's words. "What you mean?" Hialeah replied confused. She looked around and realized that Lucas had driven away from town. "Where you takin' me?" Hialeah asked worriedly. "Ain't Mr. Jackson tell you? You gone be havin' dinner with him and his mama." Lucas remarked. Hialeah was at a loss for words. No sooner than Lucas finished his sentence, he drove up to Jackson's home. Hialeah's eyes widened in shock. She was speechless. Her shock turned into rage when Jackson stepped onto the porch with the bouquet of roses he had purchased her and headed toward the carriage.

Hialeah wasted no time in opening up the door and storming out of the carriage. She angrily popped open her parasol to protect her from the vicious sun and furiously began marching back down the road away from the Harding home. Jackson hastily set the roses on a small table on the porch and raced after Hialeah. With a few short strides, Jackson caught up with Hialeah and grabbed her arm. Hialeah snatched her arm from Jackson's grasp and turned on him menacingly. "What you mean by bringin' me here?" Hialeah demanded. "We're having dinner, remember?" Jackson replied. "You ain't say nothin' bout bringin' me here and I ain't goin' nowhere near that woman." Hialeah spat. "Miss Nokosi…" Jackson began. "Don't you dare Miss Nokosi me. That woman done talked down to me one too many times. I ain't fixin' to let that happen again." Hialeah remarked angrily. "Hialeah, if you will allow me to explain." Jackson said. "Ain't nothin' to explain." Hialeah replied adamantly. "Hialeah, it was my mother's idea to invite you over for a family dinner." Jackson replied. "She ain't no family to me." Hialeah spat. She set out marching back down the road. Jackson remained put and simply crossed his arms grinning devilishly. "She agreed with you." Jackson called out. Hialeah stopped her angry march and spun on her heel to face Jackson. She refused to take another step toward him and placed her hands on her hips in utter defiance. "What you mean, she agree with me?" Hialeah replied curiously. "Oh, I don't know. She said something along the lines of Sara Williams not being the woman for me and that it was wrong of her to choose who she thought would make a perfect wife for me." Jackson remarked casually. "She say that truthfully?" Hialeah asked suspiciously. "Indeed she did. She also made mention that she whole heartedly approves of you becoming Mrs. Jackson Harding. In fact, she insisted upon it seeing as how I am her only child and she wishes me to be happy." Jackson replied simply. "However, if you'd prefer to leave and disappoint both my mother and Mama Lilly who has prepared a delicious meal in your honor, then I shall have no other recourse than to inform your future mother-in-law that you have declined her generous and humble invitation. I am sure she would understand. However, I don't think Mama Lilly..." Jackson began. Hialeah hurried over to Jackson. She truly didn't wish to upset Miss Lilly. She was a stern woman and offending her would not go over well. Frankly, the woman terrified her.

Jackson stifled his laugh as he held his arm for Hialeah to take. He looked down at her smiling. "What made you change your mind?" Jackson asked teasingly. Hialeah responded by pinching Jackson's arm. Her response brought a bout of laughter from Jackson as he escorted Hialeah toward the house. He was sure that the mention of Miss Lilly struck a tad bit of fear in Hialeah.

The closer they walked toward the house, Hialeah's grip on Jackson's arm tightened. Jackson caressed Hialeah's fingers to calm her obvious nerves. Just as they were approaching the steps that led to the front door, Hialeah released Jackson's arm and refused to go any further. Jackson's brows furrowed as he glanced down at Hialeah. "What is it?" Jackson asked. Hialeah looked up at Jackson. "What you doin'?" Hialeah replied in a whisper. "I can't go in that way." Hialeah said. Jackson followed Hialeah's gaze. It was clear to him that Hialeah feared entering through the front door. Jackson took a hold of Hialeah's hand and placed a kiss on the back of it. Hialeah said nothing. She exhaled softly and placed her arm through Jackson's once again and allowed him to escort her up the steps. Jackson retrieved the roses from the small table and presented them to Hialeah with a wink. Hialeah felt her cheeks warming. She thought about Jackson and the ladies at the vendor. She was pleased with the four roses that she saw Jackson purchase but receiving a full bouquet was delightful.

Samuel, the Harding's butler, opened the door and Jackson ushered for Hialeah to enter before him. Hialeah was reluctant to enter but was immediately reminded of Miss Lilly's encouraging words in the lunch line. Hialeah straightened up her back and walked through the door. She was immediately attacked by the aroma of Miss Lilly's cooking. Jackson casually took her parasol from her wrist and her roses and handed them to Samuel. "Samuel, Miss Hialeah Nokosi. Miss Nokosi, Samuel." Jackson said. "Miss Nokosi." Samuel replied with a nod of his head. "Nice to meet you, Mr. Samuel." Hialeah replied nervously. Jackson escorted Hialeah further into the house and they were met by a female servant carrying a glass of wine and a glass of lemonade on a silver serving tray. Hialeah felt uneasy being served by a woman that looked like her and very close in age as she. She hoped that she didn't appear uppity to Jackson's colored staff. "Lavinia, Miss Nokosi. Miss Nokosi, Lavinia." Jackson said. "Ma'am." Lavinia replied with a slight nod of her head. Jackson grabbed both drinks and handed the lemonade to Hialeah. "Thank you." Hialeah said softly. She watched as the Lavinia disappeared into the kitchen. "Lavinia assists Mama Lilly with the cooking and cleaning." Jackson said. Hialeah smiled faintly at Jackson. Jackson's brows furrowed. He was perplexed by the sudden change in Hialeah's demeanor. "Are you alright?" Jackson asked. "I don't feel right bein' served by colored folks." Hialeah replied in a whisper. "Slavery is long over. When Mama Lilly and Lavinia and Samuel and most working in the tobacco fields were freed, they had every right to leave here and start their lives new; as free people. Of course, Mama Lilly been free long before slavery was over. My father offered anyone willing to stay on a very generous wage to take back to their families." Jackson remarked. "Some that are employed here came from other plantations and Mama Lilly and Samuel why they practically run the place. Well, Mama Lilly does run the house." Jackson said smiling. "I'm sure." Hialeah replied. "My parents would no doubt run around like headless chickens if she were to ever leave." Jackson remarked jokingly. Hialeah covered her mouth to stifle her laughter.

Jackson was pleased to see Hialeah smiling. He took a drink of his wine and Hialeah did the same with her cold glass of lemonade. Before she could put the glass to her lips for another drink, Georgina called out to Jackson from the dining room. Startled by Georgina's voice, Hialeah gasped in surprise and her glass fell from her hands crashing onto the floor. She glanced quickly at Jackson in horror and dropped to her knees. "I so sorry Jackson. I so very sorry." Hialeah rushed out nervously retrieving as many pieces of the broken glass as she could. Jackson knelt down beside Hialeah. She was too humiliated to face him. Jackson took a hold of Hialeah's wrist and turned it gently until every piece of broken glass she had collected had fallen back onto the floor. "Stop." Jackson said soothingly. Hialeah looked in Jackson's eyes. Her lips were trembling. "Hialeah, it was an accident." Jackson said. Hialeah felt light headed. She could almost hear what Mrs. Harding would say to her. "Breathe." Jackson said calmly. Hialeah inhaled deeply and slowly exhaled. "Better?" Jackson asked smiling. Hialeah shook her head and Jackson chuckled. He stood and held his hand out for Hialeah. "I'm here mother." Jackson called out. Taking another quick breath, Hialeah hastily grabbed Jackson's hand and allowed him to assist her to her feet before Georgina could see her kneeling on the floor. Jackson chuckled. "That ain't funny." Hialeah whispered giving Jackson another pinch on his arm which brought out more laughter from him.

    Hialeah barely had enough time to gather herself before she and Jackson were joined by a smiling Georgina. Hialeah's knees felt as if they would buckle from under her at the sight of Georgina Harding. She found herself standing slightly behind Jackson her nerves overtaking her as she stood near the broken pieces of glass. Georgina's smile faded as she noticed the mess on her floor. "Why what on Earth happened here?" Georgina asked surprised. Before Hialeah could open her mouth to speak, Jackson interjected. "It was quite careless of me." Jackson replied. Georgina raised a curious brow. She was not fooled by Jackson's attempt to cover for Hialeah's mishap with her glass as Jackson was still holding onto his glass of wine. "Well accidents do happen." Georgina remarked lightly. "That they do." Jackson replied. Hialeah stood frozen with her hands clasped tightly in front of her. "Lavinia." Georgina yelled. Lavinia hurried from the kitchen. "Yes ma'am." Lavinia replied. "Do clean this mess up. It appears my son has dropped his glass." Georgina remarked. Hialeah swallowed hard as Lavinia glanced in her direction. She followed Lavinia's gaze as she too noticed that Jackson's glass was still in his hand. "Right away, ma'am." Lavinia replied before disappearing into the kitchen.

When Lavinia reappeared, she was carrying a broom and a hand towel. Georgina instructed her to make sure that the floor was cleaned properly before requesting that Jackson and Hialeah join her in the dining room. Jackson took a hold of Hialeah's arm as they followed Georgina. Hialeah couldn't resist the urge to look over her shoulder at Lavinia. She felt awful that Lavinia had to clean up her mess when she clearly had much to do. Lavinia cut her eyes in annoyance as she wiped up the lemonade from the floor. Hialeah quickly turned her head. She truly felt miserable for causing such a mess but kept silent as Jackson led her into the dining room.

Hialeah's eyes nearly popped from her head at the sight of the Harding's dining table. It was set impeccably. Hialeah never knew that so much went into having a dinner. She couldn't fathom that so many types of forks and spoons and cutlery existed. She immediately dreaded being invited to the Harding's for dinner. Hialeah groaned inward yet forced a smile on her face. She felt out of place and under dressed. Jackson was dressed in a fine pair of dark gray trousers with a crisp white shirt and matching gray suit jacket while Georgina was dressed in a light green taffeta dress that formed to her somewhat plump body.

Jackson insisted that his mother sit at the head of the table so that he could dine across from Hialeah. In true gentleman fashion, Jackson pulled out Georgina's chair then repeated the gesture for Hialeah. Hialeah nodded her head slightly in appreciation as she took her seat. Her stomach was tied in complete knots. She sat with her hands clasped in her lap as she waited for Jackson to take his seat. Hialeah pressed her lips together and glanced around the table. She felt her shoulders slumping from nervousness. She feared making an absolute fool of herself in front of Jackson and his mother. Jackson noticed the display of terror on Hialeah's face. He followed her gaze as she glanced at the table. Without uttering a word, Jackson cleared his throat to attract Hialeah's attention. She lifted her eyes to meet Jackson's and calmly straightened up her shoulders. Jackson reached for his napkin and unfolded it before placing it in his lap. He nodded his head slightly in Hialeah's direction hoping that she would understand the cues that he was sending her.

Hialeah followed Jackson's cue and placed her napkin on her lap. Jackson winked affectionately in her direction. Hialeah felt her cheeks warming. She was grateful that Georgina missed their exchange. Feeling a tad at ease, Hialeah felt it appropriate to thank Georgina for her gracious invitation to her home followed by a generous compliment on her elegant appearance. Georgina gushed at Hialeah's praise of her choice of dinner attire. Not one to hold her tongue, Georgina questioned Hialeah about her dress. Unsure if Georgina was genuinely interested or if her inquiry was an attempt to insult her, Hialeah spoke proudly of her mother's dress and of the Seminole women. "It is a true work of art." Jackson said. "Well I am inclined to agree." Georgina replied. "You do look quite fetching." Georgina said. "Thank you, Mrs. Harding." Hialeah replied. Georgina simply nodded her head and offered a kind smile to Hialeah before ringing a small bell that set next to her. Hialeah jumped at the sound of the bell. "Forgive me. It's the dinner bell." Georgina said casually. Hialeah blushed, slightly embarrassed. "I do hope you're hungry. Miss Lilly prepared a wonderful meal." Georgina said. "Henka. I mean yes." Hialeah rushed out. "Henka?" Georgina said curiously. "It means yes in Creek. Hialeah's father taught her his tongue." Jackson replied. "Oh, well I'll be sure to remember that." Georgina replied sweetly. Hialeah smiled faintly. She scolded herself for speaking her father's language.

Miss Lilly entered the dining room followed by Lavinia who carried a huge serving tray with three bowls of a savory beefy broth. Hialeah reminded herself to sit straight while Miss Lilly served her. She smiled her appreciation all the while trying to keep from laughing as she imagined Jackson's words of Georgina and Henry running around like headless chickens if Miss Lilly were to ever leave their employment. Jackson noticed the amused expression on Hialeah's face as he was served and although he was clueless as to her amusement he grinned in her direction. Georgina bowed her head to bless the meal and Hialeah quickly followed her lead. After the blessing of their first course, Jackson caught Hialeah's attention by casually tapping on his soup spoon. Hialeah reached for her utensil and watched as Jackson dipped his spoon into his beef broth and scooped his soup away from him before bringing the spoonful of soup to his lips. Hialeah mimicked Jackson's every move until her bowl was empty.

Throughout the course of the meal, Jackson tapped on the proper utensil for Hialeah's benefit and led the conversation to keep his mother from possibly saying anything that would upset Hialeah. He focused on subjects that Hialeah knew well such as her gardening and her love of horses. Jackson sat pleased as his mother requested advice from Hialeah on gardening as she too was an admirer of flowers and shared a passion for horses. The longer the women spoke of their shared commonalities, the more Georgina drank. Jackson chuckled at the sight of his mother becoming more and more intoxicated from her multiply servings of wine. Hialeah had warmed up to the idea of sitting with Georgina and decided to join her in having a glass of wine. Before long, Georgina had begun to slur her words and her giggles became full blown bouts of laughter. While both women were engrossed in their conversation, Jackson removed the bottle of wine from the table and set it next to his chair. He then called for Miss Lilly to clear what was left of their dessert plates and to assist his mother to bed.

Georgina was aided to her feet by Jackson and stumbled on her way from the dining room. She laughed hysterically at her own clumsiness and bid goodnight to her son and to her dinner guest. Hialeah was thoroughly amused by Georgina's intoxicated state. "I like her this way." Hialeah whispered. "She is quite entertaining to say the least." Jackson replied dryly as he set the bottle of wine back on the table and rose to his feet. Hialeah pushed herself away from the table and stood up as well. Her ill manners received a frown from Jackson. "What you look at me that way for?" Hialeah asked with a frown of her own directed at Jackson. Before Jackson could speak, it dawned on Hialeah almost immediately that she was to remain seated until Jackson pulled her chair out as he had done before their meal began. She quickly sat back in her chair and pushed herself back to the table. Jackson chuckled at her sudden remembrance of etiquette. "I won't forget next time." Hialeah said. "I'll know which fork to use too." Hialeah remarked. "I have every confidence in you." Jackson replied matter-of-factly as he slid Hialeah's chair from the table and assisted her to her feet. He gently caressed her hand before bringing it to his lips to place a soft kiss on the back of it. Jackson's tenderness brought a smile to Hialeah's lips. "This was a truly pleasant evening." Hialeah said. "It was indeed, however, I must admit our evening is not yet over." Jackson replied with a naughty grin on his face. Hialeah furrowed her brows confused as to what Jackson meant. "Come with me." Jackson said as he escorted Hialeah from the dining room and out the front door.

Hialeah followed behind Jackson down the steps of the Harding's pillared front porch and through the gate. "Where you takin' me?" Hialeah asked confused. Jackson stopped on the dirt road and removed his coat. He tossed it onto the grass and turned to face Hialeah with a sinister grin on his face. Hialeah raised a suspicious brow. "What you givin' me that evil look for?" Hialeah asked. "This is the look of a winner." Jackson replied boastfully. "What you goin' on bout?" Hialeah remarked. "Clearly you have forgotten our challenge of speed. No walls just one long road." Jackson replied pointing from their starting point to the end of the road. "You can't mean to race…" Hialeah began before letting her words trail off as she took off running down the Harding's road. "Bloody fuck." Jackson groaned. There was no way he was going to be bested by Hialeah once again. Jackson bolted down the dirt road. Hialeah's boisterous laughter ringing out in his ears fueled his need to catch her. He would never live it down if she beat him.

Jackson marveled at her speed. She was like a lioness after her prey but he refused to be daunted. Jackson barreled down the road his long powerful strides matching Hialeah's. Her persistent taunts ceased as she glanced over at her rival. Jackson had not only caught up to her but was leaving her behind in their challenge. It was now Jackson who taunted Hialeah with a victorious laugh as the end of the road was mere feet away. Hialeah found herself distracted by Jackson's protruding back muscles that were all too visible through his shirt and the masterful strength of his legs as she chased him down. His taunts were lost on her as her focus shifted from the race to Jackson's well defined frame. Hialeah slowed her steps as Jackson crossed over their make shift finish line raising his hands in victory.

   Hialeah clapped sarcastically conceding her defeat to Jackson. She slowly approached him and in one swift motion jumped into Jackson's arms wrapping her legs around his body. Hialeah gazed longingly into Jackson's eyes. She could feel his heart pounding in his chest. "Kiss me, Mr. Harding." Hialeah said seductively. Jackson was all too eager to oblige. He captured Hialeah's lips in a passionate kiss as he held her close to his chest. Hialeah wrapped her arms around Jackson's neck as Jackson invaded her mouth with his tongue. She melted against him hearing reveling in the growl that erupted from his chest. Breaking their kiss, Hialeah smiled lovingly at Jackson. "Ecenokecvyet os. (ih-chih-no-kih-chuh-yeet ose)" Hialeah said. "I love you, too." Jackson replied. Hialeah placed a quick kiss on Jackson's lips and unwrapped her legs from his waist. Jackson peered down into Hialeah's eyes. He had never betrayed her and he dreaded doing so now, however, his duel with Judge Williams was to take place at dawn and he was well aware how Hialeah felt about it. Hialeah slowly shook her head as her brows furrowed from Jackson's sudden change in demeanor. "What is it?" Hialeah asked. "I called off the duel." Jackson replied. Hialeah gasped in surprise. "You mean it?" Hialeah asked. "I mean it." Jackson replied. "And Judge Williams, he forgive you?" Hialeah remarked. "All is well." Jackson replied. Hialeah squealed happily as she embraced Jackson. She felt as if she could burst into tears of joy. Jackson held onto Hialeah cursing himself for deceiving the woman who captured his heart.

Chapter 12

After having such a lovely dinner, Jackson personally drove Hialeah home. He thought it best if he returned to his mother's side after her intoxicating performance at the dinner table. Hialeah shared Jackson's concern much to Jackson's surprise. He was however pleased to know that Hialeah had warmed up to his mother considering how Georgina had behaved to the woman he loved. Jackson held Hialeah in a long embrace, whispered his love for her in her ear and left Hialeah touching her lips after their shared lingering kiss. Hialeah stood on her porch as Jackson drove away. She retired inside when he was out of her sight.

Hialeah was so overjoyed that Jackson and Judge Williams had agreed to put an end to their differences and cease their duel she could hardly get any rest. She woke up earlier than usual surprisingly with not only Jackson in her thoughts but Georgina as well. Their shared passion for flowers gave Hialeah a perfect idea. Although Georgina Harding was not her ideal choice for a mother in law, she was Jackson's mother and it would truly please him to see the two of them getting along.

Hialeah passed on breakfast and hurried to her garden to gather a fresh bouquet of tulips. She wanted to gift them to Georgina before she left for church and time was of the essence. Hialeah didn't bother to hitch her wagon. She hastily saddled her horse and hurried to the Harding estate taking in the beauty of the early rising sun through the clouds as she rode.

The Harding estate was calm as Hialeah rode through the gate. She slowed her horse as to not disturb Georgina or Henry Harding. There were no workers in the fields aside from a few footmen, one whom approached Hialeah and took a hold of her reins as she dismounted from her horse. Hialeah thanked the gentleman before heading toward the Harding's front door. She stopped in mid step contemplating whether or not to knock on the front door. She didn't dare cause a disturbance so early in the morning. She was, however, bringing a gift to Georgina. Perhaps she was still sleeping. Hialeah exhaled, straightened her shoulders and walked up the stairs leading to the front entrance. She knocked gently hoping that Samuel would hear and allow her entrance without a fuss. Hialeah waited patiently, listening closely as the sound of footsteps approaching could be heard from inside. She took a step back to prepare herself for whoever it was on the other side of the door.

Hialeah breathed a sigh of relief. She wasn't expecting Miss Lilly to answer the door but she was grateful for the familiar face. Miss Lilly furrowed her brows and Hialeah's heart began to race nervously. Clearly she had disturbed the house. Hialeah immediately held out the tulips and mustered a faint smile to her lips. "Good morning…" Hialeah began. "Ain't no good morning with all this foolishness goin' on." Miss Lilly interjected. "Foolishness?" Hialeah replied confused. "Ain't you hear bout what's fixin' to happen?" Miss Lilly remarked. Hialeah shook her head. "No ma'am. What you mean?" Hialeah replied. "What I mean is Jackson done gone out to Milliner's Pond to kill Judge Williams. They's fixin' to duel. Shoot at each other." Miss Lilly remarked. Hialeah's blood went cold. "That ain't right. Jackson tell me they make amends. Say they ain't fightin'." Hialeah replied. "Jackson leave here a short time ago. Mrs. Harding, too." Miss Lilly remarked matter-of-factly. Hialeah dropped the tulips at her feet and raced from the front porch. She hurried to her horse and grabbed the reins from the footman.

General Bradford Stevens was called to mediate the duel. He was a trusted friend of the Harding and Williams' family. He looked over the guns making sure that both were loaded with one bullet each. Both Jackson and Harland were relieved of their personal guns and given to General Steven's servant to assure that the duel was fought fair. A physician had been called to declare the death of the unfortunate loser of the battle. Sara stood next to her mother while Georgina stood next to Lucas praying that the outcome would end in Jackson's favor. Jackson was attired in black from head to toe while Harland Williams donned a white shirt and black trousers. General Stevens instructed both men of the rules and handed Jackson and Harland their respected weapons. "Is there no chance of either you reconciling?" General Stevens said. "None." Harland spat. "None." Jackson growled out. Hearing both men refuse to end their disagreement brought a wail of despair from Harland's wife. Sara wrapped her arm around her mother to comfort her. "Gentlemen you will both take your positions." General Stevens replied. Jackson and Harland did as they were instructed. They took their marks and stood back to back ignoring the tearful pleas of their loved ones to cease their duel. "On my count you will both take a step forward. You will turn on ten and fire. Is that understood?" General Stevens asked. Both Jackson and Harland agreed to their understanding. General Stevens began his count. Jackson gripped his revolver and cleared his mind.

Hialeah thundered down the road her heart pounding in her chest. Clouds of dirt trailed behind her as she urged her horse on. She fought back the tears that stung her eyes as she reached Milliner's Pond and her eyes fell upon Jackson. Unable to contain the gut wrenching fear that consumed her, Hialeah screamed for Jackson; her voice echoing through the air. Jackson swiftly turned his head toward the sound of Hialeah's voice. General Stevens halted his count at six just as Hialeah barreled her horse between Jackson and Harland refusing to dismount. Georgina inhaled a sharp breath. Jackson kept his back turned. He would not allow himself to be distracted. "Get out of the way, Miss Nokosi!" Jackson yelled. "You lied to me." Hialeah replied angrily. "Get out of the way!" Jackson remarked threateningly. "Monks!" Hialeah fired back giving way to her tears of anguish. Enraged by Hialeah's interruption, Jackson let out a menacing growl. He quickly holstered his revolver and turned swiftly on his heel. Jackson closed the short distance between himself and Hialeah and roughly grabbed her by both arms and dragged her from her horse.

Hialeah struggled against Jackson's powerful hold to no avail. He slapped her horse on his flanks and Hialeah screamed as she pummeled Jackson's chest with her fists. Harland's patience had worn thin. He was livid that his daughter had been tossed aside for a colored woman. He was even more outraged that Hialeah had dared to show her face in the presence of Sara. "This is who you left my daughter for!" Harland yelled waving his weapon. His outburst caught the attention of all in attendance. "A filthy worthless half-breed nigger!" Harland screeched. He aimed his revolver at Hialeah's back. "Harland!" Jackson fired out. Hialeah looked over her shoulder and inhaled in shock. Jackson quickly released Hialeah's arms and shoved her toward his mother just as Harland fired his gun. Georgina screamed in terror at the sound of Harland's gun shot. Hialeah regained her footing and turned around just as Jackson stumbled backward from the impact of Harland's bullet striking his left shoulder. "Fuck!" Jackson yelled out. In one swift motion, Jackson grabbed his revolver from its holster and fired striking Harland in the middle of his forehead. "Father!" Sara cried out as Harland fell to the ground. She raced to her father and fell to her knees beside his lifeless body. Sara's mother collapsed at the sight of her now dead husband. General Stevens hurried to her aid and lifted her from the ground.

Georgina burst into tears frozen where she stood. Jackson dropped his revolver and walked toward a distraught Georgina. She fell into her son's arms sobbing uncontrollably against Jackson's blood stained shirt. Hialeah covered her mouth to contain herself. She glanced into Jackson's eyes. He showed no signs of being effected by Harland's bullet. His icy glare bore into her as he stood rigid while Georgina continued to weep. "Murderer!" Sara wailed. Hialeah was shaken by Sara's cries. "Hialeah." Jackson said softly reaching out his hand to Hialeah. Hialeah shook her head slowly. She had never been so terrified. She had never seen a man die so swiftly in front of her. She had witnessed how ruthless Jackson could be as she watched him pummel Willie into a bloody mess on the sheriff's floor. He was relentless. Unable to bear the horrendous scene before her, Hialeah ran away. "Hialeah!" Jackson called out. "Lucas, take my mother home." Jackson commanded handing Georgina off to their driver before giving chase after Hialeah.

Running frantically through the trees surrounding Milliner's Pond in search of her horse, Sara's agonizing cries deafened Hialeah to Jackson's command. The images of Jackson getting shot and Harland's body falling to the ground consumed her. Blinded by her tears, Hialeah stumbled and fell to the ground. She hurried to her feet, her escape now barred by Jackson's domineering frame standing before her. Jackson roughly pulled Hialeah toward him and starred menacingly into her horrified eyes. "You grieve the bloody son-of-a-bitch who tormented your mother and gave no thought of killing you?" Jackson growled out. "Why?" Jackson demanded. "I ain't got no care for that man one way or another." Hialeah replied. "Your tears suggest otherwise." Jackson spat. "You lied to me." Hialeah replied angrily through her tears. "What would you have had me do? The bastard wouldn't put an end to his madness." Jackson fired. "What I do if he killed you? Or don't you care none that you standin' here with a bullet in you?" Hialeah cried. "Of course I fucking bloody care. The little shit hurt like hell. Damn me if it doesn't, but all that matters is that I'm standing and so are you." Jackson replied angrily upset that Hialeah faulted him for Harland's death. He released his hold on Hialeah and turned to walk away. "Jackson." Hialeah said her plea falling on deaf ears as Jackson widened the distance between the two of them. "My Jackson!" Hialeah cried out. Jackson spun on his heel to face Hialeah remaining where he stood. "Yes, I am your Jackson! Have you no faith in me!" Jackson yelled. Hialeah ran toward Jackson and threw herself into his arms her tears beginning anew. Jackson growled out in pain. His rigid stance softened. "This all my fault." Hialeah wailed against Jackson's chest. Jackson cupped Hialeah's face tenderly into his hands and gazed down at her tearful eyes. "None of this is your fault." Jackson replied soothingly. "It's my fault cause I fall in love with a man I ain't got no business lovin'." Hialeah remarked. "You're everything to me. Do you understand?" Jackson replied. Hialeah nodded her head. "No matter what you may hear in town, this is my doing. Judge Williams died by my hand." Jackson said. "I don't ever wanna come here no more." Hialeah replied softly. She would never step foot on Milliner's Pond after such a tragedy. "I'll take you home." Jackson remarked. "Please." Hialeah said.

  Jackson held Hialeah as they walked in silence. The approaching sound of a horse caught their attention. Jackson turned around as General Stevens rode toward them. Hialeah continued to walk ahead to allow Jackson a private moment. She remembered vividly what Jackson had told her of the general. He was a slave owner at one time. Hialeah had no desire to be near the man. Jackson stood with his feet slightly apart and his hands clasped behind his back a brooding glare on his face. He waited for the general to dismount his horse. General Stevens closed the distance between him and Jackson and climbed down from his horse holding Jackson's gun. He stood mere inches shorter than Jackson. His once black hair now gray. His blue eyes were dulled from his years fighting in the army and his tanned skin was weathered from the sun. He was broad shouldered and well built and still handsome in his sixty years. "Jackson, I thought you'd like to have this back." General Stevens said. Jackson retrieved his gun and placed it back in its holster. "Thank you." Jackson replied. "The good doctor has kindly taken possession of Judge Williams' body." General Stevens remarked. Jackson simply nodded his head. "I've always considered myself a good friend to your father and to Harland. It is a shame to have things end this way. I will, however, tell the truth of what went on here today." General Stevens said. "I appreciate it." Jackson replied. "God speed on your father's recovery." General Stevens remarked. "Thank you." Jackson replied. General Stevens looked over Jackson's shoulder at Hialeah who stood watching from a distance. He returned his gaze to Jackson who remained in his position; his cold demeanor warning the general to be on his way. General Stevens kept his tongue and returned to his horse. Jackson kept a sharp eye on the general until he had ridden off.

Hialeah was relieved to see General Stevens ride away. She whistled a loud tune that she had taught her horse to recognize. A trick her father had taught her when she was a girl. Jackson turned at the sound of Hialeah's high pitch whistle. He cocked a brow in amazement as Hialeah's horse came into view and walked up to her. Hialeah led him over to Jackson; a smile coming to his lips. "You are brilliant." Jackson said. He mounted Hialeah's horse grimacing from the pain in his shoulder. Fearful of damaging Jackson's shoulder further, Hialeah mounted her horse from the other side. She held onto Jackson's waist until they reached her home.

Hialeah quickly jumped from her horse and raced to open the front door. Jackson climbed down from Hialeah's horse, and followed her inside. "Here. Come sit." Hialeah called out from her bedroom. Jackson's arm was beginning to feel numb. He did as Hialeah ordered and sat on the bed. Hialeah immediately began removing Jackson's blood soaked shirt. She grimaced at the sight of the bloodied hole in Jackson's shoulder. Hialeah looked into Jackson's eyes. "This don't look good. I best go for the doctor." Hialeah rushed out. Jackson quickly grabbed Hialeah's arm. "I hate doctors." Jackson replied. "That bullet gots to come out." Hialeah remarked. "Yes it does." Jackson replied his tone spoke volumes. Hialeah knew what Jackson meant. "Alright. I'll be right back." Hialeah remarked. She left Jackson's side and hurried to start a fire to boil water. She filled her black kettle with water and hung it over the fireplace to heat up. She then hurried outside to find a thick stick for Jackson to bite down on. Returning to her kitchen with a formidable size stick, Hialeah set it on the table before scurrying to her cabinet. She grabbed a jug of whiskey that had belonged to Mr. Hastings and carried them both into her bedroom. She set them both on the small table that set next to her bed. Jackson raised a curious brow at the sight of the whiskey. Hialeah followed his gaze. "It belonged to Mr. Hastings. Now lie back." Hialeah commanded sternly busying herself with the task of gathering towels and her Bowie knife. "I'll ruin your bedding." Jackson replied. "You a wealthy man, Mr. Harding, I suppose you just gonna have to buy me new bedding." Hialeah remarked sarcastically while scrubbing her hands with soap at her wash basin. Jackson managed to chuckle as he laid back against Hialeah's pillows. "I suppose I'll have to buy you new pillows as well." Jackson replied teasingly. "You just hush." Hialeah remarked sternly hurrying over to Jackson with her supplies. She placed her Bowie knife next to the whiskey. Jackson cringed at the size of it. "Have you nothing smaller?" Jackson asked. "This is the small one." Hialeah replied before exiting her bedroom to fetch the water and her sewing utensils. "Bloody fuck." Jackson groaned.

    Hialeah returned wearing an apron and her hair was pulled atop her head in a bun. She poured the heated water into a large mixing bowl and set to work cleaning the dried blood from Jackson's shoulder and arm. She tossed the bloodied towel into her wash basin and refilled another bowl with more water. "How you know how to shoot the way you do? Real fast like." Hialeah asked. "A lot of practice followed by more beatings." Jackson replied. "What you mean?" Hialeah remarked. "I mean I ran away quite often from that horrid school."

Jackson replied. "Where you go?" Hialeah remarked. Jackson smirked. "Ah anywhere my father's money could take me. Most nights, I traveled by train to the absolute worst parts of London. I met a few blokes; real gritty sons-of-bitches, best I ever seen with a gun and I was hungry to learn. They taught me well and I paid them well. Of course, when the headmaster discovered my adventures, I was beaten upon returning." Jackson replied. "That why you don't mind bein' round seedy folk; cause you one of 'em?" Hialeah asked. "Could be." Jackson replied nonchalantly, with a flirtatious wink to Hialeah. She reached for the whiskey and poured a generous amount into a cup for Jackson to down in hopes of dulling some of the pain he was sure to suffer. She nodded her head at Jackson to drink. Jackson took the cup with no hesitation and downed the whiskey. "You've done this before?" Jackson asked. "The women folk in my daddy's tribe took care of the men when the white man threatened harm. I seen it done plenty." Hialeah replied. "I trust you." Jackson remarked reassuringly. Hialeah said a short prayer and offered Jackson the stick. Jackson bit down on the stick as Hialeah doused his wound with the whiskey. Jackson groaned deep from his throat. Hialeah exhaled quickly to calm herself. She instructed Jackson to place his arms to his sides. Jackson did as he was told. Hialeah climbed on top of Jackson to hold him steady. She reached for another towel to wipe away the constant spewing of Jackson's blood. Hialeah looked Jackson in the eyes. "I ready now." Hialeah said her voice slightly quivering. Breathing yet another deep breath to calm herself, Hialeah reached for her Bowie knife. Jackson looked away and tightened his fist against his thighs. His chest was heaving as he bit down on the stick in preparation for the agonizing pain that was sure to ensue.

    Hialeah dug her Bowie knife into Jackson's bloodied flesh. He threw his head back and let out a fiercely deep groan as Hialeah's knife tore into his skin. "Calm yourself." Hialeah said mustering as much comfort as she could. She wiped at Jackson's shoulder with her apron and continued on. Hialeah's knife scratched against the bullet's surface. She pressed her lips together and wiped at her forehead smearing some of Jackson's blood onto her face. She began coaching herself through the procedure by softly singing a song in Creek as she dug at the bullet once more raising it slightly from Jackson's shoulder.

Jackson winced in pain but his body began to relax as Hialeah absentmindedly sung to herself. Jackson found himself listening to Hialeah's song and his fists slowly unclenched. Assured that the bullet was reachable with her fingers, Hialeah carefully used her nails to grasp the bullet using her knife as leverage to raise it from Jackson's shoulder. Hialeah kept her focus on her task. She held firmly onto the bullet and slowly began to ease it from Jackson's shoulder. "Don't move." Hialeah said cautiously. Jackson held his breath, stiffened his body and stared blankly at the ceiling. He could feel Hialeah freeing the bullet from his shoulder. Hialeah propped the bullet with her knife releasing another groan from Jackson's lips. Satisfied with the amount of leverage, Hialeah pulled the bullet from Jackson's shoulder and tossed it into an empty bowl. Hialeah exhaled and poured more whiskey onto Jackson's shoulder. Jackson tried to rise from the bed only to have Hialeah push him back down. She dried his arm and quickly took to threading a needle to stitch Jackson's shoulder. Thinking to teach Jackson a lesson for lying to her, Hialeah removed the stick from Jackson's mouth and tossed it from his reach. "Hard part's over. This might hurt a bit though." Hialeah said simply. "I take it you're preparing to punish me?" Jackson replied. Hialeah responded by sticking her needle through Jackson's shoulder. "Bloody fuck woman, I'm not a torn garment." Jackson remarked wincing from the prick of his skin. Hialeah ignored Jackson's sarcastic comment and took her time stitching his shoulder. She found Jackson's profane language quite amusing. After nearly twenty minutes of being tortured with Hialeah's needle, Jackson had had enough. He had used all of his best curse words. Swiftly rising from the bed, Jackson knocked Hialeah from his midsection onto her back. Pinning her to the bed, Jackson gazed down at her blood smeared face. Hialeah pressed her lips together to keep from laughing. "You are a cruel and merciless woman." Jackson said teasingly. Hialeah burst into laughter. "You think it's funny do you? Dress my wound if you must, but you'll not stick another needle in me." Jackson remarked grinning. "Next time I just cut your arm off." Hialeah replied simply. "Merciless." Jackson teased placing a quick kiss on Hialeah's lips before allowing her to go free to bandage his shoulder.

Jackson sat on Hialeah's bed with his left arm slightly elevated while Hialeah knelt in front of him quietly bandaging his arm. Jackson was ill at ease with her silence. A wave of guilt washed over him. Hialeah's startled and tearful face flashed through his mind. He scolded himself for dragging Hialeah into his conflict with Harland. Hialeah could feel Jackson's eyes on her. She pretended not to notice. Jackson ran his fingers through Hialeah's sleek black locks. Hialeah lost focus and looked up at Jackson. "What're you doin'?" Hialeah asked. "Are you angry with me?" Jackson replied. Hialeah returned her attention to Jackson's bandage. "Just wanna put this awful day behind me." Hialeah remarked. She secured Jackson's bandage and stood. Jackson took Hialeah's hand and caressed it while he stood to his full height. Hialeah gazed up into Jackson's eyes. "Answer me." Jackson replied low. Jackson's intense glare, gentle caress and deep tone left Hialeah at a loss for words. "Miss Nokosi?" Jackson said his tone insistent. "I ain't angry. I worried what folks gonna do." Hialeah replied. "They'll do noth…" Jackson began. His words were cut off by the approaching sound of horses. Hialeah rushed to her window and peered out the curtains. She inhaled sharply and quickly turned around to face Jackson; her face etched with fear. "What is it?" Jackson demanded. "There's five white men on horses ridin' up." Hialeah rushed out. Jackson pulled his gun from its holster. "Stay here." Jackson ordered before racing from Hialeah's bedroom.

Jackson swung the front door open and stepped bare-chested onto the porch. Hialeah listened closely from the threshold of her bedroom door. "You gentlemen are either lost or looking for trouble. Which is it?" Jackson demanded. Hialeah crept back into her bedroom and took another glance out of her window. All five of the men were poorly dressed. Their hair plastered to their faces with sweat and dirt. Hialeah's heart pounded in her chest. She had already witnessed Harland Williams lying dead in front of her at the hand of Jackson. She shuddered at the thought of five more bodies lying lifeless on her property. Hialeah prayed that the men's presence didn't rile Jackson. "We ain't come for trouble, Mr. Harding." One of the men replied nervously. "You know me?" Jackson remarked sarcastically. "Yes sir." The leader of the men replied. "Well you have me at a disadvantage." Jackson remarked coolly. "My name's Harley Joe, these here my brothers, Luke, Jacob, Bobby and Steven." Harley Joe replied. Jackson cocked his gun. "My patience, gentlemen. I have none." Jackson remarked threateningly. "Word in town is that you killed Judge Williams." Harley Joe replied. "I have six bullets in this gun. One of you will be twice as unlucky as the rest." Jackson remarked. Hialeah closed her eyes tight fearfully anticipating the sound of Jackson's gun firing. "We just come to thank you for what you did." Harley Joe replied. Hialeah's eyes popped open in shock at Harley Joe's words. "Is that right?" Jackson asked his tone dripping with sarcasm. "Yes sir." Harley Joe replied. His brothers mumbled their agreement. "Now why would a bunch of well mannered chaps such as yourselves be thankful of a man's death?" Jackson asked curiously. "That son-of-a-bitch took our farms away. He own the land. Say we owed money on the land but there weren't no truth in it. We paid him what he due on time each month. So we come by here to personally thank you for riddin' us good hard workin' folks of that scoundrel." Harley Joe replied. "If it's all the same to you, next time you feelin' like gunnin' down a Williams, take good aim at that rotten princess he called his daughter." Jacob spat. Jackson raised a curious brow. "Do tell, I'm most eager to hear what horrid act Miss Williams has committed that warrant the same fate as her repulsive father." Jackson replied sarcastically. "Horrid act? What you say to murder?" Harley Joe remarked. "Murder?" Jackson replied, skeptical of the five brothers. "That's right. If she had her way, Jacob here would be without his wife." Harley Joe remarked. Jackson turned toward Jacob. "Go on." Jackson replied. "Yes sir. Well around last year, right when we's losin' our farms, they's had a county fair what had a pie bakin' contest. My Molly a sure fit to win with her peach pie. That Miss Williams try her hand at bakin' and well it ain't go over too well with the judges. Just as we figured, my Molly win the blue and the twenty-dollars prize what went along with it. We needed the money after losin' our farm and all. Woo wee, that Miss Sara was right sore for sure but she played real cool bout it. She offer my Molly a job cookin' and cleanin' and what have you. Molly goes over to the Williams' place to discuss her wages and she given a glass of iced tea what Miss Sara done put rat poison in." Jacob remarked. Jackson raised his brows in astonishment. "Rat poison?" Jackson asked incredulously. "Rat poison indeed. Got my

Molly right sick. Says she doubled over and fall from her chair. Says Miss Sara whisper in her ear that bein' white trash is almost as bad as bein' a nigger. Leave Molly right there on the floor to die. Ain't sure how she got the strength to get to the wagon but she did. Went straight to Sheriff Willard tell him what happen but that crooked sheriff and Sara's pa ain't believe not a word from my wife. Judge Williams threaten to see Molly hang for makin' up lies and not one lawyer willin' to take the case. Say it's my wife's word against Miss Sara's. I tells you, the lot of them rich sons-of-bitches, they's all stick together." Jacob said in disgust. "That Sara Williams ain't one to cross. She's downright evil. That woman got it in for you, she ain't one to stop 'til she get what she after." Harley Joe replied. "And what she after is your colored lady gal...and you." Jacob remarked matter-of-factly. "Much obliged for the warning, Jacob, Harley Joe. Oh and Harley Joe." Jackson remarked. "Yes sir." Harley Joe replied. "That colored lady isn't too keen on trespassers nor am I." Jackson remarked low. Harley Joe caught Jackson's meaning. The whole town knew of Jackson's duel and the affection he carried for coloreds and the half-breed woman he had chosen over Sara Williams. Harley Joe didn't want to cross paths with Jackson Harding. Where he laid his head and with whom was none of his concern. "You or your lady friend ain't got no trouble here, Mr. Harding." Harley Joe replied. "Good man." Jackson remarked. Harley Joe turned his horse and his brothers followed. Jackson watched the men until they were out of his sight. Hialeah exhaled a grateful sigh. She was relieved that Jackson hadn't lost his temper with the strangers. She was in no mood for burying bodies.

Jackson holstered his gun and returned inside. Hialeah didn't like the scowl on Jackson's face. "Your shoulder painin' you?" Hialeah asked. "Yes." Jackson replied casually. "You want me to take a look at it once more?" Hialeah remarked. "No. I want you to gather your things." Jackson replied sternly. Hialeah furrowed her brows. "What for?" Hialeah remarked. "Because I don't want to have to kill Harley Joe and his brothers." Jackson replied simply. "Kill 'em?" Hialeah replied stunned by Jackson's calm response. "Why you need to kill 'em for?" Hialeah asked. "I don't like the idea of five strange men coming to your door." Jackson replied. "Jackson, I live here a long time with the Hastings. I ain't ever had no trouble. Besides, they say they right happy Judge Williams is dead." Hialeah remarked. "There will be many who aren't. I'll hitch your wagon. Get your things." Jackson replied sternly. Hialeah hurried to her room. A sudden sense of fear came over her. She knew Jackson was right. Judge Williams was a well known man with a lot of powerful friends.

Jackson hurried to the barn to prepare Hialeah's wagon while she packed what she needed. When Jackson returned, Hialeah was standing on her front porch with her bags and the rifle that had belonged to Mr. Hastings. Jackson hopped down from the wagon and took Hialeah's bags placing them into the back of the wagon. "Mr. Hastings left this to me." Hialeah said handing the rifle to Jackson. Jackson inspected the rifle before handing it back to Hialeah. "I don't expect we'll have any problems on the way but you shoot to kill." Jackson replied. "Where you takin' me?" Hialeah remarked. "You'll stay with me where it's safe. I don't want you going anywhere without my knowledge." Jackson replied sternly. "Dead man can't hurt nobody." Hialeah remarked. Jackson lifted Hialeah onto the wagon. He climbed in next to her and took the reins. "A dead man with a vengeful daughter is not to be trusted." Jackson replied. "You think she come after me?" Hialeah asked. "I think she'll do whatever she can to cause me the same pain she's feeling now." Jackson replied. "Kill me?" Hialeah said. "Yes." Jackson replied simply. "I ain't afraid of her, Jackson." Hialeah remarked. Jackson took Hialeah's hand and placed a kiss on the back of it. "I know, but I'll not risk you getting hurt on account of my rejecting her." Jackson replied. Hialeah nodded. "I stay close." Hialeah remarked. "Promise me." Jackson said. "I promise." Hialeah replied. She took a hold of Jackson's hand and gave it a gentle squeeze. Jackson tapped Hialeah's horse with the reins. Hialeah looked over her shoulder at her home as they rode off. "I know what you're thinking." Jackson said. Hialeah laid her head on Jackson's shoulder but said nothing.

Hialeah was wary of her surroundings as she and Jackson traveled to his home. She dismissed the thoughts of leaving her home and focused on every passerby they encountered on the way. The Hardings and Williams family were close neighbors and many of the carriages they passed along the way were leaving the Williams' home after having paid their respects to Mrs. Williams and Sara on their dearly departed. Many mouths were left agape as Jackson continued on with Hialeah by his side. Hialeah found herself tightly gripping her rifle. She found it rather difficult to make eye contact with those they rode by. She could only imagine what foul thoughts were running through their heads. She glanced over at Jackson a time or two. His demeanor was void of any expression. He was now a pariah to many. An obvious fact that Jackson clearly didn't give a damn about. No one wanted any trouble. Silent gawkers that Jackson paid no heed to.

Georgina was unable to regain her composure; her mind wandering frantically of her son's whereabouts. She ordered Samuel to inform her the very moment Jackson walked through the door. No sooner than Georgina finished her sentence, Jackson and Hialeah rode up the path to his home. Georgina nearly burst through the front door in her haste to get to her son. Jackson halted the wagon and turned to face Hialeah. "Stay here." Jackson said. His mother's worried face troubled him. Jackson climbed from the wagon and rushed to his mother. Georgina threw her arms around Jackson. "Dear Lord, you had me worried." Georgina said her words muffled by Jackson's chest. She looked up at her son. "Where have you been?" Georgina said worriedly. "Miss Nokosi tended to my shoulder." Jackson replied. "Merciful heavens, your shoulder. I'll send for the doctor. He'll see to it that your shoulder is properly cared for." Georgina remarked. "That's not necessary. Miss Nokosi has taken care of it." Jackson replied. Georgina offered Jackson a faint smile. "Of course." Georgina said. She glanced over Jackson's shoulder at a waiting Hialeah. "There was no other way to keep the both of you safe." Jackson said before Georgina could utter a word. "There will be talk." Georgina replied in a hushed whisper. "There has been talk since I were a boy." Jackson remarked. "Sara and her dear mother have received constant visitors coming by to pay their respects." Georgina replied. "Your respects will not be wanted." Jackson remarked assuredly. "Jackson it is the decent thing to do." Georgina protested. "Mrs. Williams has always been a close friend." Georgina said. Jackson placed his hands on his mother's small shoulders and gazed down into her eyes. "You are the mother of the man who took her husband's life. I promise you, you will not be welcomed between the walls of her home." Jackson remarked. "Until this tragedy is no longer on the tongues of our neighbors, I won't have you nor Miss Nokosi venturing into town unescorted. Do you understand?" Jackson said. "I know you're right." Georgina replied. "I am." Jackson remarked. "I'll have one of the servants' room prepared for Miss Nokosi." Georgina replied. "Servants' room?" Jackson asked his brows furrowed. "You'll not sin under my roof Jackson Harding." Georgina replied matter-of-factly. "Go on with you now." Georgina remarked before making her way back to the house.

Jackson watched his mother disappear into the house. Hialeah drove her wagon the short distance toward Jackson. He climbed back onto his seat and took over the reins. "Where you suppose I go?" Hialeah asked. "What do you mean?" Jackson replied. "Your mother, she don't want me here." Hialeah remarked. "My mother is preparing a room for your stay." Jackson replied. "How long that gonna be?" Hialeah remarked. "As long as need be." Jackson replied. "My father's investors will be here in two days time. This whole ordeal with Judge Williams could ruin my family." Jackson said. "Maybe explain to 'em that you didn't want this to happen." Hialeah replied. "I pray it will be that easy." Jackson remarked. "I never took you for a prayin' man." Hialeah replied. "I'm not, but maybe I'll start. Come on, we'll get you settled in and I'll drive you to your preaching." Jackson remarked. "Ain't goin' to preachin'." Hialeah replied somberly. Her confession gave Jackson pause. He stopped the wagon and turned to Hialeah. "You've never missed your reverend's sermon." Jackson said curiously. "Too much goin' on round here to be concerned bout that now." Hialeah replied simply keeping her eyes focused ahead. "You don't think me to believe that?" Jackson asked. "I just don't feel up to it and that's all there is to it." Hialeah replied. "Alright then." Jackson remarked. He turned the wagon away from his home to Hialeah's surprise. "What you doin'?" Hialeah rushed out. "I'm taking you to church." Jackson replied simply. "No, Jackson please." Hialeah remarked pleadingly. Jackson stopped the wagon suddenly. "The truth. Now." Jackson demanded his hazel eyes piercing through Hialeah. "I can't go back there." Hialeah replied. She could feel her eyes swelling up with tears. She cast her eyes down in an attempt to avoid Jackson's intimidating stare. "You think it just your people what don't want us together?" Hialeah said. She exhaled before finding the nerve to face

Jackson. "He say he gonna tell everyone I your whore." Hialeah said. "Isaac?" Jackson replied dryly. "I try not to let it bother me none but I see myself walkin' in that church and everyone turn around in their seats and stare and whisper bout how I give myself to a white man." Hialeah remarked as she looked into Jackson's eyes; tears falling from her own. "I swear I ain't shamed to love you…" Hialeah began. "Stop. Isaac. My father's investors. It all stops." Jackson replied sternly. He gently wiped the fallen tears from Hialeah's eyes before guiding her horse back toward the house.

Jackson stopped the wagon and handed the reins to one of the footmen. He climbed down and instructed for Hialeah to remain seated. Jackson walked toward the back of the wagon and grabbed Hialeah's bag and the rifle from her lap before entering the house. Hialeah waited patiently in the wagon. Several minutes passed before Jackson emerged from the house wearing a clean white shirt and a black Gambler hat. He climbed back onto the wagon and retrieved the reins from his footman. Hialeah gave Jackson a look of shear curiosity as they started off down the road. "Where we goin'?" Hialeah asked. "To church. If folks want to talk, we'll give them something that'll keep their tongues wagging for years to come." Jackson replied. "What you fixin' to do to Isaac?" Hialeah asked her faced etched with concern. "You don't think I'll result to violence in the Lord's house?" Jackson replied teasingly. Hialeah replied with a cock of her brow. Jackson was all too aware that Hialeah's sarcastic gesture was in response to his duel and the death of Judge Williams. Jackson held his tongue. He didn't wish to go down that road again. Perhaps going to church with Hialeah would be beneficial. He hadn't attended church since he was a boy. An uplifting sermon could very well clear his mind and his conscious.

Hialeah and Jackson could hear the powerful words of the preacher as they approached the church. Jackson stopped the wagon and lifted Hialeah from her seat. Jackson straightened his coat and Hialeah caught a glimpse of Jackson's pistol. It was now she who held her tongue as Jackson offered her his hand to escort her through the church doors. Jackson could feel Hialeah's hand tremble in his. He gave her hand a gentle squeeze and looked down on her visibly nervous face. "The Lord welcomes all into his house remember?" Jackson said. Hialeah pressed her lips together and nodded slightly. Jackson opened the church door and Hialeah hesitated before finding enough courage to take a step inside. Hialeah's heart was pounding wildly in her chest. The sight of Jackson standing in the middle of the aisle brought silent stares throughout the church. Hialeah's stomach dropped as her eyes fell on the seat in the back row where she usually sat now occupied by Isaac. She quickly cast her eyes away from his heated stare. Miss Lilly rose from her seat with a welcoming smile on her face. Jackson removed his hat and nodded his head in greeting as he led Hialeah toward the front of the congregation where Miss Lilly graciously offered them seats next to her. Hialeah's nervousness melted away as Miss Lilly patted the empty space next to her. Hialeah took her seat between Miss Lilly and Jackson and clasped her hands on her lap. She released a long held sigh of relief when the preacher carried on with his sermon. Hialeah stole a quick glance at Jackson whose attention had been taken away by the preacher's words. Jackson absentmindedly reached out and took a hold of Hialeah's hand. Hialeah smiled and focused her attention on the sermon.

When the sermon ended, the preacher called for a song from the choir. Jackson briefly released his hold on Hialeah's hand. He had held it throughout the entire service. Jackson reached into his inner coat pocket and pulled out his hymn book. Hialeah's eyes widened in utter shock. Miss Lilly stood as did the rest of the congregation to join the choir in song. Jackson opened his hymn book stunning Hialeah as he too began singing. Hialeah leaned closer to Jackson. "How you know this song?" Hialeah whispered. Jackson continued singing without the use of his hymn book. He flipped to the front of the book and pointed out the inscription to Hialeah. Hialeah inhaled sharply as she read the words on the first page of Jackson's hymn book, 'To my dear Jackson, love always, Mama Lilly'.

The service ended after a final prayer. Hialeah felt the blood rush from her face as the preacher approached Jackson. Glancing up at Jackson, Hialeah was confused as to why Jackson was smiling. Reverend Tucker held out his hand. Jackson accepted the reverend's hand and gave it a firm shake. Both men were full of smiles. "Young

Mr. Harding." Reverend Tucker said beaming. "Reverend Tucker." Jackson replied. "Why I haven't laid eyes on you since you were a young boy taggin' along behind Miss Lilly." Reverend Tucker remarked. Hialeah was sure she was hearing things. "I've been away." Jackson replied. "I remember. Well it is a blessin' to have you back." Reverend Tucker remarked. "Thank you, sir." Jackson replied. "You will stay for lunch?" Reverend Tucker asked. "Of course." Jackson replied. Reverend Tucker nodded his head and tapped Jackson on the shoulder before taking his leave. Jackson was relieved that the reverend didn't offer his friendly tap on his injured shoulder. Hialeah waited until the reverend was out of ear shot before she poked Jackson in the stomach. Jackson groaned and looked down at Hialeah who was tapping her foot with her arms crossed. "What was that for?" Jackson asked his brows raised. "Why you ain't tell me Miss Lilly bring you here when you was a boy?" Hialeah replied in a hushed whisper. Jackson cocked a grin. "You never asked." Jackson remarked teasingly. Before Hialeah could open her mouth, Miss Lilly called her away to assist with the lunch preparation. Jackson leaned in toward Hialeah. "You best get going. Us men are practically starved." Jackson said teasingly with a wink.

    Hialeah left the men to their business and followed the women to prepare for the Sunday luncheon that always followed the service. She glanced over her shoulder at Jackson a feeling of pride washed over her. He never ceased to amaze her. Here she was apprehensive about stepping into her own church and Jackson, as always showed no sign of fear. Hialeah couldn't get over his calmness. He wasn't in the slightest threatened by Isaac. Isaac? Hialeah thought to herself. He wasn't in the church with the other men. Wherever he was, Hialeah continued with her thought as she stepped out into the hot sun, she was relieved that he couldn't cause her any trouble. Her feelings for Jackson were out for everyone to see. Hialeah found herself breathing a sigh of relief as she made her way toward the other women. She stopped short at the sight of Isaac and his brother, George standing near the Leonard's family wagon. Squaring her shoulders, Hialeah looked straight ahead and ignored Isaac's scowling face. Not one to be snubbed, Isaac matched Hialeah's stride and roughly grabbed a hold of her arm. "What you doin' bringin' your massuh here?" Isaac said heatedly. Hialeah pulled her arm away from Isaac's hold. "You keep your hands off me Isaac Leonard." Hialeah spat. "This here church for colored folks and your white boy ain't welcomed here." Isaac replied through gritted teeth. "The Lord welcomes all to his house." Hialeah remarked using Jackson's words to defend his appearance at the church. "I told you I was gonna tell everybody that you ain't nothin' but a whore for the white man, and I aims to do just that." Isaac replied. "You go right on ahead. Ain't no secret no more." Hialeah remarked. "Ain't no secret what your massuh did to Judge Williams either." Isaac replied. "He kill his own for me. What you think he gonna do to you he see you handlin' me like you doin'?" Hialeah said their heated exchange witnessed by Miss Lilly who immediately marched her way over to Hialeah and Isaac.

Miss Lilly stood between Hialeah and Isaac with her hands placed aggressively on her hips as she glared up at Isaac. "Ain't got no time for you to be standin' round. Folks ready to eat." Miss Lilly said. "I ain't fixin' to eat with no willin' bedwench." Isaac spat angrily. His harsh words received him a stinging slap across his face. Hialeah jumped, startled by Miss Lilly's swift slap across Isaac's smug face. "You get on and get those there tables together you hear?" Miss Lilly ordered. Humiliated, Isaac stormed off to do what was told of him. George cringed from where he stood. Fearing Miss Lilly's wrath, George hurried after his brother. Miss Lilly turned to face Hialeah. Her face had softened once Isaac had left the two of them alone. "I'm sorry for my nephew's rude behavior toward you." Miss Lilly said. "Your...your nephew?" Hialeah stammered out stunned. "That's right and he always been that way. Not one to take rejection easy." Miss Lilly replied. "I ain't mean to hurt him but Jackson, well he done stole my heart." Hialeah remarked. "And after Isaac say he gonna tell anyone who willin' to listen that I love a white man, it scared me somethin' awful to come here." Hialeah said. "Well I know it had to be somethin' cause you ain't the kind to miss the preachin'." Miss Lilly replied. "No ma'am." Hialeah remarked. "Miss Lilly, how exactly you and Isaac kin?" Hialeah asked. "His mama, Louise and me, well we sisters. We both were bought by Jackson's daddy from another family. We just young girls then. Maybe a tad younger than you, I wager. Louise, she married Isaac's daddy and I, well I married my Amos.

Amos Willis." Miss Lilly said. "Isaac tell me he ain't know Jackson." Hialeah replied. "That's true. Isaac's daddy, he was trouble for Mr. Harding. He had him sold away. Mr. Harding sold my sister, too. He sell 'em off to one of Judge Williams' friends. I begged him not to but he ain't wanna deal with him no more. Their new owners weren't too kind and I ain't see my sister for a good many years. Amos and me, we just keep the Hardings happy. Do as we were told. Got on their good side. When Jackson come along, his mama was miserable. I delivered him into this world, but that Miss Georgina, she ain't want nothin' to do with her own boy. Oh, she despised bein' a mother. She cried bout how Jackson ruined her fine figure. I cared for that boy like he my own." Miss Lilly said. "How horrible for Jackson. I can't imagine not wantin' what the good Lord give me. That why Jackson call you Mama Lilly?" Hialeah replied. "Ain't no other reason. He went everywhere I went the moment he could walk. On Sundays, Mr. Harding allowed us to have church near the stables and Jackson he come right along with me. Afterwards, we'd eat and Jackson would play with the other slave children. Miss Georgina ain't want Jackson pickin' up our slave habits and negro songs but Jackson, he sang them all the time. No matter how many times that boy got beat, he would sing with us and play with our children. Most nights, he would sneak outta the house and come down to sleep between my Amos and me. Then one day, Jackson and the other children go for a swim. Jackson weren't too good a swimmer right yet and he went too far out in the water and he nearly drowned. Miss Georgina screamed and yelled for someone to save her baby. My Amos jumped right in that water and pulled Jackson out. It was somethin' to see. Mr. Harding was indebted to my Amos. He said he could have anything he wanted. Amos say that he wanted to be free and wanted his brother and his family back. Mr. Harding agreed and he give Amos and me our freedom. He buy my sister and her children back too. Amos wanted to go up north start life new as a free man but Mr. Harding and Miss Georgina, they ain't know what to do bout Jackson. He too colored for their likin'. I took to him from the day he was born and I couldn't imagine what they do to him if I was to go up north. His beatings were all I could stand. Mr. Harding convinced Amos to stay. Once we got our papers sayin' we was free, we come here to this church and Jackson come with me. Mr. Harding paid Amos real good and gave him land on his property." Miss Lilly said. "That your house what sit back near the tobacco barn?" Hialeah asked surprised by the news of Jackson's raising and Miss Lilly's life. "Sure is. Been there a long time. Thought my heart would rip clear outta my chest when they take Jackson away from here. Seven years old and cryin' the worst sound you ever wanna hear. He write me letters and I write back. I tell him to be strong and that I be here whenever he comes home. We wrote each other plenty. Then the war start and he tell his folks he happy that all the slaves gonna be free and that made his daddy right sore. They stop writin' him letters and sendin' him money. When his mama find out he made a name for himself, why she proud as can be. She start tellin' anybody who would listen how rich he was. He tell her he ain't never comin' back here. I tell Amos I ain't wanna be here no more if my boy ain't returnin' but then my Amos took ill and died. He buried nearby. I ain't never gonna leave him." Miss Lilly said. Hialeah nodded her head in understanding. "Then Jackson write me, tell me he comin' home for holiday, maybe get married." Miss Lilly said. "What I don't much understand is what Isaac got against Jackson if he ain't never knowed him." Hialeah said. "Isaac ain't got to know Jackson. In his mind, no colored woman ought be with no white man. He took a likin' to you round time we's celebratin' at the Independence festival. He believe Jackson steal you away from him." Miss Lilly replied. "That ain't true. I sure I took a likin' to Jackson the moment I seen him come into town. Even though I tell him I ain't much care for him right off." Hialeah remarked. "Don't go worryin' yourself over Isaac. He'll find him a good girl and leave you be soon enough." Miss Lilly replied. "I hate to think what happen if them two go at each other. I sometime think it best if Jackson find himself a white woman to love him." Hialeah remarked. "That's downright foolish talk. Jackson gonna love who Jackson gonna love. Besides, the two of them goin' after one another, ain't never gonna happen, you hear?" Miss Lilly said. "Yes ma'am." Hialeah replied. "Well now that you know all there is to know bout Jackson, we best get this food to the tables. Ain't nothin' worst than a hungry man." Miss Lilly remarked lightly.

Hialeah followed Miss Lilly to join the other women. Hialeah kept on Miss Lilly's heels as she walked by a still scowling Isaac who took to moving tables with George and several of the other men. Once all the tables were in order, the women of the church covered them with table cloths before placing the various dishes on them to be served. Hialeah kept at her task while anxiously awaiting Jackson and Reverend Tucker to emerge from the church. She could feel Isaac's heated glare on her like a ravenous dog in search of a bone. Hialeah stuck to Miss Lilly setting up whatever needed done. In her angst to keep a clear distance from Isaac, Hialeah bumped into Louise Leonard who was carrying a freshly baked cake to one of the tables. Without a second thought, Hialeah reached for the cake, in an attempt to keep it from falling onto the ground. She smiled faintly at Louise and assisted with carefully placing the cake onto the table before quickly heading in the opposite direction of Isaac's mother. Hialeah sneaked a glance over her shoulder at Louise. The older woman shared the same scowl as her son. By the bothered expression on her face, she too shared the same disgust as her son.

Hialeah was more than relieved to hear the lunch bell ring. The tables were set and the men took their seats while their respective wives went about serving their men. Jackson and Reverend Tucker exited the church, their faces full of smiles. Whatever their conversation had been it brought raucous laughter from the both of them as they made their way to the many tables. Reverend Tucker invited Jackson to sit with him and other distinguished members of the church. Reverend Tucker was a widower and Miss Lilly had always taken it upon herself to see that the head of their church was served. Just as Hialeah was reaching for a plate to serve Jackson, Violet collided with her. Her cold demeanor and icy glare at Hialeah was indicative that she was still quite angry at having been attacked in the Harding's tobacco field. Surrounded by her friends, Violet seized the opportunity to make a snide remark in Hialeah's direction. "I see someone's fixin' to serve their massuh." Violet said. Her spiteful comment received giggles from her friends. "I fixin' to serve the man I love just like you fixin' to do." Hialeah replied heatedly. "My man colored like me." Violet remarked coldly. "Maybe, but your man work for mine." Hialeah fired back her voice low and equally cold as Violet's. Overhearing the heated exchange between the two women, Miss Lilly stepped in between them and puffed out her chest like a protective mother bird. The smiles of

Violet's friends immediately left their faces. Miss Lilly starred daggers into Violet. "Get what you gonna get and mind your own affairs." Miss Lilly spat. "Humph." Violet replied. She grabbed her plate and went on about her business followed by her friends. "Take care of your man and don't let them cacklin' hens get to you." Miss Lilly said. Hialeah nodded her head and continued on with making Jackson a plate of food. She was disgusted that she had allowed Violet's comment make her feel ill at ease. She was sure that Violet wasn't the only one who found humor in her serving a white man. Hialeah glanced quickly over her shoulder at Jackson. He smiled and offered her a loving wink while in the midst of his conversing with the reverend. Hialeah found herself blushing. Violet's crude comment instantly left her mind as she piled Jackson's plate high with food before preparing her own lunch.

Returning to the table, Hialeah set Jackson's plate in front of him. His eyes widened at the amount of succulent food before him. "Miss Nokosi, are you trying to fatten me up?" Jackson teased. "Miss Lilly say there ain't nothin' worst than a hungry man." Hialeah replied smiling. "Wise woman." Jackson remarked before shoving a fork full of food into his mouth and growling for emphasis. The men around him burst into laughter. Hialeah laughed as she left the men to their end of the table. She joined Miss Lilly and a group of older women at their end. Hialeah sat where she could watch and revel in Jackson's light. She admired how he felt truly at ease with colored folks. Miss Lilly caught Hialeah eyeing him and stifled a laugh. Hialeah glanced toward Miss Lilly realizing she had been caught. Her face warmed up and she quickly took a bite of her lunch.

Isaac sat with a group of his friends at a table across from Hialeah. From his seat he had a clear view of the woman who had rejected him time and again. While his friends chatted amongst themselves, Isaac could only focus on Hialeah. He found himself glancing at Jackson's backside. Consumed with envy of the man who stole his woman from him, Isaac couldn't bear to be in Hialeah's presence. He angrily tossed his fork onto his plate and rose from the table. Hialeah took immediate notice of Isaac. Her heart began to race as she looked down the table at Jackson whom was engrossed in laughter with the reverend and the other men from the church. Fearful that Isaac had intentions of confronting Jackson, Hialeah slowly began to rise from her seat fully prepared to warn Jackson. Miss Lilly followed Hialeah's worried gaze and looked over her shoulder. Miss Lilly's eyes locked onto Isaac. Both she and Hialeah kept their eyes on him as he mounted his horse and angrily rode away from the church. Relieved that there would be no trouble, Hialeah sat back down to finish her lunch.

When the service and lunch had concluded, Hialeah joined Jackson in her wagon as they made their way back to his home. Hialeah nestled her head against Jackson's shoulder. She always felt protected when he was near. "Your shoulder still botherin' you much?" Hialeah asked. "Not so much. I had a real fine doctor fix me up." Jackson replied smiling. "Miss Lilly tell me stories bout when you was young." Hialeah said. "Did she now?" Jackson replied lightly. "She tell me how much she love you. How you like her own son and how it broke her heart when you left." Hialeah remarked. "Not one of my fondest memories." Jackson replied. "She say it was her Amos that saved your life. Kept you from drownin' and your daddy give 'em their freedom." Hialeah remarked. "She remained close in my heart through many troubled times." Jackson replied. "She a mighty fine lady." Hialeah remarked. "That she is." Jackson replied. "She also tell me how she tanned your behind a time or two." Hialeah remarked teasingly. Jackson burst into laughter. "That she did. A firm hand indeed." Jackson replied. "What about you? Who took a firm hand to little Hialeah?" Jackson said. "Oh that's easy. My puse. My grandmother. There were many times when I found myself wanderin' instead of learnin' and she would take my hand, lead me away from the other children and warm my behind but good." Hialeah replied lightly. "I don't think we've ever discussed it. Why didn't you marry and have a family within your father's tribe?" Jackson asked. "I was promised to a man named Lamochattee. It means Red Eagle. He was one of the sons of my father's good friend." Hialeah replied. "What happened? Did you not love him?" Jackson asked. "Monks. I cared for his younger brother, Kikikwawason. It means Lightening." Hialeah replied. "Let me guess. The elder son had to marry before the younger?" Jackson remarked. "Henka, but I could not bring my heart to love Lamochattee." Hialeah replied. "Why is that?" Jackson remarked. "Lamochattee was prideful and arrogant, even more so than you." Hialeah replied. Jackson found Hialeah's innocent description of him amusing. "Am I so horrible?" Jackson asked lightly. "I gettin' use to it. Not like Lamochattee. His arrogance caught the eyes of many girls in the tribe and he liked it plenty. He fought all the time with the other warriors and boasted when he won. He never lost. I would hear stories of him takin' lovers. Sometimes it would upset me but most times I was grateful. I would beg my daddy to break his promise to his friend. To find me a worthy husband but he wouldn't hear of losin' a trusted friend on account of my jealousy. I often times would plead with my mother to speak to my father to allow me a husband that would love me like he did her but he would dismiss her and they would argue. My father loved me but he insisted on keepin' his word. The day I was to marry Lamochattee, it was discovered that he had fathered a child with another woman. The arrangement was broken by Lamochattee's betrayal. He was forced to marry and I was free to marry Kikikwawason." Hialeah replied. Jackson stopped the wagon and turned to Hialeah. "Then you took him as your husband?" Jackson remarked curiously. "Kikikwawason was killed durin' a hunt for food. He was thrown from his horse. His neck was broken from the fall. My daddy find me another husband, but I refuse him. He get real sore and we argue somethin' terrible. He tell me I follow his rules. That when I decide to go away." Hialeah replied sadly. "You defied your father." Jackson remarked. "I disappoint him in doin' so. My mama stay behind. That's how I come to be here; alone." Hialeah replied.

Jackson remembered his previous conversation with Hialeah. She had refused to open herself up to his inquiry about her family. He now knew why. It pained her to leave them behind. "You cared for him greatly. I'm sorry you lost someone so dear to you. This Kikikwawason." Jackson remarked gently. "It was a long time ago." Hialeah replied softly. "Why didn't you go back? You have family there." Jackson remarked. "My puse understood why I had to leave. Why I had to find my own way and I found you." Hialeah replied. Jackson nodded his head and took Hialeah's hand and placed a soft kiss on it. "That you did." Jackson remarked gently.

After having told Jackson more than she cared to remember, Hialeah rode the rest of the way to the Harding home in silence. She placed her head back on Jackson's shoulder and closed her eyes as the wind blew gently through her hair. Comforted by the man who now captured her heart, Hialeah erased Lamochattee and Kikikwawason from her thoughts. She did, however, miss her mother and father and thought of them often. Just as Hialeah was beginning to relax, Jackson stopped the wagon at the entrance to his home. He climbed down from the wagon and walked over to Hialeah and assisted her from her seat before handing the reins to one of his footmen. Jackson barely had enough time to brush the wrinkles from his trousers before Samuel burst through the door. "Mr. Jackson come quick!" Samuel exploded excitedly. "Your daddy, he awake! He awake, Mr. Jackson!" Samuel exclaimed. Hearing the exciting news, Jackson bolted up the front steps and through the door of his home. He raced by the servants and took the grand stairs two at a time. Jackson stopped his mad rush at the entrance to his parents' bedroom. Henry Harding was sitting up for the first time since he fell ill. Georgina sat next to her husband on their bed holding his hand. Both Georgina and Henry turned to face a smiling Jackson. "Father." Jackson said before entering further into his parents' room. Henry's nurse quietly left the family alone and closed the door behind her.

Chapter 13

Upon returning from church, Hialeah thought it best to leave Jackson to his family. She was sure there was much to discuss. She found herself walking the length of the Harding's garden on through the tobacco field where she came upon Miss Lilly's home. Hialeah was in awe of Miss Lilly's flowers that lined her steps in their small pots. The door was open and from Miss Lilly's front yard, Hialeah could hear the older woman singing a church hymn. Hialeah didn't wish to intrude on Miss Lilly's privacy. She sat on the steps and leaned her head against the rail and closed her eyes as she sun beamed on her skin and the soothing sound of Miss Lilly's song relaxed her. Hialeah, too was familiar with the hymn and she absentmindedly began to sing along.

From inside her house, Miss Lilly could hear the soft accompanying yet strange voice. She continued singing as she walked to her front door. She recognized Hialeah's small frame and she suddenly stopped singing and smiled as she left Hialeah to do the singing. Engrossed in her thoughts, Hialeah had yet to notice that she was now entertaining Miss Lilly. She finished the song and received a kind applause from Miss Lilly. Startled, Hialeah bolted from her seat and turned around nervously to face a grinning Miss Lilly. Hialeah quickly clasped her hands in front of her. "That was very nice." Miss Lilly said stepping out onto her porch. "I…I didn't mean to intrude on your privacy." Hialeah stammered out. "No intrusion at all. I welcome the company." Miss Lilly replied. "Mr. Harding feelin' better now. I thought it best to leave Jackson to his family affairs." Hialeah remarked. "Well you more than welcome to come sit a spell while they tend to their family business." Miss Lilly replied. "Mvto. (Muh-doe) I mean thank you." Hialeah remarked. "Got some nice cold ice tea settin' on the table. I was just bout ready to have myself a glass." Miss Lilly replied.

Hialeah followed Miss Lilly into her home. Hialeah loved how comfortably decorated it was. Flowers set on the table and small handmade pillows set on the kitchen chairs. Hialeah especially loved the white lace curtains that hung in the windows blowing in the breeze. She sat across from Miss Lilly and watched as she poured two glasses of iced tea and offered Hialeah a slice of freshly made chocolate cake. Jackson was right. Miss Lilly was one fine cook. The cake was delicious and Hialeah complimented her friend on her tasty dessert.

The sun had begun to set and for the first time in several weeks, Henry Harding joined his wife and son at the dinner table. Miss Lilly was off duty on Sundays so the care of dinner was left to Lavinia. Her culinary skills were not up to par with Miss Lilly's but she was capable in her own right of serving a tolerable dish. Georgina had taken it upon herself while Jackson attended church to inform her husband of his close friend's passing. Henry had sent word of his condolences to the now Widow Williams by way of Samuel. Henry hated to hear that his friend met his demise at the hand of his son. He was even more so sickened that their duel had been on account of his son's lust for a colored woman. Georgina attempted to soften the shock by informing her husband that Jackson wanted nothing to do with the duel. That he had insisted on calling it off but that Judge Williams wouldn't hear of it and even threatened their good name. Hearing his wife's testimony removed some of the sting of his friend's death but the elder Harding remained unpleased with his son's love of a half breed. Georgina came to Hialeah's defense. She felt it was her duty as a woman to inform her husband that had it not been for Hialeah's knowledge of tobacco that their crops would have been burned by their neighbors. However, in saying as much, Georgina kept the secret from her husband that Hialeah would be staying with them as a guest. She would leave that up to Jackson.

After dinner, Henry questioned Jackson the books and accounts. Jackson assured his father that all was well but to appease him, Jackson brought the books and went over every transaction and every detail with his father. In the midst of going over the accounts, Jackson went into further detail about his duel. He showed his father his wounded shoulder and how he had Hialeah to thank for removing the bullet. He explained to his father the danger he believed Hialeah would be in if he left her alone and that she would be staying as a guest until the news of Judge Williams' death was no longer a topic of discussion in the town. Henry was adamantly having no part of sharing his home with his son's colored whore. Hearing his father speak so viciously toward the woman he desired to have as his wife infuriated Jackson. Their calm conversation had erupted into a heated debate.

    Miss Lilly and Hialeah sat and talked for hours sharing stories of their lives. Miss Lilly told Hialeah how it was and what it meant to be a slave. Hialeah told of her life living as a mixed blood Seminole with her father's people and what it was like for her to come to a town where she wasn't welcomed. She also shared her mother's own story of how she got away from Judge Williams. Hearing the hardships and heartache of each other's stories brought both women to tears. They chatted for hours losing track of time. The sun had begun to set. Hialeah thanked Miss Lilly for her warm hospitality and excused herself wishing Miss Lilly a good night. Retracing her steps in the darkness, Hialeah found herself humming the church hymn that she and Miss Lilly had sung earlier as she continued on toward the main house. From where she stood in the gardens, she could hear boisterous voices coming from the house. She quickened her steps and instantaneously her heart fell to her stomach. Jackson's booming voice mingled with that of his father's echoed in her ears. Hialeah cautiously inched her way forward and the gut wrenching pleas of Georgina begging her son and husband to cease with their argument froze her in her spot. Hialeah hung her head low. She undoubtedly knew that she was the cause of the heated argument between father and son. She could hear Jackson coming to her defense against his father's cruel tirade and barrage of insults thrown at her. Unable to bear any more, Hialeah crept into the house through the huge back double doors. Her pulse quickened as she quietly walked toward the servants' rooms. She opened the door slowly to her would be quarters and quickly retrieved her bags. Jackson would no doubt be sore with her once again. Dismissing Jackson's impending reprimand, Hialeah exited the room and walked carefully down the hall toward the back doors. She stopped in her tracks as the fight now carried on into the great hall. There could be no possible way for her to escape without being noticed.

Hialeah exhaled and walked into the light of the great hall with her bags in her hands. Her appearance was immediately noticed by Henry who fell silent as Hialeah's eyes locked on his. Jackson and Georgina furrowed their brows confused at Henry's sudden silence. They both followed his gaze. Georgina inhaled sharply. "Miss Nokosi." Georgina said nervously breaking the silence. "Hialeah what are you doing?" Jackson asked. "I standin' here fixin' to go home." Hialeah replied calmly. "Hialeah…" Jackson began. "It's alright, Jackson." Hialeah interrupted. "No it isn't." Jackson replied walking toward Hialeah. Hialeah took a step away from Jackson. Her action gave Jackson pause and Georgina's hand slowly covered her mouth. "Hialeah?" Jackson said in disbelief. "I ain't got not doubt in my head that you care for me; love me even. You say you wanna marry me; make me your wife." Hialeah replied. "Yes." Jackson said. "I be waitin' for you when you ready, but not here." Hialeah replied. "I'm coming with you." Jackson remarked sternly. "Monks. Your daddy, for all his hollerin' and carryin' on, ain't right strong enough to protect your mama if anyone come lookin' for you. Your place is right here." Hialeah said. "My place is with you." Jackson replied heatedly. "Some day." Hialeah remarked turning on her heel to leave. "Hialeah…" Jackson replied. "I see myself out." Hialeah remarked casually with nothing more to say left Jackson standing rigidly in the great hall with both Henry and Georgina looking on. "You insufferable bastard." Jackson spat. He turned to face his father. "Jackson." Georgina rushed out. "Not this time mother." Jackson warned. Without saying another word, Georgina ran up the stairs to her bedroom. She drowned out the overbearing sound of her son and husband at each other's throats. She found what she knew would please Jackson.

Georgina hurried back down the stairs where Jackson stood pacing the great hall alone. Henry had retreated to his study with a slam of the door. "Jackson." Georgina said. "I don't want to hear it mother." Jackson replied angrily. "You will hear it and you will listen." Georgina remarked curtly. Jackson turned to face his mother. "Go after her." Georgina replied holding out a small black box. Jackson's brows furrowed. Georgina opened the box to reveal a magnificent solitary diamond ring. "Mother?" Jackson said curiously. "It belonged to your great aunt, Mary. Take it and you go after her." Georgina replied. Jackson was dumbfounded. "Are you certain?" Jackson remarked. Georgina smiled while nodding her head. "I've never been more certain. Now hurry on." Georgina replied. Jackson took the box from his mother and embraced her. Feeling her son's arms lovingly around brought a burst of tears from Georgina. "You're crying." Jackson said teasingly. "You just hush and go on will you." Georgina replied through her tears. Jackson kissed his mother on her cheek and hurried out the back doors in search of Hialeah.

Stepping out into the night, Jackson noticed a shadowy figure marching toward him from the gardens. Jackson stood his ground, his hand on his pistol. After what had transpired earlier between himself and Judge Williams, Jackson was not taking any chances on anyone getting the better of him. "Who's there?" Jackson demanded gruffly. "I'm here." Miss Lilly replied in her no nonsense tone. Jackson exhaled and removed his hand from his pistol as Miss Lilly approached him. "Mama Lilly what are you doing out this time of night?" Jackson asked. "What I do every night since you were a boy. I'm goin' inside to prepare for tomorrow's breakfast. Lord knows a body can't get no rest with you and your daddy goin' round actin' like the both of you ain't got a lick of sense between you carryin' on like you doin'." Miss Lilly replied. "I'm sorry, Mama Lilly." Jackson remarked. "I come out here and what do I see? I see your woman leavin' here in the dead of night." Miss Lilly replied. "Where is she?" Jackson rushed out. "She at my place where she gone stay until you and your daddy can come to your senses." Miss Lilly declared. "Just downright ridicu…" Miss Lilly began, her tirade cut short by Jackson's quick display of the black box in his hand. Miss Lilly furrowed her brows curiously. "What's that?" Miss Lilly asked. Jackson smiled in the moon's light. He opened the box and presented his great aunt's ring to Miss Lilly. She inhaled in shear surprise. "Oh my word." Miss Lilly said. "I've come to my senses." Jackson replied. "I'm so thrilled I could burst." Miss Lilly remarked happily. "Get on over there and make sure you get yourself a slice of my chocolate cake." Miss Lilly said. "Chocolate cake? I was never allowed chocolate cake before bed time." Jackson teased. Miss Lilly placed her hands on her hips. "Jackson Harding, you ain't too big for me to take a switch to you." Miss Lilly replied in her all too familiar motherly tone. "No ma'am." Jackson remarked with a chuckle before placing a kiss on Miss Lilly's cheek. "Did I ever tell you how much I love you?" Jackson asked. "Boy if you don't get." Miss Lilly replied. "I'm gettin'." Jackson remarked playfully. He closed the box and placed it in the pocket of his trousers before hurrying through the gardens.

Miss Lilly had heard the commotion coming from the main house and arrived just as Hialeah was taking her leave. She insisted that Hialeah stay with her and not return to her own home at least until Jackson was healed and able to properly protect her. Hialeah agreed and took Miss Lilly up on her generous offer to stay with her in the spare bedroom. Hialeah unpacked her things and made herself at home. She curled up on the bed and decided to relax with a book. Deeply engrossed in her reading, Hialeah paid no heed to the door opening or the sound of footsteps coming from the other room. She continued with her reading assuming Miss Lilly had returned from the main house. It wasn't until she heard the familiar humming of her mother's song that Jackson had invited himself in. Hialeah closed her book curious as to what Jackson could possibly be doing in Miss Lilly's kitchen.

Jackson had made himself quite comfortable at Miss Lilly's table. He sat with a huge plate of chocolate cake and milk in front of him and the small black box centered in the middle of the table. Jackson pretended not to notice Hialeah peeking her head from the bedroom. "What you doin' here?" Hialeah asked curiously. "Mama Lilly said there was chocolate cake." Jackson replied before taking a bite of his dessert and washing it down with a sip of milk. Hialeah eyed the black box. Her curiosity piqued. "What's that there?" Hialeah asked. "Not sure." Jackson replied simply sliding the box toward the edge of the table in Hialeah's direction. "You're more than welcome to take a look inside." Jackson remarked casually before taking another bite of cake. "Ain't my business to go lookin' in what don't belong to me." Hialeah replied. "Nor mine." Jackson remarked before downing what was left of his milk. Hialeah walked further into the kitchen with her arms crossed. "You gonna tell me what inside that box or ain't you?" Hialeah asked in a huff. "Nope." Jackson replied fighting the urge to smile. He stood with his plate and cup and walked over to the sink. Her curiosity getting the best of her and receiving no answers from Jackson, Hialeah marched over to the table, picked up the black box and proceeded to shake it. Jackson burst into laughter. "Open it already." Jackson said smiling. Hialeah didn't trust Jackson's smile but she was dying to know the contents of the box. She set it back on the table and opened it slowly. Hialeah frowned as she peered into the empty box and looked over at a smiling Jackson who held up his great aunt's ring between his fingers for her to see. "I was hoping to find a brilliant and beautiful and brave woman to be my wife. Would you happen to know of any such woman?" Jackson said teasingly. "Henka." Hialeah replied softly rushing over to Jackson and throwing herself into his arms. Jackson burst into laughter once more as he held Hialeah against his chest. "Will you marry me and love me for the rest of your life, Miss Hialeah Nokosi?" Jackson asked. Hialeah was at a loss for words. She could only manage a nod of her head. "Is that a yes?" Jackson said teasingly. Hialeah looked into Jackson's eyes with her now tear filled ones. "Yes. Forever." Hialeah replied breathlessly. "We'll make it official." Jackson remarked. He took a hold of Hialeah's left hand and placed his great aunt's ring on her finger.

Hialeah's heart felt as if it would burst at any moment. Her legs were like jam beneath her. She admired the ring on her hand beaming with sheer joy. "Do you love it?" Jackson asked. "It's the most perfect thing I ever did see. I ain't never gonna take it off. Not ever." Hialeah replied gazing into Jackson's eyes. "Are you sure? Forever is mighty long." Jackson teased with a grin. "Not ever." Hialeah replied. Standing on tip toe to reach Jackson's lips, Hialeah sealed her promise with a kiss witnessed by Miss Lilly who watched the exchange from the doorway. "What a blessin' this is." Miss Lilly said startling Jackson and Hialeah. Hialeah could feel her cheeks warming having been caught in Jackson's embrace. It was evident by Hialeah's biting of her lower lip that she was slightly embarrassed. Miss Lilly chuckled at her young friend. "Ain't no shame in bein' in love with a good man. Now come let me see that ring on your finger." Miss Lilly said. Unable to contain her excitement, Hialeah practically raced over to Miss Lilly. She extended her hand for Miss Lilly to see. "Oh, it is just beautiful." Miss Lilly replied. "I'll leave the two of you alone to discuss whatever it is women chatter on about in private."

Jackson said teasingly. Before taking his leave, Jackson placed a kiss on Hialeah's now ringed hand and a gentle kiss on Miss Lilly's cheek. "Goodnight." Jackson said. "Goodnight Jackson." Hialeah replied with a smile on her face.

After Jackson had left Miss Lilly and Hialeah alone, the two friends chatted well into the night drinking tea and enjoying what was left of the chocolate cake. Hialeah had never been to a wedding. She listened intensively to every fascinating detail that came from Miss Lilly's lips as she described the décor of the numerous weddings she had attended; both slave weddings and white folk weddings alike. Hialeah was enamored with the idea of jumping the broom as well as wearing a lavish white dress and carrying fresh flowers for her bouquet. She even considered dressing in the traditional style of the women in her father's tribe. So many wondrous ideas floated through Hialeah's mind she could hardly remember them all. She decided the first thing she would do when she woke the next morning would be to write them all down before she dressed for Rose's nuptials. Oh! Hialeah thought to herself. How wonderful Rose must feel to be taking a husband of her own. Hialeah could hardly wait to fall asleep. She would dream of nothing but of her own wedding.

Miss Lilly's stories left Hialeah restless in her bed. Each time she closed her eyes, she could see herself walking arm in arm with Jackson down an aisle as their invited guests looked on in wonderment as she became his wife. Oh how she wished her mother and father were here to share in her moment. Hialeah found herself wondering if they would approve of her marrying a white man. Perhaps, they would treat Jackson the way his family treat her. How horrible would it be to have two families at odds with each other over mere skin. Hialeah thought it best to dismiss the horrid thought. She would think of only happiness. Jackson loved her and she loved him. Smiling in the darkness of her room, Hialeah drifted off to sleep.

The morning sun was hotter than usual. Hialeah's skin was sticky and covered with sweat. She brushed her soaked hair away from her face then slapped her hands down on her knees. The sun beamed off her ring and caught her attention. Hialeah smiled and squealed like a child at the sight of her engagement ring. She practically bolted from the bed and jumped up and down with excitement. She was getting married! Married! Rose's wedding was only mere hours away. Hialeah hurried to her bag and searched for a fitting dress to wear to Rose's wedding. She was particularly fond of the dress she had made from the gifted fabric from Mr. Nesbit. She loved the look of yellow against her skin. Satisfied with her choice, Hialeah hastily began her morning cleansing routine.

After dressing and styling her hair in a loose bun atop her head, Hialeah walked out of her room and stopped short in Miss Lilly's kitchen. She noticed a plate covered by a cloth napkin setting on the table. Miss Lilly had left a plate of fresh biscuits and jam, fresh fruit and a generous slice of smoked ham for Hialeah's breakfast. Hialeah had barely sat down to eat when Miss Lilly's door swung open. Jackson burst into Miss Lilly's home carrying a handful of healthy green tobacco leaves. He marched toward the table, a huge smile on his lips and placed the leaves on the table. "You, Miss Nokosi, are a miracle worker." Jackson said proudly. Before Hialeah could utter a sound, her lips were taken by Jackson's in a passionate kiss that left her breathless. She could taste the aroma of Jackson's cigar on his lips. An aroma that Hialeah had grown quite fond of. When Jackson released her lips, Hialeah was teased by Jackson's wink. She felt herself blushing. "Aside from being a wondrous miracle worker, you look absolutely breath-taking." Jackson said. "Well I should say the same for you, Mr. Harding." Hialeah replied. "My father's investors have arrived. They're awaiting me at my father's club. Our meeting is in minutes." Jackson remarked. "You'll do fine." Hialeah replied. "I have no doubt." Jackson remarked confidently. "How your shoulder feelin'?" Hialeah asked. "Quite sore, but I'll survive. Mama Lilly changed the bandage. What about you? You're a might over dressed for the tobacco fields." Jackson remarked with a smile. "Wasn't fixin' on workin' today." Hialeah replied. "No? Is there a church meeting then?" Jackson remarked. "A weddin'. I fixin' to go to a weddin'. My first ever." Hialeah replied matching Jackson's smile with her own. "A wedding?" Jackson asked his brows furrowed. "It's the first I'm hearing of this wedding. Who's getting married?" Jackson asked. "My dear friend, Rose Leonard. She fixin' to get married today. She invited me." Hialeah replied. "Leonard?" Jackson asked, his brows still furrowed. Hialeah didn't like the look on Jackson's face. She had doubts in her heart that Jackson wouldn't approve once he learned the whole truth. She turned back toward her plate and began absentmindedly picking at her breakfast. "Hialeah?" Jackson said calmly. "Henka." Hialeah replied softly. "Look at me please." Jackson remarked. Hialeah slowly turned in her seat to face Jackson's stern face. "I don't want you leaving without me by your side." Jackson replied. "Why? Cause she a Leonard? Cause Isaac gonna be there?" Hialeah remarked stubbornly. "I don't want you leaving because Judge Williams is dead and I can't be certain that those who were close to him won't retaliate against you to get at me and yes because Isaac will be there." Jackson replied sharply. "Jackson…" Hialeah began. "I don't trust him, Hialeah. I'm sorry but you'll not be attending." Jackson said adamantly before grabbing the tobacco leaves from the table.

Hialeah took a hold of Jackson's hand. Her sorrow filled eyes welled up with tears as she looked up at Jackson. "Rose the only friend I got here aside from Miss Lilly and she gonna be there, too." Hialeah said softly. "Mama Lilly's going as well?" Jackson replied. Hialeah nodded her head. "They's all kin. She'll keep Isaac in line just like at the preachin' yesterday." Hialeah remarked. Jackson raised a curious brow. "What do you mean? What happened yesterday?" Jackson demanded. "Nothin' Miss Lilly couldn't handle." Hialeah rushed out. "She give him a good sound slappin' for mouthin' off." Hialeah said. "What happened?" Jackson growled out, his temper beginning to flare. "Isaac didn't take too kindly to seein' you there at the preachin'. He grab me and tell me so." Hialeah replied. "He put his hands on you?" Jackson growled out menacingly. "I fine Jackson. I swear I am. Miss Lilly put him in his place." Hialeah pleaded. "Why didn't you tell me?" Jackson remarked angrily. "Cause the way you lookin' at me now." Hialeah stammered out. Jackson swiftly grabbed Hialeah's arm bringing her mere inches from his massive frame. His icy glare left Hialeah speechless. "I feel no remorse for putting a bullet through Judge Williams' head. I assure you I will not hesitate to do the same to Isaac." Jackson said menacingly. Hialeah swallowed hard. She was afraid to breathe while in Jackson's tight grasp. "Blood is blood no matter the skin of the man it comes from and I assure you, I will spill

Isaac's if he harms you in any way." Jackson threatened. "I promise, I stay close to Miss Lilly. I won't dance with no one neither." Hialeah replied, her voice quivering. Jackson released his vice like grip from Hialeah's arm. He could hear the fear in her voice as well as see the fear on her face that his words caused her. He wanted her to enjoy herself but he despised Isaac. He despised him even more hearing that he had put his hands on the woman he loved. "I'm not a monster, Hialeah. It is a wedding after all." Jackson remarked. He caressed Hialeah's cheek. "I just can't bear the thought of anything happening to you without my protection." Jackson remarked soothingly. "I got my dagger." Hialeah replied reassuringly. Jackson grinned. "Use it." Jackson remarked. "So you fine with me goin'?" Hialeah asked. "No, but I understand. She is a friend." Jackson replied. Hialeah threw her arms around Jackson's neck and on tip toe kissed his lips. Jackson let out a playful growl that made Hialeah giggle. "You start that, Miss Nokosi, and neither of us will be on time." Jackson remarked teasingly. Hialeah placed a quick peck on Jackson's lips. "Enjoy your meetin'." Hialeah said. "Enjoy your wedding." Jackson replied smiling. Hialeah watched as Jackson left Miss Lilly's home and she returned to her breakfast.

Hialeah had barely begun to chew her first bite when Jackson returned. Looking over shoulder, Hialeah fought the urge to smile with a mouthful of food. Jackson leaned leisurely against the front door frame grinning like a naughty boy who had just played a prank on his teacher. Hialeah swallowed her breakfast and fully turned in her chair curious as to what reason Jackson had for returning. "What you doin' back here so soon?" Hialeah asked. "I had a thought. No a brilliant thought." Jackson replied. "What would that be?" Hialeah remarked. "For you to join me in my meeting." Jackson replied. "Join you? Jackson, they don't want me there." Hialeah remarked. "I want you there. Our tobacco surely would have been burned to nothing if it had not been for your knowledge of the Black Shank." Jackson replied. "Yes, but the letter…" Hialeah began. "Damn the letter and damn my father's investors." Jackson replied. "My family and the investors, as well as everyone here who depends on the tobacco crop, owe you immensely for what you've done. I want them to meet the woman responsible for saving our asses." Jackson said. "But the weddin'. It starts at 2:00." Hialeah replied. Jackson glanced at his pocket watch and chuckled. "Hialeah, it's nearly only 11am. I fear you've dressed prematurely." Jackson remarked. "What that mean?" Hialeah asked frowning. "It means you have more than enough time to join me and make the wedding with adequate time to spare." Jackson replied. "Come on." Jackson said, extending his hand out toward Hialeah. "What your daddy gonna say?" Hialeah asked worriedly. "Until my father is prepared to return to his duties, I am in charge." Jackson replied. "I afraid they gonna say somethin' awful to me." Hialeah remarked. "I'll beat the life out of them if they dare." Jackson replied matter-of-factly. "I afraid of that, too." Hialeah remarked grinning sheepishly. "I'll be on my best behavior then." Jackson replied with a wink. Hardly convinced of Jackson's vow to behave, Hialeah reluctantly stood and walked over to Jackson and took his waiting hand. "Your best behavior, huh?" Hialeah remarked smiling. "Alright, well close to it." Jackson replied laughing.

Hialeah was beyond nervous as she sat across from Jackson on their way to meet up with his father's investors. Judge Williams' death was still very much the talk of the town. Hialeah sat in disbelief as she watched Jackson calmly flip through his documents without so much a care of what was going on around him. She was apprehensive about appearing alongside Jackson. She vividly remembered the words from the letter. The threat of Jackson's father's investors refusing to do business with the Harding family if it was true that she and Jackson were lovers. Hialeah sank into herself. Jackson was taking a huge risk but his face remained void of any worry. The sound of Jackson turning page after page in his ledger was driving Hialeah insane. She clasped her hands together in her lap. The sun's ray beamed off the diamond of her engagement ring. Hialeah slowly and nonchalantly placed her right hand over her left hand to cover up her ring. She was overjoyed to be marrying Jackson but dreaded the outcome of the meeting.

Unable to bear the silence any longer, Hialeah cleared her throat in an attempt to garner Jackson's attention. Jackson was deep in thought and remained focused on his papers. Hialeah frowned and cleared her throat yet again. Jackson fought hard to a smile from forming on his lips. Hialeah's effort to attract his attention was most amusing. Her final attempt was a long sigh. Jackson grinned yet kept his eyes cast down on his work. "Miss Nokosi, is something troubling you?" Jackson said nonchalantly. "I worried Jackson. I really worried what they gonna say." Hialeah replied, her voice quivering. "Is that why you've hidden your ring?" Jackson remarked, looking up from his work. His stern eyes made Hialeah even more nervous. "You read that letter same as me." Hialeah replied. "I don't give a bloody damn about the letter." Jackson remarked firmly. "I do. They say they gonna take their business elsewhere if it true that you love me." Hialeah replied. "Hialeah..." Jackson began. "I don't want no part in your daddy losin' money. Folks around here depend on the tobacco money." Hialeah interjected. "Miss Nokosi, no one will lose money." Jackson said. "But they say..." Hialeah said. "I am very capable of running this business. Do you understand?" Jackson replied. Hialeah nodded her head in agreement. She was still, however, worried about the meeting. Jackson returned to his work and Hialeah sat quietly until they reached town. She decided she would remain quiet. She didn't dare embarrass Jackson while he discussed his family's business.

Lucas stopped the carriage in front of The Worthington; the most expensive restaurant in town. "What we doin' here?" Hialeah rushed out. Hialeah's nerves instantly got the best of her. She immediately noticed the stares she and Jackson were receiving. "The meeting is here." Jackson replied simply. Passersby stopped in their tracks and gawked. Hialeah caught the eyes of several of the town's people who whispered and pointed in her general direction. "I ain't allowed in there. The man who runs the place told me so." Hialeah remarked. Jackson chuckled. "You mean Lincoln?" Jackson replied lightly. "Don't know his name but he tell me he call the sheriff if I step foot in there." Hialeah remarked. "I assure you, you have nothing to worry about." Jackson replied with a grin on his face. "You may not be worried cause you rich and know how to shoot, but I ain't fixin' to go to jail." Hialeah remarked matter-of-factly. "To jail?" Jackson said teasingly. "Where you think they send folks what break the law?" Hialeah replied. "Miss Nokosi, you won't be going to jail." Jackson remarked assuredly. "Why, cause you friends with that mean ol' sheriff?" Hialeah asked. Jackson chuckled once more at Hialeah's words. "No, because The Worthington belongs to my father.

Worthington is my mother's maiden name." Jackson replied. "Wait. You mean to tell me this here place belong to your family?" Hialeah remarked stunned. Jackson replied with a casual wink. "Why you ain't never tell me before?" Hialeah said. "Miss Nokosi, you never asked." Jackson replied smiling. "Now do let's not be late." Jackson remarked. Hialeah hurried to put on her gloves. She held her breath as she reached for Jackson's extended hand. She took notice of the elegant appearance of several of the women. Mindful of their straightened backs and rounded shoulders, Hialeah followed suit; adjusting her composure to fit in. She lifted her head high and held onto Jackson's arm praying that her fear wasn't evident on her face.

Jackson led Hialeah inside of The Worthington where they were greeted by Lincoln and the melodious sound of a woman entertaining the guests with her musical selections of the harp. The shocked expression on Lincoln's face was disturbing to Jackson. He could feel Hialeah tighten her hold on his arm. Lincoln was average in height with a smug look to his face. His brown eyes were very telling that he thought less of coloreds. His blond hair was combed neatly and he prided himself on his dapper appearance. Lincoln forced a smile to his thin lips. He too had heard the rumors that Jackson Harding had eyes for a colored woman but damned if they were true. However, seeing the proof with his own eyes took him aback. Lincoln knew better than to speak ill of his employee's son. He had also heard of Judge Williams' challenge against Jackson that led to his death. Lincoln cleared his throat and addressed Jackson. "Will the lady be joining you?" Lincoln asked in an uppity tone that Jackson despised. Jackson was mindful of Hialeah's presence but couldn't resist putting Lincoln in his place for causing her to feel unwanted. "Indeed the lady, whom I prefer to address as my fiancé, will be joining me. Mind how she is treated." Jackson warned. "Yes...yes of course, Mr. Harding. May I show you to your table?" Lincoln replied stammering. "No." Jackson remarked coldly. Lincoln nodded his head nervously and took a step back. He found himself gasping as Jackson led Hialeah away. For a brief moment, Hialeah relaxed her grip on Jackson's arm. Her ease was short lived. She and Jackson were the centers of attention of the diners. As if on cue, a silence fell upon the room. Jackson met the eyes of the harpist and raised a stern brow in her direction. She immediately continued on with her selection. Jackson felt the tightness of Hialeah's grasp on his arm once again as they approached his two guests awaiting his arrival.

Hialeah released her hold on Jackson's arm and planted her feet. She stood mere inches behind Jackson. Both gentlemen were having drinks and were deep in conversation as Jackson and Hialeah neared their table. Jackson cleared his throat instantly attracting their attention; forcing both men to strain their necks to meet Jackson's full height. Hialeah found herself in absolute awe of The Worthington's décor. It was a magnificent place. Each table was covered in a white linen tablecloth with candles set in the middle of each table. Hialeah glanced upward and marveled at the spectacular crystal and gold chandeliers that lined the ceiling. The sun's rays played perfectly off each piece of crystal. The delectable aromas that wafted from the kitchen seduced Hialeah's nostrils. She was oblivious to the few patrons that had stopped their dining to gaze in disapproval of her being there. She was also unaware that Jackson had announced her name to his father's investors. Jackson turned around to face Hialeah. "Miss Nokosi?" Jackson said. Hialeah was deeply engrossed in the splendor of everything that was The Worthington. Jackson placed his hand in the small of Hialeah's back slightly bringing her forward. "Miss Nokosi?" Jackson said. Hialeah snapped out of her daze. "Henka." Hialeah rushed out. "I mean…yes." Hialeah stammered out. "Mr. Howard DeWitt and Mr. Harvey Baldwin of DeWitt and Baldwin." Jackson said casually. Hialeah managed to nod her head and offer a faint smile in her nervousness.

Out of respect of their business companion's son, both men stood in Hialeah's presence. Jackson pulled out a chair for Hialeah and she quietly took a seat. Jackson sat next to Hialeah. He noticed that Hialeah's hands were tightly clasped together in her lap and her eyes were slightly cast down to avoid contact with either of the strange men who sat across from her. It had been years since Jackson had seen his father's investors. He remembered being present at a meeting with the two men along with his father when he was a boy. It was his father's attempt to introduce him to the Harding family business. Howard DeWitt and Harvey Baldwin had been long time investors. Both men slightly resembled the other. They were both balding and stout men; equal in height. They both even shared the same colored dull brown eyes that matched their thinning brown hair. Jackson couldn't escape the amusing thought that they both dressed in gray suits. How pathetic their lives must be. He managed to suppress his urge to laugh in their faces. He was, after all, there for business purposes. Jackson cleared his throat. "Gentlemen, I'm sure you're wondering as to the reason why I brought Miss Nokosi here." Jackson said calmly. "It is quite evident that since you're here you received our correspondence." Howard DeWitt replied. "Obviously." Jackson remarked nonchalantly. "Then it is evident that you brought Miss Nokosi here in total disregard of our warning." Harvey Baldwin chimed in. "How so?" Jackson remarked. "The entire town of Charleston is speaking on the death of Harland Williams by your hand." Howard DeWitt said. "A duel that Judge Williams instigated and refused to call off." Jackson replied. "Nevertheless." Howard DeWitt remarked sternly. "Gentlemen may I call your attention to the fact that had it not been for Miss Nokosi's knowledge of the Black Shank disease that threatened our tobacco and many of the other tobacco growers crops, The Harding Tobacco Company would have suffered a tremendous loss." Jackson replied heatedly. "We owe Miss Nokosi our gratitude." Jackson remarked. His words received a sarcastic scoff from Harvey Baldwin. Jackson shot heated daggers in the old man's direction. Hialeah could feel her heart slamming against her chest. "We owe her nothing of the sort." Howard DeWitt replied matter-of-factly. He reached into his inner coat pocket and produced the contract between the two companies and placed it on the table. "It is the sole duty and responsibility of The Harding Tobacco Company to produce more than an adequate amount of tobacco to keep our company invested in your business and if you cannot do such, we reserve the right to terminate all dealings." Howard DeWitt remarked smugly. Howard DeWitt's harsh comment sent chills through Hialeah's skin. "We are not in the habit, Mr. Harding, as our correspondence stated in doing business with someone with such low moral standards that they would proudly parade around and share the bed of a half-breed mongrel." Harvey Baldwin spat with as much smugness as his companion.

Jackson had held his temper long enough. Seething with pure rage and ignoring the diners he bolted from his seat and swiftly grabbed Harvey Baldwin by his coat front. Hialeah and Howard DeWitt simultaneously jumped from their seats as Jackson practically pulled Harvey roughly across the table by his coat spilling the two men's drinks onto the contract. A barrage of gasps echoed through the dining room. Hialeah's hand flew quickly to her mouth cover her stunned gasp. Jackson stared menacingly into Harvey Baldwin's eyes. "Take care of how you speak of the woman I intend to marry, Mr. Baldwin. I promised Miss Nokosi I would be on my best behavior, but you sir, have made a liar of me." Jackson growled out. He roughly drug Harvey across the table to the shock of all who witnessed the spectacle and unceremoniously released his hold on Harvey's coat front spilling the older man onto the floor along with the soaked contract and Henry Harding's ledger. "How dare you!" Howard DeWitt shouted. Jackson grabbed his father's now fallen ledger along with the contract from the floor and directed his anger toward Howard DeWitt. "Consider our business terminated, Mr. DeWitt." Jackson growled out. He handed his father's ledger to Hialeah before ripping up the contract in front of his father's now former investor. "You'll never receive another dime from The Harding Tobacco Company." Jackson threatened dropping the torn contract onto the floor. "On what authority? Your father will never allow it." Howard DeWitt fired out. "On my authority, sir! On mine!" Jackson fired back. Taking a firm hold onto Hialeah's arm, Jackson furiously exited The Worthington leaving Harvey Baldwin a crumpled mess on the floor.

    Jackson assisted a stunned and very silent Hialeah into the carriage before entering himself. "Home please, Lucas." Jackson said calmly. Hialeah thought it best to remain silent after what had transpired. She focused her gaze on the passing scenery as she and Jackson rode home. Jackson set his father's ledger next to him and began tapping nonchalantly on it. Without warning and much to Hialeah's surprise, Jackson began to chuckle. Hialeah turned her attention to Jackson. "Pathetic bastard." Jackson said simply. "You think this funny?" Hialeah replied in disbelief. "I warned him." Jackson remarked smoothly. "They told you what would happen if they learned you fall in love with a colored woman." Hialeah replied.

"I'll not have two bigots dictate to me who I can and cannot love nor will I ever stand idly by and allow vicious slurs be spoken about what is mine. You had every right to be there and I'll not apologize for your presence." Jackson remarked heatedly. "I don't expect you to apologize or be on your best..." Hialeah began. "Then don't. It'll never happen where you're concerned. It is my duty to protect my wife and I will do just that." Jackson replied. "So you just fixin; to go around beatin' up anybody who talk bad bout me?" Hialeah remarked. Jackson captured Hialeah's eyes with his. "If need be, yes. Consequences be damned." Jackson replied sternly. Hialeah nodded her head. "Alright then, how you fixin' to explain this to your daddy, Your Lordship?" Hialeah remarked teasingly. Jackson found himself smiling and chuckling at Hialeah's use of his title. He was sure she had forgotten about it. "I'll handle my father." Jackson replied casually. Hialeah raised a cocked brow but kept quiet. She wasn't one to interfere in family affairs.

After their tumultuous meeting, Jackson instructed Lucas to carry them home. Jackson hopped out of the carriage once they reached the Harding Estate while Lucas drove Hialeah to Miss Lilly's home. Hialeah practically bolted from the carriage before Lucas could hop from his seat to assist her. Raising a cocked brow, he hunched his shoulders and continued on about his way. Hialeah raced up the stairs and onto Miss Lilly's front porch. She burst through the door startling Miss Lilly whom had just placed her hat atop her head; the finishing touch of her ensemble for her niece's wedding. "Lord child, what done got into you?" Miss Lilly rushed out holding her hand to her chest. Hialeah hurried to Miss Lilly and placed both her hands on the older woman's shoulders. "It be Jackson." Hialeah replied breathlessly. "There's fixin' to be a ruckus." Hialeah said nervously. "What you carryin' on bout?" Miss Lilly remarked. "Jackson carry me to his meetin' with them investors from West Virginia. They say some awful things bout me in front of Jackson and he give it to 'em good. I thought he fixin' to kill somebody. These men, they real old and real rich and Jackson, he ain't pay that no never mind. He toss that old man right onto the floor and tear up his daddy's business paper right there in front of everybody to see." Hialeah said. "Miss Lilly, I think he done plum lost his mind." Hialeah said. "Well be that as it may. That between Jackson and his daddy. You stay outta that, you hear?" Miss Lilly replied. Hialeah swallowed and nodded her head in agreement. "Now you go on and wait for me while I grab my wrap. We got us a weddin' to attend." Miss Lilly said. "Yes ma'am." Hialeah replied. She exhaled to calm herself and did what was asked of her.

    The moment Hialeah stepped outside, an overwhelming wave of nausea took over her body. She raced down the stairs frantically searching for a place to vomit. She hurried to the side of Miss Lilly's house and vomited near her flower bed. In a panic, Hialeah kicked dirt onto the mess she had made and quickly wiped her mouth. Disgusted that she had gotten vomit on her gloves, Hialeah eagerly pulled them from her hands and tossed them into her small handbag. The distaste of vomit in her mouth, Hialeah pulled a mint leaf from a nearby mint plant and popped it into her mouth; chewing hastily. She swallowed a bit of the juice to freshen her breath and spit the remaining leaf onto the ground. Hialeah then hurried her steps to the front of the house and straightened her dress just as Miss Lilly walked out her door. Hialeah forced a smile to her lips as Miss Lilly joined her. They walked side by side to Miss Lilly's small carriage that awaited them in the tiny stable that Amos had built many years ago. Miss Lilly took the reins and as they rode through the gate, just as Hialeah feared, a disturbingly heated argument could be heard from inside the Harding Mansion. Hialeah said a silent prayer in hope that all would be well on their return from Rose's wedding.

Chapter 14

    Miss Lilly and Hialeah pulled up to the church and Hialeah's thoughts of Jackson and his argument with his father faded at the very moment she laid her eyes on the beautifully decorated church. The door was adorned with a multitude of brightly colored flowers and everyone in attendance wore their best. Hialeah was in awe. The queasiness in her stomach had resided and was replaced with butterflies. Seeing Rose's massive turnout of guests that included family and friends brought cheerful tears to Hialeah's eyes. She could only wonder how her very own wedding would be. "This is quite the celebration." Miss Lilly said snapping Hialeah from her thoughts. "Yes ma'am it surely is." Hialeah replied. "You alright child? I heard your sickness from my window." Miss Lilly said. Hialeah nodded her head. "I sorry bout that. I reckon I just worried bout Jackson." Hialeah replied softly, slightly embarrassed at having been heard by Miss Lilly. "No sense in worryin' yourself. You know as well as I do that Jackson can take care of himself." Miss Lilly remarked. "Besides, we got ourselves a weddin' to attend." Miss Lilly said smiling. Hialeah smiled in return and both women climbed down from the small carriage. "Let's get inside and find a good seat." Miss Lilly said. Hialeah spanned the crowd and almost immediately she locked eyes with Isaac. She hurried to catch up to Miss Lilly.

    Hialeah's eyes lit up the moment she stepped foot into the church. White ribbons lined the pews and hung from the ceiling. Two huge flower pots set on each side of the preacher's stand filled the same brightly colored flowers as the door. Oh how joyful Rose must feel Hialeah thought as she took her seat. She could barely contain herself. Everything was just perfect.

    Miss Lilly took to mingling with several ladies and her sister Louise. Hialeah kept to herself glancing around the room at all the cheerful faces her hands clasped together in her lap. She began absentmindedly toying with her ring; smiling at how perfectly it fit on her finger. Hialeah's presence had not only caught the attention of Isaac but Violet and her circle of friends as well. Violet led the way down the aisle toward Hialeah, a smug look on her face. Hialeah kept her eyes cast down on her ring unaware that she now had an audience. Standing over Hialeah with her arms crossed, Violet cleared her throat. "What are you doin' here?" Violet asked arrogantly. Hialeah glanced upward at the smug face staring down at her. "I invited here just like you." Hialeah replied sternly, fighting the urge to slap the smirk from Violet's face. She didn't bother to stand. She had already bested the older woman once, she had no doubt she could do it again but Rose's wedding was not the place and she would not dare make a spectacle at such a cherished event. "I see your massuh let you come out." Violet replied, her remarked garnered several snickers from her friends. "I was born free and I gone die free. Can't say the same for the lot of you. You do well to go on away from me unless you aimin' to get yourself another black eye and sore lip." Hialeah remarked spat. Violet scoffed and marched off followed by her cohorts. Hialeah simply rolled her eyes and bit her lip to keep from laughing.

Reverend Tucker approached his stand and signaled for the church pianist to begin playing soft music to bring the guests' attention on him. Once all eyes were on him, Reverend Tucker announced that the wedding was to begin and to all in attendance to take their seats. Miss Lilly took her seat next to Hialeah. Hialeah was beside herself with anticipation. The lady pianist was given her cue to start the wedding music and the church doors swung open. Hialeah was filled with angst. Her mouth hung open as Ruby and two of their female cousins entered the church wearing white gowns. Their hair adorned with flowers that too matched the doorway. Ruby was escorted by her brother, George. Hialeah had never met the other two gentlemen but she had seen them in church. She stared in sheer joy as the wedding party made their way down the aisle; the men gathered to the right and the women gathered to the left. Hialeah leaned in toward Miss Lilly. "They all look so perfect." Hialeah whispered. "Yes they do." Miss Lilly replied. Hialeah's eyes lit up brighter than the sun at the very first sight of Rose arm in arm with Isaac. The guests stood as the bride entered the church. Hialeah hurried to her feet. She leaned this way and that way to get a better look at Rose. Hialeah inhaled a deep breath. Rose was absolutely stunning in her white dress. Her hair done up in braids that resembled a crown atop her head. Hialeah adored the white daisies elegantly placed in Rose's hair. She especially loved that she carried them in a bouquet. It was everything Hialeah could do to keep from bawling at her friend's good fortune. She had forgotten that Isaac was even present. Rose was the most delicate bride she had ever seen. Hialeah was truly happy for her friend and honored to have been invited.

After the reciting of their vows and the tradition of jumping the broom, the ceremony concluded and practically every woman hurried to gather around Rose. Hialeah was no exception. She leapt from her seat and squeezed in between two robust women to catch a glimpse of Rose. Rose locked eyes with Hialeah and bee-lined to her friend embracing her tightly. "I so glad you here." Rose squealed. "I can't keep from cryin'." Hialeah replied happily. "Me neither." Rose remarked, releasing her hold on Hialeah. "Can you believe it? I got me a husband." Rose said. Hialeah nodded her head smiling. "He right lucky to have you too." Hialeah replied. Rose beamed from her friend's words and embraced Hialeah quickly once more. "Your turn is comin' soon." Rose whispered in Hialeah's ear before releasing her friend. Hialeah wiped at her eyes and took several steps back to allow the other guests to wish Rose well. Her friend's kind words brought even more joy to Hialeah's heart. Hialeah caught Ruby's attention. She smiled at Hialeah. Hialeah returned the warm gesture. Ruby's smile was welcomed. She hadn't spoken to Hialeah since siding with Violet after their altercation in the tobacco field.

The church had gotten a little too stuffy for Hialeah's liking. It was loud and it was hot and she needed some air. She quietly slipped out and walked aimlessly through the grass. Isaac was engaged in a conversation with several men and quickly excused himself the moment he spotted Hialeah alone. Hialeah toyed with her ring, smiling to herself unaware of Isaac's nearness. He stopped walking and casually leaned his frame against a tree. Hialeah breathed in the fresh air reveling in her friend's joyous occasion. The jubilant song of the choir, Reverend Tucker's heartfelt message of love and togetherness, Hialeah embraced it all. Oh, if it was only her she thought to herself.

She would be the happiest woman ever. Hialeah briefly closed her eyes and for a moment she imagined it was her. Swept away in Jackson's arms; his wife. Hialeah let out a soft sigh, opened her eyes and turned around. Her blood instantly froze, her smile faded from her lips as Isaac stood watching her a smug smirk on his face. Hialeah squared her shoulders and avoided Isaac's gaze. She kept her eyes fixed on the church doors and made her way toward the building. Isaac stepped away from the tree and followed Hialeah barring her steps as she tried to walk by him. Exhausted and annoyed at his childish game, Hialeah crossed her arms and stared heatedly up into his eyes. "You done actin' like a child, Isaac Leonard?" Hialeah said sternly. "I just wonderin' what you doin' here at my sister's weddin'." Isaac replied. "Rose invited me here and I ain't in no mood to go messin' around with you." Hialeah spat. "I ain't see your white boy here." Isaac remarked mockingly. "I come here with Miss Lilly so I suggest you leave me be or she'll give you another sound lickin' across your face." Hialeah replied threateningly. Amused by Hialeah's threat, Isaac bowed mockingly and stepped from Hialeah's path. Hialeah angrily marched away from Isaac. "I see you at my place for dinner." Isaac called out. Hialeah stopped in her tracks and spun around to face Isaac. "What you mean by that?" Hialeah demanded. "Ain't no drinkin' allowed at the church. Folks headin' back to my place for drinks and good food." Isaac replied smirking once more. "Well I ain't gone be there." Hialeah remarked matter-of-factly. "Oh, so you fixin' to upset my sister after she kind enough to invite you to her weddin'?" Isaac said sarcastically. Hialeah glared menacingly at Isaac before continuing on her way toward the church. She scolded herself. That fool Isaac was right. She couldn't dare leave. It would be rude of her to snub Rose's generosity. Curse that Isaac Leonard, Hialeah thought. What she wouldn't give to scratch his eyes out.

Hialeah mumbled every mean spirited thought that came to mind on her short walk to Miss Lilly's carriage. She found herself plopping in her seat like a child who didn't get their way while she waited for Miss Lilly to leave the church. Hialeah hoped that her escort wouldn't tarry too long. It was terribly hot and beads of sweat began to trickle down her breasts. She was so annoyed by Isaac's smugness she had half a mind to walk back to the Harding Estate. Instead, Hialeah opened her parasol and welcomed the tiny amount of shade the parasol offered as she sat patiently waiting for Miss Lilly to arrive.

Hoards of Rose's guests exited the church and headed toward their wagons full of smiles and good cheer. Miss Lilly was escorted from the church by Reverend Tucker. They walked arm in arm toward her wagon. Hialeah pressed her lips together to keep from smiling. It was quite obvious that the pair had taken a liking to each other but Hialeah kept her tongue. She didn't dare embarrass Miss Lilly in front of the reverend. The Reverend Tucker held onto Miss Lilly's hand as he assisted her to her seat. Miss Lilly nodded her head graciously. Reverend Tucker turned his attention to Hialeah. "Miss Nokosi, what you think of the ceremony?" Reverend Tucker asked smiling. "It was right fine, Reverend Tucker." Hialeah replied returning the reverend's warm smile. "Yes it was." Reverend Tucker remarked. "I do hope to see you both for refreshments." Reverend Tucker said. "You surely will." Miss Lilly replied. "That's good to hear." Reverend Tucker remarked. He took a step back and tipped his hat before Miss Lilly made her way from the church yard along with the other guests who were eager to get to the fine meal prepared for the special occasion.

The ride to the Leonard's home was a short one. Hialeah could hear the sound of banjos and fiddles playing as she and Miss Lilly pulled up to the Leonard's home. There was barely any room to park the wagon. Miss Lilly made due with a spot a short distance from the house. Their little wagon was met by Reverend Tucker and to Hialeah's dismay, Isaac. Reverend Tucker boasted a huge smile as he held his hand out for Miss Lilly, who was more than gracious for the escort. Isaac followed the reverend's example and waited for Hialeah to take his hand. Hialeah glared daggers at Isaac before reluctantly taking his extended hand. Reverend Tucker and Miss Lilly walked a few paces ahead of Hialeah and Isaac. Assured that her rudeness would not be witnessed, Hialeah pulled her hand away from Isaac's and hurried her steps to distance herself from him. Isaac's chuckle from behind infuriated Hialeah. She allowed the reverend and Miss Lilly to walk on ahead before turning on her heel to face a grinning Isaac. Hialeah marched up to him and placed her hands on her hips. She was seeing red and fought the urge to strike his arrogant face. Isaac found her expression amusing. "What you givin' me that look for?" Isaac said teasingly. "Don't you dare play the gentleman with me after what you put me through." Hialeah spat. "Fixin' to tell bout my carin' for Jackson." Hialeah continued heatedly. "Pfft. That white boy ain't here now is he? Just good food, good music for dancin' and plenty of drink." Isaac replied lightly. "Say what you want. I plan on enjoyin' myself but it ain't gone be with you." Hialeah remarked stubbornly. She turned on her heel once again but her escape was intervened by Isaac. He caught Hialeah's arm before she could march away. His annoying grin had left his lips as he peered down into Hialeah's eyes. "We had us some good times. Swimmin' with just the sun on our bare skin, lyin' in each other's arms laughin', dancin' and sharin' kisses. You can't say that none of it ain't meant nothin' to you." Isaac replied. Hialeah pulled her arm away from Isaac's grasp. "I enjoyed the time we spent together, but in the back of my mind, I always think bout Jackson." Hialeah remarked calmly. She nodded her head and left Isaac standing alone.

Hialeah joined the festivities and was greeted by a smiling Ruby who carried a tray with two drinks on it. Hialeah returned Ruby's smile as she had done in the church. Ruby nodded her head toward the drinks offering one to Hialeah. Hialeah didn't much care for Jackson's gin and she wasn't sure of the contents in the cup but she didn't wish to offend Ruby. She took the cup and brought it to her nose. Ruby giggled and took the other cup and downed the drink. Hialeah laughed loudly. She couldn't be out done and followed Ruby's lead downing the drink. Her bold antic brought on a bout of coughing. Whatever was in the cup burned her throat immensely. Hialeah could feel the liquor coursing through her blood. Ruby let out a loud cheer. Hialeah burst into laughter yet again. Ruby led her to a table where a bottle of whiskey set unattended. She slyly grabbed the bottle and put it to her lips. Hialeah's eyes widened in surprise as she watched Ruby take a massive swig of the whiskey. She was even more surprised when Ruby passed the bottle to her. Hialeah bit into her bottom lip before turning the bottle up mimicking Ruby. Her boldness earned her yet another enthusiastic cheer.

Seated next to his brother devouring his meal, George was thoroughly entertained by his sister's ability to handle the bottle. He nudged Isaac and nodded in Ruby's and Hialeah's direction. Isaac looked up from his plate and followed his younger brother's nod. Isaac's lips formed a sinister smirk. He remained silent and stuffed a forkful of roast pig into his mouth all the while keeping a sharp eye on Hialeah as Ruby led her to a table. Isaac raised a devious brow enthused by Hialeah's unsteady footing. He could hear both his sister's and Hialeah's drunken laughter from where he sat. Perhaps, Isaac thought to himself, his sister's wedding could prove quite eventful after all.

Hialeah dropped unceremoniously into her seat; still full of giggles from the effects of the whiskey. She swayed in her seat clapping her hands and stomping her feet to the sound of the music. A roar of applause and cheers rang out when Rosie and her new husband took to dancing in the middle of the crowd. Ruby set a plate of food in front of an uninterested Hialeah. What she craved was more of the spirits that set in the bottle within her reach. It was a celebration after all. Her dear friend becoming a bride was much to celebrate. Convinced that one more drink would do her no harm, Hialeah grabbed the bottle and just as she had done before, she placed her lips around it and swallowed more than a generous amount of the blood boiling moonshine. She placed the bottle back on the table and wiped at her mouth with the back of her hand. Hialeah felt an enormous bubble growing in her stomach and she quickly covered her mouth just as she let out a boorish belch. She giggled to herself; tickled by her unladylike behavior. A behavior that Jackson surely wouldn't approve of.

In a drunken panic, Hialeah stumbled to her feet and scanned the guests in search of Miss Lilly. If Jackson's former nanny learned of her unrefined antics, she would no doubt inform Jackson. Hialeah suddenly felt as if she couldn't get enough air. In her angst, she pushed herself away from the table and fell from her chair. Occupied by the new couple's dancing, no one took notice. Hialeah drunkenly attempted to stand. She was taken aback by the sudden firm grasp on her arm assisting her to her feet. Swaying awkwardly on her feet,

Hialeah stood face to face with a grinning Isaac. Humiliated being caught in such a position, Hialeah unceremoniously pulled away from Isaac. Her sudden movement nearly caused her to lose her balance. Isaac quickly reached out and took a hold of Hialeah's arm to steady her. He released her without hesitation and chuckled as she marched off toward a shady tree. Isaac nonchalantly followed and leaned his frame against the tree. Hialeah turned away and crossed her arms. She had hoped that Isaac would leave her be. He, on the other hand, found her stubbornness more than amusing. Isaac reached into his jacket pocket and pulled out a small flask. "You know I ain't never took you for a drinkin' girl." Isaac said casually. Hialeah scoffed; keeping her back to Isaac. "What you fixin' to do, go flappin' your lips to Jackson?" Hialeah replied with a slur of her words. "Now what I go and do somethin' like that for?" Isaac remarked with a smirk behind Hialeah's back. He removed his flask from his coat pocket and dangled it over Hialeah's shoulder. "This here a happy celebration. If'n you want to celebrate, you got every right to, ain't you?" Isaac said smoothly. Hialeah turned around to face Isaac's grinning face. She furrowed her brows. "What you got in there?" Hialeah asked suspiciously. "Same thing in that there bottle over there." Isaac replied. Hialeah looked passed Isaac's broad shoulders to the bottle that set on the table. Isaac chuckled. "What, you don't believe me?" Isaac asked. Before Hialeah could respond, he opened his flask and took a sip from it. "Pure moonshine, nothin' more." Isaac said reassuringly. Hialeah gave Isaac a heated glare before taking the flask. She put it to her lips and took a simple sip. Reassured that it was indeed whiskey, Hialeah took the liberty of having another drink. "Woo wee, ain't nothin' sweeter than a hot blooded woman that can best a man in a drink." Isaac said teasingly, with a slap to his knee. His overzealous compliment made Hialeah laugh.

The band struck up another boisterous song and Isaac began clapping to the music. Hialeah continued laughing. "That's right good dancin' music." Isaac said cheerfully. He held out his arm for Hialeah to join him in a dance. She took another drink from the flask and handed it back to Isaac. He placed his private drink back into his pocket. Hialeah rolled her eyes mockingly and reluctantly agreed to

Isaac's dance invitation. He was all smiles as he and Hialeah joined the other guests.

Jackson watched from his father's office Miss Lilly and Hialeah ride away for the evening. He had yet to discuss the details of his meeting with DeWitt and Baldwin. After a much needed drink of scotch, Jackson joined his father in the study. He wasted no time in informing Henry Harding what had transpired and as expected, his father exploded. Jackson stood peering out the window with his arms crossed while his father unleashed a tirade that shook the rafters. Georgina hurried to the study and rushed to her husband's side. "My word Henry, what ever are you carrying on about?" Georgina rushed out. "Have you any idea what your son has cost me!" Henry fired. Georgina glanced at Jackson whom continued staring out the window. She threw her hands up and left the room without another word. Dealing with two Harding men was enough to drive anyone insane.

Henry's tirade lasted longer than Jackson was willing to endure. He turned away from the window and casually walked over to the sofa. He sat down and propped his long muscular legs on the coffee table and crossed them at the ankles. Henry had winded himself and was desperate for a seat. Once seated in his leather chair across from his arrogant son, Jackson rose from his seat and walked leisurely to his father's bar. He poured his father a glass of water and set it on the table in front of him and returned to his seat. Jackson calmly waited for his father to quench his thirst after his tantrum before explaining his proposal. Henry was seeing red as he downed the refreshing water. He drank every drop and slammed the glass on the table. Jackson rose an unimpressed brow and crossed his legs. With the assistance of his cane, Henry struggled to his feet. Jackson leaned back in his chair and rolled his eyes. His father's feeble attempt to stand was as dull as watching grass grow. "Do you care for my assistance?" Jackson said dryly. "You've done enough." Henry snapped. "On the contrary father, I have much more to do." Jackson replied sarcastically. "Well, you'll do it alone." Henry remarked heatedly. "Now what fun would that be?" Jackson replied mockingly. "Fun? My God, Jackson. You beat my investors to a bloody pulp and you dare speak to me of fun?" Henry spat. "They were useless. You don't need them." Jackson replied calmly. "You do not tell me who or what I need." Henry fired. "A partnership." Jackson replied, his voice ever so calm. "A what?" Henry remarked in disbelief. "A father and son partnership. Me as your investor." Jackson replied. "You can't be serious." Henry remarked. "I've gone over your books numerous times since you've been ill and your dears DeWitt and Baldwin simply aren't the trusted allies you think them to be." Jackson replied casually. "What are you getting at?" Henry remarked suspiciously. "They were cheating you, father. Skimming money from your pockets. Simple mathematics. You were being robbed quite frankly." Jackson replied.

Henry's curiosity was piqued. He needed a seat. Jackson slid his father's ledger over to him. Henry reached into his pocket and pulled out his spectacles. He grabbed his ledger and silently and briefly went over the numbers. "Robbed." Jackson said simply. Henry slammed the ledger and tossed it onto the table. "Satisfied?" Jackson asked smoothly. "Those conniving sons-of-bitches." Henry spat angrily. "A well deserved beating wouldn't you say?" Jackson replied sarcastically. "What are you thinking?" Henry remarked. "As I said, a partnership and a tad more." Jackson replied with a cock of his brow. "More?" Henry asked with a brow raise of his own. "A grand horse stake. The finest thoroughbred race in the state in your honor. The Harding Stakes Race." Jackson replied. Henry sat back and contemplated his son's proposal. "As I see it, there is still much tension surrounding Judge Williams' demise." Jackson said. "You think to ease the blow with a spectacular race and a grand prize?" Henry replied in agreement. "Music, food, vendors, drinks and a lot of gambling." Jackson remarked with a wink. Henry couldn't contain his joy. He burst into a hearty laugh; a laugh that was joined by Jackson.

Both Harding men sealed their partnership with a bottle of Henry's aged scotch and Spanish cigars. Jackson presented his father with outlined and detailed plans while Henry listened intently. He hung onto his son's every word and marveled at Jackson's precision. Jackson handed his father the written proposal. While Henry went over every line, Jackson sat back in his chair; his mind consumed by Hialeah. He anticipated her return. He was sure she would be thrilled of his renewed relationship with his father.

Hialeah carried on dancing in the arms of Isaac. Between dances and nibbles of refreshments, Isaac kept his flask full of whiskey and served it to Hialeah as the festivities continued on into the evening. Many of Rose's guests had departed for home after having their fill of food and drink. Hialeah could barely stand on her own and Isaac seized the opportunity to whisk her away to his family's barn. Miss Lilly spent her time in the company of Reverend Tucker. By the night's end, after having inquired about Hialeah's whereabouts to no avail, Miss Lilly accepted Reverend Tucker's invitation to see her home assuming that Hialeah had left early.

Louise, Ruby and few other their kin helped to tidy up before bidding farewell to Rose and her new husband. Louise sent George off to search for Isaac to see his younger sister off. George returned shortly to his mother's side alone. Louise stood perplexed. Isaac had gone missing for some time now. Rose's husband had grown inpatient waiting for his new brother-in-law to make his appearance and rightfully so. He was, after all, a newlywed and his anticipation to start his life with his cherished wife was apparent on his face. Louise said her goodbyes to her daughter and embraced her tightly. George and Ruby joined their mother in wishing their sibling well. Rose waved and blew kisses while her husband drove them away under the evening's moon.

Isaac stood in the darkness of the barn and ignored his brother's call. He had waited all night to get the woman he loved alone and he wasn't about to miss the opportunity to claim what was rightfully his. He peered through the slabs of wood of the barn as Rose rode away and waited for his family to retreat into the house.

George retired into the house with an extra serving of food while Ruby and Louise made themselves comfortable on the porch to quench their thirsts with glasses of sweet iced tea. Mother and daughter chatted on aimlessly about the day's event and how beautifully attired the guests were how much in love Rose appeared with her husband. After a brief moment of silence, Ruby decided to follow her younger brother and retire for the evening. She leaned in to embrace her mother and a flicker of light from the barn caught her eye. "Mama, you leave a lantern burnin' in the barn?" Ruby asked curiously with furrowed brows. "Now why would I have a lantern goin' in the middle of the day?" Louise replied sarcastically. "Cause there's a light on." Ruby remarked. Louise followed her daughter's gaze. She stood slowly from her chair. "Go on and fetch Bessie." Louise replied softly. Ruby hurried to do what was told of her. She returned quickly and handed Louise her rifle. She grabbed a sharp cutting knife for her own protection. "I'll go and get George." Ruby whispered. "Ain't no need. Whoever in there gone be real sorry." Louise said matter-of-factly. She quietly stepped off the porch with Ruby close on her heels.

Isaac lit the lantern and shone it on Hialeah's now unconscious body. Shortly after being led into the Leonard's barn, she collapsed drunkenly in the hay. Isaac hung the lantern on a small hook hurried to Hialeah's side. He admired her in the dim light and brushed a wisp of her hair from her face. He traced the outline of her parted lips with his thumb before lowering his head to capture them in a lingering kiss. In her intoxicated state, Hialeah smiled and moaned faintly. Her faint smile and soft moan excited Isaac. He wasted no time in sliding Hialeah's dress up to reveal the lush dark caramel skin of her thighs. He allowed his hand to travel the length of her leg caressing her silken skin resting his hand between the warmth of sweetness. Hialeah let out a soft exhale and once again, Isaac took her lips; darting his tongue inside to deepen his kiss. Her soft breathing aroused Isaac immensely. He teased her woman's spot and was rewarded with another moan. Her soft sighs convinced Isaac she wanted him inside of her and he would willingly oblige her his pleasure.

Kissing Hialeah one last time, Isaac lowered his trousers and gently parted her legs as he mounted her. He was anxious for her to receive him. He was even more anxious to spill his seed deep within her waiting cove. His hardened shaft throbbed and he ached to feel himself inside of her. "You're mine and you's always gone be mine." Isaac vowed gazing down at Hialeah. He readied himself over her and smirked maliciously; Jackson Harding be damned. This here was his woman and she would feel every bit of him, Isaac thought to himself. Isaac guided his pulsating erection between Hialeah's legs. He caressed her softly yet again eager to hear her moan in his ears. Satisfied and yearning to take her, Isaac raised Hialeah's legs just as Louise burst through the barn door her rifle pointed at the intruder. A startled Isaac, leaped to his feet. "Isaac!" Louise shouted, stunned at the sight of her son with his trousers around his ankles and Hialeah lying crumpled in the hay. "Mama, what you doin' with that gun?" Isaac replied surprised by his mother's appearance. Louise handed her gun to Ruby before rushing inside the barn. Ruby's mouth fell open in shock. She remained frozen as her mother marched her way into the barn. "What you doin' with that girl and pull your britches up you hear? You hear!" Louise exploded. "Mama." Isaac said, his hands up. "Don't you mama me none! You rape that girl?" Louise demanded. "You think I a fool to do a thing like that?" Isaac replied while he adjusted his trousers. "What you doin' with that white man's girl?" Louise bit out, her hands placed adamantly on her hips. "I tell you before, this here my girl and ain't no white man fixin' to take her from me." Isaac spat. "She belong to Jackson Harding and everyone around here know it." Louise said heatedly. "You think I ain't had her before? You think I ain't laid in her bed; pleasurin' her and the like?" Isaac replied. "I don't care none what you done did with this girl. Judge Williams dead on account of her. You think Missuh Jackson won't hesitate to skin yo' black self alive?" Louise yelled. "She belong here with me and that's where she fixin' to stay." Isaac replied stubbornly. His disobedience angered Louise beyond belief. She marched over to Isaac and struck him across the face stunning Ruby as she looked on in terror. "You damn fool boy! You take her home! You hear? You take her home!" Louise ordered. "Ruby Jean!" Louise barked to her daughter. "Yes ma'am." Ruby stammered out. "Fetch the wagon." Louise ordered. Ruby placed Bessie against the barn and dropped her knife and hurried to do what was ordered of her.

Ruby was in near panic as she climbed on the wagon. She rushed back to the barn but remained in her seat. She was shaking violently. "Ruby climb down here and grab Bessie." Louise said. Ruby obeyed her mother without a word. She grabbed the rifle, placed it on the floor of the wagon and hopped back in her seat to await any further instructions. Louise returned her focus back on her son. "Pick her up and get her in that wagon. Your sister's gone go with you so you don't try no more foolishness." Louise said sternly. Disgruntled by his mother's interference, Isaac cursed under his breath as he lifted Hialeah over his shoulder and marched out of the barn with Louise close behind him. Isaac laid Hialeah in the back of the wagon and covered her with the blanket his mother kept in the back. "Hurry up and get movin'" Louise ordered. Isaac climbed next to Ruby and commanded the horses to move on. When her children were out of sight, Louise retrieved her knife and hurried to the house.

Ruby and Isaac rode in silence through the darkness with Hialeah in tow. She prayed that Jackson wasn't waiting at Hialeah's home for her to return. She was most certain that if he caught wind of what her brother had attempted to do, there would surely be blood shed and her brother, for all his strength, would end up like Judge Williams. Her mother was right. Isaac was indeed a fool. Even if what her brother said was true, that he had shared intimate moments with Hialeah, she had made her choice and it wasn't him. Ruby kept her thoughts to herself. Soon this horrendous night would be over. A night that she felt was partially her doing. A night that, the good Lord willing, Hialeah would not remember and her Aunt Lilly would never know about.

Reverend Tucker followed Miss Lilly home to assure her safety. When both their wagons arrived at the Harding's estate, they were greeted by Jackson who stood on the porch having a cigar. The massive porch was lit by several lamps. Jackson tossed what was left of his cigar, smiling, he casually walked down the steps to assist Hialeah from Miss Lilly's wagon. He was eager to tell her of his partnership with his father. His smile fell from his lips and his brows furrowed the moment he saw Miss Lilly alone in her wagon. "Mama Lilly, where's Hialeah?" Jackson asked curiously. "Why ain't she here with you? She left the party a long time ago." Miss Lilly replied. Jackson felt the blood drain from his body. Without another word to either Miss Lilly or Reverend Tucker, he raced toward the stable to saddle his horse. It took mere minutes for Jackson to mount his horse and with a sense of sheer urgency, he sprinted down the road his mind a blur of emotions.

Isaac and Ruby arrived at Hialeah's home. They stopped the wagon on the side of the house to avoid possibly being seen. Handing his sister the reins to keep the horses steady, Isaac climbed down from his seat in a huff and took his time getting to Hialeah. He leaned his tall frame against the wagon and like a stubborn child, crossed his arms. His nonchalant demeanor upset Ruby. She wanted nothing more than to be home. "What you standin' there for?" Ruby whispered harshly. "What you scared of?" Isaac replied mockingly. "I wanna go home." Ruby remarked sternly. "Then go." Isaac replied, his teeth clenched. "If'n you don't get movin', I swear to the Lord, mama gone hear bout this." Ruby hissed. "Damn women." Isaac replied heatedly. He uncrossed his arms and slammed the back of his fists against the wagon. Ruby closed her eyes to remain calm while Isaac reluctantly made his way to the back of the wagon. He uncovered Hialeah and scooped her in his arms. Ruby hurried from her seat to join her brother. She grabbed a lantern and a small box of matches that set next to Hialeah and quickly lit the lantern. Leading the way, Ruby made haste to the porch and tried the door handle. She breathed a sigh of relief when the door opened. Using the lantern to guide their way, Isaac followed his sister to Hialeah's small bedroom. Ruby stepped aside and placed the lantern on the nightstand. Her nerves getting the best of her, Ruby dashed from the house to await Isaac outside.

Fuming with jealousy, Isaac placed Hialeah onto her bed and hurried to undo the buttons on her dress to expose her breasts. Smirking maliciously, he lifted Hialeah's dress baring her backside. The sound of rapidly approaching hooves gave Isaac pause. He quickly seized the lantern and darted from the room. Isaac sped from the house and jumped into the wagon. Frantic, Ruby grabbed the reins and raced away.

Jackson's horse pummeled the earth in break neck speed to reach Hialeah. Unsure of what he was seeing before him, Jackson briefly slowed his horse. He blinked several times to focus his eyes in the darkness. Disbelieving his own eyes, Jackson dug his heels into the sides of his horse. When he reached Hialeah's home, he jumped from his horse, hastily grabbed his gun and stormed inside. The moon's light illuminated her tiny frame on her bed. Jackson hurried to her table to light the small lantern she kept there and cautiously walked into her room with his gun drawn. The sight of Hialeah's bare breasts and backside quickened his steps. He set the lantern down and brushed her hair away from her face. Hialeah let out a soft sigh; her breath wreaked of whiskey. Jackson gently caressed her cheek and spoke her name. Smiling faintly in her sleep, Hialeah softly whispered Isaac's name. Gut-wrenched from what Jackson had just heard and witnessed, there was no more proof needed. Isaac Leonard had taken what was his and the woman he vowed to spend his life with was a willing participant and had played him for a fool.

Chapter 15

Hialeah had awaken in an awful state. She had a severe headache and her stomach was in knots. Tossing her bed sheet aside, Hialeah placed her feet on to the floor. She was too weak and dizzy to stand on her own. Using her nightstand for support, Hialeah was able to awkwardly stand. Her legs felt like jelly beneath her; as if they would give out at any moment. She continued to rely on the small nightstand to steady her footing. Hialeah breathed in deeply and was suddenly overcome with a wave of nausea. In a frantic panic, Hialeah covered her mouth and ran from her room. She practically threw herself over the porch railing a spew of vomit escaping her that brought her to her knees.

Overwrought, Hialeah leaned back against her house and shut her eyes briefly. She counted to ten and with every bit of strength she could muster, she grabbed a hold of the railing and struggled to her feet. Fearing that careless night of drinking had poisoned her, Hialeah thought it best if she sought out the doctor.

It seemed as if hours had passed before Hialeah had finished her task of dressing; foregoing her hair. She hadn't the energy or desire to style her hair. She felt dead inside as she sluggishly made her way to her barn to hitch her wagon. After several agonizing attempts to climb onto her seat with the sun beating down on her, Hialeah was on her way; praying to the good Lord to keep her seated. She was ever so grateful that the trip to Miss Hattie's was less than a mile. She doubted her ability to make it any further surrounded by the tumultuous heat and overwhelmed with her throbbing headache.

The heat had taken its toll on Hialeah. Drenched in sweat, she slumped over in her seat a few feet away from Miss Hattie's home. Engaged in her needlepoint, Miss Hattie hastily placed her work aside and hurried as quickly as her legs could carry her hefty frame to Hialeah's motionless wagon.

Miss Hattie was a doctor in her own right. She had tended to the illnesses of many slaves and white folk alike with her herbs and brews. She acted as a midwife; delivering children of both colored women and their masters' wives. She was well known and well respected. Her gray hair resembled her gray eyes. Her skin was nearly as white as her former master's. Miss Hattie's mother had been a slave and bore her master a child. She like many others were children of the plantation. She had been mistaken for a white woman many times but always stood firm and proud of her slave blood. For as many children that she had brought into the world and cared for, her own five children had been sold away. Four years after the civil war she was reunited with her children.

Hialeah thought she was imagining the light touch on her cheek and the calm voice in her ears. Her eyes slowly opened to a familiar yet concerned face. "Come on child." Miss Hattie said soothingly. She took a hold of Hialeah's arm to guide her from the wagon. Still quite unsteady on her feet, Hialeah's knees buckled. Miss Hattie locked arms with Hialeah. Her burly size and stature was more than enough to hold Hialeah upright. "What's ailin' you child?" Miss Hattie said. Hialeah responded with a slur of her words. Miss Hattie ceased her steps. "I give you the best care I can but you gone have to speak words that I understand. I ain't familiar with red man talk." Miss Hattie replied. Hialeah furrowed her brows. "You ain't speakin' words that I know." Miss Hattie remarked plainly. "I say I think I been poisoned." Hialeah mustered out. "Poisoned?" Miss Hattie remarked with a chuckle as she led Hialeah to her home. "What you say poison, I say downright drunk. I see you yesterday at the weddin'. You goin' mighty hard with the spirits." Miss Hattie said lightly. "I don't feel right at all. Feel like somethin' tryin' to come outta me." Hialeah replied. "Too much of the spirit will do that to ya. Besides, you just a sprite of a girl. Got no business drinkin' like you did." Miss Hattie remarked matter-of-factly.

Once inside, Miss Hattie led Hialeah to a small bedroom and offered her a cold glass of water. Hialeah hastily downed the drink grateful for Miss Hattie's hospitality. They had never formally met, however, Hialeah desperate. She opened right up and informed the older woman of her vomiting spells and lightheadedness. Hialeah assumed it was the heat. Miss Hattie thought otherwise. She questioned Hialeah regarding her last menses. "I ain't right sure. Been a while, I reckon." Hialeah said. Miss Hattie instructed Hialeah to remove her dress. She inquired if Hialeah had noticed a change in her breasts. "They's been kinda achin' some. Ain't never felt like this before." Hialeah said innocently. "That cause you ain't never been with child before." Miss Hattie replied simply. "With child?" Hialeah remarked confusedly. "That's what I say. Done seen it too many times. You with child." Miss Hattie replied. Hialeah swallowed in disbelief. "You know this for sure?" Hialeah asked. "Like I say, I done seen it many times." Miss Hattie replied reassuringly. Hialeah sat stunned on the bed. "You go on and get yourself fixed up." Miss Hattie said. She left Hialeah alone to get dressed.

Hialeah took longer than what was needed to get herself together. She didn't know whether to laugh or sob. She was with child. Jackson's child. What ever would he say? Hialeah exhaled. Regaining her composure, she left the bedroom and thanked Miss Hattie for her care.

Hialeah rode home in a daze. Miss Hattie's words played over and over in her head. Her mind was in such a whirlwind of emotions she hadn't realized that she had just crossed paths with Isaac on horseback. Isaac frown, perplexed at the odd expression on Hialeah's face. He had finished running an errand for his mother, yet was curious as to Hialeah's visit with Miss Hattie. Women sought out Miss Hattie's expertise for one reason. Isaac's brows shot up in surprise. He quickened his pace reaching the older woman's home in a matter of seconds.

Isaac leaped from his horse and met Miss Hattie on her porch as she had returned to her needlepoint. He wasted no time in greeting Miss Hattie. He demanded to know the purpose of Hialeah's visit. Miss Hattie looked up from her needlepoint. She had known the Leonard family for a long time. "She come here believin' she been poisoned." Miss Hattie said. "Poisoned?" Isaac replied surprised. "Ain't no poison. Just a whole lot of spirits. Seems to me you wake up just fine. The two of you carryin' on like a couple of drunkards." Miss

Hattie remarked. "We just havin' a good time is all." Isaac replied sheepishly. "No woman fixin' to be a mother ought to be behavin' like some loose trollop." Miss Hattie remarked sternly. "Fixin' to be a mother?" Isaac replied, shocked by Miss Hattie's confession. "That's what I say. Now unless you expectin', get on your way." Miss Hattie ordered. Isaac nodded his head quickly and hurried to his horse. It was nearly time for him to start his day at the tobacco field. Smirking devilishly, Isaac galloped away.

News of Hialeah's intended birth spread across the tobacco fields. Isaac boasted proudly that he was to be a father. Several of the Harding workers made light of Isaac's claim. They had all heard the rumor going around of Jackson Harding falling for a half-breed woman. Many of the workers had even witnessed the two in each other's company. Isaac would not be put off. He continued his story with a simple explanation. That he had shared Hialeah's bed in secret many times before their employer had arrived in South Carolina. He professed that Hialeah may have indeed taken their boss for a lover but the child she was carrying belonged to him. Drawing a crowd of mostly men, Isaac puffed his chest out and went so far as to describe in lusty detail how often he and Hialeah made love and in the throes of passion, how she cried his name. His story was well received. A few of the workers elbowed each other playfully, slapping their knees; thoroughly entertained by Isaac's zest for storytelling.

Jackson rode like a mad man away from Hialeah's home. The echo of Hialeah's voice whispering Isaac's name and the faint smile on her lips stirred in his mind as he pushed his horse riding for hours through the night to escape his own thoughts. Unable to bear his self inflicted torture, Jackson found himself at the very spot where he had encountered a disgruntled Hialeah; Terell Grisby's place. Scowling, Jackson sauntered into the rank establishment demanding the table in the back of the room that was occupied by fellow patrons. Hearing how Jackson sent Judge Williams to meet his maker, the two men rushed from their seats. Hailing for a barmaid to bring him a bottle of scotch, Jackson spent the evening refilling his glass until he was numb.

In his drunken stupor, Jackson managed to throw himself onto his horse and at a snail's pace, guided his horse to his father's office. He threw one leg over and fell to the ground. He laid motionless while chuckling at his ridiculous carelessness. After a brief moment lying on the road, he dragged himself to the little bench that set outside his father's office. Jackson propped his feet and crossed them at the ankles. He closed his eyes; conceding defeat to the bottle of scotch.

Jackson woke to unfamiliar female voices surrounding him as well as a myriad of footsteps walking up and down the sidewalk. His face was covered with his hat and his tall frame outstretched the bench he had made his bed for the night. Reaching for his pocket watch, Jackson slightly raised his hat to reveal that it was passed noon. In no hurry to leave his make-shift bed, he returned his pocket watch to his coat. The conversation of the chattering women piqued his interest. He listened intensely as one of the women explained to her friends why she had been late arriving. Jackson could deduce from their voices that they were older women. His ears perked up when the woman made mention that she had been visited by a half-breed woman claiming to have been poisoned. She went on with her entertaining story, much to Jackson's pleasure, describing in great detail that the woman hadn't been poisoned but rather was with child. Never one for gossip, Jackson couldn't bring himself to ignore their private conversation. They were, after all, speaking over his head.

Jackson found it most amusing that women, no matter the color, had nothing better to do than share idle gossip. His own mother was guilty of such a fault, however, this bit of news was too engaging to ignore. Jackson had half a mind to beg the woman to go on with her beguiling tale. As if his mind was read, the name of the new mom to be was inquired. However, the woman leading the story hadn't asked the young woman's name. Insisting that the woman spoke some injun tongue, Jackson was fully alert. It couldn't be possible that the woman was speaking of Hialeah. His brows furrowed, Jackson's jaws clenched when the woman carried on about how Isaac Leonard came by right pestering her demanding information. Jackson's expression turned dark at the mentioning of Isaac's name. "I tells you, why that girl want to go and get herself with child with the likes of Isaac Leonard is beyond me." Miss Hattie said matter-of-factly. "He work hard and drink harder. Damn fool ain't fit to raise a mangy dog." Miss Hattie said in disgust.

Jackson bolted from the bench startling the three women. He had heard enough. With much haste, he untethered his horse from the hitching post, mounted his steed and fiercely rode out of town, his blood boiling with every tumultuous step.

Preparing to hitch her horse to her small wagon, Hialeah could hear the roaring sound of hooves approaching her property. She led her horse from the barn and quickly dropped the reins as Jackson, riding wildly, closed the distance between them. Hialeah could feel her pulse quickening. She hurried to meet Jackson; an overwhelming feeling of joy coursing through her. "Jackson, wait til you hear." Hialeah rushed out gleefully. Jackson had barely halted his horse before dismounting. His hardened glare froze Hialeah. Jackson stormed to her side and gruffly grabbed her arms pulling her to meet his chest. "How did you arrive here?" Jackson growled out. His tone left Hialeah stunned. "Mama Lilly was in the company of Reverend Tucker so I'll ask again, how did you arrive here?" Jackson demanded. Hialeah managed to swallow nervously. "I...I ain't sure what you mean." Hialeah stammered. "Well allow me to make it bloody clear for you." Jackson spat. "Jackson." Hialeah replied softly. "You were with him weren't you! You were with that bastard, Isaac Leonard!" Jackson erupted. "It was a weddin', Jackson. Folks were havin' a right good time." Hialeah rushed out. "Damn the wedding!" Jackson fired. He released Hialeah's arm, slightly pushing her away from him. "How did you arrive here, Miss Nokosi, and do not lie to me!" Jackson exploded. Hialeah shook her head. She was trembling. "I ain't sure." Hialeah cried. "Surely, you take me for a fool." Jackson replied low. "I never say such a thing." Hialeah remarked, her lips quivering. She took a step toward Jackson. "Don't!" Jackson shouted. Hialeah's hand flew to her mouth as she burst into tears. "Please tell me what got you so sore." Hialeah pleaded. "Sore?" Jackson scoffed. "Livid, Miss Nokosi." Jackson replied through gritted teeth. "Please tell..." Hialeah began. "I saw him!" Jackson rushed out angrily. "I saw that wretched son-of-a-bitch with my own eyes running from your door!" Jackson said. "That ain't true." Hialeah sobbed out. "And you lying in your bed barely clothed." Jackson spat. "That ain't true." Hialeah replied tearfully. "I caressed your cheek and you uttered his name in your drunken sleep." Jackson remarked in disgust. "No!" Hialeah screamed in angst. "You gave yourself to him! Lord knows how many times! It is even being said that you carry his child!" Jackson replied, his voice booming. "I swear to you..." Hialeah implored. "Do not swear to me!" Jackson shouted. "I ain't with child!" Hialeah screamed frantically. Her outburst ceased Jackson's tirade. Hialeah took a brief moment to regain her composure. "Speak." Jackson replied angrily. "Isaac, he find himself another girl like me; he tell me so. Say he gone start a family with her." Hialeah remarked with as much calmness she could muster. "Except that doesn't explain why he was here." Jackson replied heatedly. "I don't know but I ain't got his child in me." Hialeah pleaded, taking a step toward Jackson. He raised a hand, halting her steps. The old woman in town never mentioned Hialeah by name. Jackson's head was near exploding. He had had enough of the whole sordid affair. He mounted his horse and sped away.

Blinded by his own fury, Jackson thought nothing would bring him more pleasure than squeezing the life out of Isaac with his bare hands. He rode fervently up the long drive to his home and without so much of care, thrashed through the tobacco leaves in search of Isaac. His workers scurried like mice to avoid being trampled. He stopped his horse amidst a crowd of astonished workers. "Isaac! Isaac Leonard!" Jackson shouted. Joseph hurried to his boss. Jackson peered heatedly down at his loyal foreman. "Where's Isaac?" Jackson said gruffly. "He ain't here, sir. I sent him off. Tell him he ain't got no place here." Joseph replied. "Why?" Jackson remarked adamantly. "Well sir, he been drinkin'. He start shovin' the men and grabbin' the women folks. Said he to be celebrated. Say he fixin' to be a pa." Joseph replied. "Where is he?" Jackson demanded. "Don't know, sir. He got in a scuffle with Zeke and Clyde. Samuel had to warn him away with a shotgun." Joseph replied matter-of-factly. Enraged, Jackson dismounted his horse. "Put him away." Jackson ordered. "Yes sir." Joseph rushed out, taking the reins.

Jackson barged through the front door. The crashing of the door startled Georgina, who leaped to her feet from the dining table. She hurried after Jackson. "Jackson Harding, what on Earth has come over you?" Georgina said. "I've outgrown this pathetic town." Jackson growled out. "This pathetic town is your home." Georgina replied. "No!" Jackson bellowed, his voice echoing in the great hall. "England is my home. I'll be returning at first light." Jackson remarked harshly. "It's that girl isn't it?" Georgina replied accusingly. "Leave it alone mother." Jackson warned. "You don't think I hear what's going on around me? She's with child isn't she?" Georgina demanded. "She denies it and I no longer care." Jackson growled out. He took the massive stairs two at a time leaving Georgina alone in the hall.

Hialeah's horrendous day turned into a torturous night. She sobbed for hours at her table, her head buried in her hands before boldly stepping into the night in search of Isaac. As she was accustomed, Hialeah mounted unsaddled horse and raced through to Isaac's home. She was met by a furious Louise who viciously turned her away; condemning her for being a worthless whore. Undaunted by Louise cruel attack on her person, Hialeah sought out her only friend. If any one could get through to Jackson, it was Miss Lilly.

Riding by the light of the moon, Hialeah encouraged herself to carry on or lose Jackson to Isaac's deceit. The very thought of raising Jackson's child alone was devastating. What would she possibly tell her child? Hialeah rode in desperation. She reached the Harding Estate and dismounted her horse at the gate. Jackson's tirade still rang in her ears. She dared not risk the calmness of his home with the sound of approaching hooves. Hialeah tethered her horse to the gate and crept up the long drive keeping in the shadows of the trees. Her heart raced desperately in her chest as she cautiously hurried up the drive. Hialeah prayed that none of the Harding's servants were awake. The air was still. She remained close to the house. Miss Lilly's small home was just beyond the garden. Hialeah took in a deep breath and with much haste, bee-lined her way toward the darkened house; her silken black hair rising with the breeze. Safely on Miss Lilly's porch, Hialeah frantically looked over her shoulder to ensure she had not been followed. She knocked just loud enough to wake Miss Lilly.

Hialeah clasped her hands anxiously in front of her. The mere minutes for Miss Lilly to wake, shine some light in her home, and investigate the late intrusion seemed like an eternity. Dressed in her sleeping robe, Miss Lilly warily pulled back her curtains and shone her lantern. Her brows raised in surprised. She quickly opened her door and Hialeah rushed inside. "Lord child, what you doin' out this time of the evenin'" Miss Lilly asked, her motherly tone tore at Hialeah. She tearfully collapsed in Miss Lilly's arms. "I gots nobody to help me." Hialeah whispered through her tears. "Come sit down." Miss Lilly replied soothingly. Hialeah followed Miss Lilly to her table and slumped in a chair. Miss Lilly gently caressed Hialeah's hair before taking a seat across from her. She set the lantern on the table. The dim light illuminated the worry on Hialeah's face. Miss Lilly reached across the table. Hialeah slowly offered her hand and lifted her eyes to meet Miss Lilly's own. "I so scared. I with child but I tell Jackson it ain't so. I say it another woman Isaac got eyes for." Hialeah confessed somberly. "You lied to him?" Miss Lilly said. Hialeah nodded her head. "I done heard the talk what's goin' round." Miss Lilly replied. "That's why I come here. Jackson, he listen to you. He do what you tell him." Hialeah remarked pitifully. "It ain't my place to go messin' with folks' hearts." Miss Lilly replied calmly. "I ain't never loved nobody else in that way 'xcept for Jackson." Hialeah remarked. "Jackson, for all his funnin', well he ain't no boy no more. He ain't right sure what to think from your lie or Isaac's. You just give him some time. When he done calm himself, you tell him the truth. Love don't live on a bed of lies. " Miss Lilly replied, giving Hialeah's hand a gentle squeeze. Hialeah nodded her head. Miss Lilly's words offered some comfort. "I sorry I wake you." Hialeah said. "You just get on home and get some rest. It won't do for Jackson to find you out." Miss Lilly replied. "Yes ma'am." Hialeah remarked. She stood and hurried to Miss Lilly's door. She looked over her shoulder, thanked Miss Lilly once more before taking her leave and disappearing in the night.

Unable to sleep, Jackson found himself wandering down the long drive. The moonlight guiding his steps, he stopped in the middle of the drive, the whinnying of a horse catching his attention. He furrowed his brows and quickened his steps. Jackson swiftly removed his pistol from its holster as he scanned his property for any signs of trespassers. The unfamiliar horse's whinny drew Jackson closer. It was unsaddled; a war bridle placed in its mouth. Jackson cocked a knowing brow and hurried across the drive, leaning his frame against a tree. He returned his pistol to its holster. Whatever game Hialeah played, he would be the victor.

    Relieved to have spoken with Miss Lilly with no intrusion by Jackson, Hialeah dashed to her horse. His persistent whinnies would surely cause alarm if anyone should happen by. Keeping to the shadows just as she had come, Hialeah gently stroked her horse's face to sooth him. He relaxed at her touch and Hialeah went to work untethering him from the fence. Jackson stepped from the shadows of the large tree. "Clearly, you've lost your way." Jackson said low. Hialeah inhaled a sharp breath and made haste with her horse's tether. Like a wild cat in search of prey, Jackson swiftly closed the distance leaving Hialeah little chance to free her horse. She quickly turned around and was met by Jackson's immense frame. He placed both hands on the fence gripping it tightly. His face hidden by the darkness of the trees, frightened Hialeah. He towered over her small frame. "I leavin'. I leavin'." Hialeah whispered pleadingly, her voice trailing off. "Why are you here?" Jackson demanded gruffly. "I come see Miss Lilly." Hialeah replied softly. "A little late to come calling." Jackson replied curtly. "Why you not forgive me?" Hialeah asked desperately. "Forgive your deceit? Your betrayal?" Jackson growled out. "I never do no such thing. My heart tell me true." Hialeah replied fighting back tears. "My eyes did not deceive me. My ears burn still from the breath you took to speak another man's name." Jackson spat. He hopped the fence and began untethering Hialeah's horse. "None of this bloody madness longer matters. You say you're not with child, so be it." Jackson said heatedly. "You say I yours! You tell me you my Jackson!" Hialeah shouted, her tears of frustration streaming down her face. "Do not dare turn your treachery on me!" Jackson fired back, tossing the rope over the fence. Hialeah took a hold of the war bridle. She lifted her skirt and mounted her horse with the assistance of the fence. From atop her horse, she gazed down at Jackson. "I never should have loved you." Hialeah spat defiantly, turning her horse away from Jackson.

Infuriated by Hialeah's callous admission, Jackson astonished Hialeah by promptly seizing her by her tiny waist hauling her from her horse. Hialeah toppled on top of Jackson landing them both in the soft grass. Jackson swiftly maneuvered, rolling Hialeah beneath him pinning her arms against her body with his firm thighs. A barrage of heated obscenities escaped Hialeah's lips as she struggled to free her arms. Jackson pressed closer; a dark scowl on his face that instantaneously silenced Hialeah. Her breasts heaved heavily. "Again." Jackson demanded threateningly. "Say it again, Miss Nokosi. You never should have...what?" Jackson growled low. Hialeah laid beneath Jackson, his intense glare captured her voice. Her slightly parted lips, tousled black tresses and rising breasts awakened Jackson. She had never looked more ravishing in this light or any light. Without warning, Jackson crushed her lips with his. The doubt of the child she carried belonging to him escaped his thoughts. He yearned to feel himself inside her velvety folds.

Hialeah wrestled against Jackson's hold of her arms. Freeing herself, she pummeled his chest futility with her fists. Jackson took hold of Hialeah's wrists and raised her hands above her head until the fight left her. She cursed him in her father's tongue, a sound Jackson had grown familiar to. Hialeah turned her head away to refrain Jackson from kissing her again. Undaunted, Jackson smirked holding Hialeah's wrists together with the use of one hand. Pulling at her skirt, Jackson's ears were abused once more by Hialeah's vicious tongue and feeble attempt to free herself. Her struggles against Jackson assisted him in his task. Her skirt fell above her knees, revealing her sinewy thighs. Jackson cocked an appreciative brow. Hialeah's fiery defiance ignited Jackson's ardor. His erection at its peak, he tore at his trousers releasing himself. Hialeah's foreign tirade was replaced with an explosive obscenity that Jackson knew all too well as he took her fervently. He plunged himself deeper with every attempt Hialeah made to restrain him. She pleaded with Jackson after each ravenous thrust left her more and more breathless. Her legs went numb beneath Jackson's crushing weight. His animalistic groans rang in Hialeah's ears. Unable to bear Jackson's savage lovemaking, Hialeah gave in to her climax. She begged for Jackson's release and he willingly obliged her. Freeing Hialeah from his captive hold, Jackson erupted his seed deep within Hialeah's woman's cove with a predatory groan of satisfaction that left Hialeah trembling.

After his ravening sexual onslaught, Jackson insisted on seeing Hialeah home in anticipation that Isaac would be there. The very thought enraged Jackson. He gripped his rein tight. He ached to give the intruding bastard the thrashing he deserved. He wanted Hialeah to witness every crushing blow. He ordered Hialeah to wait for his return while he saddled his horse. In her brief moment of solitude, Hialeah thought of what she would say when it came time to tell Jackson she was with child. When he returned to her side, they rode in tense silence. Accustomed to riding astride, Hialeah was crucially sensitive in her woman's spot. She rode side saddle to ease the throbbing soreness; a decision Jackson surely noticed. She winced with every step her horse took; a gesture Jackson took note of as well.

Reaching her home, Hialeah rode ahead to light the lantern that set on her porch. She dismounted and handed her rope to Jackson. He held the horses steady while Hialeah lit the lantern. Illuminating her porch, Jackson's brows furrowed. He rushed from his horse and brushed by Hialeah. "Light." Jackson said sternly. Hialeah lifted the lantern and inhaled sharply as Jackson tore down a folded message that had been nailed to her door. "What is it?" Hialeah asked suspiciously. "Read it." Jackson replied low, handing the message to Hialeah. Trembling, Hialeah reluctantly took the message from Jackson's hand. "Read it aloud." Jackson ordered. Hialeah nodded her head and lowered her eyes to the message. "'Miss Nokosi, I sure had a swell time at the weddin'. Holdin' you close, feelin' your soft skin against mine reminded me of the time I held you close after...'" Hialeah's words trailed of. Her lips began to quiver. "Finish the bloody letter." Jackson said through clenched teeth. "I can't." Hialeah replied softly. She could feel the stinging of her tears threatening to fall. "Finish the letter." Jackson remarked angrily. "After lovin' you. Isaac." Hialeah whispered tearfully. "Where is he!" Jackson roared. "He ain't here, Jackson." Hialeah cried out. "It's you he desires not this imaginary person you think me foolish to believe." Jackson replied furiously. "Somebody's toyin' with you." Hialeah replied. "Do I look to be in a mood for games!" Jackson remarked ferociously. "This ain't come from Isaac, Jackson. He can't read or write none." Hialeah protested. "What does that matter? Do you not think it possible for someone to write his words?" Jackson replied. "It don't make no never mind." Hialeah sobbed. "Where is he!" Jackson demanded, storming from the porch. "He ain't worth hangin' for." Hialeah pleaded, following after Jackson. "That is my decision to make!" Jackson replied enraged that Hialeah would dare protect the man that meant her harm. He mounted his horse and stared icy daggers at the woman he swore to love. "You play the bloody innocent very well, Miss Nokosi." Jackson spat before leaving Hialeah standing alone.

Determined to rectify her relationship with Jackson, Hialeah hurried into town to meet Jackson before he busied himself with his father's finances. Ignoring Alice, Hialeah raced up the stairs and barged into Jackson's office. "What do you want?" Jackson said bluntly, keeping his eyes on his work. "You. You're my Jackson." Hialeah replied. Jackson closed his father's book. He stood to his full height. "Am I?" Jackson remarked sarcastically. "Yes. I love only you." Hialeah replied. "Then you'll be my wife?" Jackson asked. "Forever." Hialeah replied smiling. She rushed over to Jackson and threw her arms around his neck. Jackson captured her lips in a savage kiss; growling deep in his chest as he forced Hialeah's lips apart with his invading tongue. He ached to fill her with his staff.

Jackson tossed all of his documents onto the floor and lifted Hialeah onto his desk gingerly lying her back. He removed his hardened staff and wrapped his arms around Hialeah's thighs bringing her closer to him before gently entering her. Hialeah moaned passionately at the size of Jackson's swollen erection invading her. "Jackson." Hialeah whispered breathless. Jackson caressed Hialeah's thighs and placed light kisses on the tips of her knees before thrusting himself fully into her. Hialeah firmly gripped the sides of Jackson's desk as he possessed her body. Hialeah closed her eyes reveling in Jackson's dominate lovemaking. "Miss Nokosi, are you there?" Jackson asked. Hialeah immediately opened her eyes. "I say are you there, child?" Jackson shouted.

Hialeah inhaled sharply, a familiar voice jarring her from her sleep. Hialeah looked around frantically; her chest heaving. There was no Jackson. She had dreamt it all. She was alone at her table where she had sobbed most of the night until her eyes drew weary. Wiping at her tear stained eyes, Hialeah hurried to her door; surprised to see Miss Lilly. She stepped onto her porch and clasped her hands in front of her. Miss Lilly had never come calling. Hialeah's heart fluttered in her chest. Miss Lilly remained in her wagon; a somber look covered her face. "I wish I could say this here a good morning." Miss Lilly said. "What is it, Miss Lilly?" Hialeah replied nervously, dreading whatever news Miss Lilly had to bring. "I just gone come right out with it. Isaac, ain't no more." Miss Lilly began. "Seems he come across Jackson at that awful Grisby place demandin' Jackson pay him what he owe. Sheriff Willard, he there too. Say Isaac come right for Jackson shoutin' and such. Jackson give Isaac his pay. Lay it right on the table, tell Isaac to be on his way but Isaac want more than he's due. Say that Jackson had Joseph fire him. Jackson tell him he get what he's owed and not a penny more. Sheriff Willard say Isaac didn't take too kindly to Jackson refusin' him more money. He start goadin' Jackson. Accusin' Jackson of bein' sore. Say he lay with you and you's got his child in you. Sheriff Willard say Jackson ain't budge none. He tell Isaac he pathetic and that's when it all went terribly wrong. Isaac charge Jackson and they scuffle with one another; breaking tables like two untamed animals. Say Isaac took a right sound beatin'. Sheriff and some men folk break 'em apart and they arrest Isaac but he ain't through with Jackson. He give the sheriff a good shovin', take his gun from him. Sheriff tell it that Jackson shoot Isaac dead before he could take aim at Jackson." Miss Lilly said. "And Jackson?" Hialeah replied her voice quivering, her hand absentmindedly going to her belly. "I so sorry, child. Jackson, he had Lucas carry him to the boat. He leave some time ago for home." Miss Lilly remarked sadly. Hialeah pressed her lips together, nodding her head in understanding. "Thank you." Hialeah said calmly, unable to bear another word. She walked back into her home and closed the door behind her. Two men dead by Jackson's hand on account she dared love a man she had no business loving.

Chapter 16

Hialeah's belly grew heavy with Jackson's child with each passing month. She was seen as a pariah amongst the members of Reverend Tucker's congregation following Isaac's death. Many members of the church threatened to boycott if Hialeah was permitted to attend the service. Hialeah cared greatly for the reverend. She couldn't allow her presence tarnish his fine sermons. Reverend Tucker was quite fond of Hialeah. He held personal sermons at her home. He insisted that during her troubled times it was favorable to keep close to the Lord. Miss Lilly accompanied Reverend Tucker and saw to it that Hialeah was cared for. She assisted her with the upkeep of her home and sold her eggs to the Nesbits. When the day's events were done, Hialeah would curl into her bed, gently stroke her swollen belly and cry herself to sleep.

The chaotic life that Jackson had known before his trip to America had resumed almost instantaneously. He spent many restless nights walking the deck of the ship condemning himself for falling victim to his own game. He had shared many beds and broken many hearts and thought nothing of it. Love and all that it entailed was a game for fools not for men of power and prestige and in England, he was both powerful and prestigious. His duel and victory over Judge Williams was quite the scandal. His reasoning for the duel had caused an even greater scandal. None of which mattered to Jackson. He delved into his work presiding over numerous trials. Accepting invitation after invitation to every high society affair and a few personal invitations to dine with some of England's most eligible ladies; most of whom were resolved to share Jackson's bed. He, however, was insistent on sleeping alone. It had taken Jackson months to clear his thoughts of Hialeah. He dared not open his heart yet again to love. Wherever Hialeah was and whomever she had given her heart was of no consequence to Jackson. He was apprehensive about the letters he would receive from Miss Lilly; fearing she would make mention of

Hialeah. Memories of her had disturbed his every waking moment and deprived him of sleep. He decided, his life was best suited without her.

Hialeah's fear for her child intensified with every waking day. She encountered a group of children on her way to visit Miss Hattie. One of the children, a young girl, had been reduced to tears for being a half-breed. Miss Hattie shooed the pests away and consoled the teary-eyed child with treats while she tended to Hialeah. Hialeah's heart shattered for the girl. She knew all too well the hardships the girl would face having been born with tainted blood. Her child, too would face such agonies. Poor and looked down on; ridiculed instead of loved. It was too much for Hialeah to take in. She had to get away. She had to get herself and her child far away from the south.

Hialeah consulted with Miss Lilly who agreed that without Jackson's protection she was risking harm to herself and to her unborn child. Jackson had made quite a few enemies. It was all Miss Lilly could do to keep George, Isaac's brother, from avenging his older brother's death. Miss Lilly had even spoken to her own sister, Louise, urging her to keep George in line. Louise wouldn't hear of it. She blamed Hialeah for Isaac's death; stating whatever happened to the filthy whore and her bastard child would be well deserved.

Miss Lilly and Reverend Tucker took to aiding Hialeah in the selling of her possessions. Nearly everything she cherished was sold away. She was left with a few articles of clothing, her rag doll, and a few trinkets that had belonged to her mother. All that remained was her home. Exasperated and hungry, Hialeah accepted an invitation to dine with Miss Lilly and Reverend Tucker at his home. She had earned enough monies to start her life anew, although she hadn't quite thought of where. During their meal, Reverend Tucker and Miss Lilly offered suggestions. Hialeah had never heard of so many places. While the reverend and Miss Lilly continued on with their suggestions while they cleared the table, Hialeah absentmindedly rummaged around in her sewing bag. She jabbed the tip of her finger on something strange. Reaching into her bag, Hialeah pulled out Jackson's ring. She inhaled slightly and dropped the ring back into her sewing bag. Miss Lilly and Reverend Tucker carried on with their suggestions during dessert.

Hialeah found it difficult to follow the conversation with Jackson's ring in her bag and on her mind. She feigned interest; nodding her head and smiling; her decision already made.

After dinner, Reverend Tucker assisted Hialeah and Miss Lilly into his wagon. Hialeah thanked them both for a generous meal and for their kindness. Hialeah sat in the back of the wagon observing her two hosts. It was evident that Miss Lilly had fallen for the reverend and he with her. She had burdened them enough with her troubles and genuinely hoped that they would find comfort in one another. She was terrified of what awaited her in her new beginnings but she would have to put that fear aside for the sake of her child.

As they traveled closer to Hialeah's home, a gust of black smoke clouded the air. Reverend Tucker rounded the bend toward Hialeah's home and hastily stopped the wagon. "Oh sweet Lord!" Miss Lilly burst out. Hialeah's barn and her home were ablaze. Without warning or so much as a thought, Hialeah hurried from the wagon. She raced toward her burning home holding her expanding belly. Miss Lilly called out to Hialeah. Reverend Tucker jumped from the wagon and rushed after. In a panic, Hialeah frantically hurried to her room. The dark smoke stung Hialeah's eyes and the fire was burning rapidly. She struggled to drag the chest filled with her mother's dresses from the room. With much haste, Reverend Tucker ran in after Hialeah covering his mouth and nose with his handkerchief. He grabbed a hold of the chest's handle and pulled it from the room ordering Hialeah to leave. Miss Lilly's screams of utter distress filled the night air. Hialeah dashed from her now engulfed home and fell to her knees gasping for air. Reverend Tucker was close behind. Miss Lilly scrambled from the wagon. She assisted Hialeah to her feet all the while tearfully scolding her and the reverend for being foolish. The reverend gathered Miss Lilly in his arms. It was all he could do to comfort her. "I sure like to know who would do something this downright sinful." Reverend Tucker said. Miss Lilly held her tongue. She had a pretty good notion who was behind the fire but now was not the time to say anything. Hialeah kept her tongue silenced as well. She took her chest by the handle and dragged it as far as she could toward the reverend's wagon before he released Miss Lilly to assist her.

After securing the chest in the wagon, Hialeah climbed in. She sat motionless; her mind free of thought the entire trip to Miss Lilly's home. Miss Lilly prepared her spare bedroom for Hialeah. Reverend Tucker made himself comfortable in one of Miss Lilly's rocking chairs. He insisted on staying the night for the women's safety. Hialeah found sleep difficult. Her child's constant movement was insufferable. She found herself wondering of Jackson in the darkness of her room. She wondered if Jackson had contained any love for her. She wondered if Jackson's child would settle itself so she could find sleep. There was much to do in the morning.

Reverend Tucker was up bright and early when Hialeah arose from what little sleep she was able to obtain. She hadn't the strength to haul her chest into town. She emptied its contents into one of her oversized sewing bags and crept out of her room. Miss Lilly had yet to awaken to which Hialeah was grateful. She walked onto Miss Lilly's porch just as Reverend Tucker was climbing onto his wagon. "Miss Lilly know you movin' on so early?" Reverend Tucker said. "No sir. She still sleepin'." Hialeah replied. "Where you off to?" Reverend Tucker remarked.

The reverend brought Hialeah to what was left of her home. She sifted through the burned rubble in hopes of salvaging any small piece of what would soon be her former life. She and Reverend Tucker turned over charred pieces of debris with no luck. Hialeah brushed her hands down her dress. Reverend Tucker knelt down; something glimmering catching his eye. He turned to face Hialeah. "I think I found somethin'. Not much, but it's somethin'." Reverend Tucker said. He stood and handed Jackson's silver flask to Hialeah. She assessed Jackson's flask. It was slightly scorched but still in relatively good condition. Hialeah dusted it off with her dress and dropped it into her bag. Reverend Tucker took a glance at his pocket watch. "You best be hurryin' if you expect to catch that boat." Reverend Tucker said simply. Hialeah smiled faintly. She had told no one of her plan to leave America for England. As if reading her mind, the reverend revealed to Hialeah how he had seen her in town purchasing her ticket. "You'll tell Miss Lilly goodbye for me want you?" Hialeah replied. "I will and you tell Jackson, I expect to see him in church whenever he in town."

Reverend Tucker replied smiling. Hialeah nodded her head offering the reverend a warm smile.

Hialeah climbed onto the reverend's wagon. Reverend Tucker humored Hialeah with as many tales of Jackson as a young boy in church to ease her obvious fear. Hialeah found herself laughing at the reverend's stories. It dawned on her that she hadn't laughed in quite a while. She sorely needed the distraction. In a short while she would be onto a venture that she couldn't fathom. She would be leaving her mother and father behind; a thought that hadn't entered her mind until Reverend Tucker stopped the wagon. He stayed by Hialeah's side until it was time to board. Hialeah scanned the hoard of people embracing their loved ones. She crammed what was left of her belongings into a small suitcase and her sewing bag. Draping her sewing bag across her body, Hialeah embraced the reverend one last time and followed her class as they were called to board the ship. Saying a quick prayer, Hialeah handed her ticket to one of the crewmen, gave her name and proceeded up the gangplank. Her nerves were quickly getting the best of her. She had never seen such a vast vessel. The chaos was overwhelming on deck. Hialeah followed the signs to the lower deck. She, like many others on board were considered steerage. Holding tight to her bag, she bustled through the other passengers making their way to their cabins. Hialeah found where she would be staying and hurried into her cabin locking the door behind her.

The tiny room was occupied by only a single bed, a chair, a single dresser with a mirror and a small table. She sat on her bed and opened her sewing bag. Miss Lilly had prepared fried chicken the night before. Hialeah helped herself to a few extra pieces for her trip and a dish of wildberries. She began eating her small meal just as the blast of the ship's horn sounded. Hialeah jumped from the ear deafening blast and hurried to her porthole. She briefly glanced out of the window and left her tiny room in a hurry. Resigned to the deck of her class, Hialeah joined with the other passengers and cheerfully waved goodbye. Her cheerful wave and smile soon waned from her lips as she looked around at the other passengers' gleeful faces. Most were returning home but she was leaving hers heading to a place she knew nothing about. No one to welcome her. No one to embrace her warmly when she disembarked from the ship.

Feeling glum, Hialeah backed away from the ship's edge and left the crowd to carry on with their cheers. She returned to her cabin and finished her meal. Kicking off her shoes, Hialeah sat and thought of her mother and how remarkably brave she had been to run away and escape her torturous life. She made a plan and she kept to it. Hialeah decided at that moment, she would do the same. She remembered Jackson saying that slavery had ended many years ago in England. Colored folks were afforded decent paying jobs and she was impressively skilled with a needle and thread. She would find work as a seamstress; perhaps for a wealthy woman who would provide room and board.

Hialeah dug into her sewing bag to assess her supplies and monies. She would only spend her money on what was necessary. Thankfully, the dining needs of the steerage passengers were looked after by the British Government. She was however, in desperate need to obtain what was needed for her child's arrival. According to Miss Hattie, she would be giving birth by the month's end. Hialeah frowned. She hadn't even considered what to call her child. Hialeah pushed that thought aside as she counted her money. It suddenly dawned on her. She had American currency. What if her money was no good? Where would she sleep? How would she eat? Frustrated with her lack of preparation and knowledge of the world, Hialeah escaped her minuscule lodging for another attempt of fresh air.

She walked the deck and found herself amongst people whose skin she had never encountered; languages she had never heard. Common people like herself smiled as they walked by. She was approached by two older women whose skin was neither white nor colored. Their eyes were slanted and their language was strange. One of the women dared to touch Hialeah's skin and hair much to Hialeah's surprise. They placed their hands together, smiled and bowed slightly before Hialeah. Unsure of what any of it meant, Hialeah mimicked their gesture and continued with her walk of the ship. She made it a point each morning to walk the ship and meet as many people as she could no matter their language. A friendly smile spoke volumes.

By the end of the nearly ten day voyage to England, Hialeah had come to meet many people. She found a colored couple that had made England their home. Hialeah remained close to the pair. When the ship docked at port, the couple guided Hialeah to the train that would take her from Essex to London. She humbly thanked them and boarded her train. Hialeah was in awe. The buildings and streets were so different than that of South Carolina. She much rather preferred the blue sky, bright sun and cotton like clouds of her home over the grayish sky of England but she would get used to it she wagered. Hialeah considered resting her eyes but feared she would miss her stop. She occupied her time by staring out of the window and every now and then she found herself eavesdropping on the other passengers' conversations. Although everyone around her was speaking English, she found their words rather difficult to understand. Jackson's way of speaking was much more clear. Hialeah considered the way some of the passengers were dressed. Their clothing wasn't as fine as Jackson's. She had heard the word 'commoner' used a lot on the ship. Perhaps, Hialeah thought to herself, that common folks was another name for poor. She had been a commoner all of her life and that suited her just fine. With that thought, Hialeah nestled into her seat and continued on with her entertaining eavesdropping.

Hialeah's train pulled into the station just as another bit of gossip was heating up. She exited the train and stepped onto the busy streets of London. Hialeah didn't know where to look first. Horse drawn carriages were nonstop. Restaurants and clothing stores lined the streets. Children tugged on the arms of their mothers begging to visit toy shops. Street vendors were out selling their goods. Burly men rushed by her carrying crates of meat on their shoulders. Hialeah took it all in; every sight and sound. She hurried her steps across the street in hopes of finding a place to sleep for the night and a seamstress shop that would hire her. Along the way, Hialeah set her suitcase down to briefly stretch her fingers. She heard two finely dressed gentlemen discussing the dire need to hear the verdict of Lord Chief Justice, Jackson Harding. Upon hearing Jackson's name, Hialeah quickly picked up her suitcase and followed behind the men. It wasn't long before she was joined by a mass of people, colored and whites alike, all heading toward the courthouse.

Hialeah climbed the stairs to the courthouse. Inside there was mass chaos. Hialeah was pushed and shoved from every direction. She guarded her belly with her sewing bag. Hialeah edged her way out of the circus of men. She eyed a wiry looking man with his arms full of documents of whatever sort. Hialeah bee-lined her way toward the man, who was in quite the hurry. "Excuse me, sir." Hialeah said, tapping the young man on the shoulder. "Madame please." The young man rushed out without so much as a glance in Hialeah's direction. "I lookin' for Mr. Jackson Harding." Hialeah remarked. "His Lordship is due in court and so am I." The young man replied sternly, hurrying on his way with Hialeah on his heels. She dug into her sewing bag and pulled out a make-shift envelope. "Can you see to it that he gets this?" Hialeah rushed out, holding her envelope. The young man stopped short, Hialeah barely missed colliding into him. He turned with an annoyed huff surprised to see that the woman causing him great distress was colored. "Please." Hialeah remarked nervously. "Fine." The young man replied, agitated by Hialeah's disturbance. He ripped the small envelope from Hialeah's hand. "Now do go away." The young man ordered.

Crowds of people were stilling filing into the courtroom. The whites used the main entrance while the colored people, Hialeah noticed, entered through a side door that led up to the balcony. Her curiosity getting the better of her, Hialeah fell in line and climbed the stairs to the over crowded balcony. She wondered just what all the fuss was about. She inched her way forward to the front of the crowd. The room was buzzing with chatter. She had never seen anything like it. There were men wearing white wigs, which Hialeah thought looked absolutely ridiculous.

Jackson's clerk entered his chamber fumbling over his documents. Jackson stood glancing out of the window. "Forgive my tardiness, Your Lordship, I was accosted by a woman." The clerk said. Jackson turned from the window. "A woman?" Jackson replied lightly.

"A black woman. She insisted that I give you this." The clerk remarked, holding out the small envelope. Jackson furrowed his brows, intrigued by his clerk's gift. He walked over to his clerk and removed the small package from his hand. Jackson's clerk turned away feigning disinterest. Jackson tore through the envelope and emptied its contents into his hand. Surprised to see the ring he had given to Hialeah in his own hand, Jackson hastily slid it into his trouser pocket. "Where is the woman?" Jackson demanded. "I don't know, Your Lordship." The clerk stammered out, taking heed of Jackson's tone. "Go." Jackson ordered. His clerk hurried from the room.

The courtroom doors swung open and two officers of the court entered followed by Jackson. Dressed in his black robe and white wig, Jackson approached the bench. The room went silent and everyone in attendance stood. Hialeah's heart fell to her stomach at the very sight of Jackson. She noticed immediately that his wig did not resemble the wigs of the other gentlemen in the room. She had learned that Jackson was ruling on a highly publicized murder case. The victim, a wealthy white business man; the accused, his black male servant.

The strike of Jackson's gavel called the room to order. "I am here, ladies and gentlemen, to rule on the Harrington versus Winthrop case..." Jackson began. Hialeah held her breath. She thought she'd never hear Jackson's voice again. She stood in a daze as Jackson spoke. His hazel eyes and booming voice commanded the attention of every spectator in the room. Jackson scrutinized the room as he spoke. His eyes briefly fell upon Hialeah and he momentarily lost focus. He ushered one of his chief officers to the bench holding a short conversation with the man. The officer returned to his post and Jackson resumed his speech going over key details of the trial. Hialeah hung onto Jackson's every descriptive word. She felt privileged witnessing Jackson at such a capacity. At his conclusion, Jackson's captive audience awaited his verdict with mounted anticipation. Hialeah closed her eyes and said a prayer for Cecil Winthrop, the servant accused of murder. "I find in favor of Mr. Winthrop..." Jackson began. The courtroom erupted in both cheers and astonished gasps from both sides. The colored spectators in the balcony roared their approval of Jackson's verdict. Hialeah was embraced and embraced again by complete strangers. Jackson struck his gavel multiple times to regain order in his court. "I find in favor of Mr. Winthrop and order his release and return to his family forthwith." Jackson commanded with a final blow of his gavel. Another resounding round of applause, cheers and whistles exploded in the courtroom. Jackson left the bench without another glance in Hialeah's direction and returned to his chamber.

It took several minutes for the balcony to clear. Practically every colored person in the balcony rushed to welcome Cecil home. Hialeah was swept away in a whirl of smiling faces and boisterous cheers. Jackson's two chief officers kept a keen eye on Hialeah. They closed in on her just as she neared the courthouse's exit. She was grabbed by both arms, to her shock, and placed under arrest for disrupting the court. Her suitcase was taken by one of the officers as she was led away from the doors. Hialeah argued that she had committed no crime. Her objections were ignored.

Terror-stricken, Hialeah was unknowingly escorted to Jackson's chamber by the two officers. She was led inside and met by a stone faced Jackson. He had disrobed and placed his wig on a nearby table. Jackson stood erect attired in all black; his arms crossed in front of his broad chest. Surely Jackson didn't despise her so greatly that he would confine her to a cell for simply observing. Hialeah's suitcase was set on the ground at her feet. The two officers exited Jackson's chamber leaving Hialeah alone to face whatever punishment awaited her. Hialeah clutched her overly large sewing bag firmly against her protruding belly. Jackson's domineering stance and hardened expression gave Hialeah chills. Her voice had abandoned her. In America, Jackson had total disregard for the law. Here, he was the law and his piercing hazel eyes said as much.

Jackson took Hialeah in. Her full breasts were practically spilling over her dress. Hialeah had boldly arrived in England in her familiar native dress. She wore her long silken hair down and her skin had a glow to it. How could it be, Jackson thought to himself, that she was even more ravishing now than when he first came across her? Hialeah remained silent. It was evident from where Jackson stood that she fought anxious tears. As if her tears had a mind of their own,

Hialeah hastily wiped at her eyes before they could reach her cheeks; resuming her position. Jackson raised a sarcastic brow. "Welcome to England, Miss Nokosi." Jackson said nonchalantly. Hialeah remained silent. "What goes through your mind?" Jackson asked. The very sound of Jackson's calm yet low voice weakened Hialeah's knees. She held her breath when Jackson sauntered near her. Her eyes closed briefly the very moment Jackson casually began to circle her. "You're trembling." Jackson said, whispering in Hialeah's ear. "Why I here?" Hialeah replied almost breathlessly. "Were you not informed of your charges?" Jackson remarked. "Those men say I disturb your court." Hialeah replied. "Contempt, Miss Nokosi, a charge that carries a hefty punishment." Jackson drawled out coolly. "I stand there quiet like a mouse. No words come from me, Jack..." Hialeah began. She paused, reminding herself of where she was. "Your...Your Lordship." Hialeah said cautiously. "Your presence, Miss Nokosi, disrupted my words. Therefore contempt." Jackson replied simply. "You sound...right fine to me." Hialeah stammered out apprehensively. "Did I now?" Jackson replied casually. Hialeah nodded her head. "Henka." Hialeah remarked softly.

Jackson placed his hand inside his trouser pocket and produced his ring; holding it up for Hialeah to view. "You traveled a great distance to return it to me." Jackson said. "I got no right keepin' what ain't rightfully mine." Hialeah replied. Jackson gave a slight nod of his head. "Very noble of you, Miss Nokosi." Jackson remarked smoothly. "I figured your heart...that your heart belong to another that you have carin' for." Hialeah replied timidly, hoping that her words were not true. "Very noble and thoughtful indeed, however, I haven't given a thought of allowing my heart to be taken so easily. My duties have not allowed for it." Jackson remarked calmly. Hialeah tried her best to contain her composure, praying her relief that Jackson hadn't fallen in love with another woman wasn't visible on her face. "You are relieved?" Jackson said. "Monks. I want nothin' but for you to be happy." Hialeah replied softly. Jackson returned the ring back to his pocket. "Then you'll be returning home soon I wager now that you've returned what's mine?" Jackson asked. "Ain't got no home to return to." Hialeah replied. She dug into her sewing bag revealing Jackson's charred flask. "This here all that's left of my home." Hialeah said.

Jackson retrieved the charred flask from Hialeah's hand. His brows furrowed as he looked it over. "What happened to it?" Jackson replied sternly. "George Leonard come after me. He burn all I had in this world to the ground. My house, too." Hialeah remarked. Jackson set his ruined flask down on his desk. "Were you injured?" Jackson replied, his temper beginning to rise at the thought of Isaac Leonard's brother doing Hialeah harm. "I still standin'." Hialeah replied confidently, hugging her sewing bag closer to her expanding belly in a futile attempt to conceal herself from Jackson. A gesture that Jackson surely observed. "Tell me, Miss Nokosi..." Jackson drawled calmly as he walked closer toward Hialeah his eyes capturing hers. "What do you keep from me?" Jackson said. Hialeah gazed up into Jackson's haunting eyes, afraid to blink.

Before Hialeah could utter a sound, Jackson raised her sewing bag, keeping his eyes firmly on hers as he placed his hands on her round belly. Hialeah held her breath. "It seems you are in a most gentle condition after all." Jackson said ever so nonchalantly. Unable to bear Jackson's hazel glare, Hialeah lowered her gaze to Jackson's chest. "I ain't come here expectin' nothin' from you. I make my own way." Hialeah replied her voice quivering. "Of course." Jackson remarked, removing his hands from Hialeah's belly. "Answer me this, and I implore you, think before you answer. Am I to be a father?" Jackson asked. Hialeah swallowed and raised her eyes to meet Jackson's. "No sir, Your Lordship... my troubles are my own." Hialeah replied stubbornly. "Very well." Jackson said coolly, with a quick nod of his head. He swiftly brushed by Hialeah without another word and left her alone in his chamber. Jackson had taken his leave so expeditiously, Hialeah hadn't realized that he had taken her suitcase with him. She turned around and was met by Jackson's two chief officers.

Hialeah was led out of Jackson's chamber into the crowded courthouse. She searched frantically for Jackson through the throngs of people. Jackson had disappeared from Hialeah's view. Her two jailers said nothing to her as they escorted her down a long corridor to the rear of the courthouse where a black carriage awaited her. Hialeah was placed inside and carted away through the streets of London accompanied by her the two officers. They remained silent keeping a stern watch on Hialeah. She was petrified by what possibly awaited her. What of her child, Hialeah thought. What would become of her child? Overcome with grief, Hialeah turned away from the two men and wiped at her eyes.

The carriage pulled onto the grounds of a vast estate. Hialeah's heart sank. Dear Lord, she thought. Jackson had sent her to face their queen for her crime against his court. Hialeah felt as if she would faint. The queen would surely lock her away at his request. She was, after all, responsible for bestowing Jackson as Lord Chief Justice. Hialeah began to silently pray that the queen would show her mercy, for her child's sake, even if Jackson wouldn't.

The carriage halted in front of more steps than Hialeah had ever seen. Two stone lions were mounted on either side of the steps. The massive doors were opened and a stout stern faced middle-aged woman attired in gray stepped into the doorway, her hands clasped in front of her. Hialeah stepped out of the carriage. Her legs felt as if they would give way at any moment. Jackson's officers stood their ground. Hialeah briefly closed her eyes and exhaled slowly. She held her belly as she took each step one at a time glancing around her. The closing of the carriage doors behind her froze Hialeah where she stood. The older woman began tapping her fingers against her hand impatiently. Hialeah reluctantly quickened her steps as she held tightly onto her bag.

The bland faced woman ushered Hialeah inside and closed the enormous doors behind them. She turned to face a visibly shaken Hialeah. "I'm Mrs. Whitford. I have been instructed to see to your care." Mrs. Whitford said sternly. "My care?" Hialeah replied confusedly. "Your care." Mrs. Whitford remarked firmly. "This way please." Mrs. Whitford commanded. Hialeah followed the stuffy elderly woman. She was astonished by the immense splendor the queen's palace held. Hialeah slowed her steps as she glanced around the magnificent structure in disbelief. The astounding cathedral ceilings were adorned with crystal and gold chandeliers, the walls were lined with elegant scones. The grand stair case was far more elegant than that of the Harding home. Mrs. Whitford looked over her shoulder. "Do come along." Mrs. Whitford said austerely. Hialeah scurried to catch up to the older woman.

Hialeah followed closely behind Mrs. Whitford through a long corridor that led to a huge set of double doors. Mrs. Whitford opened the large double doors and ushered Hialeah into the room. Hialeah scanned the room. It was rather charming decorated with a floor length mirror, a chaise, a dressing screen and an elaborate vanity table. Hialeah smelled the air. "What's that scent?" Hialeah asked suspiciously. "That would be lavender." Mrs. Whitford replied. "Now, do you require assistance removing your dress?" Mrs. Whitford asked. Hialeah frowned. "What I remove my dress for?" Hialeah asked uncertain of Mrs. Whitford's intent. "Because one does not bathe in their clothing." Mrs. Whitford replied simply, pulling the dress screen aside. On the other side of the screen was an embossed porcelain tub with a golden rim. "Why it matter to your queen if I smell like lavender when she fixin' to see to it that I rot away in prison?" Hialeah demanded. "Prison?" Mrs. Whitford replied incredulously. "For heaven's sake, what are you chatting on about? The queen does not reside here nor is it a prison." Mrs. Whitford remarked matter-of-factly. "Then you tell me what I here for. Why those two men from the courthouse force me to this place?" Hialeah insisted. "You were brought here by order of The Lord of Hampshire. Now come along, he has requested your presence." Mrs. Whitford urged. "What about my charge?" Hialeah asked. "He will see to your charge and I will see to it that you're properly dressed to receive him." Mrs. Whitford replied in a hurry before leaving Hialeah alone. Hialeah scoffed and began to undress. "I dressed just fine you old cow." Hialeah muttered, allowing her dress to fall to the floor.

Hialeah tested the water before stepping into the tub. The lavender essence tickled her nose. On a small table next to the tub were an assortment of scented soaps, a bathing cloth and a fluffy white towel. Hialeah sniffed each of the scented soaps. She decided to use one after the other. While she bathed, her belly shifted. Hialeah rubbed her hand along her round bump and began to sing her favorite song in Creek. Her unborn child settled and she hurried on with her bath. As Hialeah bathed, it dawned on her that no one knew her in England. Who was this Lord of Hampshire and just how would he see to her charge, Hialeah thought in a panic. She tossed the scented soaps back on the table and carefully managed to stand. Grabbing the towel, Hialeah flung it around her and rushed to dry her skin. She was interrupted by Mrs. Whitford and a red-haired thin maid who followed behind her. The young maid carried a light blue satin dress with low heeled shoes of the same fine satin. Mrs. Whitford instructed the young maid to lay Hialeah's garment on the chaise. "This is Abigail, she'll assist you into your gown and see that your hair is nicely styled." Mrs. Whitford said. Hialeah tightened the towel around her frame. "I don't need your help. Don't need no help from your master neither." Hialeah replied stubbornly. Mrs. Whitford took offense to Hialeah's tone. "The Lord of Hampshire is not my master, he is my employer." Mrs. Whitford remarked offensively. Abigail knelt down to collect Hialeah's soiled dress. "You touch my mama's dress and I pound you good." Hialeah threatened. Abigail stood and took several steps back. Mrs. Whitford huffed her displeasure. "You are in a most delicate nature and your behavior is not becoming of a lady. I shall inform My Lord that you have refused his generosity. Come along Abigail." Mrs. Whitford said sternly.

Both Mrs. Whitford and Abigail left Hialeah alone. Apprehensive of what this Lord of Hampshire would have done to her, Hialeah hastily made her way to the chaise and picked up the gown. She admired it briefly in the floor length mirror and hurried to dress and brush her hair. Giving herself a final glance in the mirror, Hialeah crept from the room following the corridor to the entrance of the house. Mrs. Whitford and Abigail were nowhere to be found. A well dressed gentleman attired in black trousers a crisp white shirt and black overcoat stood in front of another pair of enormous doors. Hialeah contemplated making a hasty retreat providing her round belly would allow it. The sound of footsteps approaching startled her. Abigail appeared carrying an armful of fresh linen. Hialeah exhaled lightly. "Through those doors." Abigail said with a nod of her head as she made her way toward the grand stair case. Hialeah followed Abigail's nod and hesitantly started in the direction of the statue like gentleman guarding the enormous doors. With his eyes cast forward, he swung the door open waiting for Hialeah to pass through. Hialeah stopped in the door way and looked over her shoulder. She stepped to the side and the door was closed behind her.

The elaborate room boasted a long dining table with equally elaborate chairs on each side and two great chairs at the head, a masterful fireplace and four chandeliers. The draperies were pulled back from the six wall length windows. The table was decorated with silver candelabras, fresh fruits, a robust variety of cheeses, smoked meats, breads and sweet rolls. Hialeah clasped her hands beneath her belly; remaining where she stood awaiting the Lord of Hampshire's arrival. The sudden sound of shuffling papers coming from the chair with its back to her quickened Hialeah's pulse. "Sir?" Hialeah said timidly. She was summoned closer by a wave of the man's hand. Hialeah slowly approached the table. Turning slightly to position herself before the master of the house, Hialeah inhaled a sharp breath stunned at the very real sight of Jackson seated before her. "Good afternoon, Miss Nokosi." Jackson said smoothly, standing to his full height. Hialeah's knees buckled beneath her. She grabbed a hold of a chair to keep from stumbling. Recovering from her near stumble, Hialeah regained her composure. "Have you eaten?" Jackson asked simply, observing Hialeah's momentary glance of the delicacies to be served. "I…I ain't hungry." Hialeah stammered out. Jackson grinned. "Your eyes say otherwise." Jackson replied lightly. Hialeah dismissed Jackson's offer of food. "How you know I here? That Mrs. Whitford say this here place belong to the Lord of Hampshire." Hialeah remarked. "I knew you were here because I had you brought here." Jackson replied. "Why?" Hialeah remarked softly, shaking her head in disbelief. "Why you bring me to the Lord…" Hialeah began. "Miss Nokosi, I am the Lord of Hampshire. This is my home." Jackson replied bluntly. Distraught and overwhelmed by Jackson's deception, Hialeah attempted to rush by him. Jackson swiftly took a hold of her arm. "How you do this to me? To my child…" Hialeah remarked accusingly. Her premature tirade was interrupted by the thunderous strike of Jackson's fist slamming down on the dining table. "My child!" Jackson roared, taking both Hialeah's arms in his tight grasp. "My child, that you vehemently denied! Why!" Jackson demanded gruffly, his hazel glower froze Hialeah to her core. "Why!" Jackson demanded, with a firm shake. "Cause I scared!" Hialeah cried out. Her unsuspecting yet painful outburst eased the fire that had built in Jackson. Hialeah turned her head away from Jackson's piercing eyes. "I scared of what you think of me cause of what Isaac do." Hialeah said despairingly. Jackson loosened his hold on Hialeah. She lifted her sorrowful eyes to meet his. "I so scared that we...that my baby, we shame you bein' tainted with the blood what runs through us. I wonder what I gone say to it when it asks me who its daddy is and how I stop its tears when children taunt it for bein' a bastard; a mutt, treated like it's nothin' same as me. I figured on goin' up north, carin' for our child on my own the best I could but I find your ring and I think real hard bout comin' here. Maybe things be different. I see you sittin' across from me in that courtroom lookin' right smart, commandin' the room, all eyes on you. It was somethin' to see. I feel so proud and frightened at the same time. You respected here. My only carin' was to save your good name. I think bout what you lose if other important folks learn of you havin' a little one with colored skin." Hialeah said. "I mostly scared cause I fear you hate me and I love you with everything in me." Hialeah said, throwing her hands up sobbing in hopeless despair. She turned her back to Jackson to shield herself from his condemning eyes.

Jackson's heart felt as if it had shattered into a thousand pieces listening to Hialeah's tortured truth. He removed Hialeah's ring from his trouser pocket and closed his hand around it gathering Hialeah into his arms, allowing his hand to gently slide down her growing bump. She trembled at his touch. "I do not hate you nor do I require your protection, though the thought is immensely appreciated. Moreover, I could never be shamed for loving the gift you will give me nor for loving you." Jackson said soothingly. Hialeah closed her eyes. She had dreamt for many months of Jackson's touch; to hear him speak of the love that still remained for her. "I so sor..." Hialeah began. "Don't." Jackson interjected. He opened his hand and took Hialeah's in his; placing her ring onto her finger. Hialeah opened her eyes. "Your hand is where it belongs. Where it shall remain. Ecenokecvyet os. (Ih-Chih-No-Kih-Chuh-Yeet Ose)." Jackson said. Hialeah threw her arms around Jackson; overjoyed to hear him declare his love for her in her father's tongue. Jackson embraced Hialeah. "I miss you somethin' awful." Hialeah tearfully whispered in Jackson's ear. "And I you. Now do have something. I'm sure my child is most eager to enjoy what has been prepared." Jackson said teasingly, releasing Hialeah from his embrace to pull a chair out. Hialeah sat and placed her hands in what little lap she had left while Jackson proceeded to serve her before preparing a plate of his own. Hialeah waited for Jackson to take his seat and pick up his fork. She burst into laughter when instead, Jackson began eating with his fingers popping strawberries into his mouth. Amused by Jackson's humorous antics, Hialeah upped the challenge filling her mouth with three strawberries and a single grape. Laughing, Jackson applauded Hialeah's victory. To make their childish game a bit more interesting, Jackson poked Hialeah in her puffed cheeks. He howled with immense laughter when the single grape escaped her lips shooting across the room.

Their private lunch was interrupted by a firm knock on the door and the arrival of Mrs. Whitford. Hialeah turned her head in an attempt to hide her full cheeks. "Your Lordship, a word please." Mrs. Whitford said. Jackson chuckled at Hialeah's distress while rising to see about Mrs. Whitford's inquiries. Jackson and Mrs. Whitford left Hialeah alone. Taking notice of the shuffled documents beneath Jackson's plate, Hialeah quickly chewed her mouthful of berries and hurried over to Jackson's chair. Lifting his plate, Hialeah began to rifle through Jackson's letters. She noticed the name of the ship that had brought her to England printed on what appeared to be a ticket. Hialeah hastily returned Jackson's documents beneath his plate. She picked up the ticket and rushed over to the door. She could hear Jackson conversing with another gentleman. Hialeah read over the ticket and inhaled a shocked breath. Jackson had purchased a ticket back to America; back to South Carolina.

Jackson's approaching footsteps startled Hialeah. She had no time to return Jackson's ticket to its proper place. Jackson entered the dining room to find Hialeah standing awkwardly with her hands placed behind her back. Jackson cocked a dubious brow; glancing over at his seat. Meticulous with his files and documents, Jackson was well aware that his boarding ticket was not where he had left it. He returned his attention to Hialeah. "Are you not well?" Jackson asked casually. "Henka." Hialeah replied reassuringly. "Shall we continue our lunch?"

Jackson asked, returning to his place at the table while Hialeah remained standing. Jackson leaned back in his chair, crossed his legs and nonchalantly tapped his fingers against his knee. "Miss Nokosi, I'm sure it's most difficult to sit whilst attempting to conceal my ticket behind your back. " Jackson said casually gesturing for Hialeah to return his ticket. Distraught that Jackson was leaving in a matter of hours, Hialeah set the ticket on the table. "You goin' home?" Hialeah asked sorrowfully. "England is my home." Jackson replied. "That ticket say you fixin' to leave." Hialeah remarked. "I had every intention of returning to America." Jackson replied. "What for?" Hialeah persisted. "It no longer matters, you're here." Jackson replied. "You tell me true." Hialeah remarked. "Leave it be." Jackson warned. "Not until you tell me why you leavin'. The truth." Hialeah replied. "Miss Nokosi, my truth is vicious but if you insist then I'll oblige you my reason for returning home, tracking down George Leonard, and placing a bloody fucking bullet between his eyes." Jackson replied low. "Is that the truth you desired?" Jackson said. Hialeah could feel the chills coming over her skin. "And after? After George dead and gone like Isaac?" Hialeah asked timidly. Jackson dug his hand into his inner coat pocket producing two more tickets which he placed on the table. "I intended to return with you by my side." Jackson replied. "I was a fool to leave you behind." Jackson said. "I ain't give you much choice. Besides, we here now." Hialeah replied softly. Jackson placed his hands on Hialeah's belly. "When will it be?" Jackson asked. "Miss Hattie say real soon." Hialeah replied smiling. "Impatient like its mother." Jackson remarked teasingly. "Come with me." Jackson said. "But I still hungry." Hialeah replied. Jackson chuckled. "Alright, we'll have our meal, then I'll show you all of Hampshire." Jackson remarked smiling.

Near bursting, Hialeah could eat no more. She took a hold of Jackson's hand as he escorted her from the dining room. In mid stride, Jackson stopped and raised a brow at Hialeah. He looked down at her floor length dress and chuckled. "Miss Nokosi, you're not wearing shoes." Jackson said lightly. Hialeah raised her dress slightly to reveal her bare toes. "That Mrs. Whitford tell you that?" Hialeah replied defensively. "She had no need. Hard floor and your feet are silent." Jackson remarked casually. "I can't walk proper in those things."

Hialeah whispered. Jackson chuckled. "And your sense of balance has gone to your middle." Jackson teased. His playful remark earned him a pinch on the arm. "You know that smarts." Jackson said, smiling. "Well I hope so." Hialeah replied. "Come on with you." Jackson remarked, escorting Hialeah up the grand stair case stopping briefly to capture her lips in a long awaited kiss that left Hialeah breathless.

Jackson guided Hialeah on a grand tour of his home. Hialeah was exhausted by the tour's end. She was led to three libraries, Jackson's elaborate kitchen where his chef was busily preparing the evening meal, the sewing room, the powder room, Jackson's personal office, the ballroom, the gallery, four studies, twenty-four guest bedrooms, the receiving room where Jackson received visitors for brief visits, the massive gardens filled with more flowers than Hialeah ever thought she'd see in a lifetime, two ponds and the stables where Hialeah was gifted several magnificent horses to ride when she was able. Her tour ended with two last stops; Jackson's overwhelming master bedroom where her suitcase had been placed and the nursery Jackson had prepared for the arrival of their child. Hialeah stepped inside the nursery; her jaw dropping in utter fascination. The room was filled with extravagant rocking chairs, a pram for walks, stuffed dolls and animals, priceless artwork adorning the walls, a vast mahogany armoire and dressing tables, and a cradle placed next to an enormous canopy bed for Hialeah to rest. "Oh Jackson." Hialeah said, her breath taken away by the majesty of her child's room. "Do you like it or would you prefer I take it all back, gather your things and see you safely returned to London so that you may go it on your own, make your own way?" Jackson replied, his tone void of all humor. Hialeah was at a loss for words. "Take care of your words. Do not ever speak of our child as your trouble." Jackson said, placing a kiss on Hialeah's hand. "Let's have a look." Jackson replied, smiling. Hialeah didn't know what to look at first. Everywhere she turned each piece of furniture was more beautiful than the next. "Try the chairs. Perfect for nursing I hear. Haven't tried it myself." Jackson said lightly. Hialeah smiled and took a seat in one of the rocking chairs. She viewed the entire room and placed her hand over her mouth. Overcome with emotion, Hialeah burst into tears. Jackson rushed to her side and knelt down in front of her. "I so sorry. I ain't sure what to think of it all." Hialeah said between sobs. "Happy tears I hope?" Jackson asked. Hialeah nodded. "I just wonder what my mama think." Hialeah replied, wiping tears from her eyes. "I think your mother and father would be most anxious as I am to welcome our child." Jackson remarked reassuringly. "I write to her after all these years. I tell her I fixin' to be a mama. I tell her bout Miss Lilly and where to find me. I tell her bout...I tell her bout you, bout us. I send that letter some time before I come here. She never say nothin' back. I know she still sore at me. She and my daddy they both still sore I disobey my daddy's rule. Maybe, just maybe the letter ain't reach her." Hialeah replied softly. Jackson kissed Hialeah's hand gently yet again. "You're fatigued." Jackson remarked, assisting Hialeah to her feet.

Jackson led Hialeah to their bedroom and insisted she rest before dinner. Hialeah was all too happy to oblige. She sank into Jackson's bed, cradled her belly and closed her eyes. Jackson had much to do while Hialeah slept. He left her alone to her comfort and hurried downstairs to ensure that everything was going accordingly.

Hialeah was startled several hours later by the sound of Abigail bustling around in Jackson's bedroom. She had set out Hialeah's clothing for dinner. Hialeah sat straight up in Jackson's bed. "Sorry to have awakened you. My Lord's instructions." Abigail said. "Instructions?" Hialeah asked perplexed. "To see that you're dressed for dinner." Abigail replied. "I already dressed." Hialeah remarked. "Of course, but now you must dress for dinner. Protocol." Abigail replied. "What that mean?" Hialeah asked suspiciously. "It means that you dress accordingly for each meal." Abigail replied. "My Lord requested that you wear something soft yet elegant. I laid your dress out for you. You'll find your shoes more fitting for your condition." Abigail said as she made her way to the door. "Wait. I sorry what I say to you when I arrive. What you must think of me." Hialeah replied. "No worries. I'm just relieved that you're finally here." Abigail remarked casually. Her words piqued Hialeah's interest. "Why is that?" Hialeah replied curiously. "Well, it isn't my place to say." Abigail remarked. "Please." Hialeah urged, tapping Jackson's bed. Abigail hurried over to the bed and took a seat next to Hialeah. "You'll not say a word?" Abigail asked anxiously. "Not a word." Hialeah replied in a whisper. "Alright then. Well, when My Lord returned home, he was rather morose; ill-tempered. Most nights, he wouldn't arrive until quite late from his visits." Abigail remarked. "Visits?" Hialeah asked confusedly. "Lady Willoughby would send many invitations requesting My Lord's company." Abigail replied. Hialeah's heart sank upon receiving such news. As if she could read the troubled thoughts running through Hialeah's mind, Abigail rushed on. "He doesn't love her." Abigail said. "No need to love somebody to share their bed." Hialeah replied. "I have no doubt she persisted, but it was your name he spoke those nights Mrs. Whitford and I saw him to bed on the rare occasion he indulged himself in drink." Abigail remarked reassuringly. "What about that Mrs. Whitford? Turning her nose up at me on account I colored." Hialeah said defensively. "Mrs. Whitford would never do such a horrid thing." Abigail replied. "How you so sure?" Hialeah remarked. "You can't tell by looking at her but Mrs. Whitford has black blood in her. Her grandmother was a black slave. She was owned by a very prominent family; The Baron and Baroness of Stratfordshire. When the baroness took ill and passed it was Mrs. Whitford's grandmother who saw to the baron's care. They fell in love and Mrs. Whitford's grandmother bore the baron two children. Mrs. Whitford's mum, Elizabeth and her brother Alfred. The baron reared them as he did his white children. It was quite the scandal so I've heard. The baron even left Elizabeth and Alfred quite a comfortable sum of money when he passed but his children with the baroness fought against it and they were left practically destitute. However, Elizabeth, Mrs. Whitford's mum was very light; practically white even and she married quite well. Of course her husband didn't have the status of the Baron of Stratfordshire but she made due and then there is of course, Mrs. Whitford. A woman of noble blood stripped from all that was rightfully hers." Abigail said sadly. "How awful for her." Hialeah replied sorrowfully. "My Lord pays her quite well. Her father, saw fit that she was taken care of. She wants for nothing." Abigail remarked. "That is good to hear." Hialeah replied. "My Lord is most generous." Abigail remarked, smiling rising from the bed. "I'd best resume my duties. I'll leave you to your dressing." Abigail said. "If you ain't much mindin' I could use your help." Hialeah replied. Abigail smiled and proceeded to assist Hialeah for dinner.

Jackson anxiously paced the floor of the grand hall attired in a black tuxedo. He glanced at his pocket watch numerous times anticipating Hialeah's entrance. Their dinner had been prepared and Jackson was most eager to start their evening. Mrs. Whitford opened the doors to the dining room to find Jackson continuously pacing. "You're quite nervous." Mrs. Whitford said. "Does it show?" Jackson replied. "I'll see what's keeping Miss Nokosi." Mrs. Whitford replied. She made her way toward the stairs just as Hialeah appeared. Hialeah's arrival halted Mrs. Whitford's steps. She turned to face Jackson and nodded her head in approval of Hialeah. "Stunning." Mrs. Whitford said, taking her leave the moment Hialeah began descending the stairs dressed in a silk burgundy gown with a chiffon underlay. Her hair was styled in a simple bun with a modest burgundy hat adorned with black feathers tilted slightly over her forehead. Jackson was beyond restraint. He climbed the stairs meeting Hialeah and extended his arm to escort her to dinner. "My God, you look exquisite." Jackson said. Hialeah felt her cheeks warming. "Mvto. (Muh-doe) Thank you." Hialeah replied shyly. "You look exquisite, too." Hialeah said. Her compliment brought a hearty laugh from Jackson.

The gentleman Hialeah had encountered at her arrival to Jackson's home was standing at the entrance to the dining room. He nodded his head and opened the doors for Jackson and Hialeah. They were greeted to Hialeah's surprise by a four-stringed quartet and a vicar. The musicians began to play softly. Hialeah turned to face Jackson. "I hope you don't mind the intimate affair, but I thought we'd get married." Jackson said, grinning. "Married?" Hialeah replied stunned. "You've not reconsidered have you?" Jackson remarked teasingly as he gestured for the vicar to approach. "Vicar Thomas, whenever you're ready." Jackson said, taking hold of Hialeah's hand.

Vicar Thomas recited the ceremonial words that would unite Jackson and Hialeah in marriage. Hialeah stood in an unimaginable haze as the vicar spoke. Her stomach was tied in knots amidst the constant movement of her child. Hialeah absentmindedly tapped her hands on her belly to sooth her little one. Jackson gave her hand a gentle squeeze. Hialeah gazed up into Jackson's eyes. He nodded his head toward the vicar. "Yes." Hialeah rushed out. "Very well." Vicar

Thomas replied. He concluded the ceremony and Hialeah was swept into Jackson's arms sealing their vows with such a passionate kiss that even the vicar blushed. Hialeah pressed her hands against her lips. She too felt her cheeks warming from Jackson's bold kiss. Jackson leaned in toward Hialeah's ear. "No worries, My Lady, we're married, remember?" Jackson said devilishly. Vicar Thomas excused himself; his matrimonial duty completed. He left Jackson and Hialeah to celebrate their nuptials.

Hialeah had never felt so special dancing in Jackson's arms. The servants retired for the evening while Jackson escorted Hialeah through the moonlit garden. Jackson gazed down at Hialeah. He placed a tender kiss on her forehead. "We should retire." Jackson said soothingly. Hialeah clasped her hand in Jackson's and led an amused Jackson inside their home. Jackson lifted Hialeah into his arms and carried her up the stairs. Hialeah frowned when Jackson carried her away from his bedroom. "Where you takin' me?" Hialeah asked worriedly. "To your room." Jackson replied. "No." Hialeah remarked softly. "You're with child." Jackson replied. "Please. I sleep too many nights without you." Hialeah remarked pleadingly. Jackson stopped in mid-stride gazing down in Hialeah's soft eyes. "As have I." Jackson replied low. "But I dare not risk harming you. You do understand?" Jackson said. "I understand." Hialeah replied softly. She laid her head against Jackson's chest as he carried her toward the room she would be occupying until the birth of their child. Jackson entered Hialeah's dimly lit bedroom and set her on the bed. "Shall I have Abigail assist you?" Jackson asked. "Monks. I can manage." Hialeah replied. Jackson nodded. "Sleep well." Jackson remarked. Hialeah smiled faintly in the dimness of her room as Jackson left her alone.

Hialeah wandered aimlessly in her bedroom. She was restless and yearned for Jackson's closeness. Upset, Hialeah walked over to her armoire. What little items of clothing she had brought with her were hanging at her disposal. Hialeah began to undress. She tossed her gown onto her bed and removed her hat. She slipped into the sheer night robe she had worn the first night she and Jackson shared her bed. Relieved to be free of her constricting gown, Hialeah made herself comfortable in front of her vanity table and released her hair from its bun. Her black tresses cascaded passed her shoulders. She ran her fingers through her hair her bedtime preparations complete.

Jackson laid in his bed staring at the ceiling his head resting on his crossed arms forcing his mind to think of nothing. The thought of taking his wife would make for a long night. He was, however, surprisingly exhausted and desperate for sleep. Jackson groaned inwardly fighting the urge to wake his wife.

As the hours slipped by, sleep continuously evaded Hialeah. She was somewhat frightened to sleep alone in such a vast room. The shadows cast on her wall from the moon's light unnerved her. She wondered if Jackson were still awake. Surely he wouldn't object to his wife joining him if just to sleep. Her mind made up, Hialeah slipped from beneath her covers and crept from her room. Reaching Jackson's bedroom, Hialeah discreetly entered. She pressed her lips together as Jackson lie soundly sleeping. Hialeah tiptoed to a spacious side of Jackson's bed. As quietly as she had slipped from her bed she slipped beneath the covers of Jackson's. Hialeah shivered from the coolness of the sheets against her skin. She slowly inched her way toward Jackson to share the warmth of his bare skin. She immediately scolded herself for not putting out the lamp before joining Jackson in bed, however, she didn't dare risk waking him climbing out of the bed. Pondering her ridiculous situation, Hialeah glanced over at Jackson. She was relieved that he hadn't stirred. Hialeah inched her way even closer to Jackson's sleeping frame. She was forced to press her breasts against his chest and gently place her leg over his midsection. Hialeah stretched her arm toward the lamp, her expanding belly preventing her from accomplishing her task. Hialeah growled her frustration unaware that Jackson had fully awakened from the touch of her leg against his skin. Grinning at his wife's frustration, Jackson startled Hialeah by casually removing his arm from beneath his head, putting out his lamp, shrouding his room with only the light of the moon. "Hello, Mrs. Harding." Jackson said smoothly. Hialeah looked up at Jackson. "Hensci. (Hins-cha)." Hialeah replied in a timid whisper, the moonlight playing off her features. Jackson gestured for Hialeah to come closer. Hialeah adjusted her gown and mounted her husband. Jackson took a hold of Hialeah's gown front and unclasped the tiny button uncovering her shoulders and freeing her breasts. He cupped her mounds in his hands and teased her nipples into taunt peaks. Hialeah inhaled softly. Jackson positioned himself just so and kissed each breast tenderly before taking one then the other into his mouth; darting his tongue around each nipple. Hialeah let out a soft moan. "You are hellbent, Mrs. Harding, on torturing me." Jackson said low. Hialeah relished being addressed by Jackson's name. "Mrs. Harding." Hialeah replied proudly. "Mrs. Harding, indeed." Jackson remarked seductively before taking Hialeah's lips in an ardent kiss. His loins aroused at the very thought of possessing his wife. Hialeah ignited Jackson's erection with sensual kisses along his neck and chest all the while stroking his pulsating staff. "My God, what you do to me." Jackson groaned out, Hialeah's teasing driving him mad. Unable to restrain himself any longer, Jackson lost all control and rammed his throbbing hardened shaft deep within his wife. Hialeah cried out in erotic ecstasy as Jackson guided her body along his erection. Hialeah arched her back fully receiving each vigorous and intoxicating thrust of Jackson's staff; breathless from the fierceness of his ravishing lovemaking. Hialeah begged Jackson to take her matching his sultry rhythm; much to his gratifying satisfaction. Deep moans escaped him as Hialeah continued her seductive movement. Jackson slid his hand beneath Hialeah's gown; caressing her gently. She inhaled softly from his touch, her climax mounting as Jackson drove himself further into her woman's cove. With each ferocious thrust, Jackson's release heightened. Hialeah cried out Jackson's name once more as her climax overtook her. Roaring deep, Jackson erupted; his body quaking from his release; their matrimonial union truly consummated.

Enraptured beyond words could express, Hialeah rolled onto her side with Jackson's assistance and snuggled close to her husband. Jackson gingerly placed his hand on Hialeah's belly and to his shock his unborn child shifted. "Bloody hell, what was that?" Jackson exclaimed, hastily removing his hand. Jackson's astonished outburst brought about a fit of laughter from Hialeah. "That be your little one. It move around most times." Hialeah replied, smiling. "My God, I think I angered it." Jackson remarked stunned. "Your little one is just fine." Hialeah replied reassuringly; taking a hold of Jackson's hand and gently placing it back on her rounding bump. Jackson's eyes widened in awe. "Does it hurt?" Jackson asked. "Not much. Most times it just uncomfortable." Hialeah replied. "Amazing." Jackson remarked, smiling. Amused, Jackson leaned in toward Hialeah's belly. "Can you hear me?" Jackson said, speaking to his unborn child. His response was yet another delightful movement from his child. "You keep that up and you will anger it." Hialeah replied teasingly. "Really?" Jackson remarked. Hialeah giggled at the concerned expression on Jackson's face. "I speak to it all the time." Hialeah replied. "Well that's because you're the mother." Jackson remarked. "Are you frightened?" Jackson asked. Hialeah nodded her head. "Henka." Hialeah replied softly. "Don't be. You are your mother's daughter." Jackson remarked reassuringly, with a tender kiss upon Hialeah's forehead. "We should get some rest. All three of us." Jackson said. Hialeah agreed lying her head on Jackson's chest.

Feeling ill at ease in the darkness of their shared bed, Hialeah began tapping her fingers absentmindedly on Jackson's torso. Jackson grinned. "Are you restless?" Jackson asked. "Not so much. Just somethin' eatin' at me." Hialeah replied. It dawned on her that she had never mentioned George Leonard wanting to do her harm yet Jackson was prepared to travel back to South Carolina. "Do tell, Mrs. Harding." Jackson remarked casually. "You won't get sore with me?" Hialeah asked. Jackson cocked a brow, perplexed by Hialeah's question. "What worries me is what ever could have piqued your interest at such an hour." Jackson replied. "George Leonard." Hialeah remarked bluntly. "George Leonard?" Jackson replied bewildered at his wife's comment. "How you know he after me?" Hialeah asked simply. Jackson exhaled. He had best be truthful. "I received a letter from Mama Lilly that I...that I immediately disposed of." Jackson said. Hialeah laid silently in Jackson's arms. "Regrettably, my heart was cold and I wanted nothing to do with the goings on in America. Yet, another letter arrived some months later. A letter I set aside tempted to open but refused. I had forgotten about it honestly until Mrs. Whitford reminded me that there were crucial documents on my desk that required my attention. In my haste yesterday morning before I was due to appear in court, I unknowingly opened Mama Lilly's letter. Its contents chilled my blood and I'll speak no more of it." Jackson said coldly, his own admission angering him. His anger quickly subsided by the gentle movement he felt against his side. A calming reminder that he would soon be a father.

The next morning, Hialeah was awakened by a swift knock on the door before it swung open. She was greeted by an overly cheerful Abigail carrying her breakfast tray. "Good morning, My Lady. I trust you slept well." Abigail said gleefully. Hialeah frowned puzzled as to why Abigail greeted her in such a manner. Noting Hialeah's confused expression, Abigail smiled as she made her way towards the bed. "T'is your title by the way. My Lady. T'is how you are to be addressed since marrying My Lord." Abigail said. "Where is my Jack...my husband?" Hialeah replied, still weary from sleep, yet overjoyed she was now a married and titled woman. "My Lord insisted that you rest. He took his breakfast some time ago before heading into town." Abigail remarked. "What I supposed to do while he away?" Hialeah replied. "I'm most certain his work will not keep him away for long. Besides, My Lady, this is your home now as well, you're free to do whatever it is that pleases you. Perhaps, spend some time in one of My Lord's libraries or needlepoint." Abigail remarked. "Needlepoint. I like that plenty." Hialeah remarked light-heartedly. "Breakfast first, My Lady. It wouldn't do well for My Lord to discover you've not eaten in your condition." Abigail replied assuredly. "I think you're right." Hialeah remarked. Abigail set Hialeah's breakfast tray on the small table. "I'll return momentarily to prepare you for the day." Abigail replied before seeing her way out.

Hialeah tossed her covers aside and rushed to her feet. She was instantly overcome by a sharp pain in her stomach. Hialeah grasped onto the nightstand and inhaled several deep breaths. She calmed herself as the pain subsided and carefully walked over to the table to have her breakfast.

Hialeah had suffered yet another pain before Abigail's return but said nothing. Inclined to believe that perhaps something she had eaten didn't agree with her. She bathed and dressed all the while chatting with Abigail; inquiring about life in England. She wanted to know everything and Abigail was only too happy to share. Their friendly conversation was followed by a visit to the sewing room.

Hialeah placed all of her needed supplies in a basket. Mrs. Whitford interrupted calling Abigail away to assist in household duties. Hialeah insisted she could manage and Abigail returned to her chores. Glancing out of the window, Hialeah was taken in by the blue sky and bright sun. She gathered her basket and decided to do her needlepoint in the luscious garden.

While Hialeah made herself comfortable on a bench. The fresh afternoon air and aromas of the flowers made for a pleasant day of needlepoint. Hialeah was most eager to get to work on her craft for her child's nursery. Glancing around the garden, Hialeah was rather envious of Jackson's gardeners. They were surrounded by such beauty and they were colored like her. Hialeah desired to get to know them. She set her needlepoint aside and rose from the bench. The gardeners halted their work, a look of confusion on their faces as Hialeah approached them. She introduced herself as Jackson's wife and graciously shook their hands. Her introduction was surprising but well received. Chatting away as if they were lifelong friends, Hialeah momentarily forgot about her needlepoint. Her interest was in the colorful paradise that surrounded her. She was inquisitive about each gardener; both male and female alike. She inquired about their homes and families and she shared her story with them as well; describing in great detail her mother's life and how she herself had come to arrive in England. Several of the servants shared how generous and welcoming Jackson had always been and some told of humorous tales of the many jokes Jackson played on them. Hialeah joined in their laughter; amusing Jackson's servants with a story of her own. The servants roared with laughter as Hialeah told of the time she had stolen Jackson's hat and he forced to chase her through the streets to retrieve it. The lighthearted mood was soon interrupted by Mrs. Whitford's appearance on the veranda. Hialeah apologized for keeping the servants away from their duties and returned to the bench and her needlepoint while Mrs. Whitford continued on with the running of the Hampshire Estate.

Jackson returned as scheduled amidst Mrs. Whitford barking out her orders. "The house looks impeccable." Jackson said. "Well it would if anyone bothered to listen, including you." Mrs. Whitford.

Jackson grinned devilishly. "Now what, pray tell, have I done to earn your disdain?" Jackson teased. "Do go on with you, My Lord. You sir, have my utmost respect, however, I simply cannot for the life of me fathom why a man in your esteemed status should go around carrying such a brute weapon. I mean honestly, you gave your fair ruling on the Winthrop matter and anyone who doesn't care for it, well, pity on them." Mrs. Whitford replied sternly. "Whilst I do agree with your very passionate argument, there are those who adamantly disagree and if my memory serves me correctly, bullets don't care much for titles or statuses nor do the heated men who insists on firing them." Jackson remarked casually. "Barbaric. Simply barbaric." Mrs. Whitford replied. Her continued argument brought a smile to Jackson's face as he made his way toward the grand staircase. "My wife? Where is she?" Jackson asked. "Behaving as a gentlewoman should in the garden working on her needlepoint; unlike her gruff husband." Mrs. Whitford replied haughtily. "I don't much care for needlepoint." Jackson remarked teasingly, laughing his way up the stairs. "Do inform Mrs. Harding I'll join her momentarily after I've changed into more suitable attire." Jackson replied.

Mrs. Whitford's task of informing Hialeah of her husband's arrival was halted by an unexpected knock on the door. Huffing her annoyance, Mrs. Whitford looked briefly over her shoulder. Jackson had already taken his leave without a word of expecting guests. The house was, of course, impeccable. There was no need to keep Jackson's guest waiting any further. Mrs. Whitford opened the doors and was quite taken aback by the man standing in front of her. He immediately removed his hat and offered a charming smile. "Good afternoon, ma'am. My name's George. George Leonard." George said confidently. Mrs. Whitford's eyes lit up. "You're American." Mrs. Whitford replied lightly. "Yes ma'am." George remarked. "Well I am sorry. If you've come all this way in search of employment, My Lord has no positions available." Mrs. Whitford replied. "No ma'am. I'm lookin' for my sister, Hialeah. I was told in town Mr. Harding lives here. My sister and Mr. Harding, well they's got real close back home. I figured I start here." George remarked casually. "My Lady didn't mention you were coming by." Mrs. Whitford replied, smiling. "No ma'am, it's a surprise." George remarked. "Well, I'll not be the one to ruin such a joyous occasion. It is unfortunate you didn't arrive sooner. Your sister and Mr. Harding were wed just last evening." Mrs. Whitford replied gleefully, stepping aside to allow George entrance. "Is that so?" George remarked, dryly. "Oh, she looked absolutely stunning." Mrs. Whitford replied. George kept his tongue and his focus. "Do come along. I'll take you to My Lady." Mrs. Whitford said. George stepped aside permitting Mrs. Whitford to lead the way.

Hialeah was making quick work of her needlepoint. The constant twangs of discomforting pain in her belly was alarming her. She thought to hail over a servant to send for a doctor but decided against it. They had their duties and she considered herself more than capable of making it to her bed to await Jackson's return. Her mind made up, Hialeah gathered her materials and placed them in the basket.

George fumbled with his coat, attempting awkwardly to conceal the gun he had placed in the back of his trousers. Mrs. Whitford silently opened the veranda doors and turned to face George. "I'll not intrude on your privacy." Mrs. Whitford said, smiling. "Go on." Mrs. Whitford continued, tapping George on the shoulder for encouragement. George stepped onto the veranda, his smile fading to a sinister smirk. Mrs. Whitford quietly closed the door behind him and returned to her work.

Frantically looking around for any watchful eyes, George reached behind his coat and removed his gun. He quickened his steps and bee-lined his way toward an unsuspecting Hialeah who sat rubbing the soreness from her lower back. George raised his gun and placed it directly against Hialeah's head. "Bet you ain't ever think you see one of us Leonards again." George spat. Hialeah sat tensed recognizing the familiar voice. "G...George." Hialeah stammered out fearfully. George responded with the cock of his gun. "You think to scream and I empty this here gun in you the same way that son-of-a-bitch did to my brother." George remarked threateningly. "How you get here?" Hialeah replied nervously. "I get here same as you. Sheriff Willard bring my brother home dead with the little bit of money he had in his pocket. My mama lose her oldest boy at the hands of that white filth you whore yourself to instead of lovin' your own." George remarked angrily.

"Miss Lilly say differently. She say Isaac demand what ain't his from Jackson. What he had no right to." Hialeah stammered out. "Damn what Aunt Lilly say. Comin' round beggin' my mama to keep me away like some fool stuck on her massuh." George scoffed. "You burn my home." Hialeah replied, her voice quivering. "That's right I burn it. I sit back and enjoy every piece fallin' down. Then I follow every step you take. I see you go into town and buy your way on the boat. I use what little money Isaac had to buy my way, too. I keep a sharp eye on you. On the train; in the courthouse too. Then you get pulled away by those white men so I find me some place to eat and sleep; start fresh in the morning. I was told where I could find Mr. Jackson real easy and I find you. Too bad Miss Sara ain't here to see you beg for your life." George remarked smugly. Hialeah inhaled a shocked gasp. "Miss Sara?" Hialeah replied in a surprised whisper. "I run into her in town. Give her and the Widow Williams my apologies on losin' Judge Williams; explain to Miss Sara how Mr. Jackson kill my brother same as her daddy and that I fixin' to find you. She real happy to hear that. She dig right in her little bag and give me more money to get whatever I need to see you dead." George boasted. "A right shame what them white boys did to her." George said. "What you mean?" Hialeah replied perplexed by George's statement. "Five brothers get even on account her daddy stealin' they land. One of 'em claim that Miss Sara tried to kill his wife. Them white boys go runnin' wild right in Judge Williams' house with guns and such lookin' for God knows what. Whatever they be searchin' for, they kill her for it. You ain't hear bout it cause you already on the boat. I lucky I get through when I did. Sheriff Willard questionin' white and colored folks alike. I get my money from her and that all that matters." George remarked simply. "George please, I with child." Hialeah pleaded, tearfully. "What I care bout your white man's heathen child? He took my brother away from me and my mama; fill him full of holes and I fixin' to do the same to you like the good book say; an eye for an eye. Let him see what it's like to mourn and cry just like my mama did for Isaac." George spat. "You kill me and Jackson gone see you dead. Then what? Your mama gone have two dead sons." Hialeah replied. "I make my peace with my mama and the Lord. I ain't never expect to get back home." George remarked matter-of-factly. "Now you stand and face me." George ordered, nudging Hialeah with the barrel of his gun. Hialeah closed her eyes tight and quickly prayed through her tears before reluctantly coming to her feet. She instantaneously succumbed to an excruciating torment. Her eyes widened in shock as a sudden burst of warmth ran down the length of her legs. Hialeah quickly lifted her skirt to reveal the liquid streaming down. George followed her panicked stare. "It too soon." Hialeah rushed out frantically. "Don't matter none. You ain't gone live to hold it." George scoffed. "You killin' a child that ain't harm you none make you a coward, George Leonard." Hialeah spat.

Mrs. Whitford approached Jackson smiling as he entered the hall; her hands clasped beneath her bosom. Her odd yet infectious smile brought a smile to Jackson's lips. "You're smiling." Jackson said lightheartedly. "Why shouldn't I be when at this very moment your darling wife is reuniting with her dear brother, George." Mrs. Whitford replied gleefully. Jackson's smile immediately faded from his lips. "George?" Jackson remarked suspiciously. "Leonard, I believe he said. They're in the gar...." Mrs. Whitford began. Jackson's eyes widened in terror. "He's going to kill her!" Jackson shouted, bolting down the hall. Mrs. Whitford chased after Jackson, halting her steps the moment Jackson swiftly maneuvered his gun from its holster; his blood draining from his face as he dreadfully watched from the wall length window, George strike Hialeah across the face knocking her to the ground. With great haste, Jackson shattered the window with his arm. The shattering glass from above distracted George from firing at Hialeah. "George!" Jackson roared. George hastily turned around responding to the call of his name; his weapon aimed at the man he truly despised. Smirking ominously, George fired two futile shots. The gunfire alarmed Jackson's servants, whom fell to the ground, unsure of what was transpiring. Mrs. Whitford dropped to her knees at Jackson's command before he promptly returned fire assailing George's body with scorching lead. His bloodied and lifeless body fell over the bench landing near Hialeah. Her frantic scream from below sent Jackson racing down the stairs jumping over the banister.

In his haste, Jackson barged through the veranda doors and stormed through the garden to find Hialeah and George surrounded by astonished servants. His heart slamming against his chest, Jackson ordered two of the more burlier men to get rid of George's bullet riddled body and inform the authorities. Jackson lifted a distraught Hialeah into his arms. "Jackson, the baby's comin'." Hialeah said anxiously. Jackson looked down at Hialeah. "Now?" Jackson replied, his face etched with worry. Hialeah quickly nodded her head, gripped Jackson's arm and buried her face in his chest as she cried out in a labored pain. Jackson swung around frantically with Hialeah nestled in his arms. Overwrought by the screams coming from his wife, Jackson fired out a command to have the doctor brought. He hastened his steps in angst at Hialeah's desperate urging.

Abigail raced ahead to prepare Hialeah's bedroom for delivery. Mrs. Whitford stood trembling at the top of the stairs. "How could you be so careless!" Jackson roared staring heated daggers in Mrs. Whitford's direction as he hurriedly climbed the stairs. The slamming of Hialeah's door and her anguished cry startled Mrs. Whitford. Overcome with guilt, she darted down the stairs in tears. Jackson placed Hialeah onto the bed and Abigail made haste to comfort her. Sitting next to his wife, Jackson took Hialeah's hand in his. Her pain stricken face and deep breathing worried him tremendously. "The doctor will be here shortly." Jackson said reassuringly. "Yes." Hialeah rushed out breathlessly. "What can I do?" Jackson replied. "Not be sore with Mrs. Whitford. It ain't her doin'. Miss Sara. She send George here." Hialeah remarked. "What?" Jackson replied incredulously. "It true. He tell me so. He say she dead, too. Harley Joe and his brothers they kill her." Hialeah remarked, nodding her head. Jackson squeezed Hialeah's hand gently. "All that matters is no harm came to you. Sara Williams, alive or dead is of no importance to me. My only concern is to see our child born." Jackson replied firmly. "Henka." Hialeah remarked. "I'll see to the doctor. Abigail, keep my wife comforted, please." Jackson said. "Of course, My Lord." Abigail replied.

Another agonizing scream from behind the closed door sent Jackson racing down the hall in a panic toward the grand staircase. Mrs. Whitford stood at the bottom of the stairs with her suitcase in one hand a document in the other. Jackson darted down the stairs and bee-lined toward the front door, swinging it open like a mad man in search of the doctor. Mrs. Whitford cleared her throat to alert Jackson to the document she held in her hand. Jackson tore the paper away and skimmed through its contents. "My letter of resignation." Mrs. Whitford said firmly. "Yes, of course it is." Jackson replied before tearing the letter in half. "I'll not accept it. Now do please send the doctor up straight away and a drink. I'm in desperate need of one." Jackson rushed out before hurrying up the stairs. A resounding knock on the door halted Jackson in mid stride. Quickly racing down the stairs once more, Jackson hurried to the door; his path cut off by Mrs. Whitford. "My Lord, do compose yourself." Mrs. Whitford huffed out. Jackson inhaled a deep breath and slowly exhaled while Mrs. Whitford saw to the door.

Dr. Nigel Claybourne was let in and Jackson hastily made his way over to shake the doctor's hand. Nigel Claybourne was a thin man with brown hair and blue eyes. He stood a good foot shorter than Jackson and insisted on wearing his glasses at the tip of his nose to appear more distinguished. A habit that Jackson thought was ridiculous. "My Lord." Nigel said. "Doctor." Jackson replied. "Are you ill?" Nigel remarked. "Hardly. My wife, however, is upstairs expecting to deliver at any moment." Jackson replied. "Your wife?" Nigel remarked surprised. "I didn't know you wed." Nigel said. "Last night. An intimate affair. Now please." Jackson urged. "Of course. Of course." Nigel replied, following Jackson up the stairs. Hialeah's tormented wails quickened both of their steps. Reaching Hialeah's room, Nigel insisted that in Jackson's state of panic, it would be best if he waited outside. Jackson agreed and Nigel closed the door behind him leaving Jackson to pace the hall. Within a matter of mere seconds, the door opened and Nigel returned, softly closing the door behind him; an astonished look on his face. Jackson hurried over to the doctor. "How is she?" Jackson rushed out. "My Lord, she's black." Nigel replied in a hushed whisper. "Of course she is, you bloody fool. What does that matter?" Jackson remarked low, refraining from raising his tone for Hialeah's sake. "Why you simply cannot expect me to deliver a black child." Nigel replied arrogantly. His upturned nose and unconcern for Hialeah sent Jackson into a rage. Without warning, Jackson grabbed Nigel roughly by the front of his shirt and slammed him against the wall; his cold glare ceased any further words from

Nigel's lips. "Either you see that my child is safely brought into this world or I'll rip you into bloody pieces and feed your bones to the mangy dogs that run the streets." Jackson threatened. Nigel swallowed and nodded his head in terror. "Yes, of course, My Lord." Nigel stammered out. Jackson released Nigel, opened the door and followed him inside. "Jackson." Hialeah rushed out, her chest heaving. Jackson hurried to Hialeah's side. He took his wife's hand and placed a kiss on it. "All is well. Dr. Claybourne will see to it." Jackson replied reassuringly, narrowing his eyes in Nigel's direction. "I assure you, My Lady, you have nothing to concern yourself over." Nigel remarked confidently. "Abigail, please see to the doctor's hat and coat." Jackson said. Abigail hurried over to Dr. Claybourne. He removed his hat and coat and handed them over. "I must say I am quite impressed with your diligence Abigail." Nigel said proudly, going over to the wash basin to cleanse his hands. Abigail retrieved Nigel's bag while he thoroughly scrubbed his hands. After handing Nigel a dry hand towel, he assessed Abigail's work station nodding his head in approval before taking a seat at the foot of Hialeah's bed. Abigail opened Nigel's bag and set out the necessary equipment he would need for delivery. Jackson cringed as each piece of medical equipment was presented.

Dr. Claybourne raised the bed sheets exposing Hialeah's bare midsection. Jackson's eyes widened; stunned at Nigel's boldness. "Have you taken leave of your senses?" Jackson exploded, coming to his feet. Hialeah quickly grabbed Jackson's arm. "This how it's done." Hialeah said calmly before she was again taken over by a labored contraction. "Do something, man!" Jackson fired out. "My Lord, compose yourself. It is not quite time." Nigel replied sternly, unruffled by Jackson's outburst. Abigail hastily wiped Hialeah's brow with a cool cloth.

Jackson could no longer bear the harrowing cries of his wife. Hialeah's suffering lasted another six horrendous hours and Jackson was beside himself. He had threatened to crush Nigel's throat with his bare hands, pummel him senseless and toss him head first out of the window. On any other occasion, Nigel would have feared confrontation with Jackson but he dismissed the Lord Chief Justice's threats as mere new father jitters. However, Nigel had no doubt that

Jackson meant every word of his previous threat. In her frustration, Hialeah insisted that Jackson leave the doctor to his work. Jackson was reluctant to leave Hialeah's side until he had spoken to Abigail. He instructed his maid in private to keep a sharp eye on the doctor. Assured that Abigail wouldn't take her eyes from Dr. Claybourne, Jackson took his leave only to make himself comfortable sitting at the top of the stairs. Mrs. Whitford joined him with two glasses of scotch. Jackson accepted the glass. His trembling hand shook the ice in the glass. Mrs. Whitford placed her hand on Jackson's shoulder and offered him a warm smile. "I don't know how you do it; give life." Jackson said. "You love her." Mrs. Whitford replied. "I'm nothing without her." Jackson remarked. Mrs. Whitford held her glass up as did Jackson with a tense smile on his lips. Mrs. Whitford downed her drink and Jackson followed her lead. No sooner than he set his glass next to him, the sound of Hialeah's scream was heard accompanied by the cry of the newest Harding. Jackson's eyes nearly burst from his head. "My God." Jackson said stunned, jumping to his feet.

    Jackson all but tore the door from its frame in his haste to get to his wife and child. Hialeah beamed proudly at Jackson while holding their child. Jackson's feet were frozen where he stood. He couldn't take his eyes from the overwhelming sight of Hialeah cradling their child in her arms as he nursed. Mrs. Whitford gave Jackson a gentle nudge. "Go on." Mrs. Whitford whispered. Jackson exhaled anxiously. Mrs. Whitford gestured for Abigail and Dr. Claybourne to leave Jackson and Hialeah to their privacy. Jackson was at a loss for words. "He ain't fit for walkin' just yet." Hialeah teased. "He?" Jackson replied surprised. Hialeah nodded her head smiling. "A son? I have a son?" Jackson remarked. "I could throw him to you if you like." Hialeah replied laughing. Jackson hurried to Hialeah's side. His mouth fell open at the sight of his son. He looked to Hialeah in shock. "He's...he's." Jackson stammered. "Bout white as you." Hialeah replied simply. "You care to hold him?" Hialeah said. "Are you mad? I'll surely break him." Jackson replied nervously. "You can't expect me to hold him forever." Hialeah remarked lightly. "Of course I do. Besides, it isn't proper to disrupt a man whilst he's enjoying a hearty meal. I'm rather jealous, I must say." Jackson replied playfully. Hialeah couldn't resist laughing at her husband's naughty display of words.

However timid, Jackson took a seat next to his wife and son. "Is he not perfect?" Hialeah asked, smiling. "Indeed he is." Jackson replied. "As are you." Jackson remarked. "I just glad it's over." Hialeah replied. "Was it terrible?" Jackson remarked. "I just tired is all. Grateful too, that you come for us when you did." Hialeah replied. "We'll not speak of today's tragedy." Jackson remarked. "Henka." Hialeah replied softly, nodding her head in agreement. Jackson rose from the bed after placing a gentle kiss on Hialeah's lips and his son's forehead. "I'll leave you two to rest. I'm sure our..." Jackson began, furrowing his brows. "What's he to be called?" Jackson asked. Hialeah grinned. "I thought we call him Jackson Henry Harding." Hialeah replied. "Henry? After my father?" Jackson remarked. "It's a fine name." Hialeah replied. "No, it won't do. My father, for all he's worth, hasn't earned the right to have my son bear his name. I'd much prefer...Jackson Nokosi Harding." Jackson remarked proudly. Hialeah's eyes lit up. "You give him my daddy's name? An indian name?" Hialeah beamed. "My son is deserving of a strong name, much like his grandfather, wouldn't you say?" Jackson replied. Hialeah nodded her head happily. "Rest." Jackson remarked smiling, before taking his leave. Hialeah couldn't contain her excitement. She repeated her son's name over and over as he continued to nurse.

Hialeah woke during the night to the sound of Jackson's voice. During her slumber, Jackson had carried his wife from her private room to their shared bedroom. He sat bare chested a few feet away from his wife in a huge chair with their son nestled in his arms. Jackson looked adoringly at Hialeah. "I'm sorry to have awakened you. My son and I are engaged in quite the conversation." Jackson said, smiling as his son continued with his little squawks. Hialeah was mesmerized at how well Jackson had taken to their little one. She was simply mesmerized by her husband. "How you do it?" Hialeah replied. Jackson grinned boyishly. "What have I done?" Jackson remarked. "You can't know that I come but you have such fine dresses and shoes for me. How can that be?" Hialeah replied. "Ah, and you believe them to belong to another whom I may have shared my bed?" Jackson remarked casually. "You loved another before me I'm sure." Hialeah replied. "My heart was never shared with anyone. However, I may have rifled through your possessions and stolen a few items for measurements' sake. Mrs.

Whitford required a precise fit." Jackson remarked teasingly. "Besides, it's a tad late to scold me, Mrs. Harding." Jackson said with a playful wink. "Although, I do believe Nokosi has just begun to scold." Jackson remarked, standing to his feet. Hialeah's brows rose in surprise. "Nokosi? Just Nokosi?" Hialeah replied. "Perhaps when he's older and has gotten into mischief I'll beckon him fully but for now, my son has quite the appetite and is eager to have his fill." Jackson remarked, handing his son to Hialeah. She lowered her gown exposing her full breasts. Nokosi's fussing ceased as he nursed. "I am jealous indeed." Jackson said smirking as he climbed into bed to join his wife and son.

Hialeah hummed a peaceful tune as she focused on feeding her son. Lying next to his wife and child, Jackson felt a calmness surround him. Hialeah glanced over at Jackson and smiled. "What goes through your mind?" Hialeah asked. "Tranquility." Jackson replied simply. "I like that." Hialeah remarked. She finished nursing Nokosi and carried him off to sleep in the nursery. She returned a short time later to find Jackson sleeping.

In the few months that had passed, Hialeah eased into her new role as mother and wife and proper lady under the tutelage of Mrs. Whitford. Hialeah wished Miss Lilly could see how proud a lady she had become. It was after all, Miss Lilly, who had told her to always keep her head up. Hialeah spoke highly of Miss Lilly and of her mother to Mrs. Whitford. She missed them both dearly and told Mrs. Whitford as much during her lesson. Saddened by the thought of possibly never seeing Miss Lilly again, Hialeah excused herself from the dining room to dress for dinner. She shared her sentiments with Jackson in the privacy of their bedroom. Jackson sympathized with his wife. She was visibly upset. He suggested that they dine outside; presuming the alluring scents of the garden's flowers would relax his wife. Jackson assured Hialeah that all would be well. He had every confidence that she would see her family again. Hialeah smiled faintly before handing Nokosi to Jackson. She held onto Jackson's arm as they reached the top of the stairs.

Jackson cradled Nokosi in his arms as they descended the stairs and made their way toward the veranda. Hialeah walked through the grand doors and gasped in utter disbelief at the joyous sight before her. Jackson had gone through great lengths to keep his miraculous surprise a secret. "I believe she received your letter." Jackson said calmly. Hialeah burst into tears as she hurried toward her mother and father throwing herself into their waiting arms. Georgina Harding, Miss Lilly and Reverend Tucker had all made the trip to welcome Nokosi Harding into the family. Miss Lilly and Georgina bee-lined their way toward Jackson eager to hold the new addition while Hialeah relished the embraces of her parents. Annie shared with Hialeah how she received her daughter's letter and the long trip to Charleston to find her and how they were taken to Reverend Tucker's church and escorted to Miss Lilly's home. Georgina had written to Jackson telling of their arrival and how he had made the proper arrangements to see them all safely to England.

Reverend Tucker led Miss Lilly away to admire the lavish garden while Georgina took the brief moment alone to sadly inform her son that his father disapproved of what he deemed his son's union with Hialeah as disgraceful and refused to acknowledge Nokosi as his grandson. Jackson glanced down at his mother. "You're here. That is enough." Jackson replied, placing a tender kiss on his mother's forehead before making his way toward the elder Nokosi.

Teary-eyed yet full of immense pride, Hialeah lovingly introduced her mother and father to Jackson as Georgina, Miss Lilly and Reverend Tucker looked on. Jackson was in awe of Annie's beauty. Her alluring ebony skin was darker in hue than that of Hialeah's. Her black hair was thick and tightly coiled with hints of gray. She stood equal height to Hialeah and her brown eyes were welcoming. Jackson thought to himself, whatever horrors she had suffered by the hands of Judge Williams, it was evident by her strong stance, her husband had loved her fears away. Jackson was equally impressed by Hialeah's father. His towering height matched Jackson's own. His shoulders were broad and his jawline stern. The elder Nokosi's skin was tanned and firm. His black waist length hair also revealed his many struggles. His dark eyes, fixated on Jackson, spoke volumes. "Mrs. Nokosi."

Jackson said warmly. "Your Lordship." Annie replied, smiling. "Jackson. Please." Jackson remarked lightly. Annie nodded her head in agreement. Jackson turned to face the elder Nokosi. "Sir." Jackson said. Hialeah's father began to speak in his native tongue. When his words were finished, he turned to Hialeah. "He say, you are not the man I would have chosen to wed my daughter, but she has spoken highly of you. She has told her mother and I of your many brave deeds. You have kept her from harm's way. Shielded her from the savages that would have taken her away. You have loved her when even I turned my back on her. You have stood against your own kind as I have done with her mother. You are a man of great integrity; a courageous warrior in your own right. I am grateful for you, Jackson Harding." Hialeah said, with proud tears in her eyes. Jackson nodded his head. "Mvto. (Muh-doe) Thank you. I am honored by your words." Jackson replied as Nokosi woke in his father's arms. "Your grandson, Nokosi Harding." Jackson said, placing his son in his grandfather's arms. "Nokosi." The elder Nokosi replied looking down on his grandson. "A fine name." Nokosi said lightly. Jackson, Hialeah and Annie laughed at Nokosi's high compliment of his own name bestowed to his grandson.

Their joyous occasion was interrupted by Jackson's servants carrying out trays of refreshments. "Let's eat." Jackson said proudly. Annie walked side by side by her husband gushing over her grandson. Hialeah took a hold of Jackson's arm and looked up in adoration at her husband. "They are here to stay." Jackson said, smiling. Hialeah's eyes lit up. "Ecenokecvyet os, Jackson Harding. (Ih-Chih-No-Kih-Chuh-Yeet Ose). My Lord." Hialeah said softly. "And I love you, My Lady." Jackson replied, placing a gentle kiss on Hialeah's lips as he led her toward their family.

The End

Tiana Washington

Tiana Washington resides in Columbus, Ohio with her husband, Daniel and two children, Tylon and Thijs.

Other Books By Tiana Washington

Novels

Camden

Tamed By Ares' Sword

Crescent Sun

Crescent Sun: Sons of Blood

Children's Books

Shanna

Shanna's Lost Ribbon

Shanna and The Big Race

Shanna and the Tag-A-Long Pup